the muse

EMMA SCOTT

The Muse
©2023 Emma Scott Books, LLC

Cover Art by Lori Jackson Designs
Proofing and Formatting by R. Anderson

No part of this book may be reproduced or transmitted in any form or by any means, electronic or mechanical, including photocopying, recording or by any information storage and retrieval system, without written permission from the author.

This is a work of fiction. Any names or characters, events or incidents, businesses or places are fictitious or have been used in a fictitious manner. Any resemblance to actual persons or demons, living or dead or somewhere in between, is purely coincidental.

www.emmascottwrites.com

content warning

The Muse contains mature content that may be triggering for some, such as mental illness (suicidal ideation, depression, panic), drug and alcohol use, graphic violence, torture, and child abuse (off the page). Sensitive readers, please proceed with caution. For more information, please email emmascottpromo@gmail.com.

playlist

Hell // Squirrel Nut Zippers (opening credits)
Hey Man, Nice Shot // Filter
El Tango de Roxanne // Ewan McGregor, Jose Feliciano, Jacek Koman *(Moulin Rouge)*
American Boy // Years & Years
everything i wanted // Billie Eilish
Heathens // twenty øne piløts
Pain // Jimmy Eat World
Wrecked // Imagine Dragons
Walkin' in the Sun // Fink
Devil Inside // INXS (closing credits)

author's note

This book can be read as a standalone, however, incidents and spoilers from *The Sinner* are referenced in *The Muse*. In the interest of not info-dumping (for those who don't wish to read *The Sinner*) or recapping (for those who have read it) I highly recommend reading the Glossary below for a brief summary of *Sinner* events, and to become familiar with this world of angels and demons. All significant terms or names are **in bold** until defined.

glossary

Ambri: (Am-BREE) Ambrosius Edward Meade-Finch (1762-1786), **demon** of lust, vanity, and excess. Former **servitor** of the demon, **Casziel**. Created by **Ashtaroth**.

Angel: A soul who manifests benevolent energy.

Anicorpus: The animal form a **demon** is assigned in order to move more freely on **This Side**. Examples of anicorpi are ravens, beetles, snakes, or flies.

Archduke of Hell: High-ranking **demon**.

Ashtaroth: Demon of Surrender, Archduke of Hell, Prince of Accusers. Ashtaroth was the liege lord of **Casziel** and Ambri and responsible for bringing them into the demonic realm.

Asmodai: (Azz-mo-DYE) Archduke of Hell, Father of Wrath, Eater of Souls.

Casziel Abisare: (Cazz-EEL) Formerly known as the King of the South, Prince of Demons, the Nightbringer. A human warrior who lived in ancient Sumer and who became a **demon** under the servitude of Ashtaroth after the murder of his wife, Li'li. He was reunited with her in present day (Lucy Dennings) and returned to human form.

Crossing Over: Moving between **This Side** and the **Other Side**. Humans can only Cross Over by dying. Powerful demons can move back and forth at will, while others will come when **summoned**.

Demon: A soul who manifests malevolent energy.

Eisheth: (EYE-sheth) A **succubus**, second in command to Asmodai.

Forgetting: The wiping of all memory of the **Other Side** and all previous lifetimes prior to beginning another life on **This Side** in order to facilitate learning. Memory is restored upon Crossing Over and erased again once a new **lifetime** has begun.

God: The Benevolent Unknown.

Grimoire: A book of spells that may also contain incantations for **summoning** spirits or demons.

Heaven: The collective term for all angels on the **Other Side**. Not an actual place.

Hell: The collective term for all demons on the **Other Side**. Not an actual place.

Incubus: A male demon that seeks to have sexual intercourse with sleeping humans.

Lifetime: Human cycles of life, death, and rebirth. A human might live hundreds of lifetimes, returning to **This Side** again and again. Others will remain on the **Other Side** as either a demon or an angel. Humans have no recollection of the Other Side between lifetimes due to Forgetting.

Oblivion: Ceasing to exist completely. Ultimate and permanent nonexistence of a soul. "Death for the dead."

Other Side: The realm a soul returns to after death, between lifetimes. The realm of angels and demons. The human mind cannot fully comprehend the Other Side, and knowledge or memory of it would defeat the purpose of living. (see: Forgetting)

Servitor: Any demon in service to a more powerful demon. High-ranking demons might have legions of servitors.

Succubus: A female demon that seeks to have sexual intercourse with sleeping humans.

Summon: The ritual by which a human brings a demon from the Other Side.

This Side: Life on Earth. Human existence.

Twins, The: Deber and Keeb, twin demon sisters. Deber contaminates humans with constant negative, self-loathing thoughts. Keeb wracks humans with fear of failure when they try to overcome Deber's whispers. The Twins are the most successful of all demonkind in keeping humans from achieving their full potential.

Veil, The: The barrier between This Side and the Other Side.

*To every artist, creator, or storyteller who's ever doubted themselves, please don't stop sharing your gifts with the world.
This one is for you.*

part i

This story is about love. —Moulin Rouge

prologue

Ambri
Paris, 1786

Sweat trickled from under my wig, and I tugged at my ruffled collar as I made my way to the Bastille. The May afternoon was unseasonably warm, and the prison would be worse.

At the entrance, I straightened my fine red coat and told the head jailer I was there to see Monsieur Armand Rétaux de Villette. I was ushered through the stony corridors to a straw-strewn cell that smelled of piss and shit. Armand was packing his meager belongings into a rucksack. His scent was just as foul but nothing that a perfumed bath at my flat couldn't cure.

"Un moment, s'il vous plaît," I said to the guards.

They took in my finery—that of nobility—then moved a few steps down the hall. On the other side of the bars, Armand slumped onto the cell's lone bench, his back to me.

"What do you want, Ambri?" he asked tiredly.

My immaculate brows furrowed at the silly question. There was only one thing I wanted—him.

"I know the sentence is hard to take," I began. "Especially since your part in the heist was so trivial—"

"Trivial? I forged letters in the Queen's hand. I'd hardly call that trivial."

"Of course, it isn't," I amended quickly. "Your talent is exceptional. I just meant you did nothing wrong! A few letters...so what? But consider your exile a gift. A chance to start over. You and I, we can build a new life together—"

"Life?" Armand turned to me, his blue eyes flaring with incredulity. "What *life*? My sweet love is set to be tortured and imprisoned, and I must say goodbye to Paris."

I winced at *my sweet love*. *I* was his love, not that harlot trickster, Jeanne de la Motte, the mastermind behind our little caper—one that got everyone imprisoned and put to trial for forgery, treason, and conspiracy to defraud Her Majesty the Queen Marie Antoinette.

Everyone, that is, except for me.

Jeanne was the reason Armand had been convicted and sentenced to exile; could he not see that? The last few months of imprisonment must've been more difficult for him than I suspected.

"I'll go with you," I said, hearing desperation creep into my voice. "I have all the money in the world. You'll never want for anything."

He snorted, not seeming to have heard. "They may as well have sentenced me to death for all they've taken from me. I have nothing. *Nothing.*"

"You don't have nothing." I swallowed. "You have me."

Armand stared for a hard moment, then began to laugh. Harsh, cutting laughter that stabbed me like a knife. He pressed his grimy face between grimy bars.

"And what are you, Ambri? A tart. A plaything. We had our fun but let's not be ridiculous."

I tilted my chin, even as each word was another stab. "It was more than that. What we have—"

"Sex, Ambri. That's all you ever were to me. A good lay. One of the best, if that's any consolation."

I stared, at a rare loss for words.

That's all you ever were to me.

Armand smirked and gave me a once-over. "Don't look so distraught. *Desperate* and *pathetic* don't suit you."

He gestured for the guards. They shoved me aside and took custody of Armand and marched him down the hall. A thousand words to call him back—to beg, to plead—rose to my lips, but it was useless. The verdict had been rendered. I'd escaped prosecution in our grand scheme but had been punished nonetheless. Exiled from my love. I watched him walk away, his back turned, his heart closed to me.

No, not again! Not again!

Throughout my twenty-four years, I'd been treated as an afterthought. Inconsequential. A plaything to be used and then abandoned...as my uncle did when I was a child.

I squeezed my eyes shut against the memories that assaulted me on a tide of shame and fear. My uncle did the unspeakable, and yet my parents cast *me* aside. That same pain was now echoing in Armand's footsteps as he walked away. He'd used me too, then discarded me like a rag.

I straightened my collar and marched out of the Bastille, head held high, while inside I was collapsing. Forsaken yet again. Jeanne de le Motte, at least, had been sentenced to a public lashing and life in prison. I considered attending her flogging to cheer me up but opted to get drunk instead.

Night fell while I wandered the volatile streets of Paris, stumbling drunk, and attempting to drown my heartache in a bottle of wine. Protests of earlier that day had morphed into a full-blown riot. News of the verdicts had spread; the *libelles* were already printed and circulating. *Affaire du collier de la reine*—The Affair of the Queen's Necklace, they called it. They claimed Marie Antoinette had commissioned an exquisite diamond necklace during a time when the people were on the brink of starvation and had blamed an innocent—Jeanne—when her ploy had been discovered. That Antoinette had nothing to do with Jeanne's conspiracy and had turned the necklace down—*twice*—was of little consequence.

Mobs of dirty peasants, I found, weren't known to let trivial things like facts get in the way of a good outrage.

I cursed and angrily shoved my way through throngs of uncouth mongrels who stank of the chamber pot, demanding the King and Queen's heads, demanding lower taxes and food for their children. A bunch of whining sops...and me caught in the midst.

I peered blearily for a street sign but saw only shouting, angry faces. I wished I'd waited until returning to my flat before drowning my sorrows. Swinging from a tall pole, an effigy of the Queen burned, lighting the dark night and casting dancing shadows, adding to the chaos. Hands shoved. I was a trout pushing upstream, the crowd thrusting me back and sullying my rich red coat with their grime.

Then a group caught me in their net, and I was surrounded.

"We have a lord among us," one man told his fellows, each stinking of sour sweat as they made a ring around me. "Are you one of the Queen's men?"

"Piss off," I slurred and tried to push past.

"He's of the Court, bien sûr," another said, the circle closing tighter around me. "Aren't you, Monsieur Dandy?"

He *dared* put his grubby fingers on me, shoving me. Too drunk to keep my footing, I stumbled back. Rough hands caught me from behind and shoved me forward. For a few terrifying moments, I was tossed among them like a rag doll. The wine bottle was ripped from my hand, the ruffled collar torn from my neck, the wig plucked from my head.

"Ah, a golden boy," one man seethed, gripping a fistful of my blond hair and painfully wrenching my head. "A cherub, he is."

"Damn you all to hell!" I cried, fear burning up the alcohol, leaving panic to streak through me like fire. "Get your filthy hands off me. Do you know who I am?"

The man hauled my face close to his.

"We know who you are," he seethed. "You're one of *them*."

His meaty finger jabbed at the burning effigy that was swinging wildly now. As I watched, it touched the roof of a distillery. A surprised cry went up as a fire blazed fast along the thatch and dry wood.

"Let it burn!" someone cried, and the shout was taken up. *"Let it burn! Let it burn!"*

The brute holding me turned back to me, eyes wide enough to show the whites. "Oui, let it burn. And you with it!"

"What? No!"

The man hauled me to the distillery door, while others shoved their shoulders against it to bust it open. The entire structure was burning now, the smoke filling the streets.

"No! I'm not of this Court! I'm not even French!" I cried, my heels scrabbling along the cobbles as they dragged me to the inferno. *"I'm royalty, you animals!"*

A poor choice of words, in hindsight.

The man's eyes flared, his lips curled, and another verdict was rendered right then and there—death. He shoved me inside the burning distillery and the door slammed shut behind me.

Coughing, eyes streaming, I threw an arm over my mouth and heaved against the door. No avail; they'd barred it from the outside.

The roof of the distillery was swallowed by orange and red flames, embers falling and igniting tufts of hay that cradled bottles of wine. I stumbled past crates of liquor, searching for another way out. I came to a corner—a dead end—and turned to go back when a blazing beam came down, barring my way.

"No," I whimpered, sinking my back against the wall and sliding to the dirt floor. "Not like this. I don't deserve this. I did nothing wrong!"

"Indeed, you didn't," came a voice in the chaos. Smooth, refined English. Like cool water.

Blinking through thickening smoke, I peered around to see a man sitting casually on a crate. He was dressed in a strange white suit, pristine and untouched by soot. His dark hair flowed down his shoulders from under a white velvet hat, and odd spectacles were perched on his nose.

"So unfair, how those peasants treated you," he said. "*You*, the son of a British lord."

"Who are you?"

"I am Ashtaroth," the man said, though even in that smoke-filled room with death licking at me from all sides, I knew he wasn't precisely a *man*.

He was...something else.

"Those filthy pigs dared to touch you, didn't they?" Ashtaroth snarled. "They put their hands on you and consigned you to death. *You*, who are infinitely superior to them in every way."

"Y-yes. Help me...please," I cried. The smoke strangled me with a merciless grip.

"How dare they!" the man-thing, Ashtaroth, cried, his face suddenly—impossibly— inches from mine with a stench so powerful that it infiltrated the smoke until I wanted to gag.

Death. He's made of death.

"I've been watching you for a long time, Ambrosius Edward Meade-Finch."

"Watching me...?"

"Your friends—criminals and swindlers, all. But it's you we want."

Despite the heat, those words sent a shiver down my spine. "We?"

"Your carnal appetites are delicious. You are powerful. Magnificent. We see it when others choose not to. Not your parents who sent you away instead of your villainous uncle. Not those vagabonds who dare to hurt you." He smiled, showing rotted teeth. "Not that cruel Armand who broke your heart."

My throat tightened, and the tears in my eyes came not from the smoke. "How could they do this to me?"

"Indeed," Ashtaroth agreed. "Say the word, and I'll take you away from it all. I can make all this disappear."

"Then do it!" I cried, my heels scrabbling as the fire licked closer. "Help me!"

"I'll give you a new existence," Ashtaroth continued, unhurried. "An existence without regrets. Without abandon. *You* will be in command. Humans will dance on the ends of *your* strings. You will be young and beautiful forever, and death will never touch you."

I nodded, tears streaming down my cheeks. "No more…*wanting*."

"No more wanting," he agreed. "It is *they* who will want *you*. You will feed on their desire for you. You will be impossible to deny, impossible to erase, as you were by those who were meant to love you."

Anger raged in me at the unfairness of it all. The *injustice*. My parents banishing me from our home, pretending I no longer existed because that was easier than bearing the shame of my uncle's actions. My official portrait absent from the family gallery. Never painted. As if I'd ceased to be.

I'd been consigned to a life of searching for belonging and love in the beds of a hundred strangers and never found it. How much easier would it be to hate them instead?

"Will you surrender, Ambri?" Eagerness dripped from Ashtaroth's words. "Will you give yourself to me?"

I could barely see him in the smoke and flame. But his hand—bejeweled and beckoning—was a lifeline. I had only to say the word. A small voice told me not to surrender, that I was making an unholy bargain for my very soul with one of Hell's own.

Because he's a demon. And I…

I'd be like him. Powerful. Untouchable. Immortal.

"I surrender," I whispered. "I'm yours."

"Excellent."

He smiled in triumph, then retreated into the smoke, leaving my hand grasping.

"Wait! Don't go! You said you'd save me!"

"So I shall," he intoned. "But first, my sweet boy…you must burn."

I gasped and then writhed as the first real agony found me. My feet were burning inside my shoes. Then the blaze found my stockings, chewing through silk and skin with teeth of flame. The fire climbed higher and higher; the stench of my own scorched flesh filled my nose. I held my hands up and watched them blacken and curl. The agony grew so intense and total, it became separate from me. Somehow, I had voice to scream as the fire consumed me…

…and I scattered like ash on the wind. I flew in fragments, disoriented by the sensation of being broken into pieces and yet whole at the same time. Black beetles the size of a man's hand—sleek and shiny—swarmed around me.

But that wasn't right.

The beetles weren't *around* me; they were… me.

I was the swarm. *I* was a hundred flitting insects.

Sweet merciful Jesus!

But I'd turned my back on all things merciful and holy. Of that, I was certain.

The beetles melded together and became a body. My new body. Huge, black feather wings sprouted from my back, and an otherworldly power, that I could just begin to taste, flooded me. I was sickened and exhilarated at the same time.

What have I done?

In a blink, I was no longer in the burning building, I was… somewhere else, whole and untouched, watching the last of my human body disintegrate. My exquisite face charred and blackened to the bone. Ashtaroth stood beside me, smiling, and there was no pain. Not here, on the Other Side of the Veil. No fiery agony and no more aching hunger for the love I'd never known.

I fell to my knees at the demon's feet, filled with unwavering devotion. Ashtaroth had saved me from the agony of living and filled me instead with beautiful vengeance.

I felt his hand on my head, petting me. Soothing me.

"My sweet, sweet Ambri," he murmured as my body burned to ash. "Welcome to hell."

one

Cole
London, present day

"And then the bloke says he wants to buy my entire *Nights in Cornwall* series, and I had to tell him it was sold out. So he says, 'Fuck me, sketch a bloody flower on a cocktail napkin so my wife doesn't kill me.'"

Vaughn Ritter, my former flatmate at the Royal Academy of Arts, shook his head with a chuckle. I smiled faintly into my pint in the crowded tavern—Mulligan's—where I worked and was currently on a short break.

"Holy crap, Vaughn, it sounds like things are going great," I said, my stomach twisting with jealousy. It felt like hunger. Or maybe it *was* hunger; I hadn't been paid yet, and garnishes at the bar had been my lunchtime salad bar.

Vaughn waved a hand. "God, listen to me. I sound like an arrogant arsehole, going on with my silly shit. Tell me about you, Cole. How's post-Academy life treating you?"

I glanced down. "Things could be better."

"Nah, you're just in a rough patch."

Vaughn crossed his legs, ankle resting on knee, and stretched one arm over the booth's worn upholstery. He looked loose, relaxed, and utterly confident in his wool blazer and jeans. His dark hair was gelled and smartly cut. Polished. By contrast, my shaggy light brown hair was falling in my eyes as I hunched over my drink in ratty jeans and jacket. Tension and stress tightened every muscle in my body so I could hardly move.

"This *rough patch* has been going on since graduation," I said, conscious that I was on the verge of whining. "I know that a degree from the Academy isn't a golden ticket to instant fame and success, but I thought I'd at least be…"

Not drowning.

"Slightly better off," I finished.

Vaughn flashed me a wide smile of white teeth. "Cheer up, mate! You look like you're ready to jump off the Tower Bridge. Is it really as bad as all that?"

"It hasn't been easy." I took a long pull of my ale. "My grandmother passed last week. I just got back from her funeral in the States."

"Bloody hell, when it rains it pours, doesn't it?" Vaughn leaned over to grip my hand. "Sorry, mate. You were close, yeah?"

I nodded. "She was basically the last family I had. But with her dementia, I wasn't able to…" I cleared my throat, grateful my black, square-rimmed glasses helped hide my tears. "I couldn't take care of her. But I was with her at the end."

"That's rough. But you know what we do as artists. We channel it all." Vaughn made a diving motion with his hands. "The pain, grief, triumphs and joys—pour it right into the work."

I nodded again, wondering what pain or grief Vaughn Ritter was channeling into his paintings. A degree from the Academy *had* been his ticket to instant fame and success. He'd been snatched up by a big-time agent—Jane Oxley—before he could frame his diploma and had had two shows in the last year alone. I was truly happy for him, but I ached for a shred of what he had. If not the success, then just the reprieve from worry and self-doubt.

A big sale wouldn't hurt either.

"There's something more?" Vaughn said, reading my face. "You can tell me."

"Nah, it's okay."

"Cole Matheson," he chastised, raising an eyebrow. "We made a pact in Uni. You and me, remember? The Yank and the Brit. Two

Musketeers: one for all and all that." He leaned in. "Do you need money? Because I—"

"No, no," I said, quickly waving my hands. "I don't need money, I need…"

I needed someone to see my work and believe in it. I needed to get out of my own head and just *paint* instead of drowning in the chorus of voices that whispered I was no good, that I'd never make anything of myself. I needed a little glimmer of hope that being a struggling artist was worth the struggle.

I forced a smile. "I needed to have a pint with you. It's been too long."

Vaughn's dark brows furrowed as he leaned over the crowded pub's table. A football game played on the TV high in the corner—AFC Richmond against Man City. Judging by the lads in red and blue at the bar—cheering and swearing in equal parts—it was a tight game.

"I know I've been busy lately with the shows," Vaughn said. "And Jane wants me in Paris next week, but I haven't forgotten about you, mate."

"You don't owe me anything, Vaughn. I'm just feeling sorry for myself and—"

"*Wrong.*" He pounded his fist on the table. "We're in this together. And you, my friend, have talent. Real talent."

"Thanks, man. Sometimes I wonder."

"Well, don't. Things are hard, I get that. But I'm not going to leave you behind, Cole. There's a little gallery in Chelsea that wants fresh blood. I'll talk to Jane, see if she can pull some strings with the director. They're friends."

"Shit, Vaughn…Really? I don't know what to say."

"Don't have to say anything, mate." Vaughn clinked his glass to mine. "We came up together. Let's fly together."

"Okay."

A tiny umbrella of hope against a deluge of doubt opened over me and lasted for precisely twenty minutes—the time it took me to get to my shabby place in Plaistow I shared with three flatmates.

They were all in the living room, watching Graham Norton in high spirits. Beer bottles lined the coffee table.

"Cole!" Stuart said when he saw me. "Come join us."

"Looks like a celebration," I said, taking a seat beside Malcolm on the couch.

"It is. We're celebrating our liberation," Caleb said. He tossed me an envelope. Inside was £300 in crisp bills.

"What's this for?" I asked, hope filling me up and draining out just as fast as Malcolm spoke.

"A payoff from Mr. Porter. He wants to kick us all out and make this a proper flat."

"Where the tenants sign actual leases," Caleb said with a grin.

Stuart nodded. "Porter's fed up with the rotating tenant situation, so he's paying us to vacate. No rent due for this month, plus three hundred quid to boot."

He clinked beer bottles with the others, while I sat back against the ratty old couch. My flatmates seemed to think impending eviction was a good thing, while my stomach felt like an iron ball of lead.

"And everyone agreed?" I asked. "Without asking me?"

"It had to be all of us," Stuart said, frowning at my expression. "Hey, it's a good thing, right? Moving is a pain in the arse, but this place is a shithole."

He was right, but it was an affordable shithole. With my savings gone, the £300 in my lap was all the cash I had. And not enough for a deposit on a new flat.

What now? Just what the fuck now?

From inside my cheap jacket, my cell phone rang.

"Call from the States," I mumbled rising to my feet. "Gotta take this…"

I had zero desire to talk to my best friend and worry her, but Lucy Dennings and I had known each other since undergrad at NYU. I put on a smile and hit *answer*.

"Hey, Luce. What's up?"

"Just checking in on you. How are you doing?"

Lucy had been at my grandmother's funeral and knew it had hit me hard. There was nothing I didn't tell her, but I was grateful this wasn't one of our usual FaceTime calls; she'd be able to see the despair wrapping its tentacles around me.

"I'm okay," I said, "How are you? How's Cas?"

"He's great," she said, and I heard the smile in her voice. "Yeah, he's…"

"A dream come true?" I teased.

"Something like that."

My best friend had been as single and lonely as me until the mysterious Cas Abisare dropped into her life. I didn't have the whole story from her—she was uncharacteristically cryptic about certain details—but she seemed deliriously happy with him. It was as if, she'd said, some missing part of herself had been restored.

"What about you?" she asked lightly. "Any new potential love interests on the horizon?"

"Nope, I've sworn off men, remember?"

"But it's been three years. He really hurt you, didn't he?"

The *he* Lucy referred to was Scott Laudner, my first boyfriend upon arriving in London from New York. Like a dope, I'd fallen for him hard and fast, even though he'd told me explicitly that he didn't believe in a "heteronormative construct of monogamy." I tried to compromise, but when he wanted a three-way with another guy he'd been dating, I couldn't go through with it.

"That was my fault," I told Lucy, sitting on the edge of my single bed in my tiny soon-to-be-ex-room in my flat. "Scott told me from the start what he could give. Stupid of me for wanting more. I'm old-fashioned, I guess."

"That's not old-fashioned," Lucy said. "You want one person to be your only person. There's nothing wrong with that."

"Yeah, well, I have bigger problems than my love life," I said.

Like impending homelessness.

But before Lucy could ask—and be more worried—I cut her off. "But my friend Vaughn wants to hook me up with his agent. There's a new gallery in Chelsea. That could be something."

I glanced at the paintings stacked against the wall of my tiny room, all done during my time at the Academy. I was a portraitist, seeking to capture an intimate likeness of my subject. Everyone's face told a story, and I wanted to be the one to tell it. But commissions were hard to come by. I'd taken a bartending job at Mulligan's so that I'd have time to paint and do all the shitty "networking" I hated—and that Vaughn Ritter was so good at. To put my work out there, which was like casting a fishing line into a vast ocean.

So far, no bites.

I rubbed my chest that felt tight while Lucy squealed in my ear.

"Cole, that's fantastic! You *have* to tell me when your exhibit will show and I'm there."

"I don't know if it'll get that far…"

"It will. You're brilliant. But exhibit or not, I was thinking of coming for a visit. Cas and me. Or maybe just me, if you prefer. I really want to see you. I miss you."

"I miss you too, but now's not a good time. I'm going to get a new place. A fresh start," I said, wishing I had a shred of optimism to go with my declaration.

"Uh huh. Cole, are you all right? Tell me the truth. Are you sleeping at all?"

I both cursed and loved how my friend knew me so well.

"Not really," I admitted. "It's just kind of a lot going on right now. But as soon as I get settled, I'd love to have you and Cas here. I need to meet this mysterious stranger. I haven't had a chance to vet him, make sure he's good enough for you."

"I want you to meet him too."

Lucy's voice was warm with love for this guy who'd swept into her life and rescued her from the loneliness that had been starting to worry me. I'd been at the Academy then, editing the arts magazine, my future seemingly bright and busy. Now, I stared out the window to the cloudy London afternoon. Fall was fast giving way to winter. A metaphor, I thought. My life had been summer green and sunny and was fast morphing to cold, barren, and gray.

You're on a roll, sad boy.

"Anyway, I have to go, Luce. Lots to do."

"Okay," she said, the note of concern creeping back into her tone. "But call me any time. Literally, any time."

"I will. Love you."

"Love you, Cole. I really do. And if you need anything—"

"Okay, thanks. Bye, Luce," I said and hung up.

I tossed my phone aside. The quiet was oppressive and I suddenly felt untethered from everyone and everything. I'd never known my dad, and my mother took off when I was thirteen. My grandma, Margaret-Anne, had been my only family and now she was gone. Even Lucy, who lived in New York, may as well have been a million miles away.

I stared out into the cold gray light, the neighborhood buildings surrounding me. Boxing me in. No money. No place to live. No family. The paintings leaning against the wall were the only thing I had to show for an education at the Royal Academy of London. Not enough.

I'm not good enough.

My thoughts raced like this, on a loop of despair and self-doubt, spinning tighter and tighter until my heart began to pound like a hammer in my chest. In seconds, the beats became too fast to distinguish one from another. I clutched my shirt that was drenched in sweat.

"Fuck, not now."

I lay back on my pillows and concentrated on the cracked ceiling. My racing pulse slowly calmed down, one breath at a time. I'd get a new place to live *and* a new job. A better job. And Vaughn was going to come through for me. It was like he said—I was going through a rough patch. That's all.

After what felt like hours, the panic attack subsided leaving me hollow and drained. It was only six in the evening, but I climbed under the covers to try to dive into the refuge of sleep that had been eluding me for months too.

Tomorrow will be better. It will.

I held onto that thought as I mercifully drifted away—gripped it with both hands—while another seemed to smile snidely.

You sure about that?

two

Ambri

"KNEEL, boy!"

I do as commanded and wince. The blood-spattered stone is unforgiving on my naked human flesh. But if I get out of this with only a few bruises, I'll consider myself lucky.

Asmodai, archduke of hell, sits on a throne of bones, fires burning all around from nowhere and everywhere at once. He's terrible to behold. Worse is being beheld *by* him. Three pairs of eyes from his three heads—ram, human, bull—are trained on me, each burning with barely-contained rage.

He seems fun.

"You know why you're here," Asmodai says with his middle human head.

He's crawling around in my thoughts; I have to be careful.

"I have a guess, my lord."

"Ashtaroth—your maker—is dead. Consigned to Oblivion."

"Terrible shame. He was like a father to me."

A father made of snakes and whose breath could kill small animals, but one couldn't be too picky.

"Casziel, the Nightbringer and your direct superior, has escaped us." He pins me with a stare. "You were close with him."

It isn't a question.

"I served Casziel for more than two hundred human years," I say carefully. "Over that time, I developed a certain…fondness for him."

On the left side of his massive neck, the bull head snorts smoke.

"Casziel is living as a human with the woman, Lucy Dennings, free from his duties to us. Ashtaroth is no more. These are consequential losses to our hierarchy, and you were the sole witness to what transpired." Asmodai leans forward, all three pairs of eyes trained on me, his clawed hands gripping the skull armrests. "Have you done nothing to subvert our agenda? Think carefully about how you answer, Ambri."

I swallow hard, wishing I was permitted to retain my demon form. I'm weak and flimsy in my human body here…which is precisely why Asmodai commanded it so. He can consign me to Oblivion with one swing of his fist.

But I'm not entirely helpless. I have my own arsenal of weapons, so to speak. In order to be believable, a good lie is peppered with facts. Those little flakes of truth flavor the lie so that the entire thing goes down easy. Palatable.

And I am a master chef.

Thinking quickly, I concoct a little dish that is *mostly* true, leaving out the icky bits that will likely get me killed.

"Casziel was tired of immortality and sought Oblivion. A terrible loss. But he loved Lucy Dennings. I figured if she were one of us, Casziel would stay, so I provided Lucy with the means to summon Ashtaroth so that he might turn her to our dark cause. I could not have predicted the interference of an angel. That holy specter destroyed Ashtaroth and freed Casziel from our ranks. I did my best to save them both." I put on my most winning smile. "If you look at it that way, I'm something of a hero."

The ram, the bull, and the human head all watch me with black eyes, and it's all I can do to keep my chin up and my gaze unwavering. The seconds tick, counted by my pounding pulse, as I wait to see if the demonlord will swallow my story or spit it back out.

"I hear you're a clever one," Asmodai says finally. "Wily, like a cockroach. Able to slip in and out of trouble. Surviving while all else perish."

I chafe at the insinuation. "Kind of you to say, but I'm more *beetle* than—"

"Ashtaroth was sloppy. He let Casziel dwell in his infatuation for the human girl for too long and didn't keep close watch on you. As your new liege lord, I won't make the same mistake."

Oh goody.

Asmodai sits back on his throne. "I feel the lies falling from your clever tongue, Ambri. I should rip it from your mouth and feed it back to you. I should flay the flesh from your human hide." He cocks his heads thoughtfully. "Or perhaps, I shall burn it off, inch by inch. Just like old times…?"

"I swear, my lord, I did nothing—"

"Aye, you did *nothing*. You failed. Or worse, you betrayed us. You *are* the cockroach of your anicorpus, a bug beneath my boot."

"Beetle," I mutter under my breath.

"If you wish to save yourself from a millennium of pain, Ambri, you must prove your loyalty to the darkness."

"Whatever you wish of me, lord. Anything. Say the word and I—"

"I want a human," he says. "Fresh. Pure. A human who shines brightly through the Veil."

"Consider it done," I say with relief. "Corrupting humans is my favorite pastime. I can do it in my sleep. In fact, I prefer it that way. Don't have to get out of bed—"

"I'm not interested in your carnal exploits, Ambri. You will bring a human to me. Here."

I frown. "We cannot kill, Lord Asmodai."

"You take me for a fool?" he thunders in three voices, and the very ether trembles with his rage. "You will be the agent of their Crossing Over. Cajole. Whisper. *Seduce.* That is your forte, is it not?"

"I seduce them to the sins of lust, my lord. Not…their own death." My frown deepens. "May I suggest Mammon? He would be much better suited to such a task. Or perhaps, Kali? Bloodthirsty little viper, that one. She once enticed a man to eat his own cock—"

"Silence!"

I fall back as Asmodai is suddenly the size of a mountain, dwarfing his throne. Behind him, the sky boils with black clouds streaked with purple lightning. Fire spews in great vomitus streams from all three of his mouths, but I hear his words emanating from the ground, the sky, from inside my own head, threatening to burst it apart.

"Prove yourself to me, Ambri. Prove you are a loyal servant of hell. Drive a human to ultimate despair. Persuade them to end their

miserable existence, and then guide them to me. Fail, and you will know eternal agony."

I fall to my knees as pain grips my head in a vise so strong, tears stream down my cheeks and onto the stone beneath me in dark drops.
Not tears, blood.

Blood is streaming from my eyes, my nose, my ears. I hold my head as if I can keep it from exploding. I squeeze my eyes shut to keep them from popping out of my skull. The agony goes on until my body is pressed flat onto the bloody stones by the unseen power of Asmodai. Like a hand crushing me to the earth.

"My lord…" I grit out. "P-please…"

Just when I feel my bones must be on the verge of cracking, the pressure is lifted. Air pours back into my lungs and my bowels unclench. Slowly, I push myself to standing, shivering and naked and undignified.

"Th-thank you, my lord," I say, wiping my face, and the back of my hand comes away crimson. "I will not fail you."

"Ashtaroth was lax," Asmodai says, reverting to his normal size in a blink. "Casziel was a lovesick fool. I am neither."

"Of course not, my lord," I say, bowing. "You are Asmodai, Father of Wrath. Asmodai, Eater of Souls." I swallow hard. "Asmodai, the *merciful…*"

"Merciful." The bull's head snorts. "Fail me, Ambri, and you'll forget you ever knew the meaning of the word."

I back out of Asmodai's crumbling fortress of bone and blood and immediately Cross Over. In the space of a human second, I'm in my luxurious flat in New York City. The midnight city rises up all around me, skyscrapers glittering through my windows.

I drag myself to the bathroom and regard my reflection in the glass.
"Bloody demons."

I shower off the filth, blood, and grime of the Other Side, and with my golden locks still damp, I wrap myself in a silk robe and flop onto my king-sized bed. Demons don't sleep, but I must wait for the exhaustion of Crossing Over to leave me. I do it frequently enough that I need not wait long, and the night is young.

I rise and go to my closet to peruse the designer clothing and expensive colognes for tonight's revelries. Perhaps, I'll find the poor soul I'm to entice to his own death at any one of the sex clubs and secret bars I frequent for my nightly conquests. Asmodai was hazy on the deadline, so to speak. No sense in depriving myself of a little fun with my victim first.

My victim...

The idea of driving a human to take their own life leaves a bad taste in my mouth. To be sure, I despise humans. The vermin caused me nothing but pain when I was one of their number. Now I exact revenge by wringing pleasure from them until they're exhausted but begging for more. More of me. My attention, my touch, my tongue on their skin. I command their bodies, wielding control, tempting, teasing. I coax them to the brink of release but grant it only when I desire.

Delicious.

That's all you are to me...

The memory stabs me; a raw wound Armand gave me at the end of my human life.

I ignore it and put on a suit of jet black and examine myself in the mirror. If one is to die and be reborn into immortal life, twenty-four is the ideal age. I'm nearly two meters tall (six feet to the Yanks) and enveloped in lean muscle. My hair is the color of gold, thick and full. My human eyes are blue-green and fringed with long, dark lashes. Full lips, straight nose, cheek bones for days...

Truly, I'm a handsome devil.

I step out into the New York night, a November chill in the air. But instead of heading to one of my usual haunts, I immediately find myself breaking into a hundred pieces, wings chittering. I take to the air in a beetle swarm and soar toward the Hell's Kitchen neighborhood, as if pulled by an imaginary string.

Damn you, Casziel.

I fly among the buildings until I find the little apartment tucked behind another. The one with an empty lot in the back and the rickety stairs that lead up to a door. The pentagram Lucy Dennings drew in the dirt is no longer there. The black candle I provided for her is long gone. So is my maker, Ashtaroth, summoned by the girl and then destroyed by her angel. Sent to Oblivion.

I do not mourn him, but Casziel…

I swarm up to the warm yellow glow of the second story window—the proverbial moth to the flame—and watch with a hundred pairs of eyes. Casziel and his love, Lucy, cuddle together on the couch watching television. Now and then, without her noticing, his gaze strays to her. His love for her is palpable, like a scent on the wind that I can sense, even in my damnation.

A hundred tiny hearts in my hundred tiny bodies stutter at the same time.

The phone on the table next to Lucy buzzes. She kisses Casziel on the cheek and steps outside to sit on the back stairs.

Quickly, I flit out of sight and attach myself, en masse, to the side of the building. Lucy is speaking with Cole Matheson, her American friend who resides in London. I've witnessed her speak to him before. Then, the FaceTime function shows me a young man with a mop of sandy brown hair and angular features. Handsome but not overly. Unique. Deep voice, deep brown eyes behind black-framed glasses.

Judging from Lucy's worry and the droning tone of misery coming from Cole's end, he isn't happy and trying to hide it.

A potential candidate for Asmodai's command?

He lives in London, the scene of dear Uncle's crimes…

I'd vowed to return to Britain only if absolutely necessary, but I had several million pounds in a London bank and kept a lovely flat in Chelsea that I hadn't seen in ten years.

And I am no longer that terrified boy in Uncle's carriage. If he could see me now…

I detach myself from the wall and fly upward again, to allow myself one last glimpse of Casziel. He's fallen asleep on the couch, his handsome face in profile, eyes closed, a small smile playing over his lips.

Sleeping, I scoff. I have no need of it. But to curl up on the couch with someone… To be held…

My hundred beetle wings twitch at the notion. That is weakness. *His* weakness. Casziel had been an archduke of hell and yet let himself fall prey to a mere human woman. An unremarkable one at that. I will never be that foolish. Never let anyone lay a hand on me unless it's to further my own desire. I am powerful now and will not give it up for anything.

On the street, I reform myself into a human, walking and thinking. I'll return to London and find Cole Matheson and—

"Destroy him?"

My words seem to hang, frozen, in the chill New York night.

It would be agonizing to Casziel and Lucy if I drove Cole to the Other Side. Asmodai would be pleased that I'd not only obeyed his command but that I'd punished the demon who escaped him and his human lover at the same time. A satisfactory outcome all around.

Especially for me.

Yet...

Why do you hesitate? Humans brutally murdered you. Casziel has forgotten you. They all deserve a little taste of the pain you've been force-fed your entire life.

I brush off the last tendrils of hesitation.

"Cole Matheson, it is."

three

Cole

"No noise after eight p.m., no parties, no girls."

I smirked behind the woman's back as we surveyed the tiny basement apartment in Whitechapel. "How about boys?"

Velma Thomas, my potential new landlady, turned and squinted at me through eyes nestled in wrinkles. She wore a shabby housedress and slippers and a perpetual frown that was etched into her jowls.

"What'd you say?"

"Nothing."

"Hmph. Rent is first of the month, not a day later. Also, no pets, no loud music, no smoking…"

As she droned on about all the things I wasn't allowed to do, I glanced around. Dim, dusty, drafty. Hardly more than a square box with walls painted black, as if Ms. Thomas held open-mic nights or taught improv here. One window showed a thin rectangle of street. Other amenities included a hot plate, a mini fridge, and a bathroom with a curtain for a door. But the flat had its own entrance down a harrowing flight of narrow stairs, and I wouldn't have to share that tiny bathroom with anyone. It was a shoebox, but if I shoved all my stuff—which wasn't much—to one side, I'd have room to paint.

No light to paint *by*, but I'd jump off that bridge when I came to it.

"Well?"

"I'll take it."

As if I have a choice.

Ms. Thomas left me to unpack—a five-minute job—and I slumped onto the bed. Dust puffed up around me and the wind whistled at the window, little tendrils of cold air snaking their way in through cracks in the caulking.

It was going to be a long winter.

Later that afternoon, a pal from the bar helped me lug my portraits, each wrapped in moving blankets, down the narrow stairs and into my place. I leaned them against the wall and rubbed my chin, contemplating the entirety of my life's work. My phone had been silent for days—no messages or texts from Vaughn. I thought about calling or maybe texting a casual, *Hey, how are you?*

"Do not be that pathetic," I muttered in my tiny place, but *desperate* was closer to the mark—Vaughn was leaving for Paris any day now.

He'd promised to contact the gallery owner through his agent, but that didn't mean I didn't have work to do. I couldn't rely on other people to make my future. I took off my jacket and put a blank canvas on the easel. My supplies were low, but I had enough for a new piece. At Uni, my professors were always telling me I had a way of looking inside the subject of a portrait and really seeing their inner selves. I needed only a glimpse of the person, and they'd be burned into my mind, allowing me to paint them from memory if they couldn't sit for me.

That seemed like a million years ago.

My pencil on the canvas was frozen. I had no model in mind. No idea for one. My thoughts were crowded with worry, stress, and self-doubt. The praise from professors must've happened to someone else. The literary magazine must've been edited by someone far more confident than me. A version of me had gone to the Academy and another had graduated. One I didn't recognize.

I let my hand fall. "Fuck."

Okay, so today wasn't a painting day. I could still venture out and try to drum up an opportunity. A show somewhere. Anything.

I put my jacket back on and headed out.

"Don't let the door slam!" Ms. Thomas screeched from out of her window above me.

"Yes, ma'am," I muttered.

I took the bus to Hyde Park. Though it was nearly four p.m. with rain threatening, artists were behind canvases, painting the Wellington Arch, the city, or the paying customer sitting in front of them. There was plenty of room for one more. I could come back tomorrow and set up shop.

Has it come to this?

It was honest work, but the last, dying gasps of my ego had me pulling out my phone and calling Vaughn. I put the phone to my ear, shivering in my worn-out jacket.

Voicemail.

Greetings! You've reached Vaughn Ritter. Please leave a message. For business inquiries, please contact my agent, Jane Oxley, at—

I hung up.

"Shit."

I stuffed my cold hands in my pockets and started to cross the street when I saw a guy—an impossibly beautiful guy—watching me intently on the corner. He wore a long black coat, the collar pulled up under his chin. Thick blond hair blew gently in the icy wind, and his eyes met mine relentlessly. A lazy smirk touched his lips, as if he were waiting for me to recognize him. Or appreciate him; he was clearly aware of how unbelievably gorgeous he was. He wore it like his coat.

Even if I hadn't sworn off men for the foreseeable future, I was in no position to make contact with a guy like this. Everything about him screamed *money* and *confidence*—two things I had in short supply.

I tore my gaze away and sprang for a cab into Shoreditch, an artsy little district. For an hour, I wandered past hole-in-the-wall galleries, clubs, and shops that lined the narrow street. But for the bars, everything was closed. I scanned gallery windows—sometimes they had open calls for artists pasted on the glass. Nada. I'd do a better online search at home, I reasoned. Night was falling fast, bringing winter cold with it.

I took the bus—no more taxis for me—back to my neighborhood and ducked into a bodega for a package of ramen and a banana.

"Dinner of champions."

Inside my basement flat, I heated my food and ate it slowly to make it last. My stomach was still grumbling when I powered up my laptop. I searched for galleries with open calls. There were none within the city limits. Querying was soul-sucking, but that was the game. Foolishly, I'd thought it'd be so much easier to play it.

My brain threatened to begin its nightly spin, revving up with unwanted negative thoughts. I shut the laptop and dove into bed, hoping to dive into sleep as quickly.

I hunched under my thin blanket that smelled like dust and shivered. Cold air was seeping into the room like long fingers, crawling over my skin and finding their way under my blanket. With a curse of irritation, I sat up to check that I hadn't left the window cracked and jerked my hand away from the sill with a jolt.

"Oh shit!"

On the window ledge next to the bed, bathed in moonlight, was a beetle. It was sleek and black and easily the size of my palm. The beetle's soft underwings fluttered from beneath hard outer wings. Its antennae flickered.

Still in my bed, I reached blindly and grabbed for the nearest weapon—one of my art history books from the stack on the floor. Hardcover. Slowly, heart pounding, I raised the book and braced myself for the *splat* that was coming.

"I'd rather you didn't," drawled a voice from the door.

"Jesus!" I dropped the book—one corner jabbing my thigh—and whipped my head.

The same handsome man I'd seen on the street was now in my room. Even in the dimness, the recognition was instant; his head of rich gold hair was like a beacon. He leaned casually against the wall, watching me, amused and wholly unmoved by my panic. Languidly, he held out his hand. The beetle on the ledge buzzed across the room and landed on his outstretched palm. I stared. Like some kind of impossible magic trick, it melded with his skin and vanished.

A lazy smile curled the man's lips. "As you can see, I'm rather attached."

What the fuck...

I scrambled backward on my bed, pushing myself into the corner, unable to tear my eyes away as the man took a step forward into a slant of moonlight. As he moved from shadow to light, his clothing changed. *He* changed. The elegant clothes somehow morphed into a velvet waist coat of blood red, black pants, and a white shirt with a ruffled collar.

*The eighteenth-century...*my brain supplied unhelpfully.

He came closer. The moonlight climbed up his chest, up his sharp chin that was now pale, bloodless white. Like porcelain. The light climbed higher, and a scream rose in my throat with it. His blue-green eyes were now black upon black. No whites, no irises, just…

Death.

As if all the light and hope in the world were being sucked into them and scorched in an inferno that never stopped burning. Eternal…

My sanity was already stretched to breaking when shadows stretched out on either side of him like wings. Because they were wings. Black feathered wings, glossy in the moonlight.

My gaze met those impossible black pits. "How…?"

This awful, beautiful creature was now standing over my bed. Fear paralyzed me, petrified me. I was hard as a rock all over, including my dick. It was as if my body had no clue what to do with what I was seeing and was short-circuiting.

"Don't ask dull questions," the man-thing said.

His accent was British; his voice was smooth black obsidian. Like his eyes, where I was trapped. Black eyes that held no irises, no pupils, but I felt them take in my erection tenting the bedsheets. A slow, lazy smile widened his mouth, making him both more terrible to behold and yet more beautiful at the same time.

"What is happening?"

"Let go, Cole Matheson," the creature said. "This life…the pain, the failure, the loneliness… Let it all go and come with me."

"Go with you…where?"

He bent down, his unnaturally white face inches from mine. I felt drunk, vision blurring under the intensity of his eyes, burning up in them. I wondered if he were going to kiss me or kill me. I was helpless either way, held in a thrall of terror, shock, and even lust. The heated vapor of his breath touched my lips and God help me, I wanted to taste it.

"Come with me and I'll give you a new life. You'll be powerful. Endlessly beautiful. Free…"

I couldn't catch my breath. My heart was pounding madly, faster than any panic attack.

I'm dying. I'm going to die…

Black wings unfolded, blood rushed to my ears, and darkness took me completely.

four

Cole

I jerked awake, my heart pounding while my skin drenched my clothes in a cold sweat. A panic attack? A bit early in the morning for it but on par for me, all things considered.

Then it came back to me on a rush of black wings.

I frantically scanned my small place. Empty. Watery morning light filtered in from the window.

"A dream, dummy," I muttered. "Of course, it was just a dream."

An extraordinarily vivid dream where my imagination, led by dark and desperate thoughts, had turned a beautiful man I'd seen in the park into a...

Fallen angel? A demon?

I shivered at the image and then realized I was hard. Again. I'd been hard in the dream too, my body reacting to the fear, I supposed. I'd heard that could happen. But now?

I threw off the covers to discover I hadn't just been hard last night but had come in my sleep. A curse fell from my lips, but I wasn't surprised. I'd deprived myself of male company for years, and my current mental state left little energy for taking matters into my own hands. An apathy of despair had settled over me like a heavy coat.

Terrifying as it was, last night's dream had been the most exciting thing to happen to me in ages.

"Exciting." I scoffed. "I thought I was going to die."

There was no response in the emptiness and quiet. The demon-creature's whispered promises filled my head and my pulse kicked up again. Just what—exactly—had my subconscious been trying to tell me?

A cold sweat came over me again. I'd given my despair and failure a physical form. Beautiful and dangerous, and I couldn't get it out of my head.

Let go…

I grabbed my sketch pad. I had to get him *out*. I sketched and sketched: feathered wings touched by moonlight, alabaster skin, black eyes with flames and death in their endless depths. I tried to capture him all at once and in bits and pieces; different angles, different degrees of light falling over him, the lines of his elegant, long fingers, the beetle's glossy shine, the twist of his lips…

When my hand was cramping from the urgency of my sketching, I set down the pen and realized I'd filled five pages with the demon. The memory of him—no, the *image*, I reminded myself—was still with me but not as visceral; I felt like I was allowed to get on with my day.

"Whatever the hell that entails."

I set down the sketchpad and picked up my phone. Nothing from Vaughn. Nothing from anyone.

Get up. Get out. Do something.

The thoughts were warnings. Flares going up through the bleakness of a thousand other thoughts that wondered what was the point of anything? Stay in bed or don't, who cared?

Come with me…

"No."

I wasn't so far gone that I was going to sit in my bed all day with my own release drying on my pajama pants. I got out of bed and headed to the bathroom, moving through the space where my nocturnal visitor had been standing in my dream.

I caught a whiff of smoke. No, it was ash. A dead fire.

"Your imagination," I told myself. I had a vivid one, after all. I was an artist. Or had been in another life. But that's over now…

"Stop it," I muttered and continued to the tiny bathroom.

I stripped out of my pajamas, and my blood went cold all over. On my thigh was a bruise about the size of a quarter.

Where the corner of the art book hit me when I dropped it...in my *dream*.

The early morning was bitterly cold and gray. I had the day off from Mulligan's—my schedule at the pub getting leaner by the minute—and took the bus to Hyde Park, juggling a small stool, my sketchbook, and a coffee. I needed the warmth, but the coffee was making me jittery.

You could've gotten the bruise from anywhere. From moving your portraits into your new place. You didn't notice it at the time, but the dream gave an explanation. That's all.

The rationale made sense; vastly more plausible than the alternative—that an actual demon-creature had visited me last night. But the uncanny *realness* of him argued back more than any bruise until I laughed at myself.

Maybe I was going crazy. That was the most plausible argument of all.

I set up shop in Hyde Park, put out a little sign that said I'd do portraits for ten pounds, per. From my backpack, I pulled a piece of cardboard on which I'd taped a few portraits—my friend Lucy among them—as a sampling of my "talent."

The jittery feeling faded under the pointlessness of it all. Resignation infused my every action, turning my world even grayer than the sky. Who was going to sit in the chill wind for a portrait? Stupid. It didn't matter that other artists were there, setting up their own mini studios. Didn't matter that the paths were busy with foot traffic and tourists.

It sort of scared me how little anything mattered at all. The nightmare was starting to make more sense.

I sat stewing in my own apathy and almost didn't notice the young couple standing in front of me, bundled in heavy coats and scarves against the cold, their arms linked. Americans, by their accents, or lack thereof.

"Ooh, he's good. I want one," the woman said.

"Go for it," the guy said, giving her a gentle nudge. "We got time."

She turned to me excitedly. "Can I?"

"Yes, of course," I said. "Here."

I gave her the stool and knelt on the hard stone a few feet away. I set the sketchbook on my thigh and flipped past the frantic drawings of the demon—the *dream* demon, I insisted; thinking otherwise felt monumentally stupid—and began to sketch.

When I set out to do portraiture, the exact likeness of my subject was as important as capturing some innate quality in them that only they possessed. Whatever made them, them.

I blew on my hands and tried to render this young woman's eyes as I saw them—pretty, long-lashed, but with an inner light that wasn't dimmed by the drab London morning. But whatever inner light *I* might've had that guided my art felt distant. Veiled. As if I could feel that it was still there but dulled. I drew the woman from rote skill and nothing more. The couple was thrilled with the accuracy when I was finished and complimented me again and again, but I knew the truth.

It was shit.

"It's amazing! Thank you!" the woman cooed.

The man gazed into her eyes. "I'm going to take it to the office so I can stare at you when I'm at work."

Newlyweds.

The guy pulled out a ten-pound note and handed it to me. "Thanks, man. Great job."

I juggled my sketchbook and went to shut it when the wind gusted, blowing pages. The guy cocked his head, catching a glimpse of a full-bodied sketch of my demon visitor.

"Holy shit, what is that?"

I fumbled with cold fingers to close the book. "Oh, that. Nothing. I had a weird dream."

"It's amazing," he said, looking disappointed when I finally managed to shut the book. "Like…wow."

"What was it?" The woman peered over his shoulder.

"It's like a…whatdoyoucallit? Fallen angel? Can she see?"

"Uh, sure," I mumbled and opened the book again. I turned it around so they could peruse. With American brazenness, they flipped pages without asking, both ooing and awing over the sketches.

"That's epic, dude," the guy said. "How much?"

I blinked. "How much…?"

"For the big one. With the wings and stuff."

"Oh, it's not for sale."

Which was ridiculous. I was as desperately short of money as this guy was to have my sketch. Inexplicably, I wasn't ready to part with it.

"Maybe that's for the best. It's kind of scary." The woman shivered. "Those black eyes…"

"Yeah, imagine this in full color." The guy released my sketchbook. "Thanks, again."

They walked away arm in arm. I hunched on the stool, the sketchbook on my knees, and traced my demon with icy fingers. To put him in color, he'd need oils. Lots of black, white, and that rich, blood red of his coat. The burnished gold of his hair…

The momentary spark of inspiration blew out with the next cold gust of wind. Oils were expensive, and my self-doubt—which grew more ferocious with every setback—told me it would be impossible to capture the image the way it needed to be captured anyway.

"Jesus, feel sorry for yourself much?"

But those words blew away in the wind too. That was the problem with depression—logic had little effect. Past triumphs and good times were starting to feel farther and farther away, as if they'd happened to someone else. The gray flatness of everything settled deeper, sapping the very energy I needed to pull myself out of it and press on. A vicious circle of numb despair that fed on itself until I felt hollowed and empty.

I did a few more portraits, pocketed a few more quid, and called it a day. By the last customer, I could scarcely feel my fingers. I took the bus back to my neighborhood, bought some soup, another hot coffee, and headed back to my flat, wondering if I should talk to someone.

A professional someone.

And tell them what? an insidious voice whispered. *You're sad because the world isn't falling at your feet for your art? Boo-fucking-hoo.*

In my little flat, with Ms. Thomas's TV droning above me, audible through the thin walls, I opened my laptop, intending to look for more open calls. Commissions. Someone wanting a portrait of their cat. Anything.

Nothing.

Try again tomorrow, I thought as I climbed into bed, though it was hardly seven p.m. *Tomorrow is a new day. A chance to start over.*

But I fell asleep to that other voice whispering with a terrible confidence that tomorrow would be more of the same. And the day after that. And the day after that…

five

Cole

I woke in the black of the night, disoriented. A strange sense that I wasn't alone. There was a presence taking up space in my small room. A weight on my bed near my feet. I reached for my glasses and turned on the little bedside lamp.

"Hello, Cole."

"Jesus!"

I scrambled back on my heels until my back hit the wall, my heart clamoring in my ribcage and sending blood rushing to my ears.

The demon had come back.

Except that had been a dream and this was real. There were no wings or black eyes but a flesh and blood man, devastating in a black suit, coat, scarf. The man I'd seen in Hyde Park the other day. He was handsome from a distance on the street, but up close…I couldn't stop staring. His face was a painter's dream—a composite of contradicting features that harmonized into something breathtaking. Chiseled and sharp in the cheeks but full and soft in the mouth. A strong nose between blue-green eyes that were fringed with long soft lashes. He was blinding. Beautiful.

A beautiful murderer. Holy shit, this is how it happens. He followed me here, and now I'm about to be murdered.

"I'm not going to murder you," he said calmly. "Not exactly."

"Not exactly?" I croaked, fumbling for my phone on the nightstand. "I saw you…on the street the other day," I insisted, yet he had the same British accent as the demon. "H-How did you get in here?"

"This room is uncommonly shabby with numerous cracks and fissures," he said, glancing around with disdain painted on his *uncommonly* handsome features. "You might consider more hospitable accommodations."

"Sure, I'll do that," I said, my fingers curling around the phone and gripping tight. "You broke in. I'm calling the police."

"Unnecessary. You are, after all, only dreaming."

"Dreaming…"

"As you were last night."

But he was too real. Too much flesh and bone, sitting on my bed, pinning me under my blankets; I could feel his weight on the thin mattress. In the dimness, I could see a glint of light off his gold hair and the sharper glint in his blue eyes. The scent of his cologne hung in the air, mixed with the faint scent of ash…

"No fucking way…" I started jabbing at my phone.

He sighed, annoyed, and got to his feet. In one smooth motion, he plucked the phone from my hand. I started to shout for help and in the next instant, his eyes were black on black. Black feathered wings sprouted from his back, filling my small space with darkness. The scream died in my throat, and I could only stare.

As fast as they'd appeared, his wings retracted and vanished, and his eyes returned to blue-green.

"As I said, dreaming."

"Jesus Christ."

He smirked. "Not even close. My name is Ambri and you are Cole Matheson. There. Now that we're properly introduced, you can stop clutching the coverlet like a frightened child."

My hands loosened their claw-like grip on the blanket, and I stared, heart pounding, as he strolled my small place. He examined my paintings that were stacked against the wall, leisurely flipping through them.

I'm losing my shit, that's all. Plenty of painters have gone mad. It's kind of our thing…

"Interesting," Ambri said, jolting me from my thoughts.

"What is?"

"Your art. All portraits." He was no longer casual now but studying my work, his brows furrowed. "You're quite good. Extraordinary, even."

"I'm not…and don't touch those," I said, still tucked in bed like a helpless dork.

Ambri ignored me. "This one is especially well done."

He held up an oil portrait—the best of the bunch. It was of one of my professors at the Academy. I'd put her in a dark green dress with a large brimmed hat. Her Cavalier King Charles Spaniel lay curled on her lap.

"Reminds me of the portraits done in my time," he said, anger tightening his voice.

"In your time?"

With a lingering glance, he set my painting back with the others. "Tell me, Cole Matheson, why are you living in this hovel when you have talent like this?"

I shrugged self-consciously. "It's been a little rough lately."

Ambri was still strolling my place, hands laced behind his back, as if touring the world's shittiest museum. He sniffed. "A *little*?"

"How do you know my name?"

"As a figment of your imagination, it stands to reason I know everything about you, does it not?"

"You seem pretty damn real to me."

Ambri's sharply arched brows came together. "Did you not just witness me in my demonic glory? *You are dreaming.*"

"Demonic." I swallowed hard. "Okay, I'll play along. Is that what you are? A…demon?"

"That's one name for our kind. It has a sleek, sexiness I appreciate."

"What do you *want*?"

"An excellent question. I had thought my task here would be rather straightforward but now…" Ambri gave another glance to my paintings, then took the room's lone chair—a ratty, wooden thing—and dropped elegantly in it. He crossed one ankle over his knee. "I'll take what I want. Eventually. The lives of humans are pitifully short, even without our interference, so perhaps the better question is, Cole Matheson, what do *you* want?"

Now that his attention was on me, I felt every bit of it. His words were laced with danger, but the promise of sex dripped from them and emanated off of him like a vapor. I remembered a flash of last night; even terrified out of my mind, I'd wanted him. I came in my sleep...

"Are you a...what do you call it? An incubus?"

His eyebrows rose meaningfully, and he ran his tongue over his full bottom lip while his gaze raked me up and down. "I can be whatever you want me to be."

Never in the history of the English language had nine words been so loaded with sex. Each syllable sank into the marrow of my damn bones. My heart was still thumping a hard, steady beat, but the outright terror had mellowed. Moreover, the incessant negative thoughts that plagued me all day and night had gone strangely silent.

Definitive proof this is a dream.

"So that's a yes?" I said, leaning into this madness with curiosity. I couldn't peel my eyes off of him and didn't want to.

"It's a distinctive *no*. Incubi pretend to be something they're not in order to get what they want," Ambri said with disdain. "More powerful is the demon to whom a human knowingly *gives*."

"You're a demon with morals," I said. "That's cute."

His gaze trailed up and down my body under the covers; I could practically feel the heat of it. "Do you find me *cute*, Cole Matheson?"

I glanced down. I was fucking hard again. I grabbed another pillow and covered my lap. "Dammit."

"Don't feel embarrassed," Ambri said. "It's what I do. An incubus feeds on the act of sex. I feed from the need. The lust. The *want*." He cocked his head. "Shall I demonstrate?"

"N-no," I managed, shocked and bewildered that I really wanted to say yes. The erection under the pillow *begged* for me to say yes.

To let go...

Ambri's knowing smile was something out of a goddamn fantasy. "Ah well, no rush. The night is young." His gaze moved to the nightstand next to the bed and landed on my sketchbook.

"What is this?" He leaned over and picked it up, opened it to the sketches of him. "Oh..."

Finally, I broke my inertia and swung my legs out of bed, reaching for my book. "Give that here."

Reality seemed to tear open right in front of me as Ambri dissolved into a swarming mass of shiny black beetles and then *reassembled* into a man near my flat's bathroom, flipping through the sketches of himself. He looked over at me with a pained expression. Almost touched.

"You drew...me."

"Well, *yeah*." I scrubbed my eyes with both hands at the insanity of holding a conversation with someone who could vaporize himself into bugs at will. "I drew it after last night's visit. Or *dream*. You make quite an impression, to say the least."

Ambri's brow furrowed again. "Of course, I do. I'm a remarkable subject."

"A couple wanted to buy one off me, but I said no."

"Because you're drowning in lavish luxury and riches?"

I didn't want to part with you.

"I have my reasons." I crossed my arms. "What kind of name is Ambri, anyway?"

"It's Latin, meaning: a pitiful attempt to change the subject."

He closed the sketchbook and moved toward me to return it to the nightstand. My space was filled with his nearness again, his heat, his power that was doing exactly as he stated—drawing my loneliness to the surface. I dug my fingers into my arms, trying to keep myself present. I had to be dreaming and yet I'd never felt more awake. My body felt attuned to Ambri, nerve endings keyed up. My hands wanted to touch him...

I cleared my throat. "I've never heard of a name like yours. How did my imagination make it up? Or the beetles or the wings? How did it make up any of this? It's all craziness, isn't it?"

"Perhaps." Ambri returned to the chair and pulled it close, so that our knees were practically touching. "Perhaps you've conjured me to alleviate a little of that stress that's coursing through your veins instead of blood."

"I'm serious."

"So am I." His grin turned suggestive.

Christ.

Being in Ambri's presence was like trying to stay sober while downing shot after shot of the richest liquor. "What do you *actually* want from me?"

"I believe I made my intentions clear." He glanced at the pillow still covering my erection. "As have you."

"I mean, if you're a figment of my imagination, then I created you. Everything about you is something in me that's trying to get out. So what is it? My career failures? Self-doubt? Loneliness?"

"Do you know what your problem is, Cole Matheson? You think too much."

I watched, hypnotized, as Ambri slid out of the chair to kneel in front of me. His hands—elegant and long-fingered—rested on each of my knees and began to slide up my thighs, over the thin material of my pajama pants. He gently removed the pillow from my lap and set it aside. Then his hands were back on my legs, his thumbs making circles along my inner thigh, inches from my cock that strained to be free, to be touched. The sudden urge to see Ambri naked ignited in me like a flare from the dark wasteland of deprivation I'd exiled myself. But was this really happening? I was dreaming this man who sometimes had wings and kept pet beetles up his sleeve?

Ambri's hands moved higher, reached for the tie on my pants.

"I can't," I said in a strangled voice. "I don't do this. I don't just…fuck random strangers. Dream or no dream."

"Who said anything about fucking?"

"Isn't that why you're here?"

"You tell me. What do you *want*?"

Him, naked. His mouth wrapped around my cock. My hand in his hair, holding him there while he sucked and licked…

Desperately, I clung to myself. "No. This is madness. I can't. We shouldn't… Get your hands off me.

"If you insist."

He lifted his hands from my thighs, and I immediately regretted it. I wanted the heat and weight of them—someone else's touch—on my skin. I swallowed, practically dizzy for want of him.

He studied my reaction and smiled like a satisfied cat. "I don't need to touch you to make you come," he said. "Relax, Cole Matheson, and let me have you."

Ambri wasn't asking me to relax but to surrender. I hesitated for another second, but the power in him was wearing me down. I *wanted* to want him. The desire to submit to him was my own hunger. It infused me like a drug. Heat and heavy need moved through my veins.

This is what he does…

With a faint nod of my head, I surrendered.

"An excellent decision." Ambri smiled and smoothly slid out of his coat—it pooled around his knees. I watched, transfixed, as he removed his scarf, his suit jacket. He wore a vest whose sole purpose was to give shape and suggestion to the slender, muscled body beneath. He unbuttoned his dress shirt, rolled up his sleeves, as if preparing to get to work.

Because he is, God help me.

But there was no God here. I'd gone off the edge of my own imagination into something dark and reeking of danger. And sex. Ambri was a walking, talking incarnation of every fantasy conceivable and a few that had yet to be.

He got to his feet and stood over me, studying me. "It's been a long time, hasn't it?"

I nodded mutely and my heart nearly exploded as he planted his hands on the bed on either side of me, forcing me to lean back. His sudden nearness made me groan. Like a hunger pang. His face was an inch from mine; the heat of his breath feathered over my cheek. His nose nearly—but not quite—brushed mine as his blue-green gaze roamed. Examined. His lips followed and it was all I could do to keep from craning my mouth to taste him.

"It's been too long since you allowed someone this close to you," he said, low and seductive. "Too long since you felt the heat of another. Since someone gazed into your eyes—your magnificent artist's eyes that see straight down a person and into their soul. That's what you want, isn't it? Someone to see into *your* soul. To see you and say, *Yes, Cole. You are everything to me. You are perfect. You are enough...*"

A sound erupted in my chest as hot tears flooded my eyes. I reached for my aching cock, but Ambri reared back, moving out of my space. Too far away.

"No touching, remember?" he scolded. "Fair's fair."

I stifled a groan but obeyed. My hands made claws in the bedsheets, barely restrained need coursing through me like thunder. Mercifully—torturously—Ambri closed in again, the timbre of his voice now moving down my neck. Fires ignited along my skin, shooting down my back, making it arch to him. I shut my eyes, my body shuddering, aching, needing...

"I need..." I moaned. Begged. "I need—"

"I know what you need," Ambri whispered with dark, seductive authority. "But not yet. You cannot come until I say you can. I want to relish your desire a few moments more. To feast on how badly you want me..."

I moaned again. In the dark of my closed eyes, I could sense his lips were maddeningly close to my skin but not touching, and I cursed myself for making him keep his word.

If he doesn't touch me, I'm going to fucking die...

"No more thinking. Lie back, Cole. All your need and want and hunger... You're going to give it to me now. It's mine. *Mine.*"

I nodded helplessly, my eyes still closed, noting with some alarm that the only thing in the entire fucking world I wanted to be was his.

But the thought was burned up in the heat of the rawest lust I'd ever known. The presence and power of Ambri pushed me onto my back. I sank onto the bed and felt him come with me, leaning over me, but still somehow so far away. My hips lifted and came down, seeking him, but there was nothing.

Finally, when I couldn't contain it another second, his honeyed voice poured into my ear. "Come for me, Cole. Come for me right now."

Instantly, my back arched off the bed, my breath coming in desperate gasps, shortening as the orgasm climbed to a peak. I couldn't help myself but opened my eyes to witness my imagination's creation—a beautifully perfect man, bringing me to climax with just his words, his presence, as if there were nothing else he wanted more. As if he were made to do only this, only for me.

My flat was empty.

My own hand was wrapped around my cock, stroking furiously. The raw, ravenous need Ambri had drawn from me coursed through me, wave after wave. I trapped a gritty cry between clenched teeth as my climax erupted hotly over my fingers, shuddering as it moved through my body in heavy, hot ribbons of pleasure.

Jesus fucking Christ.

I sucked air in harsh gulps, my heart pounding and then slowing. Disappointment swooped in as the ecstasy faded. Ambri's absence was a cold bucket of water just when I'd finally begun to thaw from my despair. When I'd *felt* something besides hopelessness for the first time in months.

When the most mind-blowing orgasm of my life ebbed away, I sat up and glanced around, dazed. If it had been a dream, I don't remember waking from it. Lingering too, was that ferocious curiosity. Whatever

Ambri was, he was impossible, but I'd created him nevertheless. Why? Who is he?

Will he come back?

That last question burned hottest.

I cleaned myself up, then slumped back against the pillows, reality returning on icy drafts. Ambri wasn't *absent*; there was no Ambri. I'd merely woken up. And now awake, the insidious whispers that plagued me returned with a vengeance.

Your pathetic neediness has taken physical form. An imaginary friend. A beautiful man who wants only you. Who compliments your paintings and calls you extraordinary. How sad.

I groaned and rolled deep into my covers, shutting my eyes against the thoughts. But they followed me into the cold night that was colder now that my dream was over.

One thought chased me down into the dark, louder and more terrifying than any other.

All of your dreams are over.

six

Ambri

I stalk the London streets instead of taking my anicorpus form. I need the chill November air to cool my cheeks. To calm my pulse and regain my composure.

"What in the bloody hell…?"

Coaxing and feasting on a human's climax is routine. I've done it a thousand times, and yet as I brought Cole Matheson to a release he desperately needed, an unsettling sensation grew within me. Unwanted emotions felt as if they were trying to wake from a three-hundred-year-old hibernation.

"Nonsense," I declare and walk faster. "He's attractive. There's no scandal in that."

Except I'd been with countless other humans over the centuries who were far more conventionally handsome. Cole was appealing, to be sure, with his arresting eyes that were the darkest shade of brown. Almost black. Sharp with intelligence and yet soft, reflecting his artistic heart. A broad mouth, broad shoulders. His unruly mop of brown hair, burnished with gold, begged my fingers to make fists in it while I crushed my lips to his…

"I do not kiss humans," I told the night.

It was a hard and fast rule. My only rule, really, when it came to what I would do or have done to me. But Cole's parted lips had started to unravel me. My control had begun to falter and instead of witnessing the fruits of my labor—the most satisfying moment—I slipped out through the crack in the window, leaving myself unsatiated. Hungry.

Wanting.

"*No. Impossible.*"

I take to the air and swarm to my flat in Chelsea. I leave windows open for that purpose and surge into my bedroom. A new curse falls from my lips as I reform as a human.

Demon…

I can smell her. Fire and cinnamon, arousal and danger, blood and sex.

"Sugar and spice and everything depraved," I mutter as I go to the living room—*my* living room—to see Eisheth, Destroyer of Men, and Asmodai's second-in-command—draped over *my* settee.

The succubus is dripping in black lace, her black hair flowing between her bat wings like silk. She not so much lies on my couch but is spilling over it with long, languid limbs. Blood red nails trail lazily up her own bare, bloodless thigh. It doesn't escape me that she's in her demon form and I am not. I'm weak in this human shell and she knows it.

"Eisheth," I say placidly. "This is unexpected."

And ominous.

"Ambri, darling. It's been too long."

I bend so that we may kiss cheeks, then move quickly out of her space. In those few short moments, I feel her crawling around in my mind, searching…

"Brandy?"

"Please."

I fill two glasses from a crystal decanter and hand her one before I sit on the chair opposite.

"What brings you to This Side?"

Her red lips turn up in a smile that makes my skin itch. "Don't play dumb. Asmodai is not a patient entity, and neither am I."

"All business, eh? A pity."

"We can still have our fun first, if you'd like." She lets her thighs fall open slightly. "For old time's sake?"

I smirk over the rim of my glass. "We'd burn the city to the ground."

"Wouldn't we just?" Her perfect eyebrows arch. "I'm surprised to find you in London. Returning to the scene of dear uncle's crime?"

"We don't discuss our human traumas, dove. It's rude."

"Our human traumas make us what we are," she says with a laugh. "But truly, you told me you were finished with Britain."

"You know why I'm here."

"I do." She sets down the glass on my Louis XVI coffee table. "Our dark lord would like a progress report."

"Already?" I ask with a scowl to conceal my unease. "I've only just begun."

"He doesn't trust you, darling. The losses of Casziel and Ashtaroth are not inconsequential." She sits up suddenly, her black-on-black eyes flaring. "Tell me truly, Ambri. Between you and me, did you send the old man to his doom?"

As if I'd confide anything in her. As if it would remain between her and me...

"Is that what they're saying?"

"Everyone is saying that you helped the human girl summon him. And that human girl had a guardian angel—"

"What was I to do? Angels are not to be trifled with," I remind her. "*Everyone* would do well to remember that."

Eisheth reclines and sips her drink. "I don't like being here on business, Ambri, when you're so beautifully intended for pleasure. But I have no choice. You're slow to obey Asmodai's command—"

"Slow?" I huff. "I attempted, first, to terrorize the human into madness by showing myself to him. He proved more resilient than that…"

Cole was brave. He held out as long as he could.

"Therefore, I returned tonight to learn more of him. To assess his faculties."

"And to play with him?"

"Can you of all people blame me?"

"No, but anything less than the human's swift and total destruction has Asmodai suspecting your motives. It should be a simple matter, after all. The Twins have been priming your target for months."

I mutter a curse. "I should've known."

The Twins, Deber and Keeb, are masters of insidious whispering that drives humans to doubt themselves. It's called "negative self-talk" nowadays, though there is nothing "self" about it. Most humans believe their thoughts are uncontrollable, and Deber and Keeb have turned that belief into an art form. It's no surprise that they've all but smothered Cole Matheson's belief in himself—artists make the easiest prey.

"They can rot, the meddling bitches," I snarl. "If anyone is going to drive Cole Matheson to ultimate despair, it's going to be me."

"Your bravado is impressive, Ambri, but that's all it is. Words."

"I have a plan."

No sooner do I utter the words, than it comes quickly, all at once. A plan so perfect, I'm rather impressed with myself. A plan that achieves my objectives while…

Allowing me to keep Cole Matheson a little longer?

"Enticing a wretched human to his demise is a noble cause to be sure," I say, "but not terribly difficult. Much more challenging to tempt one who has reached the pinnacle of fame, wealth, and success." I count on my fingers. "Elvis, Hendrix, Marilyn… Our victories, all. Victories that make waves."

Eisheth's dubious expression softens. "You're going to raise this pathetic boy to Hendrix-like heights?"

"Something like that. He's going to paint me."

She sniffs. "Of course. Your ego always did require as much stroking as the rest of you."

"I won't take advantage of the Twins' work, I'll undo it. I'll lift Cole Matheson up and give him everything he's ever wanted. When his every dream has come true, I'll plummet him into final despair. None shall question my loyalty then."

And if I happen to remedy my erasure from the family lineage with a portrait of myself at the same time, so be it. I deserve that, after all.

"The hierarchy doesn't approve of our kind being rendered realistically," Eisheth says. "There can be no proof of our existence. You know this."

I roll my eyes. "I don't know when last you Crossed Over, dove, but there are countless dark and depraved images floating around This Side. Perhaps you've heard of the internet?"

A rhetorical question. The internet was an idea whispered into humans by one of our own—Sheerree, Queen of Madness—during the latter part of the last century. The celebrations were epic and lasted eons. I still have the bitemarks.

"Besides," I say. "You've seen renderings of us in the grimoires. All hooves and tails."

"Seems unnecessary," Eisheth says after a moment. "Your human is on the brink; you need only push him over."

"Aye, *I* am to push him over," I declare. "*I* will deliver him to Asmodai. He is my charge, not Deber or Keeb's. The glory belongs to me and me alone. I will not share it." I press a finger to my chest. "He is *mine*."

The strange thrill those words inspire in me is unlike any I've felt in all my years as a demonic entity. It's warmer, softer, and yet just as potent as my usual hunger. Dormant emotions trying to wake. My finger, I note, is resting directly on my heart.

Bloody hell.

I reach for my glass and down the brandy, wishing it had any effect on me. For a long moment, dread fills me that Eisheth will read the weakness painted all over my face. She'll take me to Asmodai where I'll spend a millennium in inconceivable agony. Perhaps I deserve that. Perhaps I'm growing soft. I shiver at the word.

But the succubus rises, her leathery wings fluttering enough to lift her from the settee onto the floor. "I admit, your plan is intriguing…if you can pull it off."

I ease a breath. "You haven't seen his talent. All will happen exactly as I say."

"I certainly hope so, for your sake." She moves to the window where she pauses. "A warning, Ambri. Because you were once my lover and friend."

"Once?"

She doesn't smile. "Mind that as you raise your human to fame and riches, you don't forget to whom the real glory is owed."

I incline my head in the smallest of bows. "Asmodai will not be disappointed."

"See that he isn't. It would be a shame if he were to cut off that magnificent cock of yours and feed it to his imps."

Her body folds inward and upward, as Eisheth takes her anicorpus form. A large bat with blood red eyes flaps obscenely in my living room, then flies into the night.

I shut the window, then lean my hands on the sill. A shaky exhale escapes me as I raise my head and see my reflection in the glass. My exquisite face is twisted in anguish. Immediately, I stiffen, stand upright and smooth my jacket. I smooth my expression too, make it impassive. Cold. Deadly.

All will happen exactly as I say.

And yet, and yet…

seven

Cole

"I'm sorry, Cole," Mark O'Shea said at the end of my shift at the pub the next day. My boss's face was a mask of genuine worry and regret. "Business is just too slow these days. A downturn."

"Right," I said, my tone flat. "I get it."

"Sorry for making you come out here, but I wanted to tell you in person." He studied my face, his brows furrowing in concern. "As soon as it picks up—the very bloody second—I'll call you."

"I appreciate that."

Mark pursed his lips. "You going to be okay?"

"Yep," I said, managing a wan smile. "I'll be fine."

My boss—*former*—boss's expression was dubious. He pressed an envelope into my hand. "Your paycheck plus a few extra quid. And you call me if you need anything."

"Right. Thanks, Mark."

"I'm sorry, Cole. I really am."

I muttered a goodbye and stepped out of Mulligan's into the gray afternoon. I'd woken that day with an odd burst of optimism. The dream of Ambri was as sharp and visceral as ever. Visions of him in his elegant suit, his beautiful hands sliding up my thighs, crowded my thoughts. He was alive in my mind in a way nothing had been in months, and I had a silly wish that he was real. To talk to, to alleviate my crushing loneliness, to maybe touch him this time and be touched…

But he wasn't real. The only way to keep him was to paint him. I'd figured after my shift at the pub, I'd use my tips to buy some oils and paint him in full color. Maybe I'd have something good. Maybe I'd make a sale…

Now, I was unemployed and couldn't afford paint. I'd have to find a new job, or I could sketch at Hyde Park, but at ten pounds per portrait, I'd have to have ten clients per day, every day, just to stay afloat. The crushing weight of failure seemed even heavier, mixed with shame that I was feeling epically sorry for myself.

On the street, I checked my phone for a message from Vaughn, knowing there wasn't one. The me of a year ago would have been appalled to be counting on someone else anyway. Now, mental exhaustion sapped my energy and colored my every thought, so that the idea of painting Ambri seemed silly and indulgent. Childish, even.

"Shut up for fuck's sake," I hissed at the destructive thoughts. The couple yesterday were agog over the Ambri sketches. That was something. I wasn't completely hopeless.

Yet.

I got back to my flat and sketched the demon version of Ambri until my hand ached, leaning into the work and leaving the negative thoughts and depression behind for a few glorious hours. When I was done, I had three full-size sketches that I thought might fetch a decent price at the park. Sketches of him in his elegant suit but with a black-upon-black gleam in his eyes. Pale skin, feathered wings, and an arrogant smirk that was all too human. I traced my finger over the line of his jaw.

"Who are you?" I whispered.

I tucked the sketches into my bag. The smaller, thumbnail sketches of his hands, the arch of a wing, a gleaming black eye…those I cut out of my sketchbook and pasted to a sheet of cardboard. Samples of my work to draw customers in. Then I stepped out into a late afternoon that was as cold and gray as ever, threatening rain, but with a tiny glimmer of hope burning in my heart.

Foot traffic through Hyde Park was light, but to my relief, the demon sketches were snapped up almost immediately. I'd priced them at twenty pounds each which I thought was risky, but every buyer told me I was underselling my work.

"I've never seen anything like this," said one guy, admiring a sketch of Ambri with one of his beetles resting on his outstretched hand. "You've got something here."

I thanked the guy—and the gods—for the bills in my wallet that hadn't felt so thick in weeks. For a few brief moments, I was free of the bone-crushing stress and dark moods that had been plaguing me lately,

By dusk, I'd done nearly a dozen portraits and was thinking about calling it a day when three lanky guys in windbreakers, two with beer bottles in their hands, sauntered over, laughing and speaking in thick Manchester accents.

"Oi, mate! What you got here?" one asked, gesturing at the thumbnails of Ambri. "You working on some kind of comic book?"

"Uh, no, it's just some stuff I thought up," I said lamely.

"Not bloody bad," said another, peering closer. His gaze was glassy with booze but cunning too as he pinned me with a look. "You got any left?"

"No, I… No."

"Sold out, did you? What else you got?"

"What do you mean?" I asked as the hairs on the back of my neck stood up. "I do portraits. Ten pounds—"

"Hear that? He'll draw yer pretty mug for ten quid, Ollie," another chortled, jostling him.

I hunched in my coat, feeling like my ten-year-old self back in elementary school, being picked on by the big kids at lunch. The guys huddled, talking and snickering amongst themselves, and then shot me a wave.

"Maybe next time, mate!"

"See you around!"

I sighed with relief as they meandered off…and cursed my lack of caution an hour later when they cornered me as I walked to the bus stop. I was shoved up against a wall between a Boots pharmacy—closed for the night—and an abandoned hair salon. Two men held my arms pinned while the third rifled through my jacket.

"Don't, please…" I gritted, struggling even as my heart crashed against my ribs like a wild animal.

"Please," mocked the guy with his hands in my pockets. He came up with my wallet—fat with today's sales—and cleaned it out. "So polite."

He balled the bills in his fist and then punched me in the stomach. Another blow came from the right to whack me in the face, knocking my glasses to the ground. I heard the crunch of glass, then again—louder—as one of the guys stepped down hard, grinding the lenses to dust. Another punch; I felt my teeth slice my lower lip and blood spattered the sidewalk. The guys holding me let go and I crumpled to the ground, curling in a ball in a feeble attempt to ward off the blows and kicks that came from all sides.

Eventually, the rush of blood in my ears receded like low tide and I realized I was alone. Pain wound around every part of me. I sat up slowly. Blood dripped from my mouth, my nose, from a cut above my eye. I gingerly inhaled. My sides ached but no broken ribs. I hoped.

For long moments, I sat against the wall and stared at the empty ally in the falling darkness. They'd taken my sketchbook, and my wallet lay like a dead bird, open and empty, on the grimy walk. What I'd earned that day would've paid for two weeks' rent. A fleeting thought that I could paint more came and went—the frames of my glasses were bent and twisted, lying in what was left of the lenses.

I examined my feelings on the matter and discovered I had none. No despair, no anxiety, no fear. I was somewhere below them all, and that should've scared me the most.

Night fell and the cold swooped down with it. I wandered the city after that. A passerby glanced at the blood on my face that I was doing nothing about and gave me a wide berth. I had no plan, no direction. Street signs were a blur to me. The Thames stayed to my right and eventually, I found myself at the Blackfriars Bridge.

The water was black and still, only a few ripples gleaming silver under the moonlight. I tucked my fists deeper into my pockets, seeking warmth that wasn't there. An exhaustion hung over me that had nothing to do with sleepless nights. It was the tiredness that comes from carrying around a heavy, invisible burden no one else can see or touch.

I glanced down along the stretch of bridge, quiet and still, and felt the urge to run. No destination in mind; just run until my lungs burned and my cheeks grew hot against the cold night wind. Run and run until I was somewhere else. Until I was *someone* else. Maybe the heavy load of being me would fall off along the way and I'd be free of it.

I turned my gaze to the black water.

Or maybe I'll just disappear.

eight

Ambri

Cole isn't at his tiny shoebox of a dwelling.

I wait as long as my patience allows—ten minutes—then take to the sky to find him. It's a monstrous thing now, this London. Since my living day, it's expanded into a colored maze of "Tube" stations, taxis, and even a bloody Ferris wheel. The Tower castle is now an easy walk to a Tesco.

But beneath the lights and modern architecture lurk my childhood memories. No amount of years or modifications will ever bury the pain that lives in the bones of this city. Against my will, memories crawl out of the shallow grave I've buried them in.

A thrill that my uncle had arrived at Hever Castle for a visit.

A greater thrill—and pride—that he wanted to take *me* in his carriage for a trip to the city.

How that thrill curdled into a nightmare I couldn't wake from.

How Uncle's liveried men sat outside the carriage's passenger quarters, out of earshot of my cries. They guided twin white horses over bumpy roads, oblivious to what my uncle was doing to his ten-year-old nephew just on the other side of the partition.

A hundred pairs of wings flicker at the memory, yet a part of me welcomes the unpleasantness. It reminds me why humans are not to be trusted but destroyed. Ruined, just as they ruined me.

High over a black London night, I turn my attention to the task at hand. Human despair has a pungent scent; the city is rife with it, but Cole emanates it like a vapor. I find him on the Blackfriars Bridge. He stands, hunched at the rail, staring into the black water.

To no surprise, the Twins lurk just on the Other Side of the Veil, as close to Cole as they dare, dripping their insidiousness in his ear like poison. I Cross Over and lunge at them with a snarl.

"Be gone, foulness," I say, my wings spread to their full width, fire and wrath burning in the black pits of my eyes. "You trespass on my property."

Keeb—in a shapeless rag of a dress—cowers behind her sister and peers at me through her stringy gray hair. Deber is bolder; she glares at me with pus-colored eyes. Both flick clear, veined wings while a cloud of flies buzz around them. They lack the sleek polish of my beetles.

"Ambri." Deber gives me a mockery of a courtesy. "With due respect, we found him first."

There is no respect in her smirk or the obscene giggle emanating from her sister behind her.

"You interfere with a task given me by Asmodai," I say. "That human is my chosen target."

"So we've heard. Yet *we* have driven him to the bridge. To the very brink—"

"He's mine!" I bellow, my wings blowing a hot wind.

"Then by all means…" Deber sweeps a wasted arm at the figure on the other side of the Veil.

Cole Matheson is hunched over, small, miserable, and—like most humans—completely unaware of his own power. But the witch is right; he's at the edge. It would take only the smallest nudge…

"I have use of him yet," I say. "Go, Deber, and take your decrepit sister with you."

"Very well, but watch that you tread carefully, Ambri," Deber says, drawing her sister close to her. "Lest your loyalty to our cause comes into question. *Again.*"

They dissipate into a cloud of flies and vanish. I pass through the Veil and emerge onto the bridge as a human, smoothing the lapels of my coat.

"Nice night for it," I say, stepping in a circle of light cast by a streetlamp.

Cole looks up, and a gasp nearly escapes me. His handsome face is beaten and bruised. His glasses are missing, and he gazes at me with eyes that are haunted and hopeless.

I'll ensure he enjoys himself before he burns out. I'll save him and ruin him, both.

"You," he says in a flat tone. "I thought I had to be asleep to dream. I can even see your breath plume in the cold air. My imagination has thought of everything."

I stand beside him and lean my arms on the rail. "You dream of me?"

"I think so. It's been hard to tell the difference, lately. You've been following me, haven't you?" He smiles faintly. "You follow me into my sleep."

His choice of words does unpleasant, fluttery things to my stomach. "I'm flattered. And what do I do in these dreams of yours?"

Cole ignores the question, frowning with a sudden thought. "You sound the same as you do in my dreams. Same voice. Same…everything. How is that possible if we've never spoken until now?"

"It's a mystery for the ages," I say. Cole will have to know the truth if I'm to get what I want but standing on the bridge in the dead of night doesn't feel like the appropriate time to reveal myself. "Perhaps we can discuss it over tea?"

He tears his gaze away from me and back to the black water. "No, thanks."

"Clearly, I've caught you at a bad time."

"*Clearly.*" He hunches into his too-thin coat. "My friend Vaughn says artists should pour their pain into their work. Do you think he's right?"

"I'm not qualified to speak on the subject. However, as it pertains to art, I have a proposal—"

"What about diving into your pain instead?" Cole says without hearing me. "How about that? It would be so easy to just…give up."

In an instant, I recall Ashtaroth in that burning distillery, promising to make my pain vanish. Did I appear this wretched to him? This painfully hopeless as Cole appears to me now?

Once again, I'm forced to brush away dusty emotions that haven't plagued me in centuries. I don't feel sorry for humans. I don't *worry about* them or *care* for their well-being. I use them, drain them, then discard them when I've taken my fill. No, Cole's pain is to be used against him when the time comes.

In the meantime, I want my bloody portrait.

"About that tea," I say. "Shall we?"

"Are you trying to pick me up?"

"No, though wouldn't that be preferable to...whatever this is?"

"Honestly? I don't know. I don't want to jump but I don't want to *not* jump." He hunches his shoulders and looks at me. "Have you ever felt like that? Like things would be so much easier if maybe you just didn't wake up one morning?"

I start to lie—I owe this human nothing. But my ruined childhood, my parents' indifference, Armand breaking my heart... They answer for me.

"Once or twice, maybe," I say in a low voice. "A long time ago."

Cole nods. "Sometimes I just get so..."

An icy draft of wind whistles over us, seeming to snap him out of his stupor. More likely, it's that I've scared off Deber and Keeb. He stumbles back from the bridge, as if shocked and horrified at his own desperation.

"No. No, this isn't me. I'm not like this. I'm just...in a bad place." He looks at me now with wide, desperate eyes. "And you... You're real but not real. What is happening? What is wrong with me? I feel like I'm going crazy."

Before I can reply, Cole's legs give out and he slumps onto the cold stony bridge. His head bows as he sobs quietly in the crook of his arm.

I stare, immobile for a moment, then awkwardly pat his shoulder. "There, there."

To my utter shock, he reaches for my hand and holds on. More shocking, I squeeze back. He pulls at me—or maybe it's my own doing—but I kneel behind him. He draws my arms around his shoulders...or maybe I wrap him in my embrace. I cannot, for the life of me, know where his need ends and mine begins.

For a few moments, I hold Cole as he rocks in his pain, telling myself this is all part of the plan. To build him up before letting him crash. To hold him together before smashing him apart.

These are dangerous waters and you know it...

My jaw clenches and I start to release him, but Cole is heaving deep, steadying breaths. He lets me go and hauls himself to standing, hurriedly wiping his eyes.

"I'm sorry," he says. "I...I don't know why I did that. I don't know you. I should go..."

I compose myself as well, smoothing the lapels of my coat. "I must insist you come with me. You're going to freeze to dea— freeze in your cheap coat if we don't get you someplace warmer. Not to mention, your wounds need tending."

Cole touches a finger to his lip, as if feeling it for the first time. "No, it's fine. Just more bad luck."

I refrain from rolling my eyes. Humans are annoyingly stoic at all the wrong times.

"We have matters to discuss. Come."

I give his sleeve a tug.

He resists. "I'm not going to fuck you."

"Presumptuous, aren't we? I told you, I have a business proposal."

"I'm not going to fuck you for money."

I smirk. "It baffles even me, but that's not what I'm after."

"What are you after?" Cole asks. His desperation and apathy are retreating, and his deep brown eyes are fixed on me and growing sharper by the moment. "Who *are* you?"

The intensity of his gaze is dangerous; something whispers in me that if I'm not careful, I might never want to leave it.

"Come with me," I say. "Get cleaned up, get warm, and we'll talk."

I take two steps, stop, turn. Cole hasn't moved.

I sigh. "I grow bored—and cold—standing on this bridge, Cole Matheson. Are you coming?"

He hesitates again, but a particularly nasty gust of wind makes the decision for him. He nods and follows me, not noticing that his dream phantom knows his name.

nine

Cole

Ambri led us through darkened London streets utterly unafraid. I followed more cautiously, jumping at shadows. The memory of my mugging flashed at me with every movement or sound.

But you'll follow a total stranger to his place. Make it make sense.

More than once, I thought of slipping away, but something kept me putting one foot in front of the other. The need to not be alone with myself again, probably. Had I really been at the bridge? Was I going to…? I shivered in the chill air, awash in shame. As if I'd gorged on something terribly unhealthy, letting my thoughts take me to the edge like that.

A bad moment, that's all. If Ambri hadn't come…

It occurred to me that I didn't actually know if his name was Ambri.

It also occurred to me that he knew my name.

Run. Now.

Instead, I followed him to a clean-swept Chelsea street, lightyears from my own place. Inside the posh building, a stately man behind the front desk nodded at us. "Mr. Meade-Finch."

"Jerome," my companion replied.

In the elevator, we stood side by side, our reflections brassy and blurred in the metal doors. "Meade-Finch?"

"It's a family name. Old. Old and forgotten."

"And your first name?"

"Ambrosius."

My heart thudded and my throat went dry. "But your friends call you Ambri?"

His gaze darted to me, then forward again. "They do."

"I knew that. You told me. In a *dream*."

"Perhaps you're psychic."

"Yeah and *perhaps* I'm crazy for coming this far."

I reached for the emergency button on the panel. Ambri's hand darted out, his fingers closing around my wrist.

"Wait."

"Let go of me."

I struggled weakly for a moment, but I was too wrung out. Too drained. Ambri pushed me against the elevator wall, and his body pressed in, his face inches from mine and fucking breathtaking in the light.

"All will be explained," he said. "I promise you, Cole Matheson, you'll want to hear my proposal. If you wish to leave afterward, I'll not stop you."

I stared, fear in the moment at war with memories of last night. Ambri's face had been close to mine then too, his voice sending electricity to parts of me that had been lifeless and dead. Like Frankenstein's monster. For a few stolen moments, I'd been alive.

I nodded mutely, and Ambri's grip on my wrist loosened, but he was slow to let go. His aquamarine eyes roamed my face, then dropped to my mouth. As if on cue, my lips parted. My body felt like it wasn't mine anymore but a puppet on his strings. My fingers touched his, stroking lightly, wanting to twine together.

What is happening right now?

Ambri's eyes widened slightly in surprise, then darkened. The elevator chimed our arrival, and he abruptly backed out of my space, taking his cologne, his heat, his *presence* with him. He strode through the sliding doors, and I must've left my last bit of common sense on the bridge because I followed him. But the entire night felt surreal—half nightmare, half dream—and I wasn't ready for it to be over.

Ambri's flat was the top floor of an old but elegant five-story building. Inside, it was a den of opulent wooden furniture, overstuffed pillows, and antique-looking decor. A canvas painted in rich gemstone colors, crystal and gold. Like stepping back in time. Standing in the middle of that wealth, I felt like a grown Oliver Twist—shabby, too thin, and shivering with cold.

Ambri had taken off his coat, scarf, and jacket, leaving him in a white dress shirt, black pants, and that black vest that made it impossible to tear my eyes off him.

"Looks like a vampire lives here," I said.

He knelt at the fireplace. "I'm going to pretend I didn't hear that."

"It wasn't meant as an insult."

"You've seen too many movies. Vampires live in caves and holes in the ground. They're vermin, not handsome actors in ruffled collars."

"You say that with such authority. But I forgot, you're a demon. In my dreams, anyway."

Ambri said nothing but poked the logs as the small flames licked the wood, then caught.

"Did you hear what I said?"

"I heard you. A demon. Fascinating." He twisted up off his knees with the grace of a dancer or jungle cat. He reminded me of a black panther—sleek, beautiful, and dangerous.

"Sit, Cole. I'll make tea."

He gestured at the stuffed chair nearest the fire and moved into the kitchen, muttering about needing servants for such menial tasks.

"You don't seem surprised," I called and sank gratefully into the chair. "Or even curious."

Ambri returned with a bowl of water and a cloth. He set the bowl at my feet and handed me the cloth. "For your wounds."

"Thanks." I held the cloth listlessly in my lap. "You had black eyes, black feather wings... Maybe some sort of fallen angel? Sounds silly to say it out loud. Just my imagination running wild, I guess. Except it earned me some money. I sketched you and you sold out immediately."

"That bodes well."

Ambri leaned an arm on the mantle above the fireplace, slender and dagger-like in black. The shadows danced in the contours of his face. It seemed more amazing to me that this man was real and *not* a figment of my sex-starved imagination.

I blinked back to reality. *My* reality.

"But that's all over now. They took all my money. My sketchbook too."

"It's not over," Ambri said. "It's just beginning."

"What is?"

"You and me, Cole Matheson."

The look in his eyes made my heart thud in my chest. The sense of danger and excitement returned, like the heat of the fire that was warming my limbs, driving out the miserable thoughts.

You and me…

The tea kettle in the kitchen whistled, breaking the moment. Ambri retreated again and returned a few minutes later with a cup of hot chamomile in an antique-looking cup and saucer. He set it on the table next to me.

I frowned. "You're not having any?"

He eased onto the sofa across from me and draped his arms along the back on either side of him. "It's pointless to eat or drink. I enjoy the occasional liquor, though it does nothing for me."

"Did you put something in it?" I demanded, my sense of self-preservation—finally—breaking the spell Ambri had over me. "Why did you bring me here? To drug me and…do things to me? Is that what happened before?"

"What was it that happened before?" Ambri asked, but he looked as if he already knew the answer.

I carved my hands through my hair. "I don't know. The dreams are getting all jumbled with reality. It seemed like you were in my place last night. But then the wings, the beetles…" I looked to him. "Were you? Were you actually in my place and I made up the rest? Have you been following me?"

He pursed his lips. "It's complicated."

"It's actually just a yes or no question." I got to my feet. "Never mind. I'm an idiot for coming here—"

"No, it's quite the smartest thing you could do, given your current situation," Ambri said. "You're not going mad, you're tormented. The proverbial starving artist. But I can change that."

"I'll bet," I said. "I don't know what plan you had in mind when you brought me here but I'm not going to be your houseboy—"

"I have no intention of you prostituting yourself for me…" He tapped his chin thoughtfully. "Though I wouldn't necessarily be opposed to it either."

I turned to the door. "I'm leaving."

"You need me, Cole Matheson," he said. "And, it just so happens, I need you. Your talent anyway. I never had my portrait done in life—a grievous sin that needs to be repaired immediately."

"In *life*?"

He sighed. "Will you *sit*? You're hovering. And you haven't tended your wounds. I won't have you bleeding all over my carpet. It's older than I am."

I slowly sank back down. "Five minutes. I'll hear you out and then I'm gone."

Ambri smirked. "It's cute that you believe you're in a position to give ultimatums, but you've had a rough night. I'll humor you."

"Thanks."

"My name is Ambrosius Edward Meade-Finch, formally of Hever Castle."

"Hever Castle. Wasn't that where Anne Boleyn—?"

Ambri flapped a hand irritably. "That skinny-necked wench has been overshadowing me for eons. Yes, Anne Boleyn grew up at Hever, but centuries later, it became *my* childhood ancestral home."

"Wait, I've been there," I said. "We took a tour at the Academy. Hever has one of the best collections of Tudor portraits, second only to the National Portrait Gallery."

Ambri's jaw clenched. "I'm aware."

"I didn't know anyone still lived there."

"They haven't. Not for hundreds of years."

I frowned. "I'm not a whiz at math but didn't you just say it was your childhood home?"

"I did. Stop interrupting. It just so happens that in the long, noble lineage of my family, there has been an unfortunate oversight. My official portrait has never been painted."

"And you want me to paint it?"

"I will pay you quite handsomely. For supplies, canvas, paints. Whatever you need."

For a few moments, hope and relief flooded me and then drained right back out.

"I don't know," I said. "I can paint your portrait and then what?"

"I don't understand."

"It just puts off the inevitable. A stay of execution." I offered a wan smile. "No offense to Anne Boleyn."

Ambri arched a perfect brow. "The inevitable?"

"Going back to…"

The bridge?

"Where I was." I shook my head. "You don't want me, anyway. I'm not very good."

"On the contrary, I've seen your work."

"My *work*. Whatever that is."

Ambri rolled his eyes. "They've done quite a number on you, haven't they?" He continued before I could ask who *they* were. "You're who I want for the job. You and no one else."

"It's a great offer," I said. "God knows, I need it. But I haven't been myself lately. What if the portrait turns out to be shit?"

"Impossible," Ambri said. "I'll be its subject, remember?"

I chuckled, but it died fast. "I don't know. It sounds pretentious but…I'm just fucking lost. What you saw tonight on the bridge isn't me. I graduated from the Royal Academy, for Christ's sake. I edited the art magazine. I had prospects for the future and somehow, they all evaporated. Or maybe I didn't do enough to keep them alive. Art is so subjective, one hundred people might love your work, a hundred might hate it, another hundred couldn't care less, and they'd all be right. Unless you're a Van Gogh or a Picasso, there's no job security."

Ambri frowned. "I doubt Van Gogh considered he had *job security*."

"You know what I mean. He's an undisputed master. Untouchable. I pushed myself to be untouchable too, to insulate myself from the criticism. Not from the outside world but from the noise in my own head. It was paralyzing, making me question every brushstroke, every line. Something I liked yesterday, sucks today. And I started to run out of the mental energy needed to push past all that and go out in the world and make a living."

Ambri arched a perfect brow. "Perhaps you'd have better success if you didn't try to talk paying clients out of hiring you."

I chuckled again, feeling lighter despite myself, and looked at this strange man who dropped into my life.

Or slipped through a crack in the window?

"All that negative shit I was feeling about my work, it was like quicksand," I said. "The more I fought against it, the more it sucked me down. Until…"

"Until?"

"Until I drew you as a demon. From my dreams, I guess. You make for a fucking beautiful fallen angel, Ambrosius. No offense."

"None taken."

"Those sketches…it rekindled the pure desire in me to paint just for the sake of painting. Like reconnecting with something I lost. It all came flooding back, and for a few, short minutes, it didn't matter what the little voices said." I gave a rueful laugh. "Sounds crazy, doesn't it?"

A short silence fell, and it seemed as if Ambri were turning something over in his mind. "No," he said, finally. "You're not crazy. And you weren't dreaming. You never were."

I leaned back in my chair. "What do you mean?"

"This part you might find difficult to believe, but you must have the truth if my proposal is to work. To keep you from sliding back into *the inevitable*."

"Okay," I said slowly. "What's the truth?"

His blue-green gaze pierced me. "I am as you say I am. A creature of the underworld. A demon."

"Oh, really? A demon?" I started to laugh, but it died swiftly at the expression on his face. "I was right. You're going to kill me, aren't you?"

"Think to the *dreams*, Cole Matheson. Do you really believe you were asleep?"

Not remotely, came the immediate answer, but I rejected it. Of course, I did. What was the alternative? That he was telling the truth?

"This is…no. Impossible. I don't believe you."

Ambri sniffed. "What you *believe* has no bearing on reality." He sat back and crossed his leg, one ankle resting on one knee. "Your primary commission will be to paint my portrait—my human portrait. You shall render a likeness of me that is befitting a member of the peerage. I presume that will take some time—full body, highly detailed and such?"

I nodded faintly.

"In between that undertaking, I'll let you paint me in my true form, as often as you like. Those renderings you may sell at will. I suspect they'll fetch you a tidy sum."

"Your true form…"

"Yes, Cole. The form in which I first revealed myself to you." Ambri stood up and moved to the window. "The form I have taken since my untimely death in the spring of 1786."

As he spoke, his blue-green eyes darkened, blackened, until they were onyx orbs. Feathered wings pushed through the fabric of his suit and unfurled.

This isn't happening...

"I chose this existence when humankind rejected me," he said, anger coloring his words. "After the betrayal of every human who was meant to care for me—my parents, my uncle, my lover... They ruined me, abandoned me, *murdered* me. But now...now, I am magnificent." He faced me, his eyes now the blackest pits in bloodless white skin, his feathered wingtips brushing the walls. "Now, I cannot be ignored."

I stared. Reality and my dreams were melting into each other, combining and intertwining, and insisting that they were not separate entities but one in the same.

"No human is meant to witness me in my glory," Ambri continued. "But I will give it to you, Cole Matheson. I'll give you all of myself so that you may sell me to the world and make your name. Your fortune."

I swallowed hard; it took me three attempts to find my voice. "This is...real?"

"Indeed," Ambri said, and in the next instant, he was a beautiful man again, standing at the window. "Few humans have encountered our kind in the flesh, and most haven't kept their sanity long after. But you will be different. Beloved. Celebrated for your artistic ingenuity. *An undisputed master.* And I'll have the portrait that was denied me in my life." He cocked his head. "Do we have a deal?"

Earlier, on the bridge, I'd been hollowed out. Drained. My self-preservation had been a pendulum swinging back and forth all night, but I wasn't ready for...whatever this was. A Faustian bargain. Or a complete dive into madness.

I pushed myself out of the chair on shaking legs and backed toward the door, never taking my eyes off of him. I hardly dared to blink. "N-no deal."

Ambri clasped his hands behind his back.

"I see you, Cole. Perhaps when no one else does. The fear is bright in your eyes but so is a spark of life. Your artistry. Your wild curiosity. I inspire you. I can taste it. I can feel its heat. You ache for me..."

"No." I stumbled for the door, fumbled at the knob. "No, I...I can't."

He smiled, unperturbed. "You know where I am if you change your mind."

"I won't."

"You will, Cole Matheson. You'll come back to take what you want from me. You're a human, after all." His confident smirk slipped. "That's what they do."

I hurried out, running down the posh hallways as if Ambri were chasing me. But he kept his word and let me go. A thought chased me instead, almost as unsettling.

He's right...about everything.

ten

Cole

I got as far as Flood Street.

The cold wind seemed to rip right through me. The hour was too late for cabs; the only things moving on the streets were the shadows and me. I hunched into my coat and trudged against the gusting wind until I couldn't go any farther. Didn't *want* to go any farther.

What did I have waiting for me? A tiny shoebox of a room with a broken window. No fireplace. No heat. Black walls and a hot plate.

And an empty bed.

I stopped and squinted into the wind, back to Ambri's building. To comfort and warmth and *him.*

"An actual demon?"

That possibility was a question I couldn't answer. But what had me turning around was exactly what Ambri had said it would be. Curiosity. Creativity. Inspiration. His human beauty stirred my blood like no man had in a long time, but his "demon" form was like a drug I wanted more of. To draw or paint him, not for whatever so-called riches he promised, but because my art had been dying and now it was revived in him.

And if he kills you?

I shivered, remembering the bridge. The black water. It scared me down to my soul that I'd been there, but living without the fire of my craft was a kind of death all in itself. Without it, I was nothing. What, honestly, did I have to lose?

Inside the lobby, Jerome was still manning the front desk. The concierge must've been pushing eighty, but he stood ramrod straight at his post. He gave me a small nod and picked up the phone.

"He's returned." A pause. "Very good, sir."

Jerome hung up the phone and gestured toward the elevators. I started for them and then stopped.

"Jerome, my name is Cole Matheson. I live in a shit flat in Whitechapel. My landlady is Ms. Thomas. My best friend is Lucy Dennings. She lives in New York City."

He arched one white eyebrow.

"Just in case *Unsolved Mysteries* comes to interview you."

"I beg your pardon?"

"Never mind," I muttered and headed for the elevators. "In for a penny and all that."

At Ambri's door, I knocked, thought about turning right back around, knocked again.

"Come in," came the faint reply.

I stepped inside to find he'd changed into black silk pajamas—a robe over pants, loosely tied, revealing the V of his chest as he lounged on the couch.

That bastard.

He shot me an arrogant, triumphant smile. "I would say *I told you so*, but I have better manners than that."

I forced myself to look at his eyes and nowhere else. "Before…anything happens, we need some ground rules."

"If you insist. Wine? Brandy?"

"No, thanks. This is surreal enough as it is."

Ambri languidly moved off the couch and poured a crystal glass full of amber liquid. "As I mentioned, it does nothing for me, but I like to keep up appearances."

"Of being human?"

"Something like that."

He resumed his seat and indicated that I should take the chair by the fire. I eased down into it and kept my eyes on Ambri, as if he were that panther about to pounce.

"You don't need to drink?" I asked.

"Or eat. Or sleep."

"What do you do all night?"

"I fuck."

Heat flushed my face instantly. "You...what?"

He grinned at my discomfort, swirling the liquor in his glass. "Before you bombard me with a thousand questions, tell me what you think you know of my kind."

"Well, not much, considering until tonight I didn't believe *your kind* were real." I ran a hand through my hair. "I've heard of Lucifer, of course. Or is it Sat—?"

"Ah-ah-ah," Ambri said, holding up a hand. "Let's not say the S-word. Safer that way. For you."

My throat went dry, and I got out of the chair to pace the room. "Okay, look, I don't know what I'm supposed to think about all this or what's supposed to happen next. I'm going to paint your portrait but also paint you as a demon?"

"That's precisely what's supposed to happen next." Ambri cocked his head. "Are you always this neurotic?"

I barked a laugh. "Right, because this happens every day. Demons just *exist* and show themselves to humans and hire them to—"

"You're doing it again, Cole Matheson. Overthinking. And you have yet to tend to your wounds." He nodded at the bowl of water and cloth still on the floor.

I sank back in the chair. "Half of me feels like I'm being epically duped and the other half of me—"

"Wants more?" Ambri smirked. He had an arsenal of those little smiles—most arrogant, all of them sexy. "Of course, you do. That's why you came back. I have that effect on, well, basically everyone."

"Because you're a...sex demon?"

He laughed, rich and throaty, and I assumed the answer was *yes* given how my body reacted. As if Ambri's voice traveled on waves that went straight down my spine to my groin and danced along every nerve ending that suddenly called out to be touched.

"That's one I haven't heard before," he said. "No, I'm not a sex demon. Not an incubus, either, as we've previously discussed. I assume you're familiar with the seven deadly sins?"

I nodded.

"I am a demon of lust and gluttony. I stoke those sins in humans and drive them to forsake all else. To become enslaved to their own need."

"Lust and gluttony…? Wait, the seven deadly sins are real?"

"Of course, they're *real*. Otherwise, my kind would be unemployed."

"Committing them can send you to actual hell?"

"There is no hell. No heaven either. Not as you imagine it. There is only the Other Side. Demons reside in one realm and angels in the other. You might call those realms heaven or hell but they're not actual places."

I rubbed my eyes. "I don't…that makes no sense."

"Of course, it doesn't. The human mind cannot fathom the Other Side. Humans return to it upon death and remain there until their next lifetime, whereupon it's Forgotten. Memory wiped. Fresh start and all that." He studied my perplexed expression. "Don't strain yourself, darling. The Other Side defies time, imagination, and the rules of the physical universe. Your human brain, with its limitations and shortcomings, cannot comprehend it."

I shook my head, trying to absorb all this. "Wait, wait, there are actual angels? And we live more than one lifetime?"

"Indeed. Love, compassion, wisdom, art—it's too much to explore in one lifetime. So, you go back, again and again, to learn. To suffer. To take one step closer toward what you'd call enlightenment." He rolled his eyes and finished off his drink. "Given the state of things, I don't have to tell you how frequently *that* happens."

"But *you* don't live lifetime after lifetime, do you?"

"No." He set down his empty glass on the table in front of him. "I've stepped out of that tedious cycle."

"How…how did you become a demon?"

There's something you don't get to say every day.

Ambri arched a brow. "That's a very personal question, Cole Matheson. I felt human existence no longer had anything to offer me."

"So you turned your back on life?"

"It turned its back on me first," he cried with sudden furor.

A short silence passed where the only sound was my heart thudding in my chest. His anger felt volatile, but underneath was a steady current of pain. Like a livewire running through it, fueling it.

Ambri smoothed his expression and smiled placidly. "The hour is late. You should sleep. I have a guest room. In the morning, we can discuss the particulars, acquire your supplies, and such."

"I don't know that I can sleep," I said. "I have a million questions and…"

"And?"

"There's a part of me that still doubts any of this is real. I've been feeling like absolute shit lately. How do I know I'm not having a mental breakdown? Or that you haven't drugged me?"

"Things usually seem more surreal or questionable in the dark of night. Sleep, and in the stark light of morning, you'll discover this is all very real, and that your fortune is about to change for the better."

"That's something else we need to talk about," I said. "Demons typically aren't into changing someone's fortune for the better unless they get something in return."

Ambri rolled his eyes. "Suddenly, he's an expert."

"What do you get out of helping me? Besides a portrait."

"Isn't that enough?"

Before I could answer, Ambri thrust himself off the couch, snatched the cloth from the bowl at the foot of my chair, dabbed it in water, and raised it to my cheek.

I reared back. "What are you doing?"

"I can't hold a serious conversation with you while you're covered in bloody filth. Now hold still."

He took my chin in his hand and swiped the damp cloth across my brow. I was only peripherally aware of these actions; my entire being was suffused with his nearness. His eyes were like gemstones—impossible to imagine them black and full of dread. His face…*Jesus Christ*, my breath caught at the perfection of it.

"I know what you're doing," I croaked. "You're trying to seduce me. Or use your…powers."

"My powers," he purred. "I like that."

I suppressed a groan, my body aching for him. But I ignored it and dug deeper, studying him, searching for what lay beneath that sexual prowess that wanted to unravel me. Ambri was ungodly handsome. Literally. But there was a softness in the chiseled angles of his jaw and cheekbones. A depth in his eyes and that pain hiding behind his sharp wit and easy smirk.

With effort, I pushed his hand away. "If this is going to happen, I need the truth."

He sighed. "Your curiosity, Cole Matheson, will be the death of me."

"Tell me. Why is a portrait enough?"

He hesitated for another moment, then went back to work, gently wiping the dirt and blood from my face, talking as he did.

"In 1736, my father, Timothy, married my mother, Katherine. They had a daughter, Jane. They're all there, in the history books, every branch in the family tree accounted for, except one. In 1762, when my mother was forty-eight—ancient by the standards of the day—she gave birth to a son."

Ambri's breath was sweet with the bite of brandy as he drew the cloth down my cheek and gently touched it to my cut lip.

"I was what they call nowadays, a 'happy accident,' though my aged parents didn't see it that way. To them, I was an afterthought. A nuisance who sapped their energy. As soon as an opportunity arose, they sent me away. Erased me. Pruned the branch, as it were."

"They never painted your portrait."

"I sound petty when you put it that way, Cole Matheson," Ambri said with a dry smile. He dabbed the cloth to my brow, his eyes darkening. "There were other…circumstances. Salt in the wound, you might say. So yes, having you *un-erase* me is enough."

"You're not telling the truth. Not all of it," I said gently, and he stiffened, his gaze darting to me. "What your parents did was shitty, but that wasn't enough to make you turn to…the dark side. Why did they send you away?"

He stiffened. "You've heard enough for one day."

He dropped the cloth in the water and started to move away, but I grabbed his hand.

"Wait."

Ambri's gaze looked to my hand gripping his, then up at me. His blue-green eyes were full of depth and humanity, but earlier that night, they'd been black. Twin abysses filled with fire. Pale, bloodless skin and wings…

"Show me again," I whispered. "Your true form. Let me see. Right now, while I'm here and not scared and desperate. Show me so I know this is real."

Ambri hesitated for a moment, and then I watched, my heart pounding a steady, heavy rhythm in my chest as the color drained from his skin. Wings emerged from behind him like shadows, but it was his eyes… His beautiful eyes blackened to nothingness. A chasm of shadow. I kept staring, feeling sucked in. I sensed, in that endless dark, a fire.

Smoke and ash.

Pain and terror.

I couldn't look away. My hand came up and touched my fingertips to Ambri's porcelain-white skin and found him hot to the touch instead of cold and lifeless. I cupped his jaw as those black-on-black eyes widened in surprise. His mouth opened slightly, and my thumb brushed over his bottom lip. And still, I fell deeper into his gaze. I could smell the smoke and feel the heat of the flames, licking…

"What is this?"

My own whispery voice sounded far away and mingled with others. Distant shouts of a mob and much closer, the pleading cries of a man. Ambri. And another… Someone—some*thing* evil. An entity of pure malevolence promising him everything.

Ambri reared back and reverted to his human form. I blinked out of a place of terror and heartache, into now.

"A word of advice: don't look too long into a demon's eyes, Cole Matheson. Not if you value your sanity."

"What did I see?"

He didn't reply but rose to stand near the fire. "You'll find the spare room down the hall, first door on the left."

I got to my feet. "What are you going to do?"

"Sit at your bedside and watch you sleep." He scoffed at my expression. "I have a job to do. Humans are waiting for me to turn them inside out with desire." He moved to the window, then turned and arched a brow at me. "Unless you'd like me to stay so that you and I—"

I coughed, a flush of heat washing over my face. "No, no. That's one of my rules, actually. *The* major rule. You and I are not going to—"

"Have any fun?"

"Yes. I don't do well with casual hookups, and it would just complicate things. Not to mention the actual fact of you being a *demon*."

"You say that like it's a bad thing."

I shot him a look.

"Fine. But if you change your mind—"

"I won't," I said. "And no more working your black magic on me. We're business partners. That's it."

He frowned in what looked like genuine confusion, then nodded. "Well? Are you going to stand there and watch me take my anicorpus?"

"Your what?"

"Anicorpus. The animal form demons take on This Side."

"The beetles."

Holy shit, it's real. This is all real.

He smirked. "I think you've had enough excitement for one night. Shoo. Off to bed with you."

I nodded, suddenly feeling the lateness of the hour; it had to be near three in the morning. I started down the hall of the opulent flat that felt ancient. Not musty or shabby but *old*. Like how a haunted house feels, with history imbedded in its walls. But the idea of Ambri going out to touch other humans… To kiss and fuck them and make them come like he made me…

"Stop it," I muttered. "You can't be *jealous*. You just told him nothing can happen. Get real."

Still, the twinge in my stomach wouldn't go away.

I found the spare bedroom—like an elegant room in a bed-and-breakfast I could never afford—and face-planted onto the pillows. I nearly groaned at how good it felt. The mattress that wasn't a hard slab, the silk against my cheek like a caress.

Against all odds, I found myself drifting off.

Even more impossibly, for the first time in months, the chorus of nasty whispers telling me I was no good, talentless, hopeless… They'd all gone silent.

And that, I thought as I drifted down, was almost worth selling my soul to the devil.

eleven

Ambri

Cole shuffles down the hall. When I hear the door to the spare room shut, I slump against the wall. The window is open, the night is waiting, but my desire to go out and feast is somehow absent.
Impossible.
And yet I remain where I am, watching the night recede with the coming sunlight, my gaze inward, recalling how Cole's hand felt on my skin and how, when he looked into my death, he was afraid. But not for himself.
For me.
This is quicksand. Tread carefully, I tell myself. *Tread very, very carefully.*
A prudent thought, but another whispers that I might already be sinking.

twelve

Cole

I woke with sunlight streaming into a room I didn't recognize. Rich, antique furniture and me ensconced in a bed that someone was going to have to pay me to get out of. Then it all came flooding back. Instead of panicking or freaking out, my heart thudded with excitement. Enthusiasm. I—Cole Andrew Matheson—was about to greet a new day without self-doubt or depression pressing me down like an unseen hand. I felt like I'd slept a hundred years to make up for all the sleepless nights I'd had over the last year. I felt…

"Normal."

Your new patron is a demon. Perfectly normal. Nothing to see here…

A chuckle began in my stomach and grew. I let it have me, laughing until I was wrung out. Then I lay on my back, staring at the ceiling.

"What. The. Fuck."

I swung my legs over the side of the bed. The room was bigger in the light of day. A desk, chair, small sofa, and king-sized bed all shared the space without crowding each other.

I cracked the window for a breath of fresh, cold air. It was nearly noon, I guessed. The day was gray and golden and full of possibility, lightyears from where I'd been yesterday.

I took the longest, hottest shower of my life in the en suite bathroom. In my old place in Whitechapel, the hot water ran out in exactly three minutes and twelve seconds. I'd timed it.

After wrapping a towel around my waist, I came out of the bathroom to find my old clothes were gone, replaced by new pants, a white undershirt, boxer-briefs, and a long-sleeved fleece. There was even a thick winter coat and a scarf. I didn't know how to feel about Ambri buying clothes for me (or that he got my measurements exactly right) but it was either put on the new stuff or walk out naked.

The possibilities that scenario created made my blood heat and I had to take a personal moment.

"Remember your own rule," I muttered, but what were rules to a demon?

I dressed in everything but the coat and scarf and headed out. The aforementioned demon was in the living room. He was dressed in a different suit of expensive slacks, shirt, and jacket, all in black, but otherwise was nearly in the same spot I'd left him last night, standing by the window. Sunlight streamed in, bathing him in gold and silver, and making his skin luminescent.

To paint him like that…

Ambri turned to regard me. "Much improved."

"Not like I had a choice. You didn't have to buy me clothes."

"This winter looks to be a rough one. I can't have you dying of pneumonia in the middle of my portrait."

"How thoughtful," I said with a smirk. "When did you get them?"

"This morning. I was out and about early. Or rather, I never came in." He offered a smirk of his own though it wasn't as sharp as his usual. "Hazard of the job."

"Thanks, but don't do it again." I noticed an open door that led to a small study off the living room. A glimpse of a bookshelf snagged my attention. "Can I?"

"By all means."

I stepped into the small study. There was another fireplace, a huge, ornate desk, and built-in bookcases along every wall, lined with antique books. Old prints and first editions. The entire collection likely cost a small fortune.

"You read all those?" I asked, returning to the living room.

He sniffed. "Of course, I've read them."

"Impressive."

"Is it? Do I now seem more attractive?"

I laughed. "Big time."

He couldn't get any more attractive if he tried.

"Despite your aversion to necessary spending," Ambri said, "today I'm going to purchase your painting supplies, no arguments. We also need to discuss the finer points of our business arrangement."

"I have to make a pit stop at the optometrist for another pair of glasses, too. But can we grab some coffee first?"

"Americans and your coffee. There's a café around the corner."

I retrieved the coat and scarf, and we stepped out. I stole glances at him as we walked along the sidewalk in the mid-morning chill, drinking him in little sips when I really wanted to—

"So," I said loudly to cut the thought off. "About last night…"

He cocked a brow at me. "Which part?"

The part where you went out and fucked someone else.

I coughed. "Just…all of it. I still have so many questions."

"Naturally."

"For instance, if you wanted to hire me to paint you, why did you come to me as a demon first?"

A muscle in Ambri's jaw ticked. "I don't know what you mean."

"When you first showed up in my flat, you wore your demon suit. You seemed like you were trying to scare the shit out of me. Mission accomplished, by the way."

His gaze slid to me and then forward. "I was testing your mettle."

"That's not a good enough answer."

He shot me a dry look. "Oh? You have a preferred method for demons appearing to you in the dead of night?"

I laughed. "No, I just mean—"

"It was to waken that spark of inspiration in you. I wanted you to need me as much as I need you, Cole Matheson."

I swallowed hard, his words running up and down my spine. "You knew I'd want to draw you?"

"Who wouldn't?"

"But it doesn't make sense. The second time, you…" My face flushed, remembering him rolling up his sleeves, kneeling in front of me…

"The second time was merely to get better acquainted," Ambri said. "It's what I do."

"Right. It's what you do." The heat in my cheeks faded. Because I wasn't the only one he visited. Not by a long shot.

We rounded the corner and Ambri nodded his head at the café called La Marais.

"This is the place. Not my favorite, but you should like it."

"You have favorites? I thought you didn't need to eat or drink."

"It's French, which brings up unpleasant associations."

"We don't have to go here—"

"It's fine. I could use the reminder, actually."

"Reminder of?"

"The cruelty of humans."

I started to ask how a *demon* could find humans cruel, but he huffed irritably. "Can we sit at a table like civilized entities before you continue your inquisition?"

"Sure," I said, chuckling. Before I could stop myself, I blurted, "You're charming as hell when you're cranky."

His brows went up. "Oh?"

"I mean it's incongruent with your refinement and expensive clothes and your perfect…face."

Dear God, shoot me now.

But the awkward train had left the station and there was no stopping it.

"It's why a super macho guy holding a basket of kittens is cute," I continued, babbling like an idiot. "The two things seem incompatible which makes them more endearing."

"Fascinating," Ambri said, though his smirk was close to becoming an actual smile. "Your mind works in mysterious ways, Cole Matheson."

"Tell me about it," I muttered, mortification climbing up my neck. But it wasn't me, it was him. I couldn't remember the last time anyone had scrambled my brain so much. If ever.

"Shall we?" Ambri held the door to the café open.

"Why not?" I muttered. "I can't say anything worse."

He grinned. "Let's find out."

thirteen

Ambri

We enter the place that is like stepping into a Parisian café. Memories batter me, but I welcome them. I'd spoken truly when I told Cole I needed the reminder. Around him, I'm becoming disturbingly soft—not a word I ever want associated with me.

He orders a coffee and a croissant, then reaches into his pocket for cash.

"These aren't my pants."

He shoots me a look, but I'm already handing the cashier a twenty-pound note and telling her to keep the change.

"I feel your stinky eye on me," I say. "Spare me the moralizing. If you get pissy every time I purchase something for you, it's going to be a tedious partnership."

We take a corner table. I unwind my scarf and lounge in the chair.

"It's stink-eye, not stinky eye," Cole says, sitting across from me. "And I'm not used to people buying me stuff, and I don't want to be."

"Is there some sort of benefit to pride that I'm not aware of? It's one of our favorite sins, after all. I fail to see how it's a virtue too."

"It can be," he says and thanks the server who sets a puffy croissant and cappuccino in front of him. "It's the suffering toward enlightenment we were talking about last night. You want to make your own way in the world and not have everything handed to you. And if you are fortunate enough to have everything handed to you, you should be grateful and try to help those who don't." He takes a sip of coffee, and his eyes fall shut. "Speaking of gratitude, thank you for this. It's one of the best I've ever had."

Cole has a bit of foam on his lip and swipes it away with his tongue. I avert my eyes. "I'll take your word for it."

"What about this place has bad associations for you?" he asks after a minute. "If you don't mind me asking."

I cross my arms and narrow my gaze at him, wondering how much—if anything to tell him. "You are an intriguing creature, Cole Matheson."

"Nah," he says. "I used to be, maybe. Once. But we weren't talking about me."

"That's what makes you intriguing. Usually, it only takes one or two questions, and I can get a human blathering on about themselves for hours on end."

He shrugs. "I like learning about other people. And you, Ambrosius, are far more fascinating than me."

Cole says nothing more, waiting for me to continue when—or if—I'm so inclined.

"Have you heard of the *Affaire du collier de la reine*? The Affair of the Queen's Necklace?"

His eyes narrow in thought, an endearing gesture I'm beginning to become familiar with.

"I think so. It has something to do with Marie Antoinette, right?" Now his eyes widen. "Holy shit. You died in 1786. That was the beginning of the French Revolution, wasn't it?"

"Close to," I say. "The Affair certainly didn't help matters for poor Antoinette."

"You were there? You knew her?"

I nod. "I was a key player in the Affair, actually, though there is no mention of my name in the history books. On purpose that time, to escape detection, which is why I kept my head."

Only to die hours later in an inferno...

Cole is listening, rapt, his coffee forgotten. "This I gotta hear."

"Very well," I say, sitting back in my seat. "There was a man by the name of Cardinal Louis René Édouard de Rohan. Like many men of the church, he was richer than his god would have approved of and had carnal appetites to boot."

"A cardinal?"

"Indeed. I recall many a party thrown at his palatial estate outside of Paris, where naked bodies writhed in every corner and occultists told fortunes." I tilt my chin, steeling myself. "My lover at the time, Armand de Villette, had befriended a woman named Jeanne Le Motte. She was a hanger-on, always trying to ingratiate herself with the nobility and trying to catch the Queen's eye. Rohan, as it turned out, had fallen out of Antoinette's graces after some nasty comments he made about her mother and was desperate to make right with her.

"Jeanne concocted a plan. She hinted to Rohan that the Queen was warming to him. She had Armand forge letters in Antoinette's hand, assuring him that a reconciliation was near. The correspondence grew more heated until finally we arranged a midnight rendezvous between Rohan and the Queen in one of her gardens."

"We?" Cole asks, his eyes wide.

"I procured a prostitute—Nicole Le Guay, sweet girl, not too bright—and dressed her up as the Queen. She bore more than a passing resemblance and often played Antoinette in street theatrics. The silly Cardinal met our Queen in the moonlight where she gave him a red rose and one of Armand's forged letters that read, *I think you know what this means.*"

"And it worked?"

"Better than we could have hoped. Not only did Rohan feel as if reconciliation was assured, he also began to believe Antoinette was in love with him. And everyone knows the way to a woman's heart is through gobs of expensive jewelry."

Cole smirked. "That's debatable but go on."

"In the fall of 1784, my Armand wrote another letter to Rohan 'from the Queen' asking him to act as a go-between in the purchase of a ridiculously extravagant diamond necklace from the royal jewelers. Rohan not only agreed, but the fool signed on as guarantor. If the necklace wasn't paid for, it would fall on him to cover the costs. But Jeanne assured him the necklace had been handed over to the Queen and that the jewelers had been paid out of the royal coffers."

"But they hadn't."

"Not remotely. We absconded with the necklace, and Jeanne and Armand cut it up into pieces and sold the diamonds in black markets all over Europe. Rohan was left holding the bag, so to speak."

"He had to pay for the necklace?"

"1.8 million livres, an astounding sum. When the Affair came out, the King foolishly demanded a public trial for Rohan, but the good cardinal was acquitted. The citizens, already believing Antoinette was spending France into starvation, decided she had ordered the necklace herself and now was using a poor commoner as a scapegoat." I wave a hand. "You know the rest. *Let them eat cake*—something she never said, by the way—and off with her head and all that. Though I never lived to see the Revolution from This Side, the Affair fanned the flames, and I tasted of those earliest flickers. To say the least."

A silence falls where those flames burn in my memory. I look up to see Cole watching me from under his tousled hair. Part of me that I'd long since believed dead—that I'd thought had perished in that fire—stirred.

"So yes, there is a reason I have bad associations with all that is French," I say quickly. "I died in Paris on the very day Armand was sentenced to exile for his role in the Affair." I lean over the small table between us. "You asked what you see when you look into the black of my eyes. You see a death, Cole. Mine."

"I thought so." His hand that's resting on the small table between us looks as if it wants to reach for mine. "This sounds odd given the context, but…do you want to talk about it?"

I suddenly find it hard to swallow.

Damn him and damn myself for the weakness that overtakes me in his presence. I have to remind myself that men such as Cole don't actually exist. Their kindness is a façade that conceals their own selfish wants. Armand had once been sweet and considerate. He'd told me he loved me, and it had all been a lie.

"No," I state. "Why would I?"

Cole sits up and puts his hand on his coffee cup, now likely cold. "No, I get it. But can I ask a question? Did *you* sell off any of the diamonds?"

"Did I profit from the Queen's downfall? No." I stiffen, regretting that I cannot tell this tale without the painful parts coming to bite me in the arse. "By then, Armand had decided he was in love with Jeanne. They cut me out of the profits. Because I was already wealthy, I pretended it didn't bother me." I force a smirk. "It all evened out in the end. They were arrested, I wasn't."

Cole nods, his gaze on his plate. "You loved him."

The three words stab me in the chest, and I don't know if it's because of Armand's betrayal or that Cole's tone is saturated with concern for me.

Like a fool, I answer truthfully. "Yes."

"Is that why you became…what you are? Because he broke your heart?"

The air seems to still and thicken, and I'm trapped in Cole's lovely dark gaze. Like an embrace I don't wish to pull myself out of.

This is madness. You're to destroy this man or else be destroyed yourself. Remember who you are!

I stand up and reach for my scarf. "Time is wasting, and we still have errands to run before you begin your work."

"Yeah, sure," Cole says, offering a small smile. He's not even angered at my rudeness, the bloody fool.

You're the bloody fool. Every door you open to frighten him only draws him closer.

We step out into the chilly day. After a stop at a doctor's office where Cole orders a replacement pair of glasses, we take a cab to an art supply store. The best in London. Cole walks the aisles like the proverbial kid in a candy store, his gaze lovingly falling on the tools of his trade. A far cry from the miserable person he was on the bridge just the night before.

I stroll down the aisle with Cole, hands in my pockets, rather enjoying his pleasure. He picks up a tube of vibrant blue paint.

"I love this shade," he says, smiling fondly. "I call it 'Chagall blue.' He uses it a lot, in his stained glass too. He was just…unreal."

And because he's Cole, he puts the tube back. I sigh and flag down an employee.

"Could you assist us? We need canvases in a variety of sizes. At least twelve to start? And oils—the best you carry in all colors. A dozen palettes, brushes, pencils, charcoal, a new sketchpad… Am I forgetting anything?"

"No, that should do it." Cole leans into me. "This is too much."

"It's everything you'll need to perform the duties I've hired you to perform. That's all."

"It's a lot, Ambri."

"Good," I say. "Then we won't need to make a return trip. For an art store, the lighting here is ghastly."

Cole laughs and rests his hand on my shoulder. "Thank you." I stiffen and he snatches his hand back. "Sorry. I have to keep reminding myself…never mind."

With a sheepish smile, he moves to confer with the store employees, leaving me with his lingering touch on my shoulder. With his guidance, they gather the supplies he prefers and ring up the sale which makes Cole's eyes bulge but is a mere drop in the vast ocean that is my wealth.

We step outside with the assurance that the store will deliver all to my flat later in the afternoon except for a large bag that contains a few items Cole will take to his quaint hovel, presumably to paint me in my demonic form.

And so begin his rise.

On the street, I tug gloves onto my hands. "I have a few rules that we neglected to cover last night. The most important being you aren't to talk about our partnership with anyone."

Specifically, Lucy Dennings.

She—and Casziel—will learn of me through Cole's paintings eventually, but by then, he'll be too entrapped to heed any of her warnings.

Cole is nodding. "Okay."

"You may say you have a patron but keep my name out of it."

"Sure. When should I start?"

"Depends. How long will the portrait take?"

Cole rubs his chin, thinking. "We'll want to make it authentic to the period. Let me do some research and then…I don't know. Tomorrow? It won't take me long. We covered eighteenth-century portraiture at the Academy. As for the actual painting, it depends on how big you want it."

"Big," I say.

"A few months?"

I nod. Months of Cole Matheson in my presence, in my flat, living under his curious, artistic gaze.

With that infuriating lock of hair falling over his brow that he won't do anything about…

"Ambri?"

I start out of my thoughts. "Yes. Fine. Tomorrow, then."

Cole smiles a smile full of the modest charm he has no idea he possesses. "Great. And…thanks again."

He gives a little wave and walks away, hoisting the bag of supplies over his shoulder.

I watch him go until he's out of sight and then head back to my flat. I'm nearly there when I catch a whiff of perfume—old and French—and hear light footfalls hurrying away. I look in time to see the train of a pale blue dress slip around a corner.

My throat tightens. Eisheth. She's not usually one for pastels but the Parisian perfume is a nice touch.

I'm being watched.

I straighten and stride on, chin up. Let them watch. I have nothing to hide. I have a plan. The rise and fall of one of the greatest artists this generation has ever seen. Any lowly servitor can torment a sad man. My triumph will be all the more glorious for the heights from which Cole Matheson will fall.

But as I walk, each clap of my shoes is like a mantra.

Quicksand, quicksand, quicksand…

fourteen

Cole

Back at my little hole in the wall, I dropped the bag of art supplies and sat on the edge of my bed.

"So that happened."

There was no more doubting what I'd seen or who Ambri was. The supplies that I could never afford on my own were physical proof. I stripped off my new coat and noticed a weight in the breast pocket—a clip of about a thousand pounds wrapped in a note:

The first installment.
~ Ambri

"It's too much," I murmured, then read the postscript.

P.S. It's not too much. Get used to being compensated for your art or find a new line of work.

I had to laugh. He was right. Even more convincing than the supplies or the money was the desire to paint Ambri. It burned in me as hot as—

The flames that killed him?

I put my hand to my chest until the ache faded. Better to focus on my new situation than what I felt about him.

Somehow, that was less complicated.

I flipped through one of my art history books. Surely, throughout time, there'd been those who'd witnessed otherworldly phenomena. I thought of the hellish paintings of Hieronymus Bosch or Francisco de Goya. Were they born strictly of imagination, or did they get a peek at something they weren't supposed to? Like me, did they know something everyone else didn't?

The questions had no answers. What I could count on was that I had a patron. I wasn't going to starve or become homeless, not for the time being, anyway.

I itched to start painting right away, but my best friend needed to know she could stop worrying about me. I owed her that. I picked up my phone and dialed Lucy Dennings's number.

"Hey you!" she said upon answering, wariness undercutting her enthusiasm. "How are you?"

"I'm great," I said. "I have some good news and wanted you to be the first to hear it."

"Oh my God, I'm *so* thrilled for you!"

I chuckled. "I haven't even told you what it is yet."

"I know but—"

"But you've been worried about me."

"Well, yes…"

"You can take five. I have a patron."

"Get. Out."

"I know. I can't believe it, either."

"Oh, I believe it. I'm just so excited for you. Who is it? What's the job?"

"He's…a very wealthy man."

I suppressed a laugh. That description of Ambri was like saying Michelangelo's David is a *very big statue*. Technically accurate but not even close to encompassing the real thing.

"He wants me to paint his portrait. A big one. Could take months."

"Damn, Cole! Who is this guy? Anyone I might've heard of?"

"I'm not allowed to say. We have a kind of confidentiality agreement."

"Oh my God, it's Prince Harry, isn't it?"

I laughed. "You guessed it, straight out the gate."

She laughed with me and then heaved a sigh of relief. "It is so good to hear you like this. Before, you sounded like you were constricted with worry and now you can breathe again. Is that true, Cole? You're doing better?"

"Yeah, Luce," I said thickly. "I'm good, I promise. And I also promise that the next time I feel that way, I'll tell you. Or tell someone."

"Good. I was just saying to Cas that I thought we should check in on you, but now you're going to be too busy with your mysterious, rich benefactor"

"I'll let you know the second I'm done," I said, already disliking the idea of being done with Ambri when we hadn't even started.

"Wait, you sound sad again," Lucy said. "Or maybe not sad, but..."

"Conflicted?"

"Yes! What is it? Is he an asshole?"

"Let's just say he's...morally compromised."

Great, now I'm a demon apologist.

"But that's only part of the problem," I added quickly and flopped back onto my hard slab of a bed and stared at the ceiling. "I think I might be developing..."

"Feelings for him?" Lucy practically shrieked in my ear.

"*No,* I'm having *thoughts.* A lot of them. And they all tend to move in his direction."

Another squeal and I had to hold the phone away from my ear.

"Oh my God, sorry," Lucy said. "It's just that it's been *three years* since you've even mentioned someone."

"Yeah, but it's not good, Luce. There are a billion ethical reasons why getting involved is a bad idea. Least of which, he's my employer."

"I see your point, but I also sort of don't care."

"You're not helping."

"Look, I know you. You're compassionate and kind and anyone who gets your attention has to be worth it somehow. Right?"

"It's a little more complicated than that." I flicked a piece of lint off my bedspread with a sigh. "We're sort of impossible."

"Oh no. Don't say that."

"It's the truth. I got a little bit infatuated with him because he's ridiculously beautiful. But I can't—and shouldn't—ignore the rest."

Lucy sighed. "Well, that sucks. Maybe after you're done working for him…?"

"He'll still be who he is. No, I need to keep things professional. Do my job and that's it," I said, wishing I felt half as convincing as I sounded.

"Well, let me know if anything changes," Lucy said. "Who knows? Maybe just being in your luminous presence will bring him around and he'll behave himself."

I smiled at the idea of Ambri *behaving* himself in any capacity.

"Miracles do happen. I gotta run. Love you, Luce."

"I love you, Cole. Talk soon, okay?"

"I will."

We said our goodbyes and I immediately set up a canvas and grabbed a pencil. The light outside was growing dim, but that seemed appropriate. I took a deep breath, inhaling the memory of Ambri standing by the window last night, feathered wingtips brushing the floor, his black-on-black eyes somehow expressive and thoughtful. Almost melancholy.

I roughed out a sketch of him in black and white, my mind's eye filling in the color. The glare of the window behind him and the lone streetlight glowing yellow. The deep maroon of the walls, the black of his suit. The entire composition came to me in moments; I could see it as if it were already finished. I dropped the pencil, grabbed a brush, and got to work.

The hour grew late. I lit a lamp.

The room got cold. I put on a sweater.

My stomach grumbled. I didn't stop. Not until my eyes began to burn. It was only then I realized I didn't have my glasses—the new ones wouldn't be ready for a few days. I was farsighted and didn't need them for this work but would need them when it came to the finer details. Time to call it a day.

Or night. My clock radio said it was after eleven p.m. I'd been painting for nearly six hours, nonstop.

I set aside my brushes and washed up. I should've been exhausted, but I felt wide awake, and I'd promised Ambri I'd do research for his portrait.

I heated up a cup of ramen—the salty-ass noodles never tasted better—and tucked myself in bed. Even the cold wind seeping in through the window didn't bother me as much.

Amazing what a little hope could do for a guy.

I flipped through my art history book that covered the Renaissance through the late 1800's. But the images passed under my gaze without me really seeing them. I already knew how I'd paint Ambri's portrait. I could envision every line, every brush stroke.

The book tilted out of my grasp as sleep crept up on me.

"I could paint you with my eyes closed..."

Dawn came in what felt like minutes later, but I jumped out of bed and examined my painting. Another few hours and it'd be done.

"Holy shit," I whispered.

I touched the edge of the canvas, half afraid it would vanish. That I was dreaming. But like Lucy had said, the self-doubt that had been squeezing me like a boa constrictor was gone and I could breathe. I was in the zone. I was doing what I was meant to do, and that was everything.

I wasn't due at Ambri's until the afternoon. I drew three full-body sketches of him as a demon—they practically flew out from under my hand—and headed to Hyde Park. I kept the price at twenty pounds and again customers told me that was cheap. Ambri was already paying me too much for his portrait, and even these sketches were a gift from him. It felt like I was taking advantage.

By noon, two sketches were snapped up, and a tall man in a brown tweed coat took the last one, studying it through round tortoiseshell glasses.

"Do you have more?"

"That's it," I said, "but I'm working on a series of paintings."

He nodded and rummaged in his pocket. He handed me a business card that read *David Coffman, Retailer and Exhibitor*, along with his contact info.

"I'm curating collections for the London Art Faire a week from this Saturday. Do you think you'll have something to show by then?"

"I...yes! Definitely."

"Stalls open at six a.m. for artists. Come see me at the office then. I'll hold a booth for you."

"I don't know what to say. Thank you."

He handed me the sketch. "You forgot to sign it."

"Oh, right."

I signed my name at the bottom right corner while he pulled a fifty-pound note from his wallet.

"I don't make a habit of buying from my vendors," he said, "but this one I'm going to keep." We exchanged the sketch for the money, and he squinted at my name. Then he tipped his cap to me. "A week from Saturday, Cole A. Matheson."

"Right. See you then." I sat back on my little stool. "Wait! You forgot your change."

He waved me off absently, his eyes on the sketch. "Trust me, this is a steal."

I arrived at Ambri's flat in the early afternoon. Jerome was at the desk. Again. Did they ever give him time off? He waved me up before I could say a word. At Ambri's door, I knocked, and he called for me to enter.

I inhaled deep, bracing myself for how he was going to barrage my senses and scramble my thoughts.

He sat on the chair near the fireplace, staring into the flames, a stormy expression painted on his beautiful face. He wore all black—dressed as if he were about to head to a photo shoot or movie premiere. His sharp glance slid to me.

"Something on your mind?" he asked. "Let me guess. You're conflicted about selling sketches of me." He rolled his eyes and turned back to the fire. "It's no wonder Fortune keeps missing you, Cole Matheson. You shun her at every turn."

"Fortune didn't miss me today, thanks to you."

I told him about Mr. Coffman and the London Art Faire.

"Thus, beginning your epic rise to fame and untold riches," Ambri said.

"I don't know about that, but it's more action than I've seen since graduation."

"So naturally, you feel guilty about it."

"It's not guilt, really." I smiled. "Well, maybe a little."

"Why? I revealed my form to you so that you might use it to make your name. My human portrait is for me."

I studied my hands, smudged with charcoal. "I know. It's just a lot and I'm grateful—"

"Then say thank you and be done with it."

His bad mood was like a storm cloud filling the flat; the air felt tight and electric. I took a seat on the couch. "Is everything all right?"

"Why wouldn't it be?"

"You tell me." I noticed his hair wasn't its usual coiffed perfection but was tousled. As if someone—*more than one someone?*—had been running their fingers through it. "Long night?"

"As a matter of fact, yes. Does that offend your delicate sensibilities?"

I shrugged, rested my elbows on my knees. "I don't know. I don't like it, but I've been wrapped up—"

"In what I could do for you?" He scoffed. "How very human of you."

"Maybe," I admitted. "I don't even know what you do, exactly. Create sex addicts? Or make people cheat on people they love? Or—"

"I don't *make* people do anything. No demon does. We only stoke that which already exists in you. It's up to you to resist us. To fight back with your power that far exceeds ours if you only believed it."

I frowned. "I just don't understand. Thousands—probably millions—of people have sexual hang ups. Are you responsible for all of it?"

"Yes," Ambri said snidely. "I'm a lusty Father Christmas who visits every bedroom in one night, delivering goodies to all the naughty little boys and girls."

"Maybe you do. I don't know how it all works."

"I have legions of servitors," Ambri said. "Lesser demons who do the same work. They—like most demons—operate from the Other Side of the Veil, whispering and enticing. I happen to prefer the personal touch. But if you're trying to exercise your moral outrage while still keeping your commission, rest assured. If I ceased to exist tonight, it wouldn't make a damn bit of difference. Another demon would come along to take my place." He gave me a look. "Feel better?"

"I don't know how to feel."

"Hmph. I don't recall you complaining the other night when you were benefitting from my particular skill set."

My face heated. "I thought I was dreaming. It won't happen again."

"You don't sound very convincing."

"It's all surreal," I admitted with a sigh. "Like there are two of you. The version that I want to paint until my eyeballs fall out of my head and then there's the version that I wish…"

I cut off my words with a cough. I didn't even know what I'd been about to say except that it was something I couldn't take back.

"There isn't one version of me without the other," Ambri said quietly. "Don't forget that."

A short silence fell and then I ventured slowly, "Do you miss being human?"

He winced—the smallest tic in his jaw. "What could possibly give you that idea?"

"You said most demons work from the Other Side. But you're here. You have your own place, your own money. You want a portrait of when you were…alive."

"I miss nothing about being human."

I smiled gently. "You don't sound very convincing."

"Fine. We're both liars."

Hope flared in my heart, stupid and bright. "You *do* miss it? So maybe if—"

"There is no *if*, Cole Matheson, and you ask too many questions. Have you done your research?"

Down to business. Good. That's what you want, right?

That was debatable, but the work was the only thing that could—or should—happen between us. I'd been protecting my heart for years; keeping my distance from a demon shouldn't have been this fucking hard.

I rummaged in my bag and brought out the art history book. I flipped it open to a section on Elizabeth Le Brun.

"Talking about Marie Antoinette yesterday gave me some ideas. Le Brun was one of the greatest portraitists of your era, known for her portraits of the queen. But this one had me thinking." I showed him Le Brun's portrait of King Stanislas II in his red coat and white wig. "Is that what you had in mind? I remember you first came to me dressed like this."

"The clothing I died in."

"But there was no wig—"

"It was torn from my head." He took in my pained expression and quickly waved a hand. "Save it, Cole Matheson. The time when kindness might've been useful to me has come and gone. I only want the bloody painting."

I shut the art book. "Maybe we could just talk about composition. I have some thoughts."

"I can't wait."

"When I do a portrait, I like to get a feel for who my subject is. If I know them better, it helps me to—"

"See directly into their soul?" Ambri snapped. "I'll spare you the trouble—I haven't got one."

"I don't think that's true," I said quietly.

His eyes flared and flashed black. "No? You know *nothing*. Nothing of the afterlife, nothing of the forces raging around you, even as we speak, and you certainly know nothing of me."

I weathered the storm of his sudden wrath, my pulse pounding. But the pain in him was as tangible as the couch under me. I didn't know what set him off today, but it was eroding my will to keep things professional with every passing minute.

"Tell me," I said and pulled out my sketchbook and a piece of charcoal. "You talk and I'll sketch, and after, we'll have a better idea about how to proceed with the painting."

What hurt you so badly?

I glanced up to see him watching me with narrowed eyes.

"You think you can help me, don't you? Me, a creature of the underworld. Do you think *talking* about being burnt alive is going to save me? Impossible. I'll never need—nor do I want—a human's pity. Ever."

The words *burnt alive* rattled around in my heart like bullets.

He sneered at my expression. "I thought so. Forget it."

"You want this portrait, Ambri. And I want it to be the best it can be. This is how we do it."

"It's too sordid for you, Cole Matheson."

"It made you who you are," I said. "That's what I want in the painting."

Our gazes met and I felt him want to give in. And then he did. The fight seemed to go out of Ambri, and he turned back to the fire.

"It matters little, I suppose, and changes nothing. But my death is the end of my ruination, not the beginning. That came earlier—a sad little tale of visiting uncles and carriage rides to hell."

I looked up sharply from my work, a sudden dread gripping my heart.

Ambri waved a hand. "Another time. Tonight, you want to hear the one about how I gave my soul to the devil."

I nodded, drawing the angle of his arm as he rested his chin in his palm. The line of his leg that was stretched out, the other bent. I knew Ambri would stop talking if he suspected I cared more than he already knew. More than *I* knew what to do with.

"His name was Ashtaroth. I can say his name aloud because he's gone to Oblivion. Destroyed by an angel, no less. But back in 1786, he was there to catch me as I fell." Ambri cocked his head, as if thinking aloud. "They call it *falling* in love for a reason, don't they? Because that's what you do. You fall and if the object of your love isn't there to catch you, you shatter into a million pieces. Or you burn to ash."

"Armand," I said gently.

Ambri winced but nodded. "He was sentenced to exile for his role in the Affair, while Jeanne was to be imprisoned for life. I thought myself lucky. They'd be separated and I'd have Armand all to myself. I'd take care of him anywhere he chose. Didn't matter to me, so long as we were together." His voice hardened, became brittle like it might crack. "But he didn't love me. He loved her. I'd outlived my usefulness to him and *he*—dirty and stinking of the chamber pot—rejected *me*."

Ambri's gaze was on the flames but far away, trapped in memories.

"It was a final blow," he said. "Another betrayal in a life that was rife with them. So I did what any poor slob in my position would do and got good and drunk. I mouthed off to some peasants and they locked me in a burning distillery. But just before the first flames found me, Ashtaroth appeared. He promised me that I'd be free from ever wanting the love or affection of another human." Ambri slid his gaze to me. "And that is how a demon is made."

He was making light of it but couldn't conceal the pain that lingered. I recalled the night I stood at the bridge, staring into the black water, wanting to vanish and the pain to vanish with me. Wasn't that what Ambri did? He'd been in agony and wanted it to stop.

But the darkness didn't snuff him out. His light is still there.

Ambri got up and headed toward the cocktail table near the window. I set aside my sketchpad and moved to block his way. "Thank you for telling me."

He frowned, but before he could speak, I put my arms around him and held him. He stiffened, but I didn't let go. I embraced six feet of lean muscle wrapped in expensive clothing and doused in cologne. Beneath, a hint of ash. Like the embers of a low-burning fire.

"What are you doing?" he asked gruffly.

"I'm hugging you."

"Why?"

"Because if you share a story with someone about being *burned alive*, the very fucking least they should do is hug you."

For a moment, I could only hear his soft inhale and our hearts beating together. I ventured one hand around the back of his neck, the other around his shoulders, still just holding him. My heart was in trouble—there was no denying it—but in that moment, this was enough. The crushing loneliness of the last few years receded, revealing a barren shore. I needed to give, too, to be there for someone. I needed a communion of souls, not merely a warm body in my bed.

It can't be Ambri. You know this. It can't be him...

I held him tighter.

After a moment, I felt Ambri's hands come up and rest lightly on my waist. I thought he'd push me away, but he pulled me closer. His lips were against my neck; the heat of his breath wafted softly. Then he leaned back, so we were face to face. My desire for him was reflected in his eyes, a mirror of want.

"What you just told me was pretty intense," I whispered. "I don't want to—"

"Your compassion is endearing, Cole," Ambri said. "But it's killing the mood."

He brought his face close to mine, our noses brushing, the blue-green of his eyes like an ocean I wanted to drown in.

"I thought you had rules," he said.

"So did I." My lips grazed his chin, seeking his mouth. "We shouldn't."

"You're right," he said, his tone still edged with anger. "You'll be another death of me, Cole Matheson, and yet..."

I can't stop wanting you.

I heard his words clear as day because Ambri wasn't free of anything. He was trapped in a darkness built with empty promises.

Or maybe I was lying to myself because I wanted him, too. It was wrong and probably dangerous, but my rules were crumbling around me with his every breath wafting over my lips. I inhaled raggedly, the need to taste him washing out every other sensation and all rational thought.

I angled my head to kiss him, but his hand came up, stopping me. His fingertips traced the lines of my mouth while his gaze roamed, as if searching my face for an answer he desperately needed.

Why you?

My lips parted, and I touched my tongue to his finger. Then licked, then sucked the tip. His eyes flared, and with his own ragged inhale, Ambri pushed two fingers into my mouth while his other hand gripped my hair at the back of my head. I sucked and licked, sliding my tongue while my hand ventured down his body to find his cock that was pressing urgently against my erection. I palmed it and gave the hard length a squeeze.

He groaned and rested his forehead against mine. I tried to kiss him again—I was fucking dying to kiss him—but he turned away.

"You can do anything to me, Cole," he said against my lips, his eyes hooded and dark. "But not that."

"You don't kiss?"

"Never on the mouth. My one and only hard limit."

I nodded, swallowing down disappointment and calling on my willpower to keep from crushing his mouth to mine.

"Then I'll kiss every other part of you instead."

With those words, our barely restrained need snapped. I stripped off his jacket. He tore off my sweater, leaving me in a long-sleeved shirt. His hands slipped underneath, exploring me until that wasn't enough. Then he tore the shirt off and stared at me in my white tank. I felt him take in the muscles of my shoulders, my chest, the tightness of my stomach.

"How…how did this happen?"

"Pushups and sit-ups," I said with a grin. "The poor man's workout."

"You've been keeping this from me, Cole Matheson," he said. "I feel betrayed…"

I started to laugh, but it was snuffed out as he attacked me with renewed heat. I responded just as fiercely, kissing and licking Ambri's neck and then biting the soft flesh there.

Finally, I felt free of the shackles I'd put on myself. Why? Because Scott Laudner had broken my heart? I could hardly remember what he looked like. My world had eclipsed to just Ambri and me in that living room.

Not kissing him was torture. We had close calls and near misses, our lips brushing but never latching on, our teeth and tongues working over jaws and necks and sucking at ear lobes when I ached to taste him and be tasted. To invade and be invaded. I took my frustration out on his clothing, yanking open his vest and sending buttons flying.

"I like this version of you," Ambri said. "The unthinking animal who takes what he wants."

Because that's what he needed me to be, but I was full of thoughts, and they were all of him. My physical need—as ravenous as it was—paled in comparison to how I wanted him in every other way. Ambri was pouring into the hollow spaces in me, driving out the cold emptiness that had lived there for so long.

My mouth sought his again—a natural instinct—but he deftly moved out of my reach.

"I'm sorry," I murmured. "I can't help it…"

My words died as desire rolled through me like a slow wave. I'd stripped him bare to the waist, and the sheer perfection of him made me lightheaded. The lines of his chest, the muscles moving under smooth skin… I rested my hand over his heart, felt it pounding under my palm.

"Jesus Christ. You're fucking beautiful."

Ambri's eyes flared with alarm. He gripped my cock over my pants and squeezed, bringing me back to the present. "Don't be sweet to me, Cole, or this ends now."

His blue-green stare was hard, but beneath, I saw a glint of fear. The same fear that lived in me—that we were playing with fire.

"Tell me what you want," I asked hoarsely.

"Rough. Raw. No useless sentiment."

He said it like a challenge I wasn't up for, but I could play this game. I could pretend this was impersonal, when in truth I wanted to take him to bed and kiss every inch of him—including his perfect mouth—for the sheer sake of being with him. I wanted to give him a taste of the release he'd given me. To make him feel taken care of.

I'll do it his way.

I took a small step back. "Make me take it."

fifteen

Ambri

"What...?"

"You heard me," Cole says thickly, those dark eyes hooded.

It must be a trick or a ploy to convince me this means nothing to him, but what did it matter? I can't resist him. A hundred times I nearly let him have my mouth. Cole is unraveling me, pulling me deeper into the quicksand, and I'm doing nothing to stop it.

No! I am still in control.

I inhale sharply through my nose and my hand snakes out to grip his hair. That lock that is forever falling over his brow, tormenting me. I use it to yank his head back. His mouth opens, his breath harsh and—goddamn him, Cole runs his tongue over his parted lips, readying himself for me. A hint of triumph is mixed with the desire that is pouring out of him.

With a snarl, I force him to his knees while freeing my cock from my pants. It rubs against his lips, but he refuses to take it. With my other hand, I grip his jaw and squeeze. I must be hurting him—I *want* to hurt him, so he'll come to his senses and escape me and my plan to ruin him. But he only grunts and keeps his mouth clenched tight.

I bend and put my lips to his ear. "You're going to open for me, Cole. You're going to open and take my cock down your throat."

He makes a sound in his chest, his eyes full of pure need as he struggles—weakly—against my grip. My thumb presses in that delicate spot just below his cheekbone, and his mouth opens with a small groan. *My* groan. Cole takes me deep the same instant his lips part, and I go dizzy at the sudden sensation. Too good. Too perfect. I release his jaw as he takes me in and out, running his tongue up and down my cock, then sucking me hard.

What is happening...?

I've done this so many times, but this is different. Something's not right...and yet it's more perfect than I've ever known. There's something behind Cole's lust. A desire for me that has nothing to do with what he can get from me.

He takes a gasping breath. "Fuck my mouth, Ambri. Give it to me."

His words are like fuel to a fire I can barely contain. My hand in his hair tightens its grip again, and my hips thrust. It's too much; his eyes are watering, but he's ravenous for me. On his next inhale, he puts a hand around my cock, never relenting while he sucks in air, and then takes me deep again.

I can't resist. My head falls back as I do something I never do—surrender. To a human. To him. To the sensations he's creating in me. Sensations I've felt a thousand times but are somehow more intense, more precious, because they're coming from *him*.

Quicksand...

The climax that is building in me is unlike anything I've ever felt. It coalesces at the base of my spine, and my entire world collapses to just Cole's mouth, his tongue, and the sounds of want he makes as he takes me, as if he wants to swallow me whole.

I shudder and tense all over as the wave crashes. Cole doesn't relent. He sucks mercilessly, then takes my cock to the back of his throat, gripping my hips as I come hard. So hard, my knees buckle and I have to prop myself on the chair. He takes everything, not slowing or stopping until I'm spent. Until he's swallowed every last drop of ecstasy he created.

Then the perfect wet heat of his mouth leaves me, and I tuck myself back into my pants and blink my eyes open. Cole is smiling and breathing hard, his eyes still wet.

"I hope that was okay," he says with that crooked, charming grin of his that threatens to wreck me.

Before I can find my voice, he stands and moves in to kiss me and I rear back.

"It's okay," he says softly. "I won't."

He plants a lingering kiss on my neck, soft and warm. I feel that kiss everywhere. Even in the parts of me I thought had been burnt out. It seeps in the cracks, infiltrating me. Making me weak for want of him. For more of this...

"Get out," I hiss.

Cole pulls back with hurt swimming in his liquid dark eyes.

"Did you hear me? *Get out!*"

He takes a step away, holding my gaze a moment longer, and I feel him reading me. There is no anger or reproach, only a small nod of understanding as he gathers his coat.

At the door, he stops. "What about our work?"

"It can wait."

"Until when?"

I don't answer and he leaves, softly shutting the door behind him. I'm still gripping the back of the chair. With a roar, I send it flying into the fire. It's an antique and smashes like kindling, the Victorian-era upholstery burning instantly.

I watch the flames lick and curl, devouring a piece of history, but what does that matter when I can still feel Cole's arms around me? I can feel his heart thudding against mine, like a communion. An intimacy I hadn't known in years. I struggle to turn my thoughts against him. He's a liar and a fraud, sucking my cock like a whore, but his eyes give everything away. They soften when he looks at me. That kiss on the neck...

I put my hand to my aching heart.

I'm not going to survive this.

But I have to. I have a command to obey or else spend the next millennium in unknowable pain. Agony worse than what was done to me in 1786. But even that memory seems distant when Cole Matheson is standing in front of me, looking at me with those dark eyes. Like staring into absolution.

Into hope.

"There is no hope for me," I say aloud.

When the hour grows late, I go out. I haven't been to London in years, but I know where to go; I can feel their need, their desire to surrender. To submit. Cole thinks I do this every night, but since him,

I haven't touched another human. I spend the long hours of the night pulling at my own hair with frustration that I've let him invade me so thoroughly, so quickly.

That ends tonight.

The club entrance is tucked into a dark alley and down a flight of stairs. A large man guards the door and asks for a password. My eyes flash black, offering a glimpse of the eternal hell in me.

He steps aside.

Down I go, through dimly lit rooms where bodies entwine and rut in corners while others watch. Cries emanate from behind closed doors—half pain, half ecstasy.

I enter one such room that reeks of perfumed oils. A man is hung from the wall, arms and legs splayed—an X in black leather and chains. Another man is holding a whip, one of many tools displayed on a wooden table in the center. Half a dozen men and women watch, sipping cocktails and smoking cigarettes. They all go still when they see me.

Without a word, I strip out of my jacket and shirt and turn my naked back to the man with the whip. I grip the edges of the table.

"Do it."

He hesitates. "Safe word?"

"I said, *do it*," I snarl, emanating just enough of my otherworldly power to command the room—disobeying me is not an option. My eyes fall shut as the leather lashes my back.

"Harder."

It comes again, biting deeper but not enough.

"Harder."

Again and again, the whip crosses my back, but for these humans, inflicting pain is only one part of the equation. Even the harshest treatment is a seduction—a trust—between the punisher and the punished. Mine is holding back. He doesn't want to hurt me the way I need to be hurt.

I turn and grab the whip as it comes down, rip it out of the man's hand, and toss it to the floor.

"Useless fool…" That's when I smell her. Eisheth. My pulse quickens and I turn. "Are you my shadow now?"

But of course she is, watching me, following me on the street. They're waiting for me to fail.

Eisheth frowns, confused, then shrugs her delicate shoulders. In her human form, she is a sharp-edged beauty reeking of danger—Cole would paint her in rubies and daggers and poison. Perfect ebony skin and hair pouring down her back. I've always felt it a shame her demon form washed out her color because she is truly one of the great beauties of the world...and one of the most malevolent.

Eisheth seems to read Cole in my thoughts and her brow arches.

"I know why you're here, Ambri, and I applaud the intention. But it's not enough, is it? No, you need something with a little more...heat." She moves to stand in front of me. "Turn. Strip."

I do as she says and brace myself on the table. Terror chokes my throat, but I need this. To be cleansed. To rid myself of the soft feelings for Cole Matheson that can have no place in my heart. Feelings that will cost me lifetimes of agony if I don't endure this now.

The room has gone silent again, wide eyes staring at the succubus and me, all instinctually knowing they're witnessing something supernatural; none will be able to explain what.

The oil is warm and slick as Eisheth pours it over my backside. It drips down the backs of my legs in scented ribbons. Murmurs and small protests ripple through our audience—she's taken someone's cigarette.

"Nothing purifies quite like fire," she says from behind me. "You, Ambri darling, know that better than any. Still...a little reminder can't hurt."

And then there is no Cole in my thoughts. There is no room for thought.

There is nothing but pain.

sixteen

Cole

I didn't hear from Ambri for three days, and it rained buckets for every single one of those three days. I worked steadily in my basement flat, churning out paintings of him as a demon. I'd done four so far—all in acrylic, which dried faster than the oils I wanted to use. I still had a few days before the art fair; I figured I could get in two more, and those six paintings plus a dozen or so charcoal drawings would hopefully be enough to fill out a booth.

It amazed me how fast Ambri appeared on my canvases. I painted him as if I were racing toward some finish I couldn't see. As if he'd vanish from my memory any second.

I paint Ambri so I can keep him when it all ends.

I took off my new glasses to rub my eyes. "This is bad."

My feelings were a fucking mess. I had no way to think about us that made sense, yet all I could do was think about us. What we'd done—what *I'd* done—the other night replayed over and over in my mind. It was shocking how fast I'd sunk to my knees for him. How desperate I'd been to have him any way I could.

Worse, I was starting to fantasize about him and me doing normal things—late night dinners, strolls through London, him in my bed as the morning light fell across his hair that was mussed because my hands had been in it all night...

"This is really bad."

I looked to my painting. It was one of the best things I'd done. Every painting of Ambri was the best thing I'd done. Not even my own natural self-doubt—which felt different from the insidious whispers—could deny it. He came alive on the canvas—a monster whose humanity emanated from every bloodless pore and feather. I painted him as I saw him: a light trapped in darkness.

"You're kidding yourself. He's a fucking *demon*," I said, trying to mentally slap some sense into myself. Thinking Ambri was suddenly going to be something he wasn't was ridiculous.

"This is why I don't do one-night stands," I muttered and set my paintbrush down. "Because I get so stupid and over-involved and I...talk to myself, apparently."

I washed up and climbed into bed, listening to the storm rage. The rain would not let up; I heard it rushing in the gutters and splattering at the window. I'd had to tuck a rag in the cracks to keep it from seeping in.

A metaphor, I thought, my eyes growing heavy. My feelings for Ambri raged like a storm that wouldn't quit; I couldn't keep him from seeping in.

Two days later, I wrapped my six frameless paintings in canvas cloth and splurged for a cab to take me to the London Art Faire. The storm clouds seemed like a permanent fixture over the London skyline, but the rain had abated to a drizzle for now.

I followed signs for the vendor entrance, and then a guy pointed me to David Coffman's office at the end of a long hallway. He was surrounded by assistants in a flurry of action. I thought he wouldn't remember me, but he shooed everyone out when he saw me at the door, then got up to shake my hand.

"Cole A. Matheson. Are you ready?"

"As I'll ever be."

"Can I see?"

"Sure." I unwrapped the bundle of paintings, and I lined them in a row against the wall of his office.

He rubbed his chin as he walked back-and-forth in front of them, his brows furrowed while I waited with sweaty palms.

I'd done a series of Ambri in a black suit, trying to let the light sources—a streetlamp, the moon, an antique lamp in his flat—define him. His pale skin seemed to glow with an ephemeral light, his black-on-black eyes glinting with a flicker of flames in their depths. In one, he held a beetle in his hand. In another, he stared at the fire, its flames a reflection of those that still burned within him.

But Mr. Coffman stared longest at the last one. Inspired by the rainstorm, I'd put Ambri outside, in a downpour. I'd made him naked from the waist up, attempting to capture the perfection of his body but also the human vulnerability he couldn't hide from me. To reveal the power in his demonic form but to put him in the rain, sodden and alone. His wings were bunched around his shoulders, water beading on the feathers like mercury. His blond hair was plastered over his pale cheeks, and his eyes faced straight ahead. The only painting in which, when the viewer stared at him, Ambri stared back.

"Jesus," Mr. Coffman muttered. "I have half of mind to take them all off your hands right now and put you on display only. How much are you pricing them?"

"I don't know. I figured maybe £450 per?"

A fit of coughing came over him. "Crikey, Cole. You're green, I can see that. And modest. But you can't let these out the door for less than £750 each. And this one…" He gestured to the last one. "This one is £2,000 and not a penny less."

I shook my head. "Oh no. That's too much."

"Rather learn the hard way, eh? Suit yourself." He went to his desk and took up a yellow slip. "You're booth twenty-one. I'd give you 666 but they don't go that high."

He had an assistant named Anne take photos of each painting to print in order to catalogue the sales. Two other assistants took the paintings to booth twenty-one while David and I followed behind. He pressed a few sheets of stickers into my hand.

"The longer ones are to write the titles; don't leave them all untitled, we need to know for cataloguing purposes and to match them with the photos. Also, buyers love named paintings. Makes for a more personal connection to the artist. The yellow stickers are for the prices, and the red are for when you sell out."

"If I sell out."

"*When* you sell out. Anne will assist you. She'll record the sales, take the payments, get buyer details, et cetera."

David shook his head, rocking back on his heels, his hands in the pockets of his tweed suit as the paintings were hung in the booth. Then he turned and shook my hand.

"I'd say good luck, but you're not going to need it."

The Art Faire was a crowded hall of vendors hawking everything from jewelry to sculptures to modern art that almost defied description. Booth twenty-one was too big for my six paintings and a couple of sketches, but I did my best to fill the space. I put the painting of Ambri in the rain front and center.

I didn't want to let myself get my hopes up, but when the doors opened, people poured in. Immediately, my booth was filled with visitors, staring and whispering. Every one of the paintings and most of the sketches were sold out within the first two hours but that didn't stop people from coming in to look.

"I'm going to go log your sales," Anne said, gathering up the paperwork. She was a no-nonsense woman with a pen tucked behind her ear. "The paintings will stay on display for the rest of the day. We'll handle distribution at closing. Come to the office for your revenue whenever you're ready, but I'd stay if I were you. Take it in."

"Thanks, Anne," I said faintly.

I felt like I was in a dream, and I'd wake up any minute to find it was all in my head. But for the next few hours, my line remained steady with attendees wanting to see Ambri. I fielded questions about my work, my process, my inspiration for the demon.

"Who *is* he?" the attendees asked again and again.

"I wish I knew," I said with a small smile and an ache in my chest.

A little after one, David Coffman approached me with another man—a trim, handsome man in his mid-thirties, wearing a sharp suit and a watch that probably cost more than my entire building.

"Sold out, Anne tells me." Mr. Coffman gave me a wry smile. "Who would've thought? Cole, this is Austin Wong."

He gestured to the young man who stood transfixed in front of a painting, murmuring to himself. "Extraordinary…" Finally, he strode to me. "Mr. Matheson. Pleased to meet you. May we talk?"

"Yeah, sure."

"I'll leave you two to get acquainted." Mr. Coffman shot me a wink and rejoined the crowd in the hall.

"I'll get straight to the point," Austin said. "Do you have representation?"

"No, I—"

"Wonderful. I'm an executive associate with Jane Oxley & Associates. Are you familiar with us?"

I nodded stupidly. "Yes, of course. Everyone has heard of Ms. Oxley. As a matter of fact, my friend Vaughn is—"

"Jane would like to have lunch with you this Monday. Are you free?"

I blinked. "I...what? How did she—?"

"Dave Coffman is an old friend. He was kind enough to show me your catalogue photos. I promptly texted them to Jane."

"Jane Oxley. Who wants to meet me for lunch."

"Monday, yes." Austin handed me his card. "We'll be in touch as to when and where. Do you have any food allergies or restrictions?"

I stared at him vacantly. "Huh? Oh, no." I chuckled. "Sorry, I'm just having an out-of-body experience."

"Fabulous. But Mr. Matheson, as a professional courtesy, I'd ask that you not entertain other offers of representation until Jane has had a chance to meet with you. She is cutting her trip to Paris short for this lunch on Monday."

"I won't speak to a soul. Promise."

"May we shake on it?"

He offered his hand and I shook it, feeling the solidity of it. This was really happening.

Austin moved back to the rain painting, the one that I'd named *Stormlight*. He crossed one arm over his suit, holding his elbow, the other hand pressed to his lips.

"The photos didn't do them justice..." He gave his head a shake, then shot me a curious look, as if he couldn't reconcile the painting and its painter. "Monday, then."

"Right," I said vaguely as he walked out, his shoes *clipping* smartly against the concrete. "Monday."

Sunday, the rain was getting worse, and there was still no word from Ambri. I was several thousand pounds richer on top of the money he'd already paid me, and it felt like I'd stolen from him. Whatever my complicated feelings, we'd made a deal and I owed it to him to keep my end.

That afternoon, I headed to his place in Chelsea. Jerome was manning the front desk and watched me approach from under bushy white brows.

"Mr. Matheson."

"Hi, Jerome. Hey, is Ambri—uh, Mr. Meade-Finch in?"

"I haven't seen him in several days, but I can try to ring him for you."

"Great, thanks."

Jerome picked up his desk phone and hit a button. He listened for a few moments, then hung up. "It would seem Mr. Meade-Finch is out."

He was out, all right. Out fucking humans, doing whatever it was he did to feed their lust and gluttony. I ignored the pang in my chest.

Get a grip and be professional.

"Do you have any stationary, Jerome? I'd like to leave him a message."

He wordlessly handed me a piece of paper, envelope, and pen, all embossed with *Chelsea Gardens* in gold. Hastily, I scratched out a letter.

CHELSEA GARDENS

Ambri,

The art fair was a huge success (you sold out pretty darn quick!) and I have a meeting with a big-time agent tomorrow. None of this would have happened without you, but it's only one half of our deal. I owe you a portrait and I'm ready to pay up. :) Hope to hear from you soon.

Yours, Cole

I cursed at myself. The *Yours* had flown out without thinking. And did I—a grown man—draw an actual smiley face?

Why don't you dot all the i's with hearts while you're at it?

I added my cell phone number at the bottom, sealed the letter in the envelope, and handed it back to Jerome. "Could you...?"

He smiled stiffly. "I'll see that he gets it, sir."

Sunday night, I got a text from Austin that said Jane would meet me at noon at the Isabel Mayfair, an uber posh restaurant a few minutes' walk from the Royal Academy. I used to pass by the place on my way to the Tube, wondering if I'd ever be able to afford to eat in its gold-lit atmosphere. Impossible at the time. I'd been too poor to afford even a drink at the bar.

"You're not in Kansas anymore," I murmured and stepped inside.

I'd worn my best outfit—jeans, a dark sweater, and the coat from Ambri. Like wearing a reminder that whatever happened at this lunch wouldn't have happened if not for him. But he still hadn't contacted me, and I was about to walk into a lunch with Jane friggin' Oxley.

Hello, imposter syndrome.

I gave the host my name and he smiled. "Your party is already here."

"Shit, am I late? I left twenty minutes early—"

"Not at all. Right this way."

The idea that Jane Oxley was waiting for *me* seemed surreal, but the host led me to a table where a woman who resembled Jessica Lange sat—early-sixties, shoulder-length blond hair, hazel eyes, sharply dressed. Everything about her was sharp, including the way she studied me as I came in and shook her hand.

"Cole Matheson," she said with a polished accent. "A pleasure to meet you."

"Same, Ms. Oxley," I said, taking a seat across from her and feeling like a colossal fish out of water.

"Please. Call me Jane."

The waiter appeared to take our drink order.

"Sparkling water, for now," Jane said, then turned to me. "So. Cole Matheson. Tell me about yourself."

"Uh, sure. Well, I'm from Massachusetts originally. I went to NYU and then came here to get a post-graduate degree from the Royal Academy of Fine Arts. I edited its magazine, and until recently, I was employed at Mulligan's Pub."

"Aside from the Art Faire, you've not exhibited anywhere?"

"No. I've been doing the starving artist thing." The memory of the bridge and the black water jumped at me. I offered a wan smile. "It's been a little tough-going, to be honest."

"I can see that; it's all in your work," Jane said, her eyes boring into me. "Now, tell me about your demon."

"Um, well, since graduation, I fell into a kind of depression. One night I had a dream, and he was in it." I shrugged. "Not much more to tell."

The lie tasted sour in my mouth, and Jane looked as if she didn't believe me. The waiter returned and sat down two wine glasses with lime wedges perched on the rim. He poured the water, and when he was gone again, Jane rested her hands on the table, gold bracelets and tasteful jewelry adorning her wrists and fingers.

"I think you're being modest, Cole. And protective. Not that I blame you. Far be it for me to pry into an artist's process, but I jumped on a plane in the middle of a very successful show in Paris to meet you. Because you have that magical, once-in-a-lifetime combination of traits that make an icon: commercial viability and genuine artistry."

Jane took a sip of water while I attempted to absorb her words. Like trying to swallow the ocean—it was too much.

"Demonic images are not unusual," she continued. "But you've infused your creature with a humanity that resonates. He's a reflection of what many are experiencing these days: depression at the state of the world, feelings of isolation, loneliness, but with a glimmer of hope still shining through. Commercial viability occurs when consumers identify with your art on a grand scale, and that's going to make you a very wealthy young man."

"I don't know about that," I said, reaching for my own glass.

"As for the other half of the equation," she continued as if I hadn't spoken. "Are you aware that the name Lucifer means 'light-bringer' or 'morning star'? Before modern Christianity turned him into the devil,

Lucifer was connected with the planet Venus, a symbol of hope and light."

"I had no idea."

"A degree in History comes in handy now and then." Jane's smile faded. "Do you want to know what I see when I look at your demon, Cole?"

I held my breath, nodded.

"I see hope and light. I see love trapped in darkness with the potential for its liberation held within it like a precious seed. It might languish in the dark and die. Or it might be nourished and thus be reborn into something beautiful. That," she said, pressing her finger into the table, "is genuine artistry and *that* is what's going to make you a legend."

I stared, stunned to hear the deepest secret of my heart repeated back to me and far more poetically than I could ever express in words. As if Jane had ripped my heart open and laid everything I'd seen in Ambri on the table between us.

No, I put it all in the paintings.

Jane sat back in her chair, mistaking my dazed expression. "You're humble, Cole, and honest. That resonates too. People are so tired of bullshit. So long as you keep that honesty, I believe you will have a long and fruitful career."

"I…I don't know what to say."

"You can say that you'd like me to represent you."

I nodded, bewildered at the speed at which all this was happening. "Yes, of course. I would be honored."

"Then we can exchange this sparkling water for champagne and celebrate," she said, flagging down the waiter. "I'd like to get you a show as soon as possible. There's a gallery not far from here that I think would be the ideal size. I'm assuming you don't have more of these paintings?"

"No, but I want to do a new series. In oil, not acrylic."

"Good. Twelve paintings, in say, six months. Is that possible? Too fast?"

"I can do that. They sort of fly out of me."

"Perfect. That puts us in April. Perhaps this rain will have let up by then," she said, smiling wryly. "I'll have Austin messenger you the contract. Or if you'd rather, we can finish our lunch and head to my offices. I want to lock you down immediately. I meant every word I said about your work, Cole. I believe in it—and you—with all my heart." She sat back, smiling. "But I also want to make us both an obscene amount of money."

I chuckled, still shaking my head. "If you say so, Ms. Oxley."

"Jane," she said. "Or, if you prefer, 'my agent.'"

The waiter returned and opened a bottle of Dom Pérignon.

"To our partnership," Jane said, holding up her glass, dollar signs dancing in her eyes.

I clinked my glass to hers thinking only of Ambri.

"To hope."

seventeen

Cole

I finished the most surreal lunch of my life, then went to Jane's posh offices in Mayfair before heading back to my dingy, dark basement flat. I itched to call Lucy and tell her my news, but it didn't seem right. Ambri was responsible for every shred of success that was coming my way and he needed to hear it first. But my phone was silent, and if I showed up at Jerome's desk again, he'd think I was a stalker.

The rain had picked up again as I left *Jane Oxley & Associates* and now lashed at the windows like an animal. I heated a cup of noodles, mindlessly jumping from one YouTube video to another. My life didn't magically feel all that different now that I had what I'd been dreaming of—someone who believed in my work. Something was still missing.

Maybe give it five minutes before you start needing more adulation?

But it wasn't adulation I needed.

I checked my phone again. Nothing.

With a sigh, I shut my laptop, stowed it on the floor, and huddled in my bed. Despite the howling wind and cold air seeping in from the cracks, I drifted off and dreamed of the Blackfriars Bridge.

I stood at the rail, staring into the cold, black water. As I watched, it rose higher and higher until it was washing over the stony ground beneath my feet. It swirled around my ankles, then climbed higher and higher, to my knees, then my waist. The scent of brackish, rank water filled my nose and my chest constricted with cold and panic. All around me were paintings of Ambri. Those I'd sold at the Art Faire and those I hadn't painted yet. The paintings for Jane's show. They were all ruined and floating away from me like postage stamps.

"No!"

I sat up shivering with cold, that same brackish smell of the Thames following me from my dream.

A cry fell out of my mouth. My flat was flooded with water, at least a foot high. It gushed down the stairs that led to my door and poured in from under it.

"Shit! Shit shit shit!" I tore out of my bed and threw on my glasses and boots. Panic made it hard to think, and I turned a useless circle, trying to decide what to grab first. My stuff, my portraits from Uni, my laptop, my supplies…

"Ms. Thomas!" I screamed. "Ms. Thomas call emergency services!"

Then I remembered my landlady had left town to visit a sister in Cornwall.

Water was still coming in and showed no signs of stopping. The old building creaked and swayed, threatening to collapse on my head. I grabbed my coat, leaving everything else, and hurried out, nearly slipping on the steps that gushed water as if a pipe had broken.

On the street, other people who were similarly flooded out of their places, huddled in the deluge, making calls to 999. I searched for a place to seek shelter. The rain smattered my glasses, breaking the night into a chaos of rushing water and lightning.

"Mr. Matheson?"

I spun around. A black SUV was parked at the curb, and a man in a suit had climbed out of the driver side and was gesturing me toward the passenger door in the back.

"This way, please."

I stared, water plastering my hair to my cheeks. The tinted window rolled down, and Ambri peered at me through the downpour. The demon's lips curled in a smile. "How about this weather, eh?"

Even shivering with cold and drenched to the bone, a flare of warm desire shot through me. "What are you doing here?"

"Rescuing you. Is that not obvious?" He cocked his head. "What is it with you and water, anyway?"

The driver held the door open for me.

"But my stuff—"

"Is replaceable," Ambri said. "Get in."

I hesitated. Sirens wailed and white and blue lights flashed. Help was coming to the others on my street. There was nothing I could do, not even call Ms. Thomas who had refused to give me—"a veritable stranger"—her sister's number.

I climbed into the SUV's plush, heated interior and sat across from Ambri, shivering and dripping rainwater all over the leather seats. The man in black got behind the wheel, and the car rolled slowly through the murky night.

Ambri sat with a cane situated between his knees, his black-gloved hands resting atop a curved, silver handle. My gladness to see him was shocking. As if I'd been starving and hadn't known how badly until food was set in front of me.

Ambri seemed to be reading my mind. He arched a brow. "Miss me?"

"How did you know to come here?"

"Call it a hunch."

I looked to the rain-splattered window. "Gone. All of it. My clothes, my portraits, my books…"

And I had twelve paintings to paint and no place to do it. I rubbed my eyes, so tired of climbing out of one hole only to fall into another.

That's life, mein Schatz. Keep going, came a thought that sounded feminine. Lucy, probably, being a good friend even in my imagination.

I heaved a steadying breath and concentrated on my other problem sitting right across from me. Ambri was too fucking beautiful for words, and it pissed me off that my entire body, mind, and heart fell into chaos at the mere sight of him.

Have some dignity for Chrissakes.

I jerked my chin. "What's with the cane?"

"You like it? The right accessories really complete a look, I think," Ambri said, but the car lurched around a turn and he hissed in pain. He gripped the cane handle so tight I could hear his leather gloves creak.

My eyes flared in alarm. "Are you okay? What happened?"

"Nothing that wasn't necessary."

"*Necessary*? Stop playing around. Are you hurt? How badly?"

"Careful, Cole Matheson, or else I'll start to think you're infatuated with me. I'm only teasing, of course." Ambri's eyes bored into me. "You wouldn't be that foolish."

My face flushed red. I lowered my voice so the driver couldn't hear. "I didn't think you could be injured."

"It's possible, but I have only to pop over to the Other Side to be healed."

"Why don't you?"

"For the same reason I'm bringing you to live in my spare room," he said. "A supreme test of will."

I sat back, even as my stupid heart thudded against my ribs. "I'm not living with you."

"Oh? Have you a second shithole flat tucked away in case of emergencies?"

"Are you serious? After the other night…" My face burned even hotter. "You think it's a good idea?"

"It's a terrible idea," Ambri said. "But as I mentioned, deprivation is a test of one's strength. Your charm and utter lack of pretentiousness make you a dangerous flatmate. One would *almost* believe your compassion isn't an act."

"It isn't," I said. "I mean, I don't know, I'm just—"

"Being yourself. Exactly. You make it too easy to share moments of weakness that are best forgotten." He wagged a finger. "You'll get no more tales of woe out of me, Cole."

"It's not weakness, Ambri," I said. "It's what you survived."

"Ah, but then I didn't survive it, did I?" he said with bitterness. "I surrendered in the end. You'd do well to remember that. Capture it and sell it, but don't look to me for something that isn't there."

He was bluffing. Or maybe I was only fooling myself that there was more humanity in him because I wanted there to be.

"I got your letter, by the way." Ambri looked amused. "I sold out, did I? You sold me out."

"In record time," I said. "And Jane Oxley is my new agent. I'm going to have a show in April, all because of you."

His smile froze, and he looked away. "I'm so glad."

The driver parked at the curb in front of Chelsea Gardens. Ambri climbed slowly out of the car, wincing with every limping step. My jaw clenched. I offered him my arm and he slid his hand into the crook of my elbow.

"Look at us," he mused. "A devil and an angel, the perfect couple's costume. Next year's Halloween is all set."

"Stop making jokes. Who did this to you?" I hissed as the driver walked ahead to open the front door. "Tell me the truth."

"I already have," Ambri said through gritted teeth, giving a nod to Jerome at the front desk as we made our way slowly to the elevators. "I needed a reminder."

"Of *what*?"

He didn't answer, but his grip on my arm tightened.

Inside his place, I helped Ambri onto the couch, noticing the room was short one chair that had been by the fire.

"Barnard, be a dove and show Cole to his room," he said, removing his gloves.

I followed the driver to the spare bedroom I'd slept in the other night. It had been converted so that half of it was living space, the other half a painting studio, complete with an easel, a tarp, and enough supplies to open an art school. The driver—Barnard—gave me a nod and went out.

"This is fucking nuts."

A quick inspection showed me the dressers were full of clothes, the closet hung with everything from suits to casual jeans and shirts. The en suite, I knew without looking, was stocked with everything I needed.

I went back to the living room in time to see Barnard leave, shutting the door behind him.

"What the hell, Ambri? How long have you been planning this?"

He rolled his eyes. "It doesn't take a seer to predict your pitiful flat wouldn't survive a drizzle, never mind a monsoon," he said, flapping a glove at the storm raging against the window. "Stop complaining, Cole. You now have space to work without the threat of a house collapsing on you."

I took off my glasses and scrubbed my hands over my face. "I can't stay here."

"Why not?"

"You know why not. You and I—"

"There is no *you and I*," Ambri snapped. "You don't have feelings for me, Cole, you have attraction, which is expected given that it's *me*. Add a pinch of sympathy thanks to my sad little story and a touch of gratitude for the rest, and that's all there is."

"Ambri—"

"Don't be a fool. You know that anything between the likes of you and me is ludicrous." He tried for a sly grin. "Of course, I'll never say no to a no-strings-attached roll in the sack. Give me a shout. I'll be just down the hall."

"I don't believe you," I said. "Yes, it's fucking crazy but—"

"Not crazy, impossible," he said, his voice hard. "You will paint my portrait because that's all I want out of you. If that's too difficult a task, go and I'll find someone else."

"You're full of shit," I spat back. "You don't want someone else. You want…" I bit off the words and fought for calm. "There's a reason you told me about your past. Why you're helping me and why you brought me here. Why you need a *reminder* about who you are."

He drummed his fingers on the cane handle. "I admit, I let myself get carried away by you, Cole Matheson. For a brief moment, I let your disarming nature—not to mention your impressive blowjob skills—trick me into thinking you're not like every other human."

"I'm not—"

"*You are.* You want what you want and will burn a city to the ground if you don't get it."

"That's bullshit," I snapped. "That's the lie you tell yourself so you don't have to feel anything real."

He held my gaze, unmoved. "I want my portrait. If we so happen to fuck now and then, I won't complain. But that's all it will be. Fucking."

"I don't work that way."

"And I don't work your way," he said and rose to his feet. "Do you want to see how demons play, Cole? How we remind one another of our true nature?" He pulled his pant leg up, revealing blistered, angry red skin that was blackened in patches.

"Jesus, Ambri…"

"Both legs, arse to ankle," he said. "It burns like hellfire and when my flesh starts to rot, I'll Cross Over to heal but not a moment sooner." He let his pantleg drop and fixed me with a hard stare. "I wiped our slate clean. You and I are starting anew. Do you understand?"

My heart felt like it was cracking in two. For the pain he'd inflicted on himself and for the hope I'd indulged in like a fool. That what Jane had said was real.

That I could save him.

Ambri read my expression and nodded. "Good." He eased himself back down with a grimace. "Consider it your little reminder too."

I nearly gave up, but as I turned to go back to my "new" room, another thought came in that strange feminine voice, like a reassurance I needed that I wasn't crazy. That he wasn't lost.

Hope is never foolish, mein Schatz. Don't give up on him.

eighteen

Ambri

I expect Cole to retreat, but he stands in my living room, dripping water on my carpet. He's shivering hard enough to make his teeth clatter, but those dark eyes of his are filled with worry for *me* and something deeper I don't care to examine.

"You're going to catch your death if you don't get out of those wet clothes." I smile suggestively. "I'd offer to help but I'm a tad—"

"Charbroiled?" he snaps with sarcasm, but his voice cracks and anguish spills out.

No! It's just the cold that grips him. He and I, like water and fire. One cannot survive in the presence of the other.

My smile stiffens. "I suggest you take a hot shower and get some sleep. Tomorrow, we'll begin my portrait. You can paint for the April show in the afternoons and evenings. Having everything you need here—in one place—will ensure you meet the demands on your artistry."

Cole glares at me. He knows I'm right, and moreover, he doesn't want to leave. My jaw clenches, and even as the lower half of my body screams in agony, I know I've made a colossal mistake in choosing Cole Matheson as my target.

Get your portrait and worry about the rest later.

"One condition," he says through trembling lips.

"You have conditions? How cute."

"I'm not painting a damn thing until you heal yourself."

"Now, now—"

"I'm fucking serious, Ambri. I'll walk out the door tonight and you'll never see me again."

I scoff. "Until I read about your great success with your *demon* paintings in the local circulars?"

"I'll quit. I'll tell Jane I lost my inspiration."

"You wouldn't."

"I would," Cole says, his eyes boring into mine. "I *will*, if you don't take care of yourself. I can't make one fucking brushstroke knowing you're suffering."

His words are like blunt shots to my chest—bruising and warm at the same time.

"You're lying," I say. "Humans don't walk away from fame and fortune when it's within their grasp."

He says nothing, only holds my gaze. I feel his conviction pouring off him as surely as the rainwater.

"Fine," I say stiffly. "But you must do the same and get out of those sodden clothes."

He crosses his arms. "You first."

Goddamn him to hell.

Then I remember that's my job.

Leaning heavily on the cane, I rise to my feet. Movement awakens fresh agony, and then Cole is rushing to me. I tear away from him before he can touch me.

"Open the window."

He does as I say, then waits again. He's shivering enough to shatter his bones, but he stands his ground.

"I'm going, I'm going," I say irritably, then level a finger at him. "But you get into a hot shower immediately before you catch the winter fever."

Before he can reply, I dissolve into my anicorpus. The agony I'd been enduring for days vanishes but all I see is him. There are a hundred Coles seen through a hundred pairs of beetle eyes, all radiating the same stoic goodness, making him more handsome. Beautiful.

I swarm out of the window and into the night.

For long moments, I fly with no purpose or aim. I need to Cross Over to make the healing complete, but the last thing I need is Asmodai sensing my presence. He'll smell my weakness instantly.

A hundred wings flit in irritation. I *burned* and yet that weakness refuses to die. Why?

Hope, mein Schatz.

The thought—and the feminine voice that carries it—makes no sense, but the word lingers in my mind like an echo. There is no hope for me, and yet…

Caszicl escaped.

He had the help of an angel. I have no angels.

I know because I looked. There is no kindly ancestor watching over me, not on This Side or the Other. Not even in death, have I known love. That pain swells brighter than the burning oil. I don't *want* to escape, I remind myself, and put myself back at the mercy of humans.

And yet…

Time on the Other Side is a nebulous thing. Angels can flit back and forth to any*when*, but demonkind are restricted. We entice humans to dwell on past failures and pain and make that misery feel unending. We're not permitted to see the future.

The future contains hope.

That damnable word again.

But I can Cross Over into the past and hide in the *when* before Ashtaroth met his unfortunate end. My liege lord will not think to look for me there, as I haven't yet betrayed our dark cause.

The hundred parts of me pause at the thought. I am admitting it; I was a traitor. I helped defeat Ashtaroth because Caszicl was heading for Oblivion, and I wanted to save him. Because he loved Lucy Dennings, and I wanted him to have what he loved.

Because you loved him. *Ah, do you see? It is not dead in you.*

I hiss in a swarm. *Be silent, Eisheth!*

I don't know why the demonwitch is taunting me in this manner, but I escape to the Other Side, passing through the Veil and reforming in my demonic self. The pain of the burning oil is now a memory—when I next take human form, my body will be as perfect and flawless as ever, such is our power. Why would I ever give that up?

On the Other Side, *when* is a suspended collection of moments defined by the human timeline chugging along on the opposite side of the Veil. I peer through it and note with a heaviness that I've returned to the *when* in which the demon Casziel is arguing with an angel, Lucy's father.

Casziel sits hunched on the ground of the back lot behind Lucy's tiny apartment in New York City, his skin pale in the moonlight, black eyes and immense feathered wings black as onyx. Her father is dressed in a trench coat and hat. His white-blue light is blinding to my damned eyes. I focus on Casziel instead, bent and miserable, tormented by his enduring love for a human that has spanned hundreds of her lifetimes.

Casziel snarls at the angel. "Tell your god, then, I'm waiting for my absolution." He rises and throws his arms and wings to the sky. "Well? Here I am. I'm ready."

I know what happens, but my breath catches anyway.

Nothing.

Not yet.

Casziel's been suffering for a millennium, but it's not yet enough. I sneer. I've suffered plenty too, but there is no angel for me to turn to as Casziel does now, his black eyes full of hope.

"Tell me what to do, priest," he pleads. "How does it end?"

"With your death, of course."

And suddenly the celestial creature is in front of me, just on the other side of the Veil. I feel the full force of his power—benevolent but strong. Stronger than anything I've felt from my kind. His eyes pierce me, as if flaying me open—every cell and sinew, both demonic and human.

"Yours too, Ambrosius."

I swarm in the bedroom window of my flat in Chelsea and reform as my human self. I flop onto my stomach on my enormous bed to let the weariness of Crossing Over pass.

"That's not what bloody happened," I mutter into the pillow.

That's the problem with angels and their ability to be any*when*—mind games and tricks. I've already died, and it wasn't an end. It was the beginning of a new existence in which I was free from wanting human love or affection.

Ashtaroth promised.

I roll onto my back and stare at the ceiling. "I'm beginning to suspect demons don't always tell the truth."

The night passes slowly, and the following morning, I find Cole in the living room at dawn. He's already set up an easel and canvas and is using one of my one-hundred-year-old end tables as a place to lay out his paint, palette, and brushes. But because he's Cole, he's thoughtfully covered it with a small tarp. The carpet too. He's wearing jeans and an undershirt only. Barefoot, hair unbrushed, glasses sliding down his nose as he mixes paint.

If I kissed him, those glasses would fly off with the force of our passion.

The thought sneaks into my mind like a crack of light. I haven't kissed a human since Armand. I'm beginning to forget what it feels like.

"You're up early," I say. "Busy bee gets the worm and all that."

"That's not how that saying goes, but yeah. I want to get in as much as possible." He searches me for signs of pain. "You okay?"

"Never better. I trust you slept well? Breakfast? Coffee? I can ring Jerome."

"No. And on that note…" He sets a brush down. "We need to make a few more ground rules if I'm going to be staying here."

I roll my eyes and flounce onto my settee, one leg dangling off. "Here we go again."

"You have to stop buying me things. I don't care if you're richer than the King. You have to let me contribute somehow."

I wave a hand. "Fine."

"Secondly, under no circumstances are you allowed to look at the portrait until it's finished."

"You intend to keep me in a perpetual state of suspense? Cruel, Cole Matheson."

"It's just how I work. You can't look at it until I say it's done. Promise me."

"Shall I pinky swear?"

"I'm serious, Ambri."

"So am I."

I haul myself off the couch and move to Cole. He's showered using the scented soaps I bought for him. His hair is soft and shining, that lock falling over his brow like a dare. I offer him my little finger and tell myself it's just because I'm a brat and not because I need to touch him.

"I swear I will not peek at your masterpiece until it's finished."

He hesitates, then hooks his pinky with mine. "Thank you."

"An unbreakable oath. The pinkies have spoken."

For a long moment, we remain linked and then he pulls away and busies himself with his paints. I retreat to the settee.

"Many eighteenth-century portraits feature monochrome backgrounds," Cole says. "I can do that, or I can add drapery, furniture, whatever you want. Or, if you're good with it, we can match your portrait to your mother and father's." He slowly pulls out his phone. "I don't know if you've seen these, but I found Lord Timothy and Lady Katherine's portraits at the gallery in Hever."

I freeze, then examine my fingernails. "Of course, I've seen them."

"No one will believe our portrait is contemporaneous, but I can match the style, if you want."

I shrug. "You're the artist."

"Okay." He puts the phone away, coughs. "I'm ready to go if you are."

The moment has arrived. It took more than two hundred and fifty years, but I'm going to get my portrait. My erasure from my family's history ends today.

"Thank you, Cole."

"I haven't started yet."

Our eyes meet and he nods.

"You're welcome, Ambri." Another cough. "Seems weird to be saying that. You've changed everything for me. I should be thanking you."

"I haven't done a thing," I say. "If you had no talent, a legion of muses couldn't make your name."

"My muse," he says, as if trying it out. He smiles to himself. "Sounds about right."

I move to stand in front of the wall near the window, directly across from Cole's easel. With a thought, I bring the clothing I died in onto my body—red coat, white ruffled shirt, black pantaloons, white stockings, black shoes."

Cole stares. "How did you do that?"

"All matter is energy. I'm able to manipulate the energy of clothing to allow for my wings, or to take my anicorpus without reforming naked later." I indicate my outfit. "These clothes are a part of me, always. My demonic DNA, so to speak. I can't get rid of them. But perhaps that is for the best. This is how I wish to be painted. But I have no wig."

"I can add one," Cole says and squeezes paint from his tubes. The competency in which he handles the tools of his trade is shockingly erotic. The deftness of his hands, the movement of his biceps under his shirt… And then the bastard tosses his head to move the lock of hair from his eyes.

"Unfair."

He looks up. "Sorry?"

"Nothing. How shall I stand? Or sit…?"

Cole rubs his chin, then looks to the cane I'd left leaning against the wall. "Try this."

He hands me the cane, and now he's in my space again. I can smell the warmth of his skin, more potent than any soap or cologne.

"Now, turn a quarter profile to me," he says. "Left hand on your hip, right arm extended, right hand resting on the cane."

He steps back to study the pose, then moves in to make an adjustment here, a slight change there. Cole's face is close to mine; he's focused on his work, but my gaze traces his jaw, his chin, the bow of his lips. The intimacy of him in my space is more than carnal. In Cole Matheson's presence, I'm safe.

Before I can stop myself, I grip his wrist and whisper, "Don't make me look a fool."

"I never would. I promise, Ambri." He smiles that gentle grin of his. "Pinky swear."

Another long, heated moment, and then he retreats. Back at his easel, he coughs again as he studies me. "Perfect."

I frown. "That's the third time you've coughed."

"You're keeping count?"

"I'm keenly observant."

"I have an itch in my throat. No big deal." Cole looks at me from behind the canvas. "Ready?"

I nod and affect what I hope is a stately stance and expression. I'd been erased from my family because of the liberties my uncle took with me. His crimes had somehow become *my* shame. He robbed me of my dignity, my sense of self, and here I am pretending to be the confident, poised human I never was.

Your glory is so much greater now. Why bother with this farce?

But I hold still and Cole paints. Being under his thoughtful, diligent gaze isn't the torture I feared it might be. True, I want to stride to him, strip him naked, and return the favor he gave me the other night. But mostly, the sense of safety washes over me and I relax.

But Cole coughs again and again. After another few minutes, I can't take it anymore. I drop my pose.

"Cole."

"I'm fine."

"You're not fine. You're ill. From last night's rain, just as I said."

"It's just a cold. I'll be okay." Cole's eyes flare with concern. "Can I get you sick?"

"Bloody hell, man, *that's* what you're…?" I scrub my hands over my face. "Put down the brush and sit down. Or lie down. Or perhaps, the hospital?"

He chuckles. "That's a little extreme. But I'll take some lemon tea with honey if you have it."

I make Cole the tea, and he insists on continuing, though his cough worsens with every passing moment. I have no idea what to do. What he needs. Human bodies are so bloody fragile, it's a miracle any of them make it past infancy.

After another bout of coughing, I toss the cane to the floor with a clatter.

"Enough. Go to bed at once."

He nods and sets his brush down. "I am feeling a little warm. Shit, I hate when you're right."

"Get used to it." I follow Cole to the spare room, and he climbs into bed. I stand awkwardly beside him. "What can I do?"

He smiles against the pillow, his eyes already closed. "Tell me a bedtime story."

"Bloody hell."

Cole laughs and that laugh devolves into yet another cough. "I'll sleep a bit and we can start again. I'm sorry, Ambri."

He sleeps, not for "a bit" but for hours. When he wakes, the sun is low in the winter sky and the room is beginning to darken. His cheeks are splotched with red, and his eyes are glassy. His coughing is worse, wracking him and bending him in half.

"Cole..."

"Do you have something for a fever?" he croaks. "A few pills and I'll be good to go."

"Will you, now? You look like absolute shite," I say to conceal the fact that my heart is thudding against my chest like a hammer. "What else? Should I call for a doctor?"

"No. Maybe some water?"

I'm already out of the room to ring for Jerome. I place an order, then bring Cole a glass of water. He struggles to sit and drinks only a little. I frown, still standing impotently at his side.

He smiles at me tiredly. "You're always too handsome for your own good, Ambri," he says. "But right now, you're beautiful. I've never seen you look more human."

I scoff. "You're clearly feverish. Stop talking nonsense and rest."

Cole chuckles, then is wracked by more coughing. "She's right," he mutters, his eyes falling shut. "I won't give up..."

He falls into a fitful sleep. I tear off my coat and yank at the ruffle at my neck, undoing buttons. I'm about to burn the city down myself waiting for the currier to bring the supplies I requested. Finally, there is a knock at my door, and a young man hands me two bags filled with cans of soup, juice, and medicines of all kinds.

I wake Cole and make him take a few pills for his fever. His skin is burning to the touch, but his eyes seem a little less glassy than they did previously. I pull a chair to his bedside, and he smiles.

"Are you going to watch me sleep after all?" He grins. "Psychopath."

"Hush. Shouldn't you eat?"

He shakes his head against the pillow and rolls on his side to face me. "This is perfect."

"I fail to see the perfection in this situation."

"If I were at my shithole flat, I'd be doing this alone." He closes his eyes for long moments. "Kind of tired of that."

"Have you no family?"

"Not anymore. Don't know who my dad is. Mom struggled a lot and eventually gave me up to my grandmother, Margaret-Anne. She raised me. Always called me her little treasure." He smiles, his eyes distant. "She was a firecracker, you know? A flower child in the sixties, a free spirit. She was full of love and joy. She was seventy-five when she died, but she always seemed younger to me. Always laughing…"

"When did she pass?"

"Last year." Cole's eyes shine. "She was diagnosed with dementia during my last year at the Academy. When it got worse, they said to stay here, that she wouldn't know me anymore. But a few months ago, I got a bad feeling, you know? I scraped together the money for a flight to Boston and got there just in time." A tear slides across his cheek and over his nose. "They were right, she didn't know me. But I think maybe she did. Somehow, she knew. I held her hand as she died. That's something, I guess."

I nod, not trusting myself to speak.

Cole coughs and wipes his eyes. "Anyway, after she passed, it seemed like my life had shrunk. I have a best friend, Lucy, and that's basically it. It's my fault though. I threw myself into the art magazine at Uni. Made no time for anyone. Then things started to fall apart." He inhales shakily. "I've been so busy struggling to stay afloat, I haven't even mourned my grandmother. I had to set that grief aside because it was too much. I couldn't deal with it all."

I have no idea what to do or say. I expect Cole to let that grief loose, but he pulls himself together and settles deeper into the pillow.

"Anyway…feel better now." His eyes fall shut. "Thank you."

"That's the medicine working."

He smiles. "Yeah, that must be it."

Cole sleeps, and when I'm certain he's under deep, I touch the back of my hand to his forehead. It's still hot, and I curse the storm, the cold, and the unrelenting fear that has come alive in me like a different sort of fever. It won't break until Cole's does.

For three days, I keep vigil. The illness that plagues him teeters on the edge of being grave and then improves, again and again, so that I'm constantly at my wit's end. Finally, in the blackest hour of night, I witness the fever release its hold on him. Sweat beads on Cole's forehead and neck, and he begins to toss and turn, as if battling with the last of the malady. He mutters and cries out, and then the grief he'd been holding in breaks too.

In his sleep, he sobs, his hands grasping for something. Without thinking, I climb into the bed behind him, my chest to his back, and wrap my arms around him. Instantly, he clutches my arms and holds on. I feel his body shudder against mine and weather the storm with him. Years of loneliness flood out. I can feel it as surely as I can feel his strong body pressed to mine.

"I'm here," I whisper against his neck.

I don't know who the *I* is I speak of, but I say it over and over until Cole's ragged breaths smooth out and deepen. I stay with him until dawn's light seeps into the room, then extract myself. He's as reluctant to let me go as I am to leave. But I slip off the bed without waking him and move to the window.

I sit on the sill. The storm has passed at last. Watery, gold light pierces through gray storm clouds that are moving away, leaving a blue sky.

In time, Cole stirs. "Hey," he croaks.

"Feeling better?"

But I can see that he is. The relief that floods me is so profound, it washes away the lies I've been telling myself—the lies Ashtaroth spun in that distillery. The emotion I feel crashes against his every false promise, breaking them to pieces. My heart is naked and raw, exposed. I burned my flesh, and it wasn't enough.

I know what I must do.

I recoil at the thought and the finality embedded in it. I'm not ready to let him go. Not yet.

I affect a casual tone. "You look improved, though that isn't saying much."

Cole nods absently. He's staring at me sitting at the window as if he's never seen me before. Without taking his eyes off me, he reaches for his sketchbook that's on the floor next to the bed. He props himself on the pillow and grabs a pencil.

"Don't move."

I wonder if he remembers last night. I hope he does and yet it's better if he doesn't. His pencil scratches against paper while I sit and watch a new day dawn over London.

nineteen

Cole
December 24

I peered at Ambri from behind the canvas, then sighed. "You have to stop doing that."

He blinked innocently. "I'm not doing a thing. Isn't that preferable?"

"Yes and no."

I raised my brush again and then let it drop. He'd resumed his pose, but the jackass was holding unnaturally still, like a living statue or a wax sculpture at Madame Tussaud's.

"Ambri, I swear to God…"

"You're a harsh taskmaster, Cole Matheson." A grin toyed at his lips. "If only you had a whip, perhaps you could make me behave."

Instantly, my face flushed red, and I had to give myself a mental cold shower. Again. Over the past few weeks, they'd been a daily necessity.

Daily? Try hourly.

"Hold still but just be…normal."

"Normal is boring."

"You know what I mean. Breathe. *Blink*, for fuck's sake."

"Don't paint angry."

I smothered a laugh. "I'm going to give you a unibrow."

"You wouldn't dare." He let the cane pivot back and forth. "I must do something to entertain myself. How is it you can paint my other self all night, every night, by memory, yet I must stand for you for *hours*?"

"It's different."

"How?"

"I don't know," I said, keeping behind the canvas. "It just is."

"That answer is unsatisfactory."

I smiled. There were few things more adorable—or sexier—than Ambri when he was being a brat. Which was frequently. It was a battle to focus on the work and not stride over and silence his constant griping with a hard kiss.

No kissing allowed, remember?

That was the fastest mental cold shower of them all.

"Hellooo?" Ambri called. "Are you still back there or have you fallen asleep too?"

"You can't sleep, dummy," I teased. "To answer your question, the demon paintings are for Jane, and the show, and my career, I guess. But I don't actually have a career yet, so I have nothing to lose. This portrait is for you. It's important. I have to get it right."

Silence on the other side of the canvas. I peered around, expecting to see Ambri in that uncanny freeze again, but his gaze was down, his expression full. Human. Like he'd looked when I'd been sick.

If I have any kind of talent, that will make it into this painting.

I couldn't tell Ambri that I'd begun to think of the demon paintings—that I worked on in my room every night, sometimes until the early morning hours—were only reflections of my imagination. With every passing day, it grew easier to pretend he was just a man. We'd fallen into an easy companionship, talking late, joking around, and flirting. (If you considered his constant barrage of indecency "flirting.") As far as I could tell, he never left at night to do whatever he was supposed to do. It was almost as if he weren't a demon at all. The light in him was growing brighter by the day.

Be careful that kind of hope doesn't someday bite you in the ass.

"But if you're bored," I said, pulling out of my thoughts, "you can tell me more about your people."

"Demons are not people, Cole," he said in a low voice.

"Right."

Apparently, Ambri wanted me to be careful too.

"Can they all do what you do? Hold still like that?"

"We have a vast array of talents."

He made a motion with his hand, and the door behind me locked itself. I jumped, staring. He turned and flicked his fingers at a book lying on the coffee table and it slid to the floor.

"Holy shit…"

"T'is nothing," Ambri said. "Most demons can perform minor acts of telekinesis. Comes in handy, especially when humans toy with Ouija boards or hold seances."

"*Most* demons can do that? Well shit, how many are there?"

"Legions."

I nearly made a misstroke, *"Legions?"*

"Don't give yourself an apoplexy. There are plenty of angels too."

"You're telling me there are a bunch of angels and demons just walking around among us?"

"Not quite," Ambri said. "Angels only come to This Side if they have unfinished business. Demons come to play. But not every demon is powerful enough to remain on This Side, disguised as a human. Most are servitors, pouring their poison into human thoughts from the Other Side of the Veil."

"How many demons are here disguised as humans?"

"Aside from me?" he said pointedly. "Not many. Perhaps a few thousand."

"A few *thousand*?"

"You're beginning to sound like a strangled parrot, Cole Matheson."

"Do I know any?"

A pause. "No."

"That answer is unsatisfactory," I teased.

Ambri didn't elaborate, so I retreated to my work, turning over his words.

"Pouring poison into thoughts… When I was in the depths of my depression, that's exactly what it felt like. Poisonous thoughts that were trying to kill me."

"You had the Twins attached to you like leeches."

"The Twins. Christ, do I even want to know?"

"They are sister demons who drive humans to despair through feelings of worthlessness."

"They're good at their job. That night, at the bridge…" I shivered. "It seemed like every thought was driving me to the edge."

"They feed existing insecurities, fears, or trauma, until there's no room for anything else. But they can't physically hurt you. No demon can. Free will and all that. Demons can lead you to the abyss, but they can't push you in."

I nodded. "I haven't heard the Twins much lately. Or at all, come to think of it."

"Because I drove them away."

I peered around the easel. "You did?"

Ambri's gaze was on the floor. When he raised his eyes to me, his expression turned sour.

"Don't look so bloody grateful. I only did it so I could get what I wanted." He nodded at the portrait. "And you shouldn't count on me to do it again if they return. You'll need to fight back." His gaze bored into me. "If any demon tries to lure you to pain, Cole, fight back."

I could practically hear the rest of his thought.

Including me.

"That's the solution?"

"It's a start. Demons didn't invent human suffering or violence or evil. As I said, we only stoke that which already exists in you."

"Evil?" I said. "I don't know about that."

"Is that so?" Ambri said snidely. "If humans don't have their own sort of evil, then explain to me parents who scream like enraged banshees at their children's sporting events."

I chuckled. "You got me there. I guess I like to think of people as inherently good."

"Even murderers?"

I shrugged. "I don't know. I don't condone any crime, of course, but there's a lot of pain in the world. It's like someone inflicts trauma on their kid, and the kid grows up and inflicts trauma too, and on and on. Not every time but enough. But if you could go back to the beginning of that thread and break the cycle, there wouldn't be so much pain at all."

"You sound quite forgiving."

"I'm just trying to make sense of it all," I said. "There's no justification for murder, and I certainly don't feel sorry for rapists or child molesters. Those motherfuckers should have their own spot in hell. Hey, maybe you can confirm…"

I peered from around the easel. Ambri had gone white as a sheet. White as he did when he was his demonic self.

"Ambri, hey," I said, taking an automatic step toward him. "You okay?"

"I've had enough for one day." He tossed the cane aside and morphed out of his eighteenth-century clothing and into a sleek black suit. He changed his demeanor just as fast; the paleness fled, making me wonder if I'd imagined it.

"It's time to end off anyway," he said. "Dinner will arrive at any moment."

"What dinner?" I asked, wiping my hands on a cloth. I carefully pulled a sheet of paper over the portrait, hiding it from Ambri.

"It's Christmas Eve," he said. "Is it not tradition to feast on this day?"

"You don't eat."

"But you do," Ambri said. "And I *can* eat, it's just unnecessary. And bland. Food is beginning to lose its flavor for me." His glance met mine. "I'm becoming less human by the day."

"Maybe not. Maybe it's just been too long." I smiled lamely. "Don't give up."

The moment hung heavy, and then he moved to the cocktail table.

"Alcohol still tastes like something, anyway. Not that it does me any bloody good." He poured himself a shot of brandy and downed it. "Would you like?"

I shook my head. "I'm not much of a drinker."

A knock came at the door, and two cater waiters entered and got to work setting the table for dinner in the space between the kitchen and living room.

"Ambri, this is too much," I said, watching them lay out a feast enough for a dozen. "And we said no gifts, remember?"

"We didn't pinky swear," he said. "Besides, this isn't your gift. That is."

He gestured with his cocktail glass to the corner of the room where a flat, square gift was peeking from behind the cadenza, wrapped in black paper with a blood red bow.

"Ambri, goddammit. You've done too much already. And we *made a deal.*"

"Please. As if you haven't broken the oath yourself."

I started to protest then laughed instead. "How did you know?"

He grinned. "I didn't. You just told me."

"Asshole!" I chucked him on the arm. "Fine, you caught me. But it's not going to be as nice as whatever that is. Just a warning."

"I'm certain it will be a very Cole Matheson gift," he murmured into his glass. "Thoughtful and perfect."

The cater waiters finished setting up. Ambri paid them and then gestured for me to sit at the table that was laden with turkey and stuffing, warm bread, green beans almondine, roasted potatoes, and Christmas pudding.

"Shall we?"

"We're going to have a dinner you can't taste?"

"Consider it a last supper, of sorts."

I glanced up. "What the hell does that mean?"

Ambri shrugged and poured the wine. "I'm being facetious. And blasphemous. A little devil humor. Stop overthinking, Cole, and eat."

Reluctantly, I let it go—the scents and warmth of the food were making my heart heavy.

"What troubles you now?" Ambri demanded. "Is this not good?"

"It's perfect," I said. "I was just thinking of my grandmother and the Christmases we had when I was a kid. She'd cook a big feast too. But it's been a long time since I've done anything for the holiday. I was always alone at the Academy, using the time off to catch up on work."

Ambri's frown deepened. "You're smiling, yet your eyes are wet with tears. I don't understand."

I wiped my eyes from under my glasses. "That's grief, for you. If you give it time, it changes until it's not just sadness anymore. The sorrow and pain are still there, but there's gratitude too."

"Gratitude?"

I nodded. "It hurts. It hurts a lot, but you wouldn't be feeling that pain if that person never existed for you to love them in the first place. The love makes the hurt beautiful." I smiled at the memory of her. "I miss my grandmother but I'm grateful for the time I had with her."

"Demons do not traffic in grief," Ambri said softly, after a moment. "That's strictly the angels' domain. Now I understand why."

I take a shaky breath. "Sorry, I got a little carried away... Actually no, I'm not sorry. Remembering my grandmother, and missing her, and wishing she was here, isn't something I should ever be sorry for."

Ambri stared at me for long moments, likely with the same expression I'd given him when he was holding himself unnaturally still—like he couldn't believe what he was seeing.

"Okay, I'm done." I laughed and waved a hand. "We can eat."

We dug into the food that was anything but bland. Ambri didn't complain either, though the two of us couldn't put a dent in the sheer amount. We drank rich red wine and talked and laughed—mostly *I* laughed at Ambri's cleverness; his mind was sharpened to a keen edge. By the end of the meal, I felt as warm and full of being with him as I was of the dinner.

"We'll have leftovers for days," I said and started to clear the table. "Which reminds me, I need tomorrow off."

"What for?"

"It's a holiday for one thing, *taskmaster*. Every Christmas Day, I volunteer at the Passage House on Longmoore, serving meals to the unhoused."

Ambri rolled his head back to stare at the ceiling. "You have got to be bloody kidding me."

I chuckled. "It's not a big deal. Having no place to go these last few years, it's a good way to spend the time. The best way, actually. Do you want to—?"

"I'm leaving."

I froze in the act of stacking plates. He'd said it so simply, I nearly missed it. "You're what?"

"Leaving," Ambri said. "London, the UK…this entire bloody island."

I nearly went dizzy at how fast my heart dropped to the floor. "When? *Why?*"

"Soon. And I have my reasons," he said, looking into his wine glass. "I have other flats to attend to in other cities. Otherworldly duties I've neglected." He flinched at my expression. "Don't look at me like that. You knew perfectly well this commission wouldn't last forever."

"Yeah, I did," I said, struggling to find my voice. "But…the portrait isn't even finished yet."

"You'll have to paint me as you do the demon images. From memory."

"Ambri…"

"Fear not, you may stay here as long as you need. Until your gallery show at least, longer if necessary. I have no doubt you will be a smashing success and the entire world will open its doors to you, Cole."

"I don't get it," I said, wishing my desperation wasn't so damn obvious. "This portrait seemed like it meant a lot to you."

"Perhaps, at one time. Things change." He rose to his feet and headed to the cocktail table. "Leave the mess. I'll have someone clean up tomorrow. Come and open your gift."

I gaped, a turmoil of emotions cycling through me—anger, hurt, and fear at the thought of never seeing Ambri again. And that he could walk away from me so easily.

"Sure," I spat. "Let's open gifts and sing carols and roast fucking chestnuts and keep right on doing what we've been doing for weeks. *Pretending.*"

"Don't be bitter, Cole," Ambri said, not taking the bait. "Doesn't suit you."

I stared for a moment, but his back to me was a wall. Not knowing what else to do, I strode to my room. I yanked open the nightstand drawer and pulled out my gift for him, wrapped in green and red. I sucked in air to calm down, but the pain that gripped my heart was breathtaking. I'd stupidly created a future that didn't exist. It crumbled before my eyes in the same instant I realized how vast I'd built it.

I hadn't known, until Ambri was leaving, how badly I wanted him to stay.

You're an idiot. He is who he is. You can paint 'the light' you think you see a thousand times, but that won't make him human.

I glanced at the gift in my hand. I'd been at Foster Books, perusing old titles to add to Ambri's collection. None jumped out and I nearly left but decided to try one more aisle. And then I found it. A rare, second-edition print of *The Adventures of Pinocchio* by Carlo Collodi. As if some instinct had guided me toward it. At the time, I'd thought it a benevolent sign from the universe. Now...

"The universe is a fucking prick."

I mustered my dignity. It was my fault, after all. I'd kept myself protected for three years and then threw it all away over a handsome face, a quick wit, and...

He's leaving.

I braced myself against the door. "Fuck."

In the living room, Ambri sat on the couch, his gift for me resting against his leg. It was about the size of a picture book but flatter.

I handed him his gift. "Here."

"There's the Christmas spirit," Ambri said wryly. "Sit. Don't be a *bah humbug.*"

"That's not how it... Never mind."

I sat next to him on the couch and watched as he unwrapped his gift. He set the paper aside and ran his fingers along the book's cover. "A child's fairy tale."

"Fairy tales resonate for a reason. This one is about a wooden boy—"

"I know what it's about," he said quietly. He held it carefully for a few moments, as if it were fragile or precious. Then he set it aside without turning the pages. "Thank you, Cole."

It was my turn. The last thing I wanted was to take something else from him, but I carefully unwrapped his gift. When the paper had fallen away, a breath stuck in my chest.

"It's only a lithograph, but it's his. Numbered and signed." Ambri smirked. "Marc Chagall, at least, remembered to sign his work."

I stared. It may have been a litho—a copy of the original work—but it came from Chagall's studio. I knew that without having to look at the certificate affixed to the back. I was holding a small fortune in my hands, but that's not what made it valuable to me.

"The Painter and His Double," I murmured.

Like most of Chagall's work, the painting was fantastical, filled with mythical imagery, symbols, and metaphor. This one was of a painter sitting on a small stool behind his canvas. A yellow sun sat low in a pale blue sky, the Eiffel Tower rising on the right. The scene was Paris but may as well have been Hyde Park. A romantic couple floated above the painter's canvas, reminding me of the honeymooners who bought my first portrait. The painter's subject was a man with white wings, standing on a cello.

"Chagall is my favorite." I touched my fingertips to the winged man. "How did you know?"

"You told me. In no uncertain terms."

"When?"

"At the art store."

I searched my memory, vaguely recalling that I'd mentioned a certain indigo color I called 'Chagall blue.'

"You remember that?"

"He seemed to move you. I took a chance."

I shook my head. "Any particular reason you chose this print with this title?"

"A coincidence," Ambri said stiffly. "Don't read too much into it. There's also a flying fish and a bird playing the fiddle, so…"

I laughed a little though, my heart felt like it weighed a thousand pounds. "Thank you."

Without thinking, I reached over and hugged Ambri, an automatic gesture of gratitude. Instantly, I was enveloped in his scent, the heat of his body and the power that emanated from it. For weeks, I'd lived in torturous proximity, getting only hints, like scraps of food thrown to a starving man. Now I held him close, absorbing the feel of him everywhere we touched.

"Cole…" he said thickly against my neck.

For a moment, the air between us tightened and filled with possibility. Then he abruptly rose and went to the window.

The wine had made me fuzzy. Or maybe it was his gift. He was too fucking smart to have picked that print by accident. Hope was the true taskmaster, I thought. Relentless. I took off my glasses and set them aside and went to Ambri.

I rested my forehead on his back and laid my hands over the places where his wings would be but weren't tonight. I moved my palms up the silk of his suit jacket, then down the sides of his shoulders so I could peel it off him.

Unwrap him…

The jacket fell to the floor.

"What are you doing?" he said hoarsely.

"Trying to keep you."

Still behind him, I undid the top buttons on his dress shirt and pulled the collar away from his neck so I could put my mouth there. One hand slipped into his shirt, against his chest and over his heart that was pounding. The other slid down to the front of his pants. He was already thick and hard against my palm. All the while, I kissed his neck, grazed my teeth against his skin, tongued his earlobe.

One of Ambri's hands shot out to brace himself against the windowsill, his breathing ragged. The other reached up to sink into my hair, making a fist and sending electric shards down my spine. I maneuvered under his waistband, under the silk of his underwear. He groaned as I squeezed and stroked, my mouth never relenting against his neck, my other arm holding him tight to me.

I thought he might let me take him to release, but he made a strangled cry and spun around. He captured my wrists and slammed me back, pinning me to the wall. To myself. To the earth. Finally, I felt connected to something other than weightless loneliness.

His face was inches from mine, our bodies flush against the other. I widened my stance to bring him closer, our hips pressed tight. I heard his inhale; it drew me to him, to his mouth. He evaded my kiss and buried his face in my neck, an onslaught of teeth and tongue and heated breath.

"Cole," he hissed against my ear. "I have to have you."

With those words, our embrace became a battle. Grasping hands tore at clothes, and mouths bit instead of kissed because kissing wasn't allowed. He yanked my shirt over my head; the bare skin of my chest met his where his shirt hung open, but it wasn't enough. I needed both of us naked, in bed, skin to skin and touching in a thousand places. I wanted his kiss, even though I knew it would ruin me forever.

I was losing sense of time and place, reckless need replacing rational thought. I was seconds away from bending him over the couch and fucking him senseless. Or I'd let him do it to me. I was desperate for him.

He'll still leave and then where will you be?

With supreme force of will, I raised my hands to his chest and pushed him away.

"I'm sorry. I can't. I shouldn't have..."

"What's wrong?" he asked, bewildered and breathless, watching me stride past him.

In front of the fire, I spun to face him. "What's *wrong*? Where should I start?" Before he could speak, I cut him off. "No, I get it. You think if we fuck, you'll get me out of your system, and we can pretend that's all it was ever about."

"Obviously." He leveled a finger at me. "And allow me to remind you that *you* started this little heated interlude, not me."

"I know. I'm sorry. I...I stare at you for hours a day, every day. All I want is to rip off your clothes and...do things. Do everything."

He gaped at me. "Bloody hell, man, what are you *waiting* for?"

I didn't know whether to laugh or cry.

"Because it's not just lust, Ambri. I can't fuck somebody who won't kiss me."

He stared, momentarily at a loss. "That's all? That's...that's nothing! A little foible of mine. It doesn't mean anything—"

"It means a lot to me. And now you're leaving," I said, my voice cracking. "That's why, isn't it? You're leaving because you're fucking scared too."

"Scared? Me? Never."

"Jesus, Ambri, you *burned* yourself to try to keep yourself from feeling anything. And now—"

"Yes," he cried with rising frustration, "I burned and yet you still haunt my every thought and waking hour." He jabbed a finger at me. "You…are…maddening, Cole Matheson. You are unraveling me one thread at a time, and it is torture! Bloody dreadful fucking *torture*!"

I started to speak but he made a cutting gesture with his hand.

"*No*. Forget it. I don't need you. I can fuck any human I want. There are hordes of them out there, waiting for me to make them forget their miserable little lives for a few moments of carnal bliss, and not a single one will give two bloody shits if I kiss them or not!"

He strode to the window and threw up the sash. I crossed my arms tightly, waiting for him to dissolve into the night. Instead, he gripped the sill, his entire body trembling.

"Are you done?"

He hunched his shoulders and loosed an inhuman cry, then brought the sash back down hard enough to send a spiderweb of cracks through the glass.

"*Bloody fucking hell.*" He whirled around and strode to me. "What is this hold you have over me? Who *are* you?"

I smiled tremulously, the calm to his storm, and took a step toward him. "I'm no one—"

"Lies, all lies," he muttered, the fight slowly draining out of him. "*You* are the angel of death. Mine. You'll be the death of me. Mark my words."

I waited a moment while he straightened his jacket and smoothed his hair.

"Ambri," I said quietly. "Don't you think I feel the same? It's not just me or you. It's us."

"There can't be an *us*, Cole," he said miserably. "Because there is no me."

"That's not true," I said, moving closer. "I fucking hate that some evil bastard told you that, because it's a lie. It's just like she said."

"Who? That voice…?"

"Jane. You have a light—"

"*No…*"

"You do. I see it."

I took another step and reached for him. He stiffened but didn't resist. I pulled him close until our foreheads were pressed together, his heart pounding against mine.

"Cole..." Ambri shook his head. "You have no idea what's at stake. I've made a terrible...miscalculation. I have to undo it before it's too late."

"Too late for who?"

He didn't answer; his eyes roamed my face. His hand cupped my cheek. "I knew. When you were ill, that's when I knew. Or maybe I've always known."

His hand slid down, touching his fingertips to my lips. The yearning in his eyes was so palpable, I thought—*prayed*—that he'd crush his mouth to mine. That we'd spend the rest of the night tangled in his sheets in a heated frenzy of need, the feelings between us finally breaking free in every touch, every kiss, and every deep, perfect thrust...

But he didn't.

Ambri let me go and turned to the window, and I was terrified that the night was going to swallow him for good if I let it.

"Wait," I said. "At least come to the show with me. It's yours anyway. Please. I'll make sure the portrait is finished by then."

He shook his head. "A folly. A dangerous gambit."

"Ambri. Please."

I held my breath, and finally, he nodded.

"I can't attend the show, that would be unwise. But I'll stay until then, and that must be the last we see of each other."

"If that's what you want," I managed.

He turned to the window. "It's what must be."

I sank into the chair nearest the fire, suddenly exhausted down to my bones. Ambri had only been in my life a short while, and yet the thought of doing the rest of it without him was like a lead ball in my heart.

I rubbed my eyes so I wouldn't have to watch him go, but when I looked up, he was standing before me. To my utter shock, he dropped to his knees. His arms went around my waist, and he rested his head in my lap.

"I can't sleep but I'm so tired," he said.

"I know." I gently raked my fingers through his silken blond hair, over and over.

"I want to kiss you, but I can't."

"I know that too. I'd never ask you for something you can't give."

"Of course, you wouldn't," he said, his cheek on my thigh. "That's what makes it all the more unbearable."

"It doesn't have to be."

"You think this will end like the child's storybook? I know your heart, Cole. You believe art shows us what love can do." He shook his head; a hot tear seeped through my pants. "There is no blue fairy. No happy ending. Not for me."

My eyes fell shut, and I wondered if he were right. If life was all just bullshit and suffering or if there was hope, even for those who turned their backs on it in their darkest hour.

No answers came.

I ran my hands over his back, his shoulders, his hair, and we stayed that way for a long time.

twenty

Cole
April

"Thanks for meeting me," Vaughn Ritter said, leaning back in his chair and taking a long drag on his cigarette. His second since we sat down at the cafe patio a few minutes ago. "I'm sure you're pretty busy gearing up for your show."

"Not really," I said. "I finished the paintings weeks ago. Jane's doing all the work."

"I'll bet she is," he said and took another drag.

I shifted in my chair. "Well...you look good. And I heard about your Paris show. Congratulations!"

"Right. The Paris show."

I frowned at his morose tone. "You sold out. And the reviews I read were all raves."

"Yeah, yeah, it was bloody fantastic. The press was very involved and asking me all sorts of questions, such as, 'Where is your agent?' and 'Hey, wasn't your agent here a moment ago?'"

"I'm sure Jane knew you were killing it and didn't need her."

"Yeah, and *I'm sure* Jane sniffed the Next Big Thing—you—and jumped across the Channel to snatch it." He stubbed out his cigarette. "Bloody hell, listen to me. Whining like a wanker when I'm actually pleased to bits about your show."

"Thanks, I—"

"But you know how it is," he said, pulling another smoke from his pack and talking around it as he lit it. "You get a taste of success and then you're bloody petrified it's going to flit away." His lip curled. "Or jump on a private jet to London. You know what I mean?"

I smiled. "Not really."

"Well, you're about to find out," Vaughn said. "Jane has been plastering the art world with promotional teasers. Little tidbits only, but what I saw was miraculous." He leaned back in his chair, dragging hard on his smoke. "I never knew. I mean, I knew you were talented but bloody hell, man. How did you come up with that monster?"

"He's not a monster," I said a little too sharply. "He's…someone I know."

Vaughn's eyes widened. "He exists, this muse of yours. Who is he? Boyfriend?"

"No, he's…"

I had no idea how to finish that sentence. Over the past few months, things had been mostly business as usual with Ambri. I painted his portrait during the day, the demonic paintings at night, and filled the in-between hours with my side project: drawings of him at his most human. As he had looked at the windowsill when I'd been sick. I'd filled a sketchbook with them, and to me, it was the most beautiful work I'd ever done. I had an inkling that they'd someday be something more, but I couldn't see what. Not yet.

In the meantime, Ambri and I talked and had a few laughs, but his impending departure felt like it was screaming toward me like a freight train, and I couldn't get off the track.

"He's a friend," I finished lamely, but Vaughn didn't appear to be listening anyway.

"You're on the precipice, Cole. Your show's going to be a smash. But let me tell you, the higher you go, the thinner the air. You catch my meaning? I've only just had a taste of success, and I'm already quite certain it's slipping away."

"But…why?"

"Because of you."

I sat back in my chair. "Me? You're a realist. I do portraits. And it doesn't matter anyway. For God's sake, Vaughn, *ArtForum* said you could be the next Andrew Wyeth."

"I know, that's why it's so bloody maddening!" He ran a hand through his hair. "I feel like I'm being tricked by my own brain. Plagued by thoughts that tell me I'm an imposter and there's no room for me now that there's you."

"I haven't even had a show yet." I offered a smile. "To paraphrase Mark Twain, reports of my success are greatly exaggerated."

Vaughn didn't crack a smile. "Oi, fuck me, I've gone mental. Don't listen to a word I'm saying."

"Hey," I said, reaching across the table and capturing his wrist with my hand. "Those thoughts you're having? They're bullshit. They're…demons whispering in your ear. Don't feed them by listening. I know it's hard, but I've been there; it can get really fucking scary."

He nodded absently. "I know, you're right. You're right. But the bitch of it all is that I thought success was the end of wanting more, but I fear it's actually the beginning." He stubbed out his smoke and tossed a few quid on the table. "I have to run. I'll see you Saturday, Cole."

"Thanks, Vaughn. It means a lot that you'd come."

"Wouldn't miss it." He clapped his hand on my shoulder. "Oh, and tell Jane that Vaughn says hi. Vaughn *Ritter*, in case she's forgotten."

———

I was on the Tube on the way back to the flat. Lucy and Cas were due to arrive that morning on a redeye from New York. I'd finally meet this mysterious guy of hers and hopefully convince Ambri to meet them. And because my heart had stupidly chained itself to his, my imagination concocted every kind of scenario where the four of us went out on double dates, or traveled together, or had dinner parties where Lucy and I—who'd both suffered our own brands of crushing loneliness—would look across the table and know for sure the other was safe and happy at last.

But Ambri was leaving. That was the period at the end of every sentence.

Christ, I'm so fucked.

On the metro, I toyed aimlessly with my phone and realized I had missed calls and texts from Lucy from the night before.

Boarding plane now but just received an email sneakpeek thingy from the gallery for your show. WE HAVE TO TALK

"Not you too, Luce," I muttered.

When I unveiled the collection to Jane and her people, I thought they were all going to need fainting couches and smelling salts. The barrage of compliments felt like too much, if not for the fact that more than one had tears in their eyes. They all teased me for being humble and modest, but the truth was, I didn't believe it was my talent that was extraordinary.

It's Ambri. You know...the one who's leaving?

"Fucking hell."

The Tube car swayed and rocked. I was about to put my phone away when it lit up with Lucy's number. I answered, putting a finger in the other ear to quiet the rumbling train.

"Hey, Luce—"

"Cole? Cole! Are you okay?"

"Of course, I'm okay. Are *you* okay?"

"I mean, are you safe? You're not in danger? Or in a bad place or...being held captive?"

In the background came a masculine voice tinged with a strange accent. "Held captive?"

"I don't know," Lucy hissed at him. "I'm freaking out."

"I'm not being held captive; I'm on the A-line. Almost the same thing. What's going on?"

"Okay, listen. Your paintings seem very...um...realistic. *Frighteningly* lifelike. Did you, by any chance, have a model? A real person sitting for you?"

"Well...yes."

"Oh, God, Cole. I don't know how to tell you this. I *can't* tell you over the phone."

"Tell me what?"

"I need to know first and foremost that you're okay. Are you?"

"Yes, but I'm starting to get really worried about *you*."

"Listen, we're about to deplane. We need to meet somewhere. Somewhere public. Just you and me and Cas. *No one else.*"

"Why Cas? No offense, but I haven't even met him yet."

"It concerns him too."

"Okay, now I'm really confused."

"Tell me a place we can meet."

"Uh, La Marais? It's a café near our flat. *His* flat. Not mine," I babbled. "I'm just staying there temporarily."
Until the show, because he's leaving.
"You're *living* with him?" Lucy screeched. "Sorry, sorry. La Marais. Got it. We'll go straight there. See you in a few, okay?"
"Sure, I—"
The phone went quiet. I stared at it for a moment, then put it away. Everyone seemed weird or was losing their minds over the show, and all I could think about was that I had four days left with Ambri. The entire city could burn to the ground, and I doubted I'd notice.

I went back to the flat to grab some cash I'd stashed so I could get Lucy some flowers and Cas a bottle of wine, though the jury was still out on him as far as I was concerned. He'd come out of nowhere and swept my best friend out of her lonely life. I needed to shake his hand and tell him thank you. Or kick his ass if he wasn't good to her.

I found Ambri sitting by the fire, dangling a glass of cognac by the rim. Spring was coming, but the mornings were still mostly gray and cold. The flat felt warm and cozy. I'd begun to feel like it was home. Our home.

I'm so very, very fucked.
"Little early for cocktails, isn't it?"
Ambri's gaze slid to me. "If they had any effect on me, I'd be quite drunk by now."

Understanding passed between us. He was hurting too, but he wouldn't hear of any other option than to vanish the moment my show was over.

"How was coffee with your friend?"
"Weird," I said, sitting on the armrest of the couch. "I think he has the Twins on him. He's super successful and already worried that it's all going to disappear."

"Isn't this the bloke who promised to help you and then haunted you?"

"*Ghosted* me," I said with a smile. "And yes, but it was never up to him to make my career. I was just desperate."

"How the tables have turned," Ambri muttered. "Serves him right."

"And Lucy is freaking out, and I have no idea why. I guess Jane sent her the press packet. Lucy saw the paintings and wants to meet with me immediately."

"She must have a *very* good reason," Ambri muttered into his drink.

I frowned. That was another sore subject. Ambri had been all over the place as Cas and Lucy's visit drew closer. Sometimes he was angry, sometimes blasé, and sometimes he seemed almost nervous. He refused to meet them, refused to attend the gallery show with us, and he insisted I not mention his name. It'd been months, and he was still just "my patron."

It wasn't enough. I tried again.

"If everyone's freaking out about the paintings, they'll lose their minds to see you. My muse." I mustered a smile. "You sure you won't come? My stock would skyrocket with you as my arm candy."

Ambri ignored the appeal to his vanity. A bad sign.

"For the millionth time, *no*," he said. "There will be press from all over, and you're sure to make a huge splash. It wouldn't do for me to be so exposed."

"Exposed to who?"

Ambri swirled the liquor in his glass. "I've overstayed my time on This Side. It would be unwise to remind my liege lord of that fact with fanfare and paparazzi."

A cold hand of dread squeezed my heart. "You don't talk about him much. I don't even know what to ask." I swallowed hard. "Will you be okay…wherever you're going?"

"Oh, I'll be bloody *brilliant*," Ambri said with sudden bitterness and sarcasm. "Not as well as others I could name, of course. Not as well as those who were granted their freedom and now nap on sofas, cuddling with their heart's desire while the rest of us are forced to watch the weeks dwindle into days, until there are none left."

My heart clenched. "Ambri, I don't know what to say except don't go. I'm a fucking broken record, I know but—"

"But it can't be helped so let's not be morose." He fixed me with a tight smile, his eyes lit with anger. "You must be excited to see your friend and…what was his name again?"

"Cas."

"Cas, of course. Silly me. And where is this private rendezvous?"

"I told them La Marais, right around the corner. Lucy wants to meet somewhere public. Honestly, I don't know what's going on with her."

Ambri's smile showed all his teeth. "I can't imagine."

"Are you okay?" I said as he stood and tossed the rest of his drink into the fire where it flared and hissed. "Now *you're* acting strange."

"I'm not okay, I'm not strange, I'm not anything, Cole Matheson. Except damned." He strode down the hall toward his room. "Of that, we can be certain."

The flower shop was more crowded than I expected, and I had to wait for the best wine shop to open. Even so, I figured I'd beat Cas and Lucy to the café since they were coming all the way from Heathrow. But Lucy was already there with two rolling bags of luggage behind her chair. She sat at a table with a handsome man with olive skin, piercing dark eyes, and a mop of loose, dark curls. My best friend looked radiant—healthier and happier than I could remember ever seeing her—but both of them sat facing the door looking strangely guilty.

"Cole!" Lucy tore out of her chair, brown hair flying, to hug me over the flowers and wine. She gripped my face in her hands. "Oh my God, it's so good to see you. You look…so good. Healthier than I've seen you in ages."

"Read my mind much?" I asked. I hadn't known how much I missed my friend until I had her back.

She frowned. "But your eyes are sad. Oh God, we need to talk. It's been way too long. Come, sit." She led me to the table. "Cole, this is Cas Abisare."

Cas stood up—he was a good two inches taller than my six feet— and offered a hand. His sharp gaze seemed to be searching me all over.

Right back at you, pal, I thought, shaking his hand.

"It is an honor to meet you," he said in a faint accent. Middle Eastern, I guessed. "Lucy has told me so much about you and she's shown me your portraits of her. I didn't think it was possible for her to be more beautiful, but you captured her spirit completely."

We all sat down, Lucy and Cas on one side, me on the other. Cas's cadence was strange and kind of old-fashioned, and I suspected he was bullshitting me with compliments to win me over. But the way he held Lucy's chair for her when she sat down and how he looked at her when she laced her fingers with his on the table made it clear he was besotted with her. I swelled with relief and happiness for her while at the same time, my heart ached with a jealous hunger.

"Thanks, Cas. I wish I could say the same about you," I said with a smile. "Maybe now I can finally hear the story of how you two met."

Cas and Lucy exchanged nervous glances.

"That's sort of why we wanted to see you right away," Lucy said. "Jeez, I seriously don't know where to begin." She looked to Cas. "Any ideas?"

Cas started to speak when his eyes widened at something over my shoulder. Lucy joined him and before I could turn, I was enveloped around the shoulders by Ambri's Armani-and-cologne embrace.

"I always feel honesty is the best policy, don't you?" He smacked a kiss on my cheek and took the chair beside me. "Sorry I'm late but then, I wasn't invited in the first place."

"Ambri..." Cas said with a growl.

I jerked in my chair. "You know each other?"

"Indeed." Ambri smiled lazily and inclined his head in a small bow. "Lucy. We meet again."

I gaped. *"Again?"*

Lucy was hunched in her coat, not denying anything, but she regarded Ambri with wariness. Cas and Ambri were locked in a staring contest. I threw up my hands.

"Anyone want to explain to me just what the fuck is going on?"

"I should have told you eons ago, but you'd have thought I was crazy," Lucy said, tucking her arm deeper in mine as we walked back to Ambri's flat. She carried her flowers while I dragged her rolling suitcase behind me; Cas had the other as he and Ambri followed, talking in low voices. We'd all agreed it was best to take our conversation outside since Ambri was prone to fits of drama.

Not that I'd want him any other way.

"I just don't get it," I said. "How do you both know Ambri?"

Lucy heaved a breath and blew it out. "Cas used to be...like he is."

I nearly stopped walking, craning my head to look at Cas, but she kept me moving. "Are you kidding me?"

"It sounds nuts just to say out loud, but it's true. We'd been married, once upon a time, in ancient Sumer. I died violently, and his grief turned him toward darkness. He's been watching over me for all my lifetimes and..." She shook her head. "It's a long story, but Cas was released of that existence so we could be together. We've been reunited."

Released from that existence...

"And how does Ambri fit into this?"

"It was a battle to free Cas. Ambri helped me, but I'm sure he did it for Cas's sake. I remember getting a feeling that he cared about him. Loved him, even."

I stared straight ahead, my head—and heart—filling with possibilities.

"Are you mad?" Lucy asked. "I'm sorry I didn't tell you. I just had no idea how. But I would've tried a heck of a lot harder had I known Ambri's been with you all this time."

"I'm not mad," I said with a small laugh. "Just the opposite. But as much as I wish that were true, he's not really *with* me."

Lucy studied my face a moment. "You love him."

"I don't know," I said, my throat thick. "I'm trying not to."

"Because you thought it was hopeless. Does he feel the same about you? Tell me everything."

I gave her an extremely abridged version of our story, leaving out the actual bridge and that cold, desperate night. Lucy listened, nodding and then smiling.

"You put everything he is in your paintings," she said. "I can see it. And after all that's happened with Cas—and now Ambri—I'm beginning to think that any demon who was once human can be saved. We have such capacity for love. It can't be snuffed out in one dark moment of despair or hopelessness." She smiled. "I can practically feel my dad telling me I'm right."

"Jesus, Luce, I hope you are too."

Her smile faded and her hand on my arm tightened.

"But Cole, you have to be careful. Ambri might want to escape, but he probably answers to a more powerful demon that won't let him go. The kind of demon that is *not* salvageable. One that might never have been human at all."

The way she spoke told me there was a hell of a lot more to her and Cas's story. I wanted to hear all of it, but one thought was clamoring in my head, over and over, louder than Big Ben at noon.

He has a chance.

twenty-one

Ambri

Casziel, formerly the Nightbringer, erstwhile commander of legions of warmongering servitors, walks in step with me, dragging a suitcase behind him like a common bumpkin. Like any old ordinary human male.

Jealousy chews at my guts.

"Ambri." His voice is low and full of warning. "What are you playing at with Cole?"

I sniff. "Jealous, are we? Too late. You had more than two hundred years to make a move on me, friend. You blew it. Or didn't, actually."

"Be serious. What is your plan? To hurt him? Or—?"

"Destroy him."

Casziel's eyes widen in horror.

"Calm yourself. It won't happen. I can't do it."

"But that was the plan?"

I lower my voice. "I was commanded to drive a human to ultimate despair."

"And you chose *Cole*," he hisses in disbelief. "Why?"

"I overheard his conversations with Lucy. He sounded halfway there already. I thought it'd be easy." I pierce him with a dark look. "And I wanted to hurt you."

"Not me. It would destroy Lucy."

"And therefore you."

"True enough," he says and shoots me a hard glance. "And how did I offend?"

"You left me."

Casziel gives a start, then shakes his head, confused. "I can't remember that life. It's a haze now. Like a nightmare that's fading."

My lip curls. "Convenient."

"I didn't forget how you helped Lucy that day. She told me what she felt from you. How you cared about me."

"A lot of good it did me. You wanted Oblivion."

"I thought I had no choice," he says quietly.

My heart softens toward him, but I ignore it. The bloody organ has done nothing but cause me grievous injury for centuries. I look to Cole walking ahead, and the ache becomes a roar. I want to roar with it.

"Pardon me if I don't cry my eyes out for you, Casziel," I snarl. "Did you think for one moment where your choice would leave me? No, of course not. Not one spare thought for your loyal servant. Your *friend*. Another abandonment. I thought I'd escaped that particular misery in life but to have it happen in death was a particularly cruel twist of the knife."

"Ambri—"

"I'm not interested in your excuses. You have your happy ending. Coming here to rub it in is overkill but not unexpected."

"I didn't..." He carves his hand through his hair. "You're as maddening as ever. I don't remember the Other Side well, but I distinctly recall you being a colossal pain in the ass."

"Flattery will get you nowhere."

Cas looks like he's trying not to smile as he glances at me fondly. "I've missed you."

I struggle to hold onto my anger too, the bastard. "Get in line."

"Behind him?" He nods at Cole.

I wince and cold despair floods me, instantly washing out any warm feeling.

"You've got us all figured out already, I see. Impressive."

"I know what I see between you," Cas says, unperturbed. "How he looks at you and you him. As if you can't stop and don't want to."

Damn him.

"You know nothing," I say and cut him off when he starts to protest. "*Enough*, Casziel. You were once my superior but no more. Now, hush. You're spoiling the stroll."

He grits his teeth but says nothing more. By the time we reach the flat, Lucy is giving me a warm smile and Cole regards me with fresh hope, likely because she's filled his head with fairy tale notions of redemption and love conquering all.

I can't look at him. His handsome face that dominates my every thought is even more beautiful now. And those lovely dark eyes look at me with something I've never seen before. Not even from Armand, who I now know was false and shallow—two words that could never be used to describe Cole.

He is honest and good, and I'm going to lose him before he was ever mine.

In the flat, I direct everyone to sit in the living room. "Make yourselves at home. I'll just open this"—I examine the bottle of wine I've been carrying—"and pour it down the sink. I have better on the shelf there."

I move to the kitchen and hear footsteps behind me. "I'm teasing, Cole. You tried—"

But it's Casziel, looking severe.

"We need to finish our conversation."

"*Need* is a strong word."

He crosses his arms over his broad chest, and I roll my eyes. "Yes, my liege. This way."

Cole has taken Lucy on a tour of the flat—I hear her squealing over my portrait in his room. It's finished, or nearly, and I haven't the slightest inkling to look at it. Like Cole's show, it's become a beacon of my impending departure.

I lead Casziel to the library, and he shuts the door behind us. I lean casually against the bookshelf. *The Adventures of Pinocchio* rests on top, not stowed with the rest. I casually trace my finger over its cover as if it were inconsequential instead of what I've been reading every night, all night, for months.

"Well?"

"I'm sorry I left you," Casziel says. "I'm sorry I didn't consider your feelings, but how was I to know you had any? You know how it is with our kind. You can trust no one."

"*Our* kind. How droll. You are no longer *my* kind. You've been freed."

Casziel takes a step to me. "I was freed because of Lucy. Because I love her. There is love in you, too. It didn't begin with Cole, but he brought it out of the shadows, and it is so very bright. Ambri, don't you see? There's hope for you too."

I want so badly to believe him, but that way lies pain. Another betrayal. Abandonment. I should storm out and yet I remain rooted to the floor, that precious book under my hand.

"You had the help of an angel," I say. "I have none."

"How do you know?"

"Because I've been wrestling with this bloody fucking assignment from the moment it was commanded of me, and there's been no help. Nothing that lets me feel that I'm being watched over, even a little. Oh, except that I'm to die. Does that sound like hope to you?" My voice cracks and I angrily blink back the tears that threaten. "There is nothing that tells me I'm not doing this alone."

"Maybe you're not listening hard enough," Cas says gently.

Outrage burns through me at his calm certainty. "I sold my soul to Ashtaroth—remember him? I burned my own flesh to remind myself of how I've been ruined time and again by humans and even that isn't enough."

"If you love Cole, nothing will be enough," Casziel says. "If you love him, you will die a thousand deaths, burn to ash a thousand times for him. To protect him. To save him." He moves closer and grips me by both shoulders. "If you love him, Ambri, you need no angel to tell you what's in your heart. That love will save you. I swear it."

"We're throwing the L word around a little generously, aren't we?" I say weakly.

He pins me with a hard look. "You tell me."

And in that moment, for the first time in centuries, I'm at a complete loss for words. What I feel for Cole defies definition. It's certainly nothing I've ever felt before—a terrifying and exhilarating blend of emotions that made what I'd felt for Armand pale by comparison. A tiny flicker to a blazing inferno.

I look to Casziel, wanting so badly to believe him and terrified down to my bones at the same time. "Let's presume what you're saying is true. How does it save me?"

"I don't think we're meant to know exactly how," he says. "Only that it will."

My shoulders slump and I pull out of his touch.

"That's very helpful, thank you," I mutter. "I'll be sure to remember that while I'm being torn limb from limb in an archduke's dungeon for all eternity."

He grimaces and I wave a hand.

"Fear not. I'm letting Cole go. The night of the show. Tell Lucy. Assure her that I won't let anything happen to him."

"What are you going to do?"

"I'll tell my liege lord that I failed. Or that Cole's not our ideal victim." I smile wanly. "I might have one good lie left in me. One that might save my arse."

But even as I speak it, I know nothing will pacify Asmodai. I'll pay for my weakness. It's the only thing I can be certain of.

Casziel is watching me. "What about Cole?"

"The Twins might come back when I'm gone. I'll warn him against them and—"

"No, Ambri," he says gravely. "What is going to become of Cole if you vanish out of his life?"

I frown, confused. "He'll have all the fame and success he's ever dreamt of."

"And a broken heart."

"Over me? Hardly. His work will sustain him. Success is a potent magnet. Adoring fans and admirers will flock to him. Other artists will clamor to be near him. He'll find someone else on whom to shower his bottomless care and compassion."

"You make it sound easier than I suspect it will be, when he loves you as he does."

I freeze, staring in agonized ecstasy to hear the words out loud. Cole can't love me. None have. Not even Armand. He said the words and then took them back when his heart found something it wanted more.

"He doesn't. He can't. You…know *nothing*," I manage. "Leave us alone. You've got your perfect life. Your perfect happiness. Leave us creatures of the dark to our misery. You are no longer one of our number."

"Neither are you."

"Is that so?"

Instantly, I morph into my demonic form, my wings outstretched to their full width, my black eyes boring into his. Casziel falls back against the desk, his eyes wide.

"How quickly you forget," I say, leering over him. "This is what you were. This is what I am. Still. Always."

Casziel recovers and swallows hard. "I don't believe that's true. I was you, yes. And I was freed."

"By your angel."

"By love."

He takes a step toward me. Before I can say another word, I'm engulfed in his strong embrace. He holds me close, even in this body, with my death burning hot in my black eyes. I stiffen and start to pull away but find myself holding on instead. Clinging to him and morphing slowly back to my human self, my demon form melting away.

"I'm not strong like you," I whisper. "I'm not strong enough to endure what's to come."

"I don't think that's true. And you're not doing this alone, Ambri. I can't believe that."

I hold him tight for another moment, my eyes squeezed shut, and then I pull away.

"What you believe and what awaits me are vastly different things," I say, straightening my suit jacket.

"You forget, I've been through hell and back," Cas says with a small smile. "Our angel—mine and Lucy's—told me to love her and let her love me. I think that's the way out, Ambri. Love Cole. Let him love you."

If that's all it took, I would have been saved months ago.

"I fear it's too late."

"Don't give up," Casziel says. "That's the only way it becomes too late."

Casziel and Lucy stay for hours, catching up and speaking of banal things such as Lucy's work with a nonprofit and Casziel's position at NYU as an adjunct professor of Ancient Civilizations.

But the damage has been done.

Sitting in my flat is living proof that there's hope for the damned. Casziel sleeps at night, has a commute, a retirement plan, and he's going to grow old with the love of his life. It's as if his time in our dark world never was.

The air feels charged now, even more so than usual. My desire to have Cole, to kiss him, to fuck him, to make him mine in every way, is a hunger I haven't felt in centuries. Worse are the softer thoughts of lying abed with Cole on cold London mornings, basking in the warmth of him—his body, his gaze, his care for me...

Cole's heated glances my way tell me his thoughts are running along the same track and with more than just "care," though I won't let myself believe it's anything stronger.

But no solution to my little dilemma arrived with Casziel and Lucy. They might have found a way out, but that doesn't mean mine is assured. I hold my hope in check, even as my will breaks down with every passing hour.

The day of the show arrives. Flowers and gifts of congratulations have been pouring in from Cole's agent and from those whom Cole explained were Big Names in the art world. He should have been over the moon, but his happiness is held in check too. It's almost as if my departure occupies him more than his imminent success.

Perhaps Casziel is right, and Cole does have the same depth of feeling for me as I do for him.

That seems impossible. Ludicrous, even.

That afternoon, while Cole changes into his suit in the next room, I stare at my reflection in my bathroom mirror. Beautiful, cold, sharp. The face of a con artist. As a human, I dodged responsibility because I thought I'd paid enough. I indulged in unbridled hedonism to escape the memories of my uncle's indiscretions. Marie Antoinette may not have lost her head until years after our folly with the necklace, but I helped pave her way to the guillotine.

And when Armand rejected me, I gave up.

I wonder if the benevolent forces are waiting for me to take a stand. To be brave. To declare to This world and the Other that I belong to Cole Matheson, heart and soul.

But I can't.

Armand wasn't half the man Cole is and his betrayal ruined me. What would become of me if Cole did the same? The thought stabs me down to my soul.

"I'll accompany him to his show and then I'll go. We can have that much."

"Ambri?" Cole calls as the sun begins to sink in the sky. "It's time. I have to go."

His voice frays at the edges, but when I join him in the living room, his mouth falls ajar, and he takes a step back. I'm dressed in a sleek black suit, one more elegant than my usual—an *art show opening* type of suit.

My own heart stutters to see him in a simple suit of blue with a slate gray tie. He's still himself—his hair is moppish as ever, his glasses boxy and unstylish. But his broad shoulders in that suit jacket are lusciously masculine and hint at the strength his body possesses. Strength I want to bash myself against like a doomed ship on the rocks of an unknown shore.

"Aren't we a dapper pair," I say lamely because Cole's gaze is undoing me. "Both of us dressed to the tens."

"Nines," he corrects absently, still staring. "Are you coming with me?"

I nod. "It is, after all, an entire gallery of *me*."

He laughs, joy radiating off of him, and takes a step toward me. "Ambri…"

I hold up a hand. "Nothing else has changed. It can't. There is just tonight, and even that might be a terrible mistake."

His smile vanishes. "Are you in danger? Because if you are—"

"There is danger for me no matter if I stay or go," I say and offer him a smile. A real one, naked of sarcasm and sharp edges. "I'll take my chances. Especially if it makes you happy."

Cole's expression is bloody heartbreaking in its beauty, and I know in that instant I would suffer a thousand tortures to preserve his happiness.
And that, Liebling, is true love.

From the street, Gallery Decora is full of golden light and packed with people sipping champagne served from trays of circulating waiters. The car drops Cole and me at the curb and he offers his arm.

"Are you ready?" he asks.

"Me? It's your glory that is imminent. I'm the…what did you call it? Arm confection."

He laughs. "It's seems surreal. I'm going to take it one bit at a time. But you…they're going to lose their shit over you."

I sigh. "Your modesty would be tedious if it weren't so genuine."

We step into the gallery and immediately, the crowd bursts into applause. An elegant woman in a red dress makes a line straight to us and takes Cole's other arm.

"Cole, darling."

"Hello, Jane."

She gives him a kiss on each cheek and nearly loses her composure to see me. Nearly.

"The muse, in the flesh. My, my."

"Jane Oxley, this is Ambri Meade-Finch."

"A pleasure to meet you," she says, offering her fingertips for me to shake. "I suppose thanks are in order. I don't know how you inspired our Cole to create such masterpieces, but I'm grateful you did."

I'll bet, I think and smile pleasantly.

She pulls two glasses of champagne from a passing waiter and hands them to us.

"We're at capacity. Every invited guest replied with a resounding *yes*. They all want to be a part of what is about to happen, Cole. To say they were here, at the genesis of your career."

Cole runs a hand through his hair. "Um, wow. I don't know what to say, Jane."

"You don't have to say a thing. Just take it in." Jane turns her eyes on me. "I beg your pardon, Ambri, but I have to steal Cole from you. There are people he needs to meet."

"By all means."

Cole shoots me a helpless smile and is whisked away into the heart of his triumph. I meander through the crowded gallery, perusing his work. In the months he'd been working on this collection, I'd kept out of his way and hadn't seen the paintings.

Now, the champagne gets stuck in my throat, the infernal bubbles stinging my eyes. They're all larger than I imagined, all incredibly realistic, the colors dark and rich with light giving the subject—me—shape and definition.

And life.

I wander, listening in on the murmured conversations of the attendees regarding Cole's work.

"I don't think it's overstating it to say his use of chiaroscuro is on par with the Dutch and Flemish masters," says one man.

"I was about to say the same," says his companion. "Note the glint on the candlestick. I could reach out and pick it up. Jan van Eyck, through and through."

Pride wells in me. When I first encountered Cole's artistry, I viewed it only as a means to an end. To attain what I wanted. But it's obvious he's a master, no matter the subject. His extraordinary talent is what packed this gallery, and I ease a sigh of relief that his renown will carry on long after I'm gone.

I move around a corner where two attendees discuss a piece.

"What is he? The angel of death?" asks a young man.

"I've never seen anything like this before," says his companion—a woman with an accent I can't place. "Marvelous, isn't it?"

"He's so fucking *real*," says the man. "Like he's going to move at any minute and bite my face off. Not that I'd mind. *Hello*, sexy."

"Darling, you're missing the point," says the woman. "There is death and danger here, but the promise of hope burns brightest. There is always hope, don't you think? There must be or else art is a lie."

Her words draw me to see the speaker, but I catch only a glimpse of a sapphire dress and the lingering scent of perfume as they move away. I turn to the painting they were discussing and my breath catches.

Cole has rendered me on a bridge—vague but with enough detail to know it's Blackfriars. A lone streetlamp casts a yellow cone of light over me, bringing detail to my feathered wings. Black eyes and black water. An expression on my face I don't recognize. There is danger, indeed, but something else too. As if Cole's painted me as a human and then overlaid the image with my damned self. As if it were a costume I could shed at any time.

"Hey," says a young man suddenly beside me. He gestures at the painting with his champagne glass. "That's you."

"Yes," I murmur. "That's me."

The night flies by. Casziel and Lucy arrive. They stand with me as Cole is surrounded, constantly occupied, speaking with the press and other artists, a bewildered smile on his face. Jane Oxley has her hooks in him as if he were her property.

I feel a soft pressure on my shoulder. Lucy's pressed her cheek to me, her eyes shining.

"Look at him. He deserves all of it. It's everything he's wanted." Then she glances up at me. "Well, almost."

Despite the champagne having no effect on me, I feel drunk anyway. Warm and reckless, my head dancing with possibilities. I look to Casziel and he reads my thoughts. He nods, as if giving me permission to reach for everything I want.

There is only one thing I want.

Cole extracts himself from the adoring throng and joins us. We only have him for a few moments before he's drawn away again. The stream of people who want to be in his presence is never ending, but eventually, the night reaches its conclusion.

Cole pulls Casziel aside for what looks like a serious conversation, then we say our goodbyes, and the car takes us back home. The energy of the night is like a spotlight over Cole that fades the closer we get to the flat. He grows quiet, his dark gaze on the city passing by the window.

Inside, he takes off his suit jacket and tosses it on the back of the couch.

"Thanks for coming tonight," he says. "I should've spent more time with you instead of getting caught up in all that hoopla."

"Is that not what you wanted?" I ask. "Your work will be celebrated far and wide."

"I guess. I'm so fucking grateful and at the same time…" He looks away. "Anyway, your portrait is finished. It's in my room if you want to see it."

I follow him to his room that's lit only by the small lamp at his bedside table. He sits on the edge of the bed and holds his head with one hand. The painting is in the corner, facing the wall.

When I remain rooted to the floor, Cole looks up. "Aren't you going to look at it?"

"No."

"Why not?"

Because then it's truly over.

I say nothing, and Cole nods miserably.

"I can't thank you enough for all you've done for me, Ambri, and I also can't watch you go." He sets his glasses on the nightstand and rubs his eyes. "I can't fucking do it."

"Neither can I."

Slowly, I go to him, feeling as if there is no floor beneath my feet and each step toward Cole is a leap of faith.

He looks up at me and swallows hard. "What are you doing?"

"I don't know. The worst thing. The best thing. I can't see it."

Words fail me as he stands up, his smile beautiful in the dimness, and I still can't bring myself to believe it's because of me.

"You're flush with the fruits of success," I offer lamely.

Cole shakes his head. "I don't give a shit about any of it."

I arch a brow.

"Let me rephrase. It was a dream come true. I loved every fucking minute, but I'd give it all back if I could just kiss you."

I fall back a step. "That's not true."

"Ambri…" His eyes shine, his voice hoarse. "This moment right here, with you? This is all I need."

No. He's lost in bliss, success, joy. He's forgotten who—*what*—I am. I've forgotten I'm supposed to leave him. To give him up before I'm ruined by Asmodai. Or maybe Cole will ruin me. I don't know which is more terrifying.

His hand comes up to hold my cheek. "You have to tell me it's okay."

"Yes," I whisper, nearly undone by his consideration. "Yes, Cole. With you, it's more than okay."

His expression is one of relief and joy—different from any he's worn all night. A joy that breaks my heart. Kindness tempered with heat. His other hand comes up to join the first, so he's holding my face as if I'm something valuable. Something worth saving.

My heart is hammering in my ribs as if it wants to break free when Cole's lips brush mine lightly. Then again, firmer but still soft. I have to close my eyes at the surge of want that wells in me. I'm suddenly fragile, I could shatter at the slightest wrong touch. I detest the feeling, but Cole's fingers slide to the back of my head and sink into my hair as he pulls me closer, and I feel more whole than I ever have. I don't kiss humans in an attempt to hold onto something that is just mine. Something that has not yet been taken from me. But Cole isn't taking, he's giving. His kiss is like a breath resuscitating me from a long airless sleep.

My mouth parts to allow him in, and his tongue finds mine. I can't stop the groan that escapes at the taste of him. He releases a sound—the deepest relief—as if he'd been drowning until now too.

For a few moments, we do nothing but gently taste and touch, arms slowly wrapping around each other, pulling closer, kissing deeper. His mouth, his lips and tongue… Cole's kiss is the best thing I've ever known. His desire simmers beneath, hot and potent, like a promise. We're going to burn the entire world away until there's nothing left but me and him.

Finally, he pulls back just enough to meet my eyes. "Now tonight is perfect." His smile falters. "Unless…is this goodbye?"

I stare, confused. *Goodbye* makes no sense. A nightmare worse than death.

"No. But Cole, we're not free. *I'm* not free. They might come for me."

"They'll have to get past me first."

His words shock me, undo me with their possessive promise. It was I who thought to ruin him, and yet he's trying to save *me*.

"No one's ever said anything like that to me," I say hoarsely.

I can tell my words pain him, but then he grins that grin that's so beautifully him. "Get used to it."

Gods help me.

I make him the same promise deep in my heart—my human heart that has never felt this alive. I'll keep him safe, and he'll never learn what I'd been commanded to do. What I could never do.

I'll die first.

One hand snakes into Cole's hair, the other around his waist, and I hold him tight to me. The desire between us shifts into something volatile; the next touch will ignite it and there will be no turning back. Cole responds just as urgently. He presses me against the wall, his body stronger and more powerful than I ever suspected. Our lips hover. We both inhale, and the tension cracks.

In the next instant, our mouths collide—an attack and a surrender both—and I'm his entirely.

twenty-two

Cole

We were held, suspended, in that torturous moment before the spark ignited. The anticipation wrapped us tight and then snapped like a whip. Our mouths crashed, melded, opened, and invaded.

Ambri took my kiss that didn't leave one bit of his mouth unexplored, and after fantasizing for months what he would taste like, I was utterly unprepared. He was fire and wine, searing and intoxicating. He let me have him and then kissed me back with equal ferocity.

Jesus H Christ in a sidecar…

The first gentle kiss was for him, to let him know he was worth more than sex to me. I thought this second, frenzied collision would help satisfy the need that had been simmering between us. But there was no satisfaction. I knew I'd never get enough of kissing him. I could kiss Ambri for the rest of my life and still want more.

And he kissed me back with an indulgence that made my heart fracture. Because with me it was okay. He knew he was safe.

What happened to him…?

But thoughts were hard to grasp and broke apart. I pressed him to the wall as if I could climb into his skin. He pulled me in tight, as if he could fuse us together. Our hands tore through hair, roamed over bodies, frustrated by too many clothes. I wanted whatever he wanted, but my need to have him was greedy, verging on savage.

"Ambri," I murmured between kisses. "I'm versatile, but I want to fuck you tonight. Christ, I want to fuck you so bad. We should probably talk about—"

"What goes where? Fear not, Cole Matheson. I want you inside me more than I want my next breath."

My eyes nearly rolled back in my head, and then his grin turned wicked.

"But not yet."

His hands worked the buckle on my pants, and he started to drop to his knees.

"Wait, wait." I pulled him back to eye-level. "When I come, I want to be buried in you."

He arched a brow. "You think you're only going to come once tonight? Who do you take me for?"

I laughed, and we shared a brief moment where the utter joy of him staying infiltrated our lust and made everything more perfect. Then Ambri's petulant-yet-hot-as-fuck scowl returned.

"I'm going to take what's mine," he said. "What I've been wanting since the moment I first saw you. You've been keeping this beautiful cock from me, Cole. I won't stand for it another minute."

Literally, I thought as he dropped to his knees between me and the wall.

Ambri freed me from my pants, and I braced myself with a palm flat on the wall, blood surging through me at the first lick—a maddening flick of his tongue on the tip. Every muscle and nerve ending tensed and trembled with anticipation as his hand encircled me and squeezed, and then my knees threatened to buckle as that obscenely sexy mouth of his took me deep. The wet heat and pressure tried to undo me, and then I felt the graze of his teeth as he came up for air, tonguing the slit.

"Fuck," I breathed and gripped a fistful of blond hair.

"Yes," he hissed. "It's my turn. Make me take it."

His words whipped at the need I was already struggling to control. I could barely restrain my hips from fucking him, but every moment that felt like too much was a moment he sucked me harder, took me deeper.

"Ambri…I'm going to come."

He made a sound of pure greed and gripped my ass to hold me still while my release ripped through me. He drank it down, then sucked long and slow to draw it out.

He was right—that orgasm turned me inside out and yet only took the edge off. In moments, I was hard again as he made his way back up my body, undoing buttons on my dress shirt along the way. He tossed it aside and kissed me. I tasted myself on his tongue, mixed with all that was him. My need took on a life of its own. I kicked aside my pants and underwear, then tore his shirt open, sending buttons flying.

He frowned. "That was new."

"I'll buy you another one," I said into his neck.

"Ah yes. You're about to be a very rich man."

"Ambri." I met his gaze. "I already am."

The words hit him and sunk in, but I knew he could only hear so much in one night. With a ferocious kiss, I drove him to the bed and blanketed his body with mine. Putting myself between him and whatever the fuck thought it could take him from me.

I'll die first.

I lay over him, kissing him until we were both breathless. His hands roamed my back, exploring, and I suspected it wasn't often someone just held him, kissing him, and letting the need flare and ebb in indulgent waves. With effort, I released his mouth and moved my tongue down his body, intending to leave no inch of skin untasted. He hissed as I took one small nipple between my teeth and sucked.

"Torture," he managed.

"Your fault. You bought me time."

"Lesson learned," he gritted out. "No more blowjobs for you."

I bit him lightly in retaliation, just below his navel. His abs contracted, became more defined, and I had to see the rest of him. I knelt and stripped him out of his pants and underwear. His cock sprang free and stood at attention, huge and hard and leaking.

"Fuck, Ambri." I took him in hand, licked that salty drop, and groaned. "So fucking beautiful."

"Kind of you to say," he said, his eyes glazed. "But if you don't fuck me soon, I'm going to think bad thoughts about you."

"Can't have that." I reached to the nightstand drawer and fished around for a condom and a small bottle of lube. "I want this to be good for you."

Now it was his turn to look somber.

"It's already perfect."

I kissed him, deep and long, then paused to slick my fingers. Propped on one arm, I lay over him and reached between his legs to gently work him open. His tightness made me groan, and I couldn't imagine my entire cock in him. I kissed his lips, his chin, his neck, and then made my way back up to his mouth that I couldn't get enough of. One finger became two, and I pressed the sensitive spot inside him, making him arch into my hand. He moaned, made fists in the sheets, as I moved my fingers in and out. Then I added a third, watching him all the while, checking in.

Finally, he shook his head, panting and sweaty. "Enough with the bloody fingers, Cole. Give me your cock."

"So demanding."

"I wouldn't have to be if—"

I silenced him with another kiss. "A perk of this new development. I finally found a way to shut you up."

He replied by snarling and biting my lower lip, and I laughed. Ambri was like an untamed wildcat, all teeth and claws.

And all mine…

I sat up, straddling his hips to put on the condom. I stroked my length with lubed fingers and then settled between his legs to align myself. Ambri inhaled and let it go. Slowly, I eased inside him an inch. His next inhale was a hiss, and my gaze jumped up.

"Okay?"

He nodded, exhaled. "More…"

I pressed in slowly. Another inch. God, he was so fucking tight.

"I know what you're doing," he said, tense with the strain of taking me. "Stop being careful."

"I refuse to hurt you."

"Now who's talking too much?" He brought my mouth to his and then he reached down to grip my hips to pull me deeper inside him until I was buried to the hilt.

"Ah, fuck, Ambri…"

I moaned at the sudden tightness all around me, gripping my dick in a perfect pressure. I pulled back slowly, then pushed back in, lowering myself at the same time, wanting more skin to skin. Our eyes met, and how good it was hit us at the same time. I couldn't keep from smiling, and Ambri…Jesus Christ, his expression in that moment nearly wrecked me.

I kissed him and moved faster. His heels dug into the backs of my thighs, driving me even deeper. My thrusts grew more urgent. The bed creaked, sweat beaded on my chin and he licked the drop, then we kissed again. A desperate mashing of mouths, broken by the grinding motions that rocked us both.

"Bloody gods, Cole," he gritted. "So good."

"Every time," I managed. "I want it to be like this every time for you."

He shook his head. "Don't. It's too much."

Anger flared white hot through me. Whoever had hurt him so badly in life had left him unable to accept kindness. Consideration. As if he didn't deserve it or know what to do with it. I vowed to change that, but in the meantime, I fucked him the way he wanted. When he reached for his cock that was trapped between us, I knocked his hand away.

"Don't touch what's mine," I gritted out.

His eyes flared. "You need a gallery show every night."

I took his hard length and stroked him in time to my driving hips. He made a strangled sound and came fast over my hand, hot and thick. I put my fingers to my mouth, tasting him, and then lowered myself to kiss him. To make him taste us both. His kiss was searing and urged me faster, our hips slamming and the raw sounds of our bodies driving me to the brink.

"Cole," he said around panting breaths that came with every deep thrust of my cock. "Come. Come in me right now."

My body obeyed, and the orgasm shuddered through me hard enough to force out a cry that felt like it had been trapped in me for years. This is what I'd wanted—the perfect harmony between raw need and connection that lived between the beating of our hearts.

Ambri took everything I had, and I collapsed on top of him, his sweat and his release sealing us together. My arms went under his shoulders so I could hold him close, one hand in his hair. He was wrapped around me, our legs tangled, his face in the crook of my neck.

"I'm heavy."

"Yes, you are," he said and held me tighter.

Our chests heaved in sync as we caught our breaths together. I carefully withdrew and rolled in a boneless heap beside him. I expected a smart-ass remark or a joke, but Ambri lay on his back, staring at the ceiling, an unreadable expression on his face.

"Hey. You okay?"

He turned his head on the pillow to look at me. "Tonight was so perfect, I fear it's a lie. Or I'll wake up to find this was a dream. Except I can't dream."

I smiled softly. "Then it must be real."

"Bloody hell, Cole…"

I pulled him close and kissed him deeply, then slipped out of bed. In the bathroom, I cleaned myself up and dampened a washcloth. I drew it over Ambri's abdomen, then climbed back into bed with him, wrapping myself around him, his back to my chest.

"I have to sleep," I murmured against his shoulder. "Just a little. Will you stay with me?"

He nodded, holding my arms that held him. "I don't ever want to leave."

I was too tired, too drained by the entirety of the night to stay awake, but I could practically hear the rest of his thought and it followed me down into the dark.

But I might not have a choice.

The morning light slanted across my eyes, waking me. For a moment, I was disoriented and confused. For years, I'd woken to a cold, empty bed, and now the warm weight of Ambri's body was pressed to me, my arms still wrapped around him.

I kissed the place between his shoulder blades and reluctantly released him.

"Sorry. I've been holding you prisoner all night."

"I'm a willing captive."

He rolled to face me, and I brushed my thumb over his lower lip. "It's sort of impossible not to kiss you now that I can," I said.

"What's stopping you?"

"My morning breath."

I tossed off the covers and headed to the bathroom.

"I don't care about such things, Cole."

When I returned, I slid back into bed and laid a soft kiss on his lips. "I care. Not if you have it but that I might."

"That makes no sense."

"I know. It's like gift cards. I hate giving them; I worry they're not thoughtful enough, yet I have no problem receiving them."

Ambri looked dryly amused. "So glad we got that sorted."

I laughed and kissed him again. Our kiss deepened and my body threatened to wake, but just lying with Ambri in my bed was worth savoring. I tucked my arm under my head. My other hand found his, our fingers tangling.

"Thank you," I said.

"For what?"

"For trusting me."

"It's only kissing," Ambri said. "Silly to withhold it, I suppose. An attempt to keep something to myself after so much had been taken away."

My heart dropped and I held his hand tighter. "I wondered if something had happened to you. I *hoped* it hadn't. But it's not silly. You did what you had to do to protect yourself."

He frowned. "You're not going to ask me what other sordid little tale I'm harboring?"

"No. I'm here if you want to tell me, but it's up to you if you feel ready."

He closed his eyes. "Cole Matheson...if only I'd met you in life, things might've turned out very differently for me."

"I'm here now. And this is still your life, Ambri."

He rolled onto his back, holding my hand, tracing my fingers with his. "Are you certain you wish to hear it? It's not pleasant but rather...shameful."

"I'm here. I'm listening," I said, while inwardly bracing myself. Pain was coming to the surface of his expression. "It might help to get it out."

"Perhaps."

He laid my hand over his heart, holding it there, his gaze on the ceiling. Just when I thought he'd decided against it, he inhaled and began to speak.

"I told you my parents had me late in life. My birth nearly killed my mother, and while my father was pleased to have a male heir, neither had the energy or inclination to raise me. To this day, I'm not entirely certain of my own birthday. I grew up with a rotating roster of tutors and governesses. I rarely saw my parents or my older sister,

Jane—a spinster who kept to herself in the west wing. The one bright spot was the visits from Uncle.

"He wasn't blood-related but a family friend. I called him Uncle. He was like a burst of light in the gray mausoleum that was Hever. A jovial fellow, always giving me treats, always ruffling my hair—always resting his hand on my shoulder or finding other reasons to touch me. His affection was platonic until I was ten years old. I suppose it was then that he'd decided that he'd waited long enough."

Oh fuck...

My chest tightened with dread. Under my hand, Ambri's heart was beating fast, belying his calm, resigned tone.

"He arrived at Hever in mid-summer from his estate in Kent and asked if I would like to accompany him to London. I'd agreed, of course. To trade the cold, drafty castle for the bustling city? What rambunctious boy wouldn't? But no sooner had the carriage door closed than Uncle made his true motivations known. His affection for me became *less than* platonic."

I gritted my teeth. *Ten years old.*

"That first journey collapsed my entire world," Ambri said, his gaze distant. "My childhood burnt up in a few short—and agonizingly long—moments. Instantly, there was no one in the entire godforsaken world in whom I could trust."

"Your parents...?" I asked helplessly.

"Raced to my rescue? Cursed my uncle for his deeds and threw him in the dungeon?" He shook his head against the pillow. "Hardly. The next fortnight, Uncle called again to take me to the city. I begged my parents not to allow it, but my pleas fell on deaf ears. They were angry at my insolence and called me an ungrateful little wretch. I was dragged kicking and screaming into Uncle's carriage, the door locking behind me. The third time Uncle came calling, I hid in the garden. The fourth time, I climbed up into the attic and had to be hauled out by the Master-at-Arms." The sharpness in Ambri's tone fell away and his voice lowered to a near whisper. "The fifth time, I stopped fighting."

My eyes fell shut, pain and rage gripping my heart in an iron fist. "Jesus, Ambri..."

"I didn't tell my parents the truth until years later. Uncle assured me they'd never believe me and would send me away in either case. He was right. At thirteen, I finally mustered the courage to speak up. It took everything I had, but I did it." Ambri's voice tightened. "And my parents called me a liar."

"Fucking hell…"

"They immediately packed me up and sent me to Europe with my inheritance. It was the last I saw of them. I ceased to be a member of the family and became a dirty little secret instead. And that's what I felt. Dirty. Shameful. As if I'd done something wrong."

I pulled him close. *"No,"* I said fiercely. "It wasn't your fault. Do you hear me? It wasn't your fault. They failed you. They all did."

"Seems foolish to be emotional over it now, doesn't it? It was a long time ago. And humanity is riddled with stories like mine, most much worse."

"It's what happened to you, and it matters," I said against his shoulder. "It matters a lot."

"Thank you, Cole." He exhaled raggedly, melting against me. "I feel as if I've been waiting centuries for someone to tell me that."

I held him tighter and then Ambri pulled away just enough so that we were face to face.

"You aren't the only person I've ever told that to, but it feels as if you are," he said. "I wonder how things might've been different if I'd spoken of it more. If I'd released the pain that was living inside me. I couldn't escape it, so I had to become it. I decided that if something could be so easily taken from me, then the only way to survive would be to make it easy to give away." He smiled wanly. "But kissing…that could be something that was just mine. *I* could decide. A small measure of control."

"Then I'm even more honored that you trusted me, but mostly, I'm sorry, Ambri. I'm so sorry that happened to you."

"Don't shed a tear for me, Cole," he said, his gaze dropping. "I don't deserve your sympathy. I've done terrible things." He inhaled and let it out slow. "Since I'm in a confessional mood…there's something else."

"You can tell me anything."

His brows furrowed and he searched my eyes. "No, another time. I've already spoiled your morning."

"You haven't spoiled anything."

Ambri hesitated another moment, then lunged forward and kissed me, pushing me back and settling himself on top of me.

"It would appear I'm more selfish than I am honest." His hips ground against me, his cock sliding against mine that grew hard almost instantly. "And I'm not ready to give you up just yet."

Two days later, Lucy and Cas returned to New York. Ambri and I saw them off at Heathrow. Before they headed for security, Cas pulled me aside and pressed a piece of paper into my hand.

"My colleague says Jules Grayson is the man to know. You can email him at this address. He'll help you if he can."

"Great. Thanks, man," I said, slipping the paper into my pocket before Ambri's sharp eyes could see it.

Cas and I shook hands and then Lucy was throwing her arms around me.

"Take care. Be careful. Call me if anything happens. I don't know what I can do, but…call me anyway. I need to know you're okay."

"I will. I promise."

Ambri said his goodbyes to Cas and Lucy, and then he had his driver take us back to the flat.

"So," he said from the plush backseat. "You and Casziel seem cozy. Think as thieves."

"It's *thick* as thieves and mind your own business." He scowled and I laughed. "I fucking love it when you're cranky. Almost as much as I love it when you butcher common idioms."

He sniffed. "You try keeping up with hundreds of years of changing vernacular from the Other Side."

"You're doing a hang-up job. Really murdering it."

"Oh, piss off."

I laughed harder and though he tried his best, Ambri couldn't help smiling too. Then his smile became a laugh, and I didn't think I'd ever seen anything as fucking beautiful in my life.

I leaned in to kiss him, vowing that I'd do whatever it took to preserve this happiness between us. But a nagging fear that he could be taken away at any time dogged every blissful moment, and there was nothing I could do about it.

Just love him, mein Schatz. There's nothing else to do.

The thought was comforting, like a mother's embrace, but my own baggage was as heavy as ever. I'd been protecting my heart for years, wanting certainty, stability, safety. Ambri and I had none of these. After being careful for so long, letting myself love him felt like the most thrilling wish of my heart and the most reckless.
He's a demon. "Careful" *left the chat a long time ago.*
I could have laughed at the irony except I realized with a pang of fear that I'd stopped thinking of Ambri as a demon.
He was just mine.

———◈

The following day, I met Jane for lunch at CORD on Fleet Street for a post-mortem of the gallery show over her duck confit and my twenty-eight pound BLT that seemed too fancy to eat, even for a sandwich.
"I don't need to tell you it was a smashing success," she said. "You were there."
"I'm so grateful for all the work you did, Jane." I toyed with my napkin. "How did they do? I mean, did we…?"
"Sell out? Nope. Nothing was sold."
"Oh," I said, sitting back. "That's a bummer."
Jane reached across the table and patted my hand. "You're too pure for this world, Cole. No one bought anything because nothing was for sale. Not yet. Forgive me for being secretive, but I suspected we needed to hold off until the responses came in, and I was right. The reviews are spectacular, the feedback has been off-the-charts, so we're going to shift gears."
"Okay," I said slowly. "What does that mean?"
"It means we're going to sell them at auction at Christie's after a European tour to drum up further interest. To whip the art world into a frenzy."
My eyes widened. "A tour?"
"Amsterdam, Paris, Madrid, Rome, Vienna, Prague, and Berlin. In that order. I've already locked in clamoring galleries, so plan to leave in about ten days."
"Holy shit," I said. "Okay, well, that sounds pretty incredible. But Jane, I don't exactly have the funds for a seven-city tour."

Jane motioned with her fork while she swallowed a bite of food. "Your accommodations will be paid for: five-star hotels, first class flights, food, drink, a publicist, a stylist—"

"A *stylist?*"

She slid an itinerary across the table. "You have interviews lined up with *ArtForum, Beautiful Bizarre, Apollo*, and *Aesthetica*, and that's *before* the tour. Some people from the agency will contact you to make all the arrangements. And of course, you must bring Ambri to Europe. He is *divine.*"

I choked and nearly sprayed the table with sparkling water. "I'll tell him you said so."

"As for funds, the appraiser has assessed your collection prior to auction. Based on his numbers, Christie's is going to advance you five percent, which amounts to £150,000. Of course, that's if you agree to consign the collection to them. Which, as your agent, I recommend you do."

If I'd been sipping water that time, I'd have spewed it for sure.

"Sorry," I said with a small laugh. "I could've sworn you said they want to give me a hundred grand."

"And a half. The appraiser estimates the hammer price of your entire collection at auction will be in the realm of three million."

I stared, my mouth hanging open like a door with a broken hinge. "You're telling me those paintings are worth a quarter of a million apiece?"

"A conservative number, to be sure."

"That's…not possible."

"I assure you it is." She speared a piece of duck on her fork, smiling. "You are the literal talk of the town, Cole. I haven't seen Christie's this excited over a young new artist since Anna Weyant."

I tried to let those numbers sink in, but they wouldn't go. I waved my hands. "No, no, I can't take that advance. If they don't sell, I'm on the hook for it, right?"

"Yes, but they're going to sell, darling. For a lot of money," she said. "Christie's buyer's fee is twenty-five percent, tacked on to the final sale price of every piece, which means they're going to more than cover your advance. Our agency's cut is fifteen, which will net you more than £2.5 million, all told."

I blew air out my cheeks. "I think my brain is going to explode."

"Perhaps that can wait until after lunch? We need to discuss your next collection," Jane said. "As beautiful as your demon is, the public is going to want something different for round two. But not *too* different. Perhaps there's a variation or new theme you might tackle?"

I nodded, thinking of the drawings that had been filling my sketchpad. "I already know what comes next."

"Brilliant!" Jane said. "You can begin right after the tour—"

"I'd rather work on the road if that's okay," I said. "It'll keep me grounded with all this madness."

Not to mention, my burning need to paint Ambri hadn't gone anywhere but had only grown stronger and more insistent.

"Even better," Jane was saying. "We'll ensure that supplies travel with you and that your hotel rooms have adequate space in which to work."

"Great. Thanks, Jane. For everything."

"It's overwhelming, isn't it?" She patted my hand again. "I understand, but all you need to do is soak it in and paint. We'll do the rest." Her cell phone next to her plate chimed, and she frowned at the notification. "Oh dear." She turned her phone over and smiled tightly at me.

"What is it?"

"Nothing. A bit of unpleasantness I'm currently dealing with. We need not let it spoil our lunch."

"Is it Vaughn?" I asked, a lump settling into my stomach.

"You must've seen the news."

"No, I just had a feeling. He never showed up at the gallery and he's not answering my calls or texts."

She sighed. "He was arrested for a DUI the night of your show."

"Oh, shit. Is he okay?"

"Minor injuries. He wrapped his Audi around a telephone pole. He's bloody lucky he didn't kill anyone."

"Damn. Where is he now?"

"That is a very good question." Jane frowned, then waved her hand. "I know you went to Uni with him, but now is not the time to become distracted by his drama. You've paid your dues. Enjoy yourself. Let me worry about Vaughn."

"I can't do that, Jane. He's my friend."

She smiled at me like an indulgent mother. "Of course, he is. I just meant, in this highly competitive business, it's very easy to let ego get in the way of friendship." She leaned over the table. "I'll put it this way—there was a reason he didn't come to your show, Cole, and it wasn't that telephone pole."

No, it was a plague of demons.

After lunch, I immediately pulled out my phone and called Vaughn. Voicemail.

I put my finger to my ear and turned my back on the street noise. "Hey, Vaughn, it's Cole again. Listen, I heard what happened and I just want to know you're okay. Call me whenever. Don't hesitate. Whatever you need, I'm here. And Vaughn…" I hunched my shoulders. "Remember what I told you about not listening to those voices in your head? I know what it's like. They had me too. Just…call me, okay? Any time."

I hung up and leaned against the wall. I waited for a few minutes, but my phone remained silent.

———

I returned to the flat to find Ambri on the couch reading a book. He tucked it into the cushion as I came in.

"Well? Did you sell me out? Again?"

"Not exactly."

I sat across from him in the chair and explained Jane's plan.

"What do you think?"

"I think she's right," Ambri said. "At the show, a pair of gents compared you to Jan van Eyck. Three million is conservative."

"I meant, what do you think about coming on the tour?"

"Paris," he said, his eyes darkening.

"I know." I moved to sit beside him, put my arm around him. "You could skip it and meet me in Madrid, but…call me a selfish asshole, but I want you with me for all of it."

Ambri shot me an imperious look. "Can't bear to part with me for even a moment? Understandable."

I grinned. "It's a miracle that I manage to close my eyes at night to your radiance. Every blink is a tiny torture—"

He snarled and took me down on the couch, settling himself over me, a dangerous smile on his lips and a glint in his eyes. Over the last few days, we'd spent a generous amount of time getting to know each other's bodies with our mouths and hands but hadn't had sex again. My breath caught, and I wondered if now he'd take his turn and fuck me until we were both spent and gasping.

"I'll tour with you, Cole," he said, his hands leisurely sliding up and down my chest over my black Henley. "Paris too. As it happens, I can't bear to be parted from you either. And a change of scenery might be smart."

"It'll help keep you hidden?"

His shoulders slumped. "*Buzz kill*, Cole Matheson. That's an idiom I know." Ambri planted a kiss on my lips and then climbed off of me. "I'll order dinner. I'm in the mood to watch you eat pasta. Italian all right?"

"Sure."

He stopped on the way to the kitchen.

"You're right to be cautious, Cole. We can't make the mistake of thinking it will always be this easy. I have much to pay for." His gaze landed heavily on me. "More than you know."

twenty-three

Ambri

Within the week, my humble little slice of Chelsea is overrun. Publicists walk to and fro, forever on the phone and saying things like, "Mr. Matheson isn't available at that time. Perhaps tomorrow at four?" and snapping at someone else to bring "Mr. Matheson" a latte or a bottle of water or a sandwich—none of which I ever hear him actually ask for.

There are interviews here at the flat nearly every day, crammed in before our departure for the European tour. A stylist had given Cole a haircut, contact lenses, and a new wardrobe of simple but impeccably stylish clothing. Gone are his ragged sweatshirts and paint-splattered pants. Now he's effortlessly handsome in light jackets, slacks, designer jeans, and many a tight-fitting long-sleeved shirt that accentuates his lean, toned body.

Except for the aforementioned shirts, I chafed at the changes, fearing they'd erase the Cole I know and replace him with a stranger. But bare of glasses, his dark eyes are somehow even more arresting. And while I mourn the loss of hair that fell over his brow, he still has enough to run my fingers through (and grip in the heat of the night).

Moreover, he's still himself. The assistants fetching him coffee and brushing powder over his face—for a photo spread in *ArtForum*—seem not to faze him. He's as gracious and kind as ever and constantly checking in with me to ensure the "craziness" isn't too much or too intrusive.

When the fawning hordes leave for the day, he works, studying his sketchbook filled with God-knows-what and gathering canvases and paints for his next collection that he'll begin on the road. I don't ask him his plans; I still haven't brought myself to look at my portrait. Something tells me that the right time will come, and I'm in no rush—I'm terrified it'll be exactly as I hoped it would be.

Cole painted it; of course it will be beyond your wildest dreams...and then what?

To be perfectly honest, I never considered what I'd actually *do* with a portrait of myself—a portrait that belongs in Hever or a museum, not in my bloody living room where the shame of my human existence would be staring down at me with my own eyes.

No, thank you.

I know it hurts Cole's feelings a little that I haven't beheld the fruits of his labor, but I also know he understands why without my having to say a word. I've come to learn acutely that for Cole, my feelings come first. His own, a distant second.

I can relate—I'd commit merciless bodily harm on anyone who threatened his happiness.

It's all going to come crashing down, and then where in the bloody hell will we be?

But as the days pass and there is no sign from the Other Side, hope starts to rear its nasty little head again. Perhaps Asmodai has grown bored with me. Perhaps the hierarchy is busy with other matters. Perhaps an angel has intervened...

The fact that I can sprout wings or dissolve in a swarm of beetles puts a wee bit of a damper on things, but as the day of departure for Amsterdam draws nearer, I breathe easier and turn my thoughts to that elusive thing that demons have no business looking toward—the future.

A future with Cole...

The mere thought feels like a secret, too precious to speak out loud. If there is such a thing as paradise, that is it.

On the eve of our departure, Cole emerges from his bedroom/studio looking extraordinary in a black Henley, jeans, and short, laced boots, also in black, that are somehow both rugged and elegant at the same time.

I'm reading *The Adventures of Pinocchio* for the umpteenth time. Cole catches me tucking it into the couch cushion.

"Again?" he teases and sits beside me. His chestnut hair is damp from a recent shower, and he smells of cologne and soap and warm skin, and I want to press my face into his neck and live there.

"It's quite bloodier and more gruesome than you likely realize," I say. "I doubt, for instance, the cartoon version includes the scene where bandits capture Pinocchio and hang him from a tree, waiting for him to suffocate."

"Disney saved that for the collector DVD," he says wryly. "Are you packed?"

"Of course."

"Good, then let's go." He stands and pulls me to my feet. "Before the tour starts and makes things even crazier, I want one night that's just me and you."

I grip him by the hips and pull him tight to me. "Why go anywhere?" I say against his lips. "Why not stay here and let me have you?"

His already nearly black eyes dilate, and he groans. We kiss, and like most kisses between us, it's impossibly good with the promise of carnal ecstasy burning beneath.

Cole pulls away. "Later," he manages. "I want that. *Badly*. But later."

"What do you have in mind? A romantic dinner? A horseback ride through Hyde Park?"

Cole chuckles. "Um, *no*. None of the above. Come on, get your coat."

"I'm not dressed to go out," I protest.

"Ambri. You're head-to-toe in black Armani. You're more than dressed. In fact, you could stand to wear less than a three-piece suit every day." He wags his eyebrows. "Make it easier for me later."

At the entry closet he puts on an elegant, form-fitting coat and hands me mine.

"Ready?"

I nod, watching him. His eyes are brighter than usual, his cheeks flushed.

"Are you feeling well?" I ask, visions of his November illness swooping back in to haunt me. I press my hand to his forehead. "You're warm. We should stay in—"

He laughs and moves in to kiss me. "I'm fine. Trust me. But let's hurry."

"Shall I call the car?"

"Nah, let's walk for a little bit, then hail a cab."

"You just said we should hurry. Delirium has already set in…"

He laughs again and tugs my arm. "I want to walk around the city a bit and show off my arm candy first. Okay?"

I consider this. "That makes sense."

We walk into a lovely London spring evening—cold and threatening rain—both of us with our hands tucked in our pockets but arm in arm. Linked.

We're a set. Can't have one without the other.

The thought makes me smile and I feel buoyant. As if I'd float away if it weren't for Cole. *Because* of Cole.

We pass the Chelsea gallery that so recently held his collection—now carefully packed away and en route to Amsterdam. His strange, electric smile fades and he checks his phone.

"Sorry," he says, tucking it back in his pocket. "No more phone tonight, but the gallery reminded me of Vaughn. Jane says he skipped his DUI hearing at the magistrate's court, and no one's heard from him since. I think he has the Twins on him."

"You mentioned."

"I wish there were something we could do." Cole glances over at me. "Is there? Can you scare them off of him?"

I shake my head. "I don't have the authority to do that."

"Why not? You scared them off of me."

I nearly stop walking. Thinking quickly, I glance at Cole. His eyes are ahead, he suspects nothing. Because he's a good man and he trusts me.

"That was different," I say.

You were already marked for damnation. By me.

I clear my throat and add quickly, "Besides, there's no certainty that those witches are whispering at him." Cole starts to speak but I cut him off. "Do we have a destination in mind, or are we just going to wander the streets all night like a pair of exceedingly handsome drifters?"

My petulance has the desired effect—Cole chuckles and breaks from me to hail a cab.

"Okay, okay. You win. Just don't roll your eyes at me when you hear it."

"Me? I *never*."

"You *always*."

The black taxi arrives, and Cole holds the door for me, then awkwardly climbs in after. "Good evening. London Eye, please," he tells the driver, then peers intently at me.

I manage to keep my face placid. The car drives for a few moments, and then I can't restrain myself. "The Ferris wheel? Really?"

Cole laughs. "Have you ever been?"

"No."

"Then what are you complaining about?"

"It just seems terribly gaudy. The city was beautiful enough in my day. Now it's draped in colored lights like so much costume jewelry."

"Give it a chance. For me."

I roll my eyes. "As if I'd refuse you anything."

His smile is beautiful as he leans in to kiss me. "Of all your eye rolls, that's my favorite."

Night has begun to fall as we arrive at the London Eye. Instead of waiting in the regular queue, Cole takes my hand and brings me around to a special office.

"Mr. Matheson and guest," the man says, consulting his computer device. "Very good, sir. If you'll follow me."

The Ferris wheel has thirty-two enclosed capsules. A sign helpfully informs us they each hold twenty-five people, and a single rotation takes thirty minutes to complete. We're ushered into an empty capsule by a man who carries a bucket of ice with champagne and two glasses. He sets them on a long, canoe-shaped center bench, then tips his cap with a smile.

"Enjoy the flight, gentlemen."

Cole is looking at me with an expectant smile. "So?"

"The fact we're not going to spend the next half hour crammed in this glass pod with twenty-three gawking tourists is a plus."

Now it's his turn to roll his eyes. "I'm so glad you approve."

"Let me rephrase," I say, pulling him to me. "I love that you did this for us and that it's just me and you."

"I always want just me and you."

Cole kisses me, then pours the champagne as the capsule begins to rise. The sun is setting in the west, casting the sky in shades of gold and purple. The vista of the city lit up for the coming night, spreads farther and farther, huge and beautiful under a darkening sky.

For so long, London had held nothing for me but memories of shame, degradation, and abandonment. I look to Cole who is taking in the view with artist eyes, possibly digesting it and re-imagining it for a future canvas. But I know what he's really doing. He's trying to give the city back to me in a new light. He's trying to give *life* back to me, by showing me it can be more than pain.

No, that it can be beautiful despite the pain and because of it.

"When did you know you were an artist?" I ask.

He blinks at the sudden question. "Oh, well…I don't know. When I was a kid, I guess. I loved to draw. Hardly ever stopped. But I didn't consider myself an *artist* until much later. Not officially. I felt like that would be arrogant or asking too much, you know? I mean, who gets to make a living doing what they love?"

"And then your incredible talent forced you to accept your fate."

He chuckles. "No, it was my grandmother. When it came time for college, she insisted I apply to NYU's school of the arts. So I did." His smile was warm and sad. "She believed in me. I think that's all it really takes sometimes. Just one person you love, who loves you, and believes in you."

"Why portraiture?" I ask because I realize I'm dangerously close to saying something dreadfully emotional and unretractable.

"I like people," Cole says. "I like looking at them and trying to get a sense of who they are. I'll never know them fully or understand them completely, but I get to capture one facet of them, one moment that I can hold still forever."

Cole feels my gaze on him and turns on that charming grin that holds so much goodness. Much more than I deserve.

"What do you think?" he asks. "You forgive me for dragging you up here?"

I say nothing but move to him and slide my free hand around his broad shoulder and into his hair. I lean in and kiss him. His lips part, and I taste the champagne—a sweet bite on his tongue—and I decide from then on that's the only way I want to taste champagne or anything else. Because he makes everything good.

The capsule plateaus and we watch the city. Cole looks pleased but that strange, nervous energy has returned. He tosses back the rest of his champagne and tugs at the collar of his coat.

"All right, tell me the truth," I demand. "What is going on with you?"

"Nothing, but…oh fuck, I'm sorry. I tried. I had another event planned, a little jazz club I hear is amazing, but I'm not going to make it."

My eyes widen in alarm. "What does that mean?"

He looks sheepish and even a bit mischievous. Though we're thoroughly alone, he leans in and whispers, "I'm wearing a toy. Beads. For you. For us, so that tonight—"

"I can take you immediately." I stare as every drop of blood in my body goes up in flames. Then I give my head a shake. "And you're telling me this *now*? When we're trapped in this pod, kilometers off the ground, and I can't do a thing about it?"

"How do you think I feel?" he says with a laugh, though his eyes are dark and glazed. "Every step I take hits that spot and makes me imagine your cock there instead."

"Bloody fucking hell."

I pour a glass of champagne and toss back the entire thing in one go, though it does absolutely nothing to help me. I refill his glass and pour another for me.

"You surprise me, Cole Matheson, I'd never have guessed you were so adventurous. And devious."

"It's your fault," he says. "You're too fucking sexy. Try toning it down a notch, will you?"

"If only that were possible…"

He laughs and we kiss again, this time with more heat and need, though time seems to have stopped entirely. Finally, the infernal capsule touches down, and we exit and head to the cab stand. I start to open the door for Cole, then stop.

"On second thought, why rush home?"

He blinks. "Sorry?"

"I'm suddenly in the mood for some classic cinema. They're playing a double feature at the Savoy."

"I hate you."

I laugh and pull him to me, kissing the smile on his lips. Then I lean in to whisper in his ear, "When we get home, I'm going to strip you naked and fuck you into the next century."

He grips my cock surreptitiously over my pants and gives it a squeeze. "That's the idea."

The cab ride is interminable. We finally arrive at my flat. No sooner is the door closed, then we're discarding jackets and undoing buckles. We maul each other with our mouths—teeth biting, tongues tangling in a battle of heated need and lust.

I drive him to my bedroom—a suite really, with a fireplace and sitting area—which has remained unused and vacant since Cole Matheson came into my life. My rotating assortment of overnight guests ceased the night I found him on the bridge. I pause our battle long enough to throw the switch on the lamp with a flick of my hand, then we resume tearing at each other's clothes until we're naked.

I jerk my chin at the bed. "On your knees."

My tone is masterful, but inside, I'm quaking with need. Cole gets on all fours, and I climb up behind him. I run my hand through his hair, then down his spine, to his perfect round ass. I move slowly and leisurely as if I'm not dying to get inside him as soon as humanly possible, but the sight of the toy nearly ends me.

"Ambri..." Cole glances over his shoulder. "What are you waiting for?"

I reply by bending my mouth and making a slow circle with my tongue over his tight flesh and the toy that stretches it.

He shudders on all four limbs and makes a strangled sound. "Jesus Christ..."

I sink my teeth into his muscled ass, then tongue him again, my hands roaming his back and backside, taking my time.

Cole is panting now. "Ambri, I can't..."

Neither can I wait one more second. Quickly, I reach into my nightstand drawer that has quite a few more toys and baubles than Cole's did and find the lube and the condom. Very slowly, I remove the toy, a device of five connected orbs of decreasing size. I toss it aside, then slip on the condom and slick my cock. He's already primed for me, and I slide inside him in one smooth thrust.

Cole's head bows between his shoulders and he struggles to remain on all fours. I'm just as undone, my thighs trembling at how impossibly good he feels, how tight, how bloody perfect.

I move slowly at first, gripping his hips and then running my hand along his spine and up into his hair. I make a fist and pull his head back, my other hand holding him still while I fuck him.

"Yes…" he grits out. "Fuck, yes…"

His desire spurs me on, and I move faster. Harder. I want to give him everything. I want every sound he's making, every strangled breath and every cry of ecstasy to come only from me.

And I don't want to give myself to anyone else but this man who has completely infiltrated my entire existence. I need more of his skin on mine, so I pull him higher, his back to my chest. The new angle elicits a pleasured cry from his throat.

"Ambri…ah, fuck. I'm going to come all over your pillows."

"Do it."

He grips himself in one hand, braces his other against the headboard. I reach to wrap my hand around his so we're both stroking his cock as my thrusts drive deeper and harder, our flesh slapping together. He makes another beautiful cry of ecstasy and comes all over my Italian silk pillow.

"So good," Cole groans. "Fuck, you feel so good in me."

I grit my teeth because his words want to bring me to the brink, and I want to stay in him forever. Cole reaches an arm around to take a fistful of my hair. He cranes his mouth to mine, and we kiss as best we can while I am pistoning into him.

Finally, I can contain myself no longer. The release crests in me and then breaks like a wave. I grip his hips tightly and come in him. Every nerve ending, cell, and sinew in my body vibrating and my awareness coalescing only to the place where we're joined and the perfection of it. The rightness of it.

I am ruined…

I slump over him and kiss his back before gently withdrawing and rolling to my side. He tosses the soiled pillow to the floor and does the same so we're facing each other and kissing again.

We kiss for long moments, and then we lie quiet, saying nothing. He brushes a lock of hair off my brow, and the gesture threatens to undo me with its simple intimacy.

I climb out of bed to clean up and return to find him dozing.

"I can't keep my eyes open," Cole says from behind closed lids. "You fucked me into the next century. Time travel is tiring."

I roll my eyes and he laughs tiredly. "I saw that."

Psychopath that I am, I watch him sleep. When I know he's deep under, I lean over and kiss his forehead. Because I can't tell him he's precious to me. The words stick in my throat, mired in the fear that it's too much, too good. This *life* we're building is too good, and I'm afraid if I speak it, it will blow away in the breath it takes to say the words.

twenty-four

Ambri
Amsterdam

The tour begins in a whirlwind. In Amsterdam, we stay at the Pulitzer Hotel—artsy and elegant. The morning of the first gallery showing, we do a little sightseeing through the city of canals and bicycles as if we were an ordinary couple—hands linked or arm-in-arm, always touching. Cole takes me to the Van Gogh Museum and I watch him take in the paintings.

"It's like it's *breathing*," he says as we stand in front of *Wheatfield with Crows*. "The wheat stalks are swaying, and the birds are alive and flying. Can you see it?"

I nod, but I'm looking at him, overwhelmed by him—his physical body, his heart and his soul, and those three most dastardly and beautiful words nearly escape my lips…

Then some assistant or another pops up to tell Cole it's time to head to the gallery and I swallow them down.

The show is a smashing success, of course, and a portent of what's to come for the rest of the tour. The art world looks at Cole's work the way he looks at Van Gogh.

Back at the hotel, we take turns bringing each other to ecstasy. After, I hold him while he sleeps against my chest, and I know—for the first time—perfect happiness.

Perhaps if I'd remained sharper, less foolish, less naïve to think that I deserved any kind of happy ending, things might've been different.

But as it always happens, by the time I know the utter horror of my mistake, it's too late.

Paris

Despite my unfortunate demise here two-hundred and fifty years ago, Paris is still one of the most beautiful cities in the world, and we stay in one of its most beautiful hotels—the Le Bristol, the erstwhile home of Josephine Baker and the American writer, Holden Parish. But being in this city works a little bit of sinister magic on me. I feel nervous and on edge the moment we arrive.

Cole's kindness and consideration make it more than bearable. He is unmoved by the chaos of the show but rises at four a.m. every morning to paint as if he is racing against the ticking of a clock only he can hear. Our time together is broken by interviews and meetings and the never-ending stream of assistants, but when we are together, it's just him and me.

On our third day in the city, Cole has an interview for *Paris Match* prior to the gallery show.

"If it's all the same to you," I say, "I'm going to take a walk and perhaps do some shopping."

"Getting boring, isn't it?" Cole asks with a grin from the living room couch of our suite.

"They all ask the same dull question of you—where do you get your inspiration?" I snort delicately. "*Me*, obviously."

"Obviously." Cole stands to take me by the lapels of my jacket to kiss me. "Some people from the agency are coming by later today. I don't know who—I can't keep track of everyone." His expression melts into concern. "Will you be okay out there? I know this hasn't been easy for you."

"I'll be fine," I say. "Ready to face my demons."

Oh, the irony.

I return several hours later after wandering through an old bookstore and taking a stroll along the Seine. In the suite, I hear voices—men and women, both. I step into the salon and every part of me seizes up. An instant petrification, except for my heart which crashes against my chest in a slow slam and then takes off at a gallop.

Cole is leaning on the arm of the couch. On the couch itself sits an older man—perhaps mid-sixties—and a blond woman in her thirties, wearing an eyepatch. Another woman stands at the window, but they're all blurred and indistinct because in the chair across from the couch is Armand de Villette.

I blink, certain that I've accidentally crossed into a different *when*, until the woman at the window turns, and I see it is Eisheth. She's in her human guise—that is to say, strikingly gorgeous in a colorful dress, her hair piled on her head and sparkling with tiny gems.

But my gaze is stuck on Armand. He is older that I knew him in life—perhaps in his forties—and in modern dress but otherwise the same. He shoots me a disgustingly smug smile and waggles his fingers. My shock subsides enough to see that the woman with the eyepatch is Jeanne de la Motte and the older gentleman sitting beside her is bloody fucking Cardinal Rohan.

What is this madness?

Cole smiles when he sees me and comes over immediately.

"Hey, are you okay?" he asks, his smile falling at my shell-shocked expression.

"No. *Yes.* I'm fine."

"Cole," Eisheth drawls from the window. "Please introduce us to your friend."

"More industry people," Cole murmurs with an eyeroll and a smile, then leads me by the hand into the den of demons. "This is Eisheth," he says. He indicates Jeanne. "And this is Daeva, that's Zerin..." Rohan gives me a nod. Finally, Cole gestures to Armand. "And this is Piccolus."

"Please," Armand says. "Call me Pico."

It takes everything I have to muster my composure. "A pleasure. But if you'll excuse me, I realize I left my parcels with the concierge and must check on them."

The last thing I want to do is leave Cole in the clutches of those demons, but I must compose myself. My life depends on it.

I make it a few paces down the hallway before I hear footsteps behind me.

"Running off so soon?" Eisheth calls.

I whirl on her, disguising my panic as anger. "Eisheth," I snap rudely. "Whatever brings you here?"

Her dress is yellow and red silk, and gold jewelry adorns her arms, ears, and neck. Her dark eyes are as shrewd as ever, cutting right through me.

"I thought it would be fun to bring the gang back together. We are in *Paris*, after all."

"But Armand? Why *him*?"

"Ashtaroth was one of our greatest collectors of souls before his untimely demise," she says pointedly. "After he collected you, he sought the rest of your cohorts from your little caper with poor, sweet Antoinette."

"I didn't know they'd been turned."

"Of course, you didn't. Ashtaroth was clever and far-seeing for our kind that cannot know the future. Perhaps he knew it would one day be useful to have all of you."

"Fine," I say, crossing my arms. "But you're flinging Armand in my face because…?"

She cocks her head, smiling in confusion. "Why, to finish your ingenious plan for Cole Matheson's downfall, of course."

I freeze as I did when Cole was painting me—it was the only way to keep the horror off my face.

"You seem surprised," she says. "It was, after all, your idea."

My idea. My fault. Whatever is to come is all my fault…

"This is how we took down Marilyn, Jimi, Janis…" Eisheth continues. "Our victories that you said yourself 'made waves.' Drugs, alcohol, fame—the trifecta that spoils many a human's rise to sudden success." She aimed a red-lacquered nail at the hotel door. "These three are Vices. They attach to a human who is flush with new money and remind them that they now have access to every drug, every drop of alcohol, every resource in the world to numb the pain that fueled their art. And they shall do the same to Cole Matheson."

I nod faintly, each of her words tearing me apart, one syllable at a time.

Eisheth paces leisurely in front of me. "It was already an ingenious plan to begin with, Ambri, but I have to admit, where you have taken him is quite extraordinary. Ambitious."

My gaze jumps to hers. "What do you mean?"

"Bringing Cole to the highest of heights is all well and good, but making him fall in love with you is a masterstroke. It will break his very soul when he learns the truth."

Those words are like little bombs dropped in the center of me. "The truth…"

"That it was all a lie," Eisheth says brightly. "This victory will ensure you'll be lauded in the halls of our hierarchy to the end of time. That was the idea, Ambri…" She cocks her head. "Wasn't it?"

I feel her studying me. Mocking me. I nod, formulating a plan so quickly that my thoughts give me whiplash. My future with Cole has burnt up in an instant, and now my entire purpose in this godforsaken realm is to protect him from "the Vices" at any cost.

"Yes, of course," I say with a haughty sniff. "Admittedly, that was not my intention at first, but when I realized how the simpleton grew infatuated with me, it seemed obvious."

I want to rip my tongue out for saying such abominations. For being so stupid. So reckless. The horror unfolding in front of me is doubly unbearable because I should've seen it coming.

Because I let it happen.

"I see," Eisheth says. "Because it would be a shame to find out you had other plans."

"What other plans could I possibly have?"

A life ever after with the man I love…

"Following in Casziel's footsteps perhaps?"

"Never," I say. "That fool gave up eternity for the love of a plain human girl."

Eisheth's dark-eyed gaze bores into me. "We've been watching your performance, Ambri. You're quite convincing."

My heart jackrabbits in my chest, caught in Eisheth's snare.

I scoff. "My life was nothing but a string of endless misery. It was pure shite broken by momentary flickers of less-than-pure shite and an orgasm or two. Why would I want to go back to that? Why would I want to grow old and sick and frail, when I can be beautiful and perfect forever?"

She holds my gaze a moment longer, then nods. "I will presume that you'll not reveal to Cole that we're all *less than human*? That would spoil our fun."

"Not a word," I grit out.

"Because if you do, we'll assume it's in betrayal of our cause. We'll have no choice but to send you to the Other Side for an eternity of pain while the Vices finish the task *you* began."

Gods, what have I done?

"I don't need their help," I blurt, putting up one last defense. "They're a trio of bloody knobs. You're telling me they're responsible for Elvis? For Marilyn? My arse."

"No, darling," Eisheth says. "They're part of a larger sect of Vices. You've told Cole Matheson your history as a human, so they've taken new names, but they're quite capable, I assure you. They did, after all, succeed in acquiring that diamond necklace."

"They *succeeded* in getting caught. I did not. I don't need their interference."

The demonwitch smiles though her eyes are frighteningly hard and devoid of anything remotely human.

"Asmodai believes otherwise."

With that, there's nothing more to be said, and she knows I know it. The devastation I've wrought blooms in my gut like a rancid flower. It's all I can do to not brace myself on the wall. If I ever ate anything, I'd surely vomit on Eisheth's Louboutins.

But in that chaos, my path is clear: I have to extricate Cole from me. He can't love me, but wounding him too quickly would make him vulnerable. To protect him, I'll have to break his heart slowly, instead of shattering him in one devastating blow. Stay close to him while I show him I'm not worthy of his love.

Because I'm not. Of that, there is no doubt.

Eisheth places a kiss on my cheek, sticky with lipstick. I smell fire and blood, and the promise of eternal pain burns in her eyes.

"Ah Paris, Ambri, darling," she muses triumphantly. "Welcome back."

part ii

Prove yourself brave, truthful, and unselfish, and someday you will be a real boy. —The Blue Fairy, *Pinocchio*

twenty-five

Cole

I frowned after Ambri as he hurried out. Being in Paris was hard enough for him and here I was, surrounded by strangers at every given moment. I wanted to follow him, but Eisheth was already moving to the door.

"I must step out too," she said. "Enjoy the champagne."

The people from the agency—I assumed Jane sent them—were very French and very colorful, like characters out of a book. Eisheth seemed to be their boss. They'd brought a bottle of something very expensive in a bucket of ice along with a handful of glasses. Pico poured, then passed them around. I took a glass but didn't drink any; it wasn't even noon.

"Tell me again what you do?" I asked.

"We're here to ensure that you have a marvelous time while you're in Paris," said Zerin. He looked to be about sixty-five and reminded me of Bill Nighy from *Love Actually*. "How do you say? A welcome wagon. If you don't mind kicking around with an old coot like me."

Picollus nodded and beamed. He was an energetic guy in his mid-forties, dark-haired, with a wide, flat face. "All work and no play would make us dull boys, eh?"

"I guess so," I said and looked at the door where Ambri had gone. I set my untouched glass on the coffee table. "But I have a lot of work to do."

"Mais, oui," Daeva said. "Paint *and* play. You must do both in a city like Paris."

Her single eye found Pico in a kind of flirty commiseration. I wondered if they were a couple.

Eisheth returned, sweeping into the room like a queen or movie star. "Come, come, let's leave Cole to prepare for the show tonight," she told them, then turned to me. "We have planned a tremendous party for you, after."

I waved my hands. "That's not necessary…"

"But you must come, mon ami!" Pico said. "You celebrate your hard work, and we celebrate *you*."

"Thanks, but I'll see how I'm feeling after the show and if Ambri is up for it."

"Oh, you must bring him as well," Daeva said. "Is he your boyfriend? Il est très, très beau, non? So very handsome."

She turned her one blue eye to Pico who made a face.

"Yeah," I said. "He's my boyfriend."

The thought made me warm all over. I'd never considered the word *boyfriend* before, but what else could Ambri be?

How about the fucking love of my life?

That thought nearly knocked me off the arm of the couch, and my face heated to see them all watching me.

"Clearly he is special to you," Eisheth said. "Your muse and your lover, both. Your paintings of him are sublime."

"Indeed," Zerin said with a smile. "Demons. I've never seen anything like them."

They all laughed and exited the suite after making me promise to at least consider an after-party. When it was quiet again, I thought about working on my next collection but couldn't concentrate.

Finally, I heard the key card in the door. I hurried from the studio to see Ambri, looking pale and nervous.

"Hey, Ambri. I'm sorry."

"For what?" he asked dully. "What could you possibly have to be sorry for?"

"It seems like Paris is too much for you," I said. "It was selfish of me to put you through that."

I wrapped my arms around him, but it was like hugging a statue—one that didn't hug back. I let him go. He was staring at me as if I were an alien life form.

"How are you so good to me?" he asked. "*Why* are you so good to me?"

I swallowed hard. "Well…there's a reason for that." My heart was pounding, sending a rush of blood to my ears. I rubbed the back of my head suddenly feeling raw and scared shitless. But also ridiculously fucking happy. Happier than I'd ever been and probably ever would be.

I heaved a breath. "Ambri, I—"

His hand shot up and he took a step away. "Don't say it."

"Sorry?"

"Don't say what you're going to say."

I smiled. "How do you know what I'm going to say?"

"Because every beautiful thought that crosses your heart emerges on your face before you speak it, and I can't." Ambri moved farther away. "I can't and I…I don't deserve it. I don't deserve you."

"Woah, woah, woah." I grabbed his arm and pulled him back. "Hey. It's okay," I said gently. "I get it. It's fucked up that we're here, and we should leave. Tonight. Forget the show—"

"*No,*" he said, practically shouting. Then calmer, "No, you must have your show. Don't mind me. I'm out of sorts, but it's nothing I can't handle." He raised his eyes to mine and the blue-green was like a stormy sea. "I *will* handle it. I have to."

"Are you sure? Because I can skip it," I said. "Jane and everybody can do the show without me."

"This is everything you've dreamt of, Cole," Ambri said. "Your art, your vision…sharing your incredible talent with the world so they see you for who you are. *That* is what is important."

I shook my head. "I used to think so too. And I love it, don't get me wrong. I'm so grateful for every moment, but Ambri, don't you see? Without you—"

He shook his head almost violently and started for the door. "The show is at eight. We must have dinner reservations. I will go speak with the concierge and have him find a place that's suitable."

"Ambri, wait."

But he was already gone, leaving me to stare after him in an empty suite.

twenty-six

Ambri

I can't do this. I can't bloody fucking do this.
I take the elevator down, tugging the shirt collar that is choking me. In the lobby, instead of finding the concierge, I head outside for some air because I'm suffocating on my own carelessness.

The courtyard is sunlit, filled with wrought-iron furniture, greenery, and a bubbling fountain. I sink onto a bench and rest my elbows on my knees, hold my head in my hands.

Footsteps approach.

Cole doesn't know—doesn't suspect—because he's surrounded by strangers every day, but I can smell my own kind. They surround me, and I raise my head, rage burning through me that these creatures are here to ruin the man I love…and me for loving him.

All three are smiling triumphantly at me. Rohan is the tallest. Jeanne and Armand stand arm-in-arm.

"Bonjour, Ambri." Armand cocks his head. "What, no kiss?"

Jeanne laughs and presses her face into his arm.

Rohan sits in a cushioned chair and lights a cigar. "Ambrosius, my boy. We had no idea you were one of us. Whatever became of you?"

"I died, obviously." I stand and roughly push past Armand. "I died young and beautiful and managed to keep both my eyes."

Jeanne's face twists in outrage. "It could've happened to anyone!"

I laugh, pretending as if this is all perfectly okay. As if I'm in complete control, when on the inside a black hole has opened in me, and it's sucking the light out of the world. I'm helpless and on the precipice of being hauled back to hell at any moment. My only hope—and it is a flicker of flame in a gale-force wind—is to somehow drive them away.

"I know why you're here," I say. "And frankly, it upsets me greatly."

"You did seem quite taken aback in the suite," Rohan says. "Terrified, even."

"Yes, terrified. Terrified that you three bumblers will ruin all of my hard work."

"Bumblers?" Jeanne screeches with none of the calculating calmness she used to possess. She's no longer the mastermind behind the Affair but a nervous mess—a result, I suppose, of having lived the rest of her short life in disgrace and desperation.

Which gives me an idea. A last, desperate idea to be rid of them.

"You're fools, all of you, and I don't need—or want—your help."

Armand's face grows red. "Watch your tongue, Ambri."

"Am I wrong?" I say, leisurely pacing the courtyard, hands clasped behind my back. "I've read your histories. Jeanne, you escaped from prison by disguising yourself as a boy, only to die in the most undignified manner. What was it? Lose your eye jumping out of a hotel window to escape debt collectors?"

She spits and curses, but I ignore her and turn to Rohan.

"And you. We duped you out of nearly two million livres and had you arrested."

He waves a hand. "Water under the bridge."

"You may have been acquitted, but no one at court liked you much," I continue. "Especially Antoinette. The king got sick of you and banished you anyway."

"Indeed," Rohan says, as if the matter bored him entirely. "I lived out my life in absolute luxury, and when Ashtaroth came for me, he promised I would continue to do so." He shot me a sly smile. "Like you, Ambrosius, I like to indulge in the finer things."

This isn't working.

But of course, it isn't. They hold every card and I have none.

For Cole...

I turn my eyes to Armand. There's not one speck of feeling left in me for him except disgust. Looking at him now, it's incredible that I ever found this oaf worthy of trading my soul. Not when such a man as Cole exists.

My eyes fall shut at the agony in my heart, but I'll give them none of it.

"And you," I say. "The great counterfeiter, Armand de Villette. Forged even the queen's hand and yet died penniless and alone—unknown—wandering the Italian countryside like a vagrant."

He snarls and pushes up on me. "You ruined me! It was your fault. *You* should've been exiled."

I shove him back. "I evaded capture because I'm more clever than all of you. Oh, but I did find our sweet little Nicole." I glance around the courtyard. "Is she coming too?"

"Now, now, Ambrosius, let's not be rude," Rohan says, puffing his cigar. "Exploiting our human demises for personal amusement is impolite."

"That's right," Jeanne says. "But do you know what we'd find if we looked *you* up, Ambri? Rien." She made a cutting motion with her hand. *"Nothing."*

Armand regains his composure and smiles like a snake. "So very true. There is no mention of sweet Ambri in the history books or…anywhere, actually. Why, I remember you once told me you weren't certain of your own birth date."

He and Jeanne dissolve into mocking laughter while Rohan looks amused.

"We may have made mistakes in life, but in death we are powerful," the former cardinal says. "We must set aside our differences if we're to ensure victory over the boy."

My throat is dry, and I cross my arms. "Well, then, what's the plan?"

"The usual," Rohan says.

"I will ruin his sleep," Jeanne says, "keeping him up at night, worrying about the pressure of all this attention. How the anticipation is too much, and the critics will call him a fraud." She smiles gleefully. "How it will all come crashing down any minute and he'll be the laughingstock."

"I'll provide our boy with pills to help him sleep and then more pills to keep him awake and plenty of alcohol in between," Armand says, looking extremely pleased with himself.

"I have a special talent for illusion," Rohan says. "Cole's 'exhaustion' will have him seeing things. Unpleasant things that will induce paranoia and erode his sense of what is real. And once you, Ambrosius, break his heart, well, that's when the real fun begins."

I feel ill. My very soul is curdling at their plan. One that I set in motion.

"Yes, we're going to have fun," Jeanne says. "We ruined that silly queen; surely we can help you ruin him too."

"He knows he doesn't have a choice," Armand tells them, inspecting me through narrowed eyes. "Your human history is lost, Ambri, but we know what happened to Ashtaroth. Our maker. Our *father*. We know you had a hand in his downfall. They whisper that you're a traitor."

"Ambrosius knows what torture awaits him if that proves to be true," Rohan says, rising from his chair. "He laid wonderful groundwork. I think this will be quite a simple victory."

The three of them move to leave, but Armand pauses to lean in to me.

"You want to know what I think, Ambri? I think you're still a traitor. I think your little act with Cole Matheson isn't much of an act at all." He sniffs in disdain and sneers. "You always were so bloody needy."

They all break into tittering laughter and leave the courtyard, trailing their stench behind them like a foul perfume. The moment I'm alone, I sink onto the bench and hold my head. It feels as if there's a fire inside my skull.

"What have I done?" I murmur. "God forgive me, what have I done?"

twenty-seven

Cole
Rome

Madrid went by in a blur. By the time we hit Italy, a cold dread had settled into me that something was terribly wrong. Ambri was acting weird and growing more distant with every passing day. We hardly spoke and when we did, he was curt and distracted. It kept me up at night, wondering and worrying, on top of the mounting stress of the tour.

Any minute now, some critic was going to break from the pack and write that I was a fraud, drawing mythical creatures instead of something serious. No one did, but that didn't stop me from tossing and turning. My days were crammed with interviews and media events, when all I really wanted was a moment to talk with Ambri and figure out what the hell was going on. Or to just curl up in bed with him and sleep, secure in his arms.

But he didn't lie with me in the bed anymore.

Am I losing him?

The thought made me sick to my stomach, and I channeled that fear into my paintings. Every morning, I got out of bed at the crack of dawn—whether I'd slept or not—and painted as if possessed, working off the sketches of Ambri I'd done in London.

Back then, I was never far from my sketchbook. I caught him in moments of pure beauty—when he looked the most human. Most like himself. I didn't know it then, but my new collection would be about transformation. Instead of painting him as a demon, I painted him as a human with the demon form hovering over his shoulder. Or lurking in the shadows. Or merging with him like a photo's double image.

I could never capture him the way I wanted, but I tried. I fucking tried, infusing every painting with as much hope as I could. The last painting in the collection would be as I saw him when I'd been sick. No demon, just Ambri as he sat in the windowsill in a white dress shirt that was open at the collar, his hair messed. His expression was heavy with worry, but his hope had shone through, as bright as the sunlight that bathed him in gold.

It was the most beautiful thing I'd ever seen, because that's when I knew I loved him and that I would always love him.

But as the tour through Europe progressed, the paintings began to reveal my fear. The human version of Ambri was like a portrait—straightforward and clean. The demon form haunting him was like a different painting on the same canvas. They became horrifying monsters that reached for him, their wings like shadows that threatened to swallow him up.

I used a wide variety of techniques and styles—whatever the painting told me it needed. I took a pallet knife and slashed brushstrokes onto the canvas, leaving waves of thick black paint. Or I'd sgrafitto a swath of color, scraping a fork, a pin, or my own fingernails through the paint to evoke desperation.

Pain.

Terror.

The fear that Ambri's dark world was taking him back.

The afternoon of the gallery show, I emerged from the studio, wiping paint off my hands to find Ambri sitting on the couch in our suite at the St. Regis Roma. He was dressed as impeccably as ever in a black suit.

"Going out?" I asked, trying to keep my tone light.

"Hmm? No. I…no."

I stood awkwardly next to the couch. "Well, I was thinking of getting lunch. Something light before the show tonight."

"Whatever you want, Cole."

I stared at the ceiling for a moment, willing back a wave of complicated emotions.

Don't give up on him, Liebling!

I didn't know where the hopeful voice came from, but I wanted desperately to believe I only had to obey, and everything would be okay again.

"Hey," I said brightly, kneeling on the floor in front of him. I rested my hands on his thighs. "Let's get out of this hotel, get some gelato, and look at some art that isn't fucking mine and just…be together." I slid my hands up higher. "Unless…you'd rather stay here and *be together* right now. Right here on this couch."

Ambri inhaled sharply through his nose, and I took that as an encouraging sign. But when I raised my eyes, he was staring over my shoulder, looking annoyed.

I shot to my feet, my face hot. "Oh, I'm sorry, am I *boring* you?"

"Yes," he said and dismissed my stricken expression. "I mean, no. Not you. I don't know." He got up with an irritated groan and went to the window, his back to me. "The entire world bores me, Cole," he said. "I made this tour when I was a child in exile from my home and then a thousand times after that."

"Okay," I said slowly. "So maybe coming with me was a mistake. Maybe it's too much for you."

"Maybe," he said coldly. "Or maybe after nearly three hundred years, it's fair to say humanity doesn't impress me anymore. I grow tired of it."

I clenched my jaw. "I see."

Ambri cleared his throat and slowly turned to face me, as if it were effort. He smiled tightly and shrugged. "What can I say? Like the food I can no longer taste, it's losing its flavor."

His words stabbed me in the chest. I crossed my arms to hold it all in. "Sure. Okay. Well, I don't know what the fuck I'm supposed to do with that information, so I'm going to go take a shower, then take a walk and…eat gelato."

I strode back to the bedroom.

And Ambri, that asshole, didn't call after me or follow me and throw me onto the bed and fuck me until all my doubts were erased and we were happy again.

After the gallery show, there was a large dinner at the hotel restaurant with Jane, Austin Wong, and the horde of publicists and stylists that seemed to follow me around. Eisheth had left us in Paris, but Daeva, Pico, and Zerin had joined the tour. They were a nice distraction from my fears about Ambri and kept me company when he vanished for hours at a time to who-knew-where.

To resume his extracurricular activities?

That night, the dinner was loud, and the wine and champagne flowed like water. I sat at the head of the table next to Jane. Ambri was at the other end, as far from me as possible while still being in the same room. I tossed back glass after glass of champagne. Someone—Zerin, I think—kept it full. I was drinking more than usual, I noticed, but it was either that or examine the gulf that had opened between Ambri and me, and that was too fucking terrifying. So I drank instead.

An instinct of self-preservation whispered that I was on a train that was speeding up, and if I wasn't careful, it was going to go off the rails.

But with Ambri's distance, the sleepless nights, and the nonstop tour, the old loneliness was coming back. I sat at the head of a table full of people who were there for me and yet I didn't know any of them.

I glanced around, my eyes tired and raw. The booze made things blurry, as if I were underwater. The whole night was a wavering mirage. On one side of the table, two women were whispering and laughing at me when I looked their way. On the other side, two critics were in a serious conversation. They both glanced at me grimly and shook their heads.

This is it. It's all going to come crumbling down and me and Ambri with it.

"Cole, my friend, you look a bit worn out," Pico said from my left. "Not sleeping well?"

"Not really," I muttered. At the other end of the table, Ambri was speaking with a handsome young guy, their heads close together.

"I have a little something to help with that, if you'd like," Pico said. "A little sleep helper. Just say the word."

"Thanks. Maybe I'll take you up on that."

Jane leaned in to me. She was glowing with the success of the shows on the tour and half tipsy herself. "Cole, you need to prepare yourself. If this tour continues like it has, that appraiser's original auction estimate is going to be blown out of the water."

I nodded absently.

She bent and kissed me on the cheek. "I'm going to retire, but you stay and enjoy yourself with your new friends."

"*My* new friends? Aren't they from the agency?"

Jane answered but I didn't hear her. I couldn't hear anything over the rush of blood in my head. Ambri had put his lips close to the guy's cheek and whispered something in his ear.

The guy nodded and smiled, and the two of them got up and left.

My heart cracked right down the middle. I was pretty sure the entire room heard it.

Fuck this.

I got to my feet, knocking over my chair. I was drunker than I wanted to be. Someone called after me to stay—Pico, maybe, but I ignored him. I made it to the elevators just as they shut. I jabbed the button as if I were trying to murder it and grabbed the next car. On our floor, I stormed into the suite. Ambri was crossing the living area.

I slammed the door shut and glanced around. "Where is he?"

"Where is who?" Ambri peered at me and grimaced. "Christ, you look like shite."

"Of course, I do," I snapped. "You've been acting like a complete stranger for days and then tonight… Tonight I have to follow you up here like a pathetic asshole after you leave with some other guy."

"I didn't leave with…" Ambri shook his head, his mouth hard. "Rohan, that bastard."

"Why?" My voice cracked. "Why are you trying to break us?"

"I don't know what you mean. I told you, I'm growing bored—"

"Of being with me?" Tears flooded my raw, aching eyes. "If that's true, then just say it and put me out of my fucking misery."

Ambri's jaw worked but no sound came out. Finally, he let out a frustrated cry and paced a circle, tearing his tie off. *"Fucking goddamn bloody fucking hell…"*

He stopped abruptly when he saw the painting on the easel in the middle of the suite. It was turned away from us and covered with a sheet.

Slowly, he raised a pointed finger. "What is that?"

"It's your portrait," I said. "The one you won't look at? I had it shipped from London. It must've arrived while we were out."

"Why is it here?"

I went to the coffee table beside the easel and picked up a manila envelope and thrust it in Ambri's hand. "Because tomorrow is your birthday."

He stared down at the envelope, then up at me. "How...how can you know that?"

"It's all in there. I asked Casziel to use his connections through the NYU history department. He connected me with a London-based historian. I knew there had to be a record of your birth and I was right. June 3, 1762." I swallowed hard. "You're not erased, Ambri. Not anymore."

Ambri stared at me and clutched the envelope in a fist.

"Why?" he asked brokenly. "Why are you doing this to me? Why are you still painting me?"

"Because," I said, "I'm scared that's all I'm going to have left of you."

"No. I'm not worth it. I'm not worth anything. Paint someone else," he said, and I heard his real meaning.

Love someone else.

I shook my head. "I don't want to *paint* anyone else. I don't want anyone else ever again. Ambri..." I inhaled raggedly. "I love you."

His face crumpled as if I'd struck him, and he broke down to a whisper. "No. You don't... You can't."

I moved in front of him, trying to force him to look at me. Because I wasn't going to let him go without a fight. "I do. I love you and I think you love me."

Ambri shook his head vigorously. "No. *No.* This entire endeavor was a huge mistake."

"You're lying again—"

"Frequently, yes. But not about this. I don't love you and no one can love me. I'm a demon. We don't love. *That's the whole point.*"

"Well, sorry to break it to you, but that's bullshit. I love you—"

"Stop saying that," he thundered. "You're drunk and high on success and it's all going to your head. You're full of fanciful ideas and none of them can come true. *Do you hear me?* None of them can come true."

I refused to let his words sink in. They were born of his fear, and the abuse he suffered as a child was still with him, working its terrible evil on him. Making him think he wasn't worthy.

"Do you know the craziest thing about getting everything I ever wanted?" I asked, my hand slipping over his cheek to cup his jaw. "It doesn't mean shit if I don't have you."

His eyes fell shut, and his jaw clenched under my fingers.

"I love you, Ambri. You don't have to say it back. You just have to believe it."

twenty-eight

Ambri

Cole's words slam into me and then settle warmly in my chest. My heart. I nearly break. I nearly confess that I'm madly in love with him too, then remember Eisheth's words.
We're watching you…
Cole waits, hope and love shining bright in his dark eyes. Then his phone buzzes from his suit pocket. He's so fucking handsome in a suit. And in paint-splattered sweats. And in nothing at all. And I want all of it. I want his every day to be my every day. A life together…and it can never be.
"Say something," he whispers, his hand slipping away from my cheek, leaving my skin cold.
But I can't. Anything I say will reveal my betrayal to the dark cause. I'll be punished, and Cole will be surrounded by the Vices. He was at the bridge once. He can be driven there again.
His phone buzzes again and this time he looks at it. "Everyone's going to a club. *Notorious.* An after-party."
I inhale and tilt my chin, striving to make my face as impassive as I possibly can, to keep what I feel for him out of my eyes. But still, I say nothing. I can't tell him to go, to throw himself at the Vices, and I can't tell him to stay and bind him tighter to me. I don't know what to

do or what to say that will save us both from this fucking mess I got us into. The danger I put him in.

My silence punches him right in the heart. He presses his lips in a thin line and nods.

"That's it?" he asks. "We had all those moments together and spent all those nights and we…we felt what we felt, but it was all bullshit. Is that what you're telling me? Or *not* telling me?"

I'm in love with you, Cole.

It's the only thing I want to say and the only thing I can't.

"Okay, so I'm going to go because I can't be in this room with you right now," he says, his voice breaking. "Have a good night."

The door shuts behind him, and the silence in the hotel room is deafening. The envelope is still in my hand, the portrait still in front of me. I pull out the documentation. There are photocopies of old records from a midwife. Civil archives of a male birth at Hever. And there is my name in black and white: Ambrosius Edward Meade-Finch, born to Timothy and Katherine on the morning of June 3, 1762.

Pain grips my heart, and slowly, I force myself to stand in front of the portrait. With shaking fingers, I remove the tarp. I behold Cole's artistry for all of three seconds and then burst into tears.

"Ah, gods…"

The portrait is everything I wanted and more than I ever dreamt possible.

Cole has rendered me in the style of Elizabeth Le Brun, the master portraitist who was famed for her paintings of Marie Antoinette. The style is replicated so exactly, it could have been from Le Brun's own hand.

There is my bookshelf of old, rare books on one side and a window on the other, with light slanting over me. Cole's embellished my red suit so that it has gold embroidery and gold buttons. My pants are black satin with a high sheen, and I wear a white wig befitting the era. There's a mischievous glint in my eye. The barest hint of a Mona Lisa smile.

And there is no shame in my expression. No hint of disgrace. Or exile. Or abandonment.

I look dignified.

I fall to my knees, and for long moments, I'm unable to do anything but weep. I weep for Cole. For me. For what was done to me. For what I did to myself. I sob until I'm turned inside out and there's nothing left.

Mein Schatz, you know what you must do.
My head snaps up, anger burning through my tears.
"*Mein Schatz, mein Schatz,*" I snap, mocking. "What does that mean? Who's there?"
But there's nothing except the truth that I don't deserve Cole. And in the same instant that I admit my love for him, there comes the certainty that I have to let him go.

The club *Notorious* is packed with writhing bodies who bounce to a DJ's thrumming music. Lights crisscross here and there in different colors. Armand and the other Vices are here; I see them at the bar, laughing in triumph because Cole is with them. He does a shot of some liquor, then pushes past them to join the dancers. The pain and anguish on his face is as clear as if he'd painted it on.

I hide in the crowd, keeping low as I approach Cole, making sure the Vices don't see me. I'll try to bury my confession under the noise of the music and the people, though I know failure is certain.

I grip Cole's arm and drag him to the back of the club before he registers it's me.

"Ambri," he says as I press him against the wall.

My heart cracks because he's so happy to see me. Because he's drunk and thinks I'm here to be with him and tell him that I love him as much as he loves me.

Because I do, more than I've ever loved anything.

"You are the most beautiful man here," he says, shouting over the noise of the club. "I'm so glad you came."

His arms go around me; he wants to kiss me, but I turn my head and press my lips to his ear.

"Run, Cole," I whisper tremulously. "Run far away from here. Go to New York. Go to Lucy and Cas."

"What? I can hardly hear you."

I want to cry. I grip his shoulders, willing him to listen and understand.

"Remember what I told you about fighting back? You're in danger. Leave those terrible people. Don't swallow their pills or their lies. Don't listen to anything they say. They're not your friends. They're—"

In the space of a blink, a dozen hands made of shadow—servitors of Asmodai—grip my arms and haul me away. They drag me through the dancing people; I pass through them like a cold wind—a ghost. Cole grows distant, like a telescope closing down, and then I'm Crossing Over to the Other Side.

There's a short moment of disorientation. When I regain my bearings, I'm in my demon form, naked, sprawled face down on the cold stone of Asmodai's realm, pinned there by servitors. The archduke gazes down on me with his three heads, the bull, the ram, and the human.

"Traitor," he says, his voice thundering through my head. "I am finished with you. Your pain begins now."

Heavy, crunching footsteps shake the foundation of the dungeon, and from my prone position—my cheek pressed flat to the stone—I see the golem. An ancient earth spirit that was imprisoned in a body of stone by demons eons ago. So long ago they're no longer fully conscious, but mindless servants. This one is nearly three meters high and stomps toward me, its stony feet making the ground shake. Its eyes are tiny yellow lights set in its rocky face. The heavy pressure of its foot on my lower back keeps me pinned to the ground, and the servitors flee. Fear courses in my veins instead of blood. My breath is like a panting dog, my pulse too rapid to count each beat.

"We'll start simply," Asmodai says. "Rip his wings off, one at a time. When they grow back, rip them off again. A decade or so to start, then we'll move on to something truly painful." His bull head nods at the golem. "Begin."

I feel more than see the creature bend over me, and then its stony hands grip my right wing.

"No. *No. NO!*"

There is a horrifying crunch of bone. Agony pierces my shoulder, straight through my chest and down my spine. My mouth opens in a silent scream. My wing is wrenched right and then left. It's stubborn, imbedded in muscle. The golem keeps at it. Bones splinter, feathers flutter, and black blood gushes over my back.

My wing comes free.

I suck in air, and my scream echoes through hell. I scream as agony floods me, and I know nothing else.

I scream until my throat is scraped raw, my black eyes wide and staring. My right side is a throbbing pain of broken bones and the fire of torn flesh. Before the shock fades, the golem takes hold of my *left* wing and begins to pull...

twenty-nine

Cole

I blinked and looked around, confused. Ambri had had me up against the wall, his hands gripping my shoulders, saying something about New York. And then, suddenly, he was gone as if I'd imagined him.

I pushed myself off the wall and staggered into the throng of dancers, searching for him. The club was a blur of strobe lights and strangers' faces. I cursed myself for being too drunk, for letting myself get out of control, and for drowning my pain instead of facing it.

I made it to the bar and asked the others if they'd seen Ambri.

"Can't say that I have," Pico said, smiling. "Have a seat, Cole. We're just about to line up another round of shots."

"Hell no, I've had enough," I said. "I'm going back to the hotel. Maybe he went there."

They tried to get me to stay, but I ignored them and headed out to hail a cab. Back at the suite, I called Ambri's name but there was no answer. The paperwork Casziel helped me find was scattered all over the floor in front of the portrait.

I was too fucking drunk to do anything but faceplant onto the bed and try to sleep it off. I felt like I hadn't slept more than a handful of hours in weeks. I closed my eyes, and as the darkness started to take me down, a horrifying dread gnawed at my guts that the darkness had come for Ambri too.

I woke up with light slicing across my eyes, making my headache throb harder. I hurried to the living room and found Zerin snoring on the couch with Daeva's head on his shoulder, sleeping off their own drunken benders.

Pico was at the window looking distraught.

"What are you doing here?" I asked. "How did you get in?"

Zerin and Daeva came awake immediately, blinking and rubbing their eyes in an exaggerated manner. Like bad actors in a play.

Pico turned, somber. "We got a little carried away last night, Cole. Apologies, but…" He held up a sheet of hotel stationary. "I believe this is for you. A letter from Ambri."

I stormed across the suite and snatched it out of his hand. "What are you doing with it?"

"I found it here by the window, and I didn't know what it was," Pico said. "But…that's his handwriting, isn't it?"

I glanced at the letter and nodded. It was Ambri's elegant script. Pico went to stand near Zerin and Daeva on the couch, all three solemn and quiet, but they fell away as I read. The entire suite, all of Rome, the entire fucking world burned away as I read Ambri's letter.

ST. REGIS
ROME

Dearest Cole,

It should come as no surprise that our little adventure has come to an end. My portrait has been painted ~ bravo! It's exactly as I hoped, but it's served to remind me of an important fact: I'm no longer made of pathetic human frailty. I'm powerful now, and I had forgotten. Your portrait has reminded me of why I chose this existence in the first place.

It's been fun, but one human (you) is never going to be enough to satisfy me. I have the entirety of time in which to play in their world. And there are so many, waiting for me to entice, to touch, to lick and fuck, and I've spent far too much time giving that to you.

Fare thee well, Cole. Don't fret! We'll always have Paris.

*Regards,
Ambri*

The paper fell from my trembling fingers to seesaw to the floor. I stared at the people in my suite, not seeing them.

"Something's wrong. This is all wrong."

Daeva leaned forward. "Bad news, darling?"

Zerin moved to stand beside me. "Love is fickle. Comes and goes. Hard to tell what is real anymore." He offered a glass of some kind of liquor. "This will help take the sting out."

I took it and stared into the glass. I could dive in and drown in it. It's what I'd been doing. What else was going to make this raging agony in my heart go away?

"Everyone get out."

They stood for a moment, exchanging uncertain glances.

"Get out!"

"Yes, perhaps we should leave Cole alone with his thoughts," Pico said.

They scurried for the door.

"We'll be close if you need us," Daeva added. "Just call and we'll come running."

When the suite was quiet, I sucked in a breath. Then another, but the pain in my chest wouldn't subside. A knife felt lodged there, heavy and stabbing with every movement.

I tossed back the shot of liquor, grabbed the bottle off the coffee table, and went to the makeshift art studio.

Vaughn Ritter once told me—a lifetime ago—to pour my pain into my work. I painted until my hand cramped and my eyes ached. I painted while the bottle grew lighter and lighter. The hours passed and I was no closer to finding the end of the hurt.

I knew I never would.

London

The tour ended a week ago with no sign of Ambri.

Because I'm a fucking idiot, I thought, standing in the mess that was my bedroom/studio in his flat.

I'd chosen to forget that he was a demon. I erased his true nature because it was inconvenient to my grand plan to end my loneliness. Because with him, I had so much more than that. There was love. True love.

I thought I had it.

I thought it was real.

And I was really fucking wrong.

"Fuck everything."

I tossed down my paint brush and lifted the bottle of whiskey.

Against all odds, the collection was nearly done. I painted and drank, and when I couldn't go on another minute, Pico was there to fulfil my pharmaceutical needs for a pick-me-up.

I knew I was walking on a razor's edge, but what did I care?

Not much.

That's a lie too.

I cared too fucking much. I'd let down the barriers around my heart and now it was a shredded heap. So I flung the torn bits of it against the canvases like blood, letting the monster version that stalked Ambri become more and more monstrous. More dangerous. The dark had swallowed him, and it was swallowing me too.

I studied the current painting. When it was finished, there'd be only one left. The most important one.

You can't paint Ambri at the windowsill while drunk or high. You know that, right?

I took a swig of booze. Maybe not, but what did it matter? How I'd seen him then was a lie.

That night, I slumped into my empty bed and tried to sleep but without much hope. My bed had become a battleground where I wrestled with the poisonous thoughts in my own head that kept me tossing and turning.

"Fuck this," I muttered and reached for Pico's bottle of "sleep helpers." I didn't like taking them—I had no idea what they actually were—but a guy can only go so long with zero sleep.

I popped two and washed them down with the water I kept on the nightstand for my post-bender ibuprofen. I sank into the pillow. Time warped and became slippery; I woke up after what felt like an hour's worth of actual sleep.

There was someone in my room.

I sat up slowly and peered at the silhouette of shadow. A tall man, sleek and slender.

"Ambri?"

He stepped into the moonlight, extraordinary in black. The light chiseled the contours of his face and glinted in the gold of his hair, turning it silver.

He didn't move or speak. I threw off the covers and approached.

"Are you…back?"

He smiled that maddening, sardonic curl of his lips I loved so much and held out a hand to me. I took it and he hauled me to him, then crushed his mouth to mine.

I sagged against him with my arms wrapped around him. He kissed me hard and deep, and my relief that he was back immediately curdled like sour milk. *He* tasted sour. And cold. His arms around me were all wrong. He felt all wrong.

I tried to pull back, but he held me tight, his mouth sealed over mine. His eyes were black-on-black but dead with no spark of life. His tongue in my mouth grew ticklish. Tiny legs, fluttering wings…

I tried to scream past the beetles filling my mouth and sliding down my throat. Then Ambri's arms around me dissolved—*he* dissolved into the swarm that poured into me. I fell to my knees, repulsed, choking and gagging, my body heaving against the invasion. Dimly, I was aware of other bodies in the room, shadowy figures with wings standing over me in silent, malevolent mirth.

Tears streamed down my face and starbursts danced in front of my eyes from lack of oxygen. My insides were crawling, swelling, stretching to contain the swarm. I staggered to my feet and tried to run. To escape. But there was nowhere to go. I bent in half, pain wracking me. Just when I thought I'd pass out, the swarm spewed from my open, gagging mouth.

I retched, my insides clenching, and when the last beetle was gone, I screamed…

…I came awake on the floor of my room with my scream dying in my throat and my phone ringing in the living room.

"Jesus Christ…"

Late morning light streamed in through the window. It was daytime. No beetles, no shadowy figures… It was only a nightmare.

Are you sure about that?

I crawled to my nightstand and grabbed the glass of water to wash the sour taste out of my mouth.

My phone rang again.

I was tempted to let it go, but I suddenly needed a connection to the outside world. One that wasn't paint and demons and missing Ambri until I could hardly breathe and then creating nightmares out of all of it.

I staggered to the living room. My phone had gone silent and then starting ringing again as I approached.

Lucy.

She'd been calling for a week, and I'd broken my promise to not shut her out. I hadn't wanted her to hear me like this but beneath the anger and the pain and the booze, there was a part of me that needed her to hear me *exactly* like this.

I sat on the couch and tried to sound more sober than I felt. "Hey, Luce."

"*Hey*, Cole," she said angrily. "Jesus Christ, I've been calling for ages. I know you're a big celebrity now, but I thought I might warrant at least a text that lets me know you're still alive."

"Sorry."

"Well...what's happening? Are you okay? What's wrong?"

"Ha. How much time have you got?"

"For you? Forever," she said warily. "But you sound drunk and it's not even noon there."

I nearly told her to piss off, that I wasn't in the mood for a lecture. But her sweet voice was the lifeline I needed. The last time I'd tried to tough shit out on my own, I'd ended up staring into the Thames from Blackfriars Bridge.

"Fuck, Luce," I said. "It's all become a huge mess and I'm a fucking idiot."

She sighed with relief that I was talking. "Tell me everything."

So I did. I explained everything that had happened with Ambri, and his letter, and the strange moment at the club.

Lucy made a frustrated sound. "Cole...why didn't you call me sooner? Have you forgotten I've been there too?"

"Well...no. Maybe." I rubbed my eyes. "I can't think. I can't sleep. I just drink and paint and feel sorry for myself. Because it's over. Luce...I've never loved anyone like I love him, and now it's over."

"Cole, listen to me," Lucy said, and I'd never heard her sound more serious. "Nothing is over. You can't believe him. Not one word of that letter was true."

"It's his handwriting. He wrote it. He put the fucking pen to the paper, and he put that shit down for me to read—"

"I know but you have to believe me. Cas tried the same crap on me. To protect me. Ambri is trying to protect you. That's all this is. I'd bet my life on it."

"Protect me from what?"

"I don't know. For me, it was another demon. Not just thoughts in my head, but a flesh and bone monster."

Instantly, Picollus, Daeva, Zerin, and that woman, Eisheth, popped into my head.

"Wait, wait..." I said, trying to think through the murk of whiskey and insomnia. "There're these people—but no, Ambri would've known if they were demons. He would've warned me or kept me away, and he didn't say a word."

"Maybe he couldn't," Lucy said quietly.

And just like that, a fragment from the club in Rome pushed through my drunken recollection. Ambri's last words to me.

...not your friends...

"He did," I breathed. "Oh, fuck, he tried to warn me...and I didn't listen. I was drunk and caught up in the tour and my success and my happiness with him. Dammit, Luce. I created a little bubble of bullshit and tried to stay in it as long as possible..."

"Of course, you did," Lucy said. "Because you love him."

A cold stone of dread settled into my gut. "Wait...if the letter is a lie, then where is he?" My voice became a strangled whisper. "Oh Christ, Lucy, where is he? What are they doing to him?"

"Cole, stay calm. You don't know he's in trouble," Lucy said, though she didn't sound all that sure either. "He's smart. He might've fooled them or...I don't know. But you need to keep yourself safe."

I shook my head, hardly listening. "They dragged him away. They took him back and...and oh fuck me, he's hurting right now. They're hurting him because of me."

"No," Lucy said. "Because of *them*. Because of who they are and what he is. But I believe there's still hope, and you should too."

I clutched my chest, making a fist out of my shirt. "Hope," I spat. "I've done nothing but love him for months. And I thought...it *felt* like he loved me too. What's it going to take?"

"I don't know, but they're *demons*. Ambri put himself in their world. Getting out is not going to be easy. It wasn't for Cas and me. It was brutal, but maybe that's how it's supposed to go."

"Oh, is it?" I snapped. "You just casually toss out that it's *supposed* to be—"

"There was nothing *casual* about watching the man I love die in my arms," she snapped back with a fierceness that I didn't remember hearing in her. Not before Cas came into her life.

"I'm sorry. I'm so sorry, Lucy. I'm being an asshole because I'm scared for him. I'm fucking *terrified* and there's nothing I can do."

"I know you are, honey. But the best thing you can do for him is to ignore the worst thoughts and fears. That's *them*. And that's exactly what they want."

"It's not just thoughts," I said. "They're real people and I never knew. Never suspected."

"How could you when they're keeping you drunk and filling your head with God-knows-what? That's what they do. If it were easy to ignore them, more people would. But it has to stop, Cole. Do you hear me? Come here if you have to but get away from them. Immediately."

"And then what?" I asked helplessly. "What happens to Ambri?"

"Honestly, I don't know," Lucy said. "But you have to stay in the light, Cole. That's the only chance he has to find his way back to you."

———

Days bled from one into the next.

I couldn't leave London. Running away felt wrong. What if Ambri needed me and I wasn't there? Moreover, running away from shit never got me anywhere. If he was facing something horrible, I would, too. I'd face it and fight. I tossed all the booze down the sink and cleaned up the flat and tried to stay in the light.

My sleep was still shit—the whispers in my head kept at it, but they'd changed their tune. Instead of whispering that I was an imposter, and the critics were going to wise up any day, they wracked me with doubt.

What if Lucy had it all wrong?

What if Ambri was in cahoots with the demons?

What if he meant what he said in the letter?

What if he never loved me?

He never said it, after all. I laid my heart bare to him and he didn't say a word.

You're letting the fear spoil what you know to be true, Liebling. Don't let it.

But all I knew was fear. Fear for what Ambri might be suffering, and that fear was the doorway that let those thoughts march right in.

Ambri had been right about that. The sinister whispering of demons didn't come from nothing. They built up what was already there—our own natural self-doubt, fears, worries—and gorged on them.

I had to cut them off, so I began the final painting.

I poured my pain and love into the work, trying my best to capture Ambri as I'd seen him at the windowsill in that beautiful moment. I called it *Morning Light,* and even before it was finished, I knew it was the best thing I'd ever done or would ever do.

Even as the tears fell, I smiled and set my brush down.

"I love you, Ambri. Come back to me. Please…come back to me."

But there was only the quiet, and the sun coming in through the window like a promise.

———>

Christie's auctioned off my first collection, and Jane invited me to lunch to discuss the details. I accepted and met her at La Pergola, going through the motions. The moment I saw Jane at the restaurant, I could tell she was bursting with good news.

"The tour was a smashing success, to say the least," she said over food I didn't have the appetite to eat. "If you recall, the appraiser's estimate was three million. I got the final number from Christie's today. Are you ready for this?"

"Sure."

"Your first collection sold for nearly seven million. *Seven*, Cole."

"Holy shit," I said. "That's a big number."

"It's a glorious number, but I think it's going to pale in comparison to the final sales price of your next collection. I want to sell it through Gallery Decora this time, instead of an auction house. Are you almost finished?"

"Yeah. A few more days."

"Marvelous. I cannot wait to see it. I know it will cement your name in the annals of the art world for the rest of time."

But will it bring Ambri back?

"That's great, Jane. Thanks."

Her head tilted. "Oh, Cole, darling, I'm so sorry. I've been babbling on when obviously you must've heard about Vaughn."

"No, I haven't heard anything. What happened?"

Jane pursed her lips. "He…passed away. Last week. I'm so sorry."

I sat back, my heart dropping. "H-how?"

"Drug overdose. It's unclear whether it was intentional or accidental, but they're leaning toward the former. Again, I'm so sorry."

She reached across the table to touch my hand, but I barely felt it. Her voice faded out, and my head felt stuffed with cotton. I mumbled something about not feeling well and walked back to the flat. The sun that had been bright that day hid behind a cloud, and the world was dark again.

And the flat was overrun with demons.

Pico, Daeva, and Zerin were standing in the middle of the living room, despite the fact I never gave them a key. Now that I was fucking awake and sober, it seemed obvious who they were. Shocking that I hadn't seen it before.

"Cole, my boy," Zerin said. "I hope you don't mind that we let ourselves in, but it's just been too long. We're worried about you."

"So very worried," Daeva said, slipping her hand into mine. My skin crawled, and it was everything I could do to not pull away from her touch and wipe my hands on my jeans.

Pico sidled up to me and put his arm around my shoulders, sending chills down my spine.

"Listen," he said confidentially, like we were old pals. "I know it's been hard for you since Ambri dumped you in Rome. Between you and me, he always seemed like an asshole. Full of himself, you know?"

I nodded stiffly, teeth clenched.

"But the show must go on, right?" He opened his hand to show me a bottle of white pills. "My gift to you. A little something to get you through the last push for your collection."

He held the bottle to me, and I remembered something else Ambri had told me—they couldn't hurt me unless I let them. Pico couldn't press the bottle into my hand; I had to willingly take it from him.

He was waiting, a tight smile on his face. The others, too. Watching. Their friendly expressions hiding a malevolence that seemed so obvious now.

Slowly, I took the bottle and feigned a look of gratitude. "Thanks, Pico. I appreciate it."

He beamed and the others relaxed.

"Plenty more where those came from. I'm here for you. We all are. Whatever you need." He clutched my shoulders. "We're not going to abandon you, Cole. We're going to stick close to you no matter what. Thick as thieves."

Think as thieves...

I swallowed down a sob and made a fist around the bottle. "Thanks for these, Pico," I said carefully. "I'm going to get to work. Maybe you guys could come back later?"

"Of course," Zerin said. His eyes were cold blue ice pouring into me. *"When?"*

"Soon. I'm almost done with this collection and then we can celebrate."

"A party!" Daeva clapped her hands. "One nice, long, crazy party."

"Exactly," I said. "The party to end all parties."

The three exchanged glances. They seemed to like the sound of that.

"Of course, my friend!" Pico said. "We'll leave you to it. But give a shout if you need more little pick-me-ups."

"I will."

They went out and closed the door behind them. I waited a few moments, then hurried to throw the locks. But what fucking good would that do? They could fly in windows or materialize out of thin air.

I let out a strangled cry and hurled the bottle of pills into the fireplace where it clattered against the wrought iron and brick. Then I slid down the door and cried. I cried until I felt hollow. For Vaughn. The Twins got him. Or maybe some other demon. They got him and they had Ambri. And there was not one fucking thing I could do about any of it except try to do what Lucy had said and keep to the light.

But for how long? How long was Ambri going to suffer?

I cried his name, softly, then louder, then screamed it with the voice of my soul.

thirty

Ambri

Right.
Then left.
Right.
Then left.
The right wing is torn out, then the left.
While my left wing lies in a heap of bloody bones and feathers, the golem takes its foot off my back and waits. It knows I'm not going anywhere. I'm immobilized by pain. Impaled by it, as if a spike has been driven between my shoulder blades and into the stony ground. A beetle pinned in a display.
I cannot move my arms. I tried once.
Once.
My naked, alabaster skin is covered in grime and black blood. My fingernails are ripped off, clawing the stone as they do, but they'll grow back, just like my wings. I figure it takes about twenty-four hours of human time for them to regenerate, but it's hard to know for sure. Constant, unrelenting agony makes one fuzzy on the details.
Right.
Then left.

When the last of the pain has faded and my huge, beautiful wings have regrown, the foot on my back returns, and the process begins anew. Because that's what it is to be on the Other Side.

Behold, the glory of immortality.

I always try to bite back my screams and I always fail. Sometimes, I vomit. Not every time but sometimes. I like to keep things interesting.

Right wing.

Vomit, it is. My cheek is pressed to the ground, but the black blood spews out with impressive force. Better distance than last time.

Then the left.

The second wing is torn free and my scream right along with it.

I lie panting in a pool of my own inky bile, shuddering in grinding agony. Twenty-six times down, 3,624 more to go. Give or take.

That's when I hear it.

A scream of anguish. An echo of my own.

Cole...

I close my eyes and listen. The cry doesn't come again. Very slowly, each movement bringing a crushing shard of pain, I lift my head and look through the Veil, searching quickly for Cole's *when.*

He's slumped against the door of our flat in Chelsea. He didn't leave London like I told him to. He's still there, in danger, sobbing for me.

Because he loves me.

I don't know how or why, but he does. Cole's love for me has breached centuries of my own self-doubt, shame, and even my demonic fate.

I let it in.

Lying on that filthy, blood-splattered floor in hell, I let myself feel his love for me. It's more astonishing than I ever could have imagined. Fuller and deeper and so rich. As rich as his brown eyes and his smile and the beauty of his soul that looked through the monster I'd become to see me.

"Thank you," I whisper to whoever is listening, because now I see the path to my salvation.

The only way to survive the next millennia of this torture is to tell Cole the truth. Tell him my terrible plan and how I could never go through with it. Because I love him. I love him with all that is left of me, and I always will. But I never said the words and now I have to say them. I can't let him believe he's gone through all this madness alone.

Even if he hates me, he'll know. I just need a few precious moments with him, and they'll see me through whatever is to come. Because Casziel was right; I'd die a thousand deaths for Cole Matheson.

I'll love him and let him love me.

I lay my cheek to the stone and wait for my bones to slowly knit together. For the torn flesh to slowly mend itself.

Inhale, exhale.

Time passes in Cole's *when*. He's no longer at the door. Maybe the Vices have him. My wings aren't remotely close to being healed but I can wait no longer. I inhale again and imagine strength is filling me instead of pain. It's not much, but it has to be enough; I'll have only one shot at this.

The dungeon is quiet. Asmodai is off torturing some other unfortunate soul. The golem stands somewhere behind me, doing nothing but waiting for fresh, strong wings to rip.

Piss off, pebble boy.

With an agonized cry, I hurl myself through the Veil and Cross Over.

I land with a heavy thud in my bedroom suite in Chelsea. My scream is cut off by the *woosh* of air that is pushed out of me. For long moments, I can't move but only whimper softly. I'd love to pass out from the pain, but I can't, and there's no time anyway.

"Ambri?"

Cole, calling from elsewhere in the flat. He can't see me like this. I try to take my human form, but I'm too weak.

"Ambri? Is that you?"

He's almost at the door. Mustering a desperate thrust of energy, I throw the lock with my telekinesis. The handle twitches and he bangs on the wood.

"Ambri! Let me in. *Let me in!*"

I pull myself along the floor on my elbows, grunting, biting back more screams, until I'm close to the curtains. Reaching out for them makes me retch, but there's nothing left in me. I grip the material in a fist. Shivering and whimpering at the pain that's coming, I grit my teeth and give it a hard yank.

The agony is a flash of white and then someone screams as if the world is ending.

I'm fairly certain it's me.

The curtain lies in a pile of velvet in front of me, but now I'm too drained to cover myself. It's useless anyway; Cole has busted open the door and he's running to me…

thirty-one

Cole
An hour earlier

Gallery Decora was packed. I had a feeling of déjà vu from my first gallery show. Gold light filled the space as champagne-drinking artists, gallerists, critics, and buyers meandered about, taking in the collection I named *Transformation*.

Jane popped up at my elbow now and then to keep me appraised of the sales. In less than an hour, the entire collection had sold out.

"The numbers aren't all in, but it's looking like it'll be in the realm of ten million, Cole," Jane whispered. "*Ten*. Not that I'm surprised. *Stormlight* was incredible, but this…" She gestured around us. "It's next level. You have officially arrived. You changed your style, changed methodology, experimented, yet kept what made your first collection so special. It's genius."

"Thank you, Jane."

"And that last painting of him in the window? *Morning Light?*" She dabbed her eye. "Jesus Christ, I'm emotional just thinking about it."

"You didn't sell that one, right?" I asked with sudden panic. "Tell me you didn't…"

"Of course not, darling," she said, giving my arm a squeeze. "I remembered to leave it off the ledger. I understand why you want to keep it, but it's a shame. A certain buyer—I won't name names, but let's just say he has *titles*—offered two million for it alone."

I sipped my sparkling water. "I'm sorry, Jane, but I can't part from that one."

It might be all I have left of him.

That and the "official" portrait I'd done of him. His two lives.

"I admire you, Cole," Jane said. "I don't know that I could walk away from two million so easily."

I looked around the packed gallery. I was more financially secure than I'd ever imagined. I had all the success and adoration I could handle...and I'd have walked away from all of it, if only I could have Ambri back. No amount of money or fame would ever be enough. He was priceless.

Where are you, baby?

I blinked hard and shook more hands and made more small talk. When the hour came where it wouldn't be considered rude if I bailed, I headed back to the flat.

Jerome was at his post, as usual. I mustered a small smile.

"Good evening, Jerome," I said, then asked the same question I asked every time I'd been out for a while. "Has Mr. Meade-Finch come in?"

"No, sir."

Always the same answer. I started for the elevator.

"Thanks, Jerome. Have a good night."

"Sir?"

This was new. I turned. Maybe it was my imagination, but he seemed as if he were fighting for composure.

He cleared his throat. "If you do hear from Mr. Meade-Finch, would you be so kind as to leave word here at the desk?"

I swallowed hard. "I will."

Upstairs, I took off my tux jacket and bowtie and tossed them on the couch. No sign of Pico and Friends. I eased a sigh and sat down. Now that *Transformation* was finished, a long stretch of time opened in front of me—the rest of my life. I couldn't let myself believe Ambri wouldn't be in it, but if I'd lost him forever, I had two choices: to give in and call Pico and drown in my pain, or I could live and channel it all into my art.

"I'm really fucking scared that second option isn't going to be enough," I said to Ambri's portrait. "I miss you so much."

He peered back at me, the barest hint of his sly smile on his lips.

Christ, if only I could kiss him one more time...

A thudding crash sounded from the back of the flat, shaking the beams, and my heart crashed with it. I tore off the couch and raced down the hallway. My door was open, my room empty. Another sound—Ambri's strangled cry—came from his room.

"Ambri? Ambri, is that you?"

His door was shut and as soon as I touched the handle, it locked. I shook at it, then pounded on the wood. "Ambri! Let me in. *Let me in!*"

There came another thud and an inhuman scream of terrible agony that ripped my heart to shreds.

"Ambri!"

I threw my shoulder against the door again and again until it gave. I charged in and then nearly fell to my knees in horror. Ambri was on his stomach near the window, naked and in his demonic form. His pale white skin was splotched with grime and what looked like black blood, and his back…

"Jesus Christ…"

Where his wings had been, was now splintered bone jutting from torn flesh, all of it splattered with that same black blood. He lay panting on the floor in agony with one hand clutching a fistful of curtain. Because he'd tried to cover himself.

To protect me from this.

I rushed to him and knelt beside him. "Ambri. Oh, God, baby, what did they do to you? What did they do…?"

Tears were choking my air, rage making my heart pound. But he needed me to keep my shit together. I covered the lower half of his body with the curtain and carefully took his hand—scraped and bloody. I put my head down to his, stroking his hair gently.

"Ambri? Ambri, can you hear me?"

His eyes opened—black-upon-black. His lips were stained black too, and black tears spilled down his cheeks.

"Cole," he said.

And then he smiled.

"God, Ambri. I have to fix this. I have to stop the bleeding…"

"No. No time. Cole, listen to me," he whispered, ragged from screaming.

How long had he been screaming?

"Gods, I missed your face." His eyes fell shut, more tears streaking inky trails down his cheek that was pressed to the floor. "I'm so bloody happy to see you. But I have to tell you something."

"I have to help you first."

"You can't. And there's no time—"

"He's right," said a smooth voice coming from the doorway. "He has no time."

My stomach clenched to see Eisheth, Picollus, Daeva and Zerin, all in their demonic forms. Pale skin, black eyes, and feathered or bat wings—and all emanating terror and dread like a stench. I saw their deaths in the depths of their eyes, full of fear, loneliness, desperation, and—in Eisheth's case—terrible violence.

I sprang to my feet and grabbed a poker from the fireplace. I brandished it like a baseball bat, keeping between Ambri and the demons.

"Take one step toward him and I'll fucking end you."

They froze...and then laughed.

"He's not worth it," Pico said. Black feather wings protruded from an old eighteenth-century coat. His breeches were dirty and threadbare. "Trust me, I know. He's good for a fuck and that's about it. Pretty little tart, he is." He tilted his head with a sneer. "Now he's not even that."

The others laughed again. My hands tightened around the iron.

"Now, now," Eisheth said. "There's no need for hostilities. Your protectiveness is sweet, Cole, but futile. We *will* take him back. But you don't have to stay behind, alone and missing him for the rest of your life. There is a way..."

"No," Ambri gritted out from behind me. "Don't listen to her, Cole."

"On the contrary, you should listen to me," Eisheth said. "Because I am providing the only means by which you two can remain together."

I swallowed hard. "How?"

"Give yourself up to us, Cole Matheson. Join us. Leave behind this human world of frailty and ego, where the opinions of a few fools wield power over your art. *You* will wield power over them. *You* will sink your teeth into their desire for recognition and feast on their desperation to be heard. You will remain powerful and beautiful. Serve our dark lord at Ambri's side and you will be together. Forever."

"She lies," Ambri snarled weakly. "It's all lies..."

I shook my head, my heart pounding, feeling as if I were in a dream. "I don't want to hurt anyone…"

Eisheth's smile hardened, and anger glinted in her eyes. "What about Ambri? Do you want him to hurt? Will you let him suffer? Because he will. He's only had a taste of the torture that awaits him." She held out her hand to me—now bloodless white. "Or you can come with us, and he'll be spared."

"He will?"

"Of course. Join us and he'll be free of his pain at last."

"Cole," Ambri cried softly. "Don't…"

His helpless agony trapped me in a limbo of terror and confusion.

"You cannot stand guard forever." Eisheth's tone was now deadly pleasant. "You must sleep and when you do, we'll take him back. He will suffer like none have suffered before. Only you can save him, Cole Matheson, by joining us. Or you can stay and live out the rest of your life, knowing you've consigned your one true love to an eternity of pain. The choice is yours."

The demons evaporated in a cloud of black dust that smelled of ash and death. I hurried to kneel beside Ambri, keeping the poker in hand.

"She's always had a flair for the dramatic," Ambri said. He peered up at me. "Don't even think about it."

"I don't *need* to think about it," I said. "I'm not handing you over to them. Now, come on. We have to get you off the floor."

"Must we? It's quite cozy down here. Need to dust under the bureau, however…"

"You're shivering," I said. "Let's get you on the bed and I'll start a fire."

Very carefully, I slid my arm under Ambri's chest. He grit his teeth as I pulled him off the floor. His breath came in heaving gasps, but he got to his knees, and then I helped him to his feet. At the bed, he gave another strangled cry as I helped him lie face down on the pillow, arms by his sides. I covered his lower half with the curtain, just below the ghastly wounds on his back where a few stray feathers were stuck to his skin.

Keeping the poker in hand, I turned on the gas to the fireplace and lit a fire, then stood helplessly. "What I need is in the bathroom, but I can't leave you."

"You can," Ambri said. "Eisheth is giving you time to think about her little proposal. My fate is unavoidable; they can take me any time they want. But if they could bring you Over, it would be a great victory."

"How do you know that?"

"Because that was my plan all along."

I stared, the poker nearly falling out of my hand. "What...? Wait. Hold on. I have to *do* something, or my brain is going to explode."

I raced to the bathroom to grab a towel, ran some water over it, and hurried back. Carefully, I climbed into bed next to Ambri and smoothed the damp cloth over his face, wiping away filth and tears. I looked to the ruin of his back but Jesus, where to begin?

Ambri's brows furrowed. "Leave it. I told you, you can't help me and why are you trying? Didn't you hear what I said?"

"I heard you," I said. "From the beginning I had a feeling there was more to your interest in me than a portrait."

"Perhaps, but the others were never part of my plan."

"Who are they?"

"My former lovers and/or associates," Ambri said. "Except for Eisheth, they go by different names, but they are Armand, Jeanne and Rohan."

My eyes widened. "From your lifetime?"

"Eisheth has a sick sense of humor."

"I don't understand. If they weren't part of the plan, why are they here?"

"To ensure I fulfilled it." Ambri inhaled, his eyes closing. "I'll tell you everything but sit closer. I'm going hoarse with all this shouting."

Not shouting. *Screaming*. He was still trembling, still wracked with pain.

"I don't know what to do for you," I said.

"Don't do anything. Just sit here and be with me."

I lay curled on my side facing him, our heads close together, the poker still clutched in my hand.

"I was commanded to drive a human to despair," Ambri said. "I didn't want to; it's not my forté. But I had no choice but to obey, so I chose you. I thought it would be easy—you were so close already."

"Why didn't you?"

"Because you opened your mouth and *spoke*, Cole Matheson. You showed yourself for who you are, and I knew I'd made a terrible mistake. But I didn't know how to stop what I'd started, so I bought time. I told them I was going to build you up before crashing you down. The pinnacle of success and all that rubbish. And it worked."

"So all of it...the millions of dollars and the fame and the interviews...it was all you?"

"It was all *you*. Your astonishing talent. I didn't have to do a thing. But it didn't matter anyway. I could never hurt you, Cole." Ambri smiled ruefully. "I was supposed to ruin you, but I fell in love with you instead."

My chest was full and warm as his words found me and sank in. "I've been waiting a long time for someone to say that to me, but I never knew it would feel like this."

"I should've told you so much sooner, but it scared me, how much I loved you. And I...didn't think it was possible you could love me back."

I smiled gently. "Well, I do. I love you so much, I can't see where it ends. I don't think it does."

"But...how?" he asked brokenly. "I betrayed you. I brought those demons into your world..."

"And now you're prepared to suffer for an eternity for it. Fuck that. There has to be another way. What Eishcth said—"

"No."

"What the hell else am I supposed to do?"

"You stay here and live your life."

"And what kind of life is it going to be knowing you're suffering? *Forever*? I can't give you up to them. I won't."

"You can't come with me, Cole. I forbid it."

"I hate to break it to you, Ambrosius, but you're in no position to forbid anything."

"You're just saying that because I can't move."

I laughed through the tears, and then there were only tears. "How can I say goodbye to you? I can't do it, Ambri. They're going to hurt you..."

"Likely, but you can't sacrifice your soul to pay for my misdeeds. You have to protect yourself, protect this life that you have. It's precious. Don't make the same mistake I did. Don't throw it away."

I shook my head. "I have to protect *you*. Save you, somehow..."

"You already have." Ambri smiled. Through blood and tears and pain, he smiled. "You showed me how beautiful life is. At the Eye, the museum, just being with you. The pain makes the joy even more precious," he whispered. "Live it, Cole. Live fully and that's how you will save me. Not by following me into the dark."

Love for Ambri, so profound, washed over me and through me. In the most dark and lonely nights, I'd dreamed of what it must feel like to love and be loved so completely. But my imagination—that people paid millions for a piece of—couldn't come close to creating this feeling. Because *he* was so much more than I'd imagined. The depth and beauty of Ambri was boundless…and about to be consigned to eternity in some hell. Lost forever.

"No. No, I can't." I got up off the bed and gripped the poker tighter. "I'm not letting them take you. I'll stay awake as long as I can and then when you're better, we'll leave. We'll get out of here—"

"There's nowhere we can go that they can't find me," Ambri said. "Put down the bloody stick and lie with me. I have a few more demands to make, and in my current state, you can't deny me anything."

I looked to him helplessly. "Ambri…" I whispered. "I'll fall asleep."

"I know, love."

The finality in his words fell over me like a shroud. I lay down beside him, as close as I could, our foreheads nearly touching. Grimacing in pain, he slowly brought his arm up, bent at the elbow, and I clutched his hand in mine.

"To set the record straight," he said, "I never touched anyone else. Not since the first night I brought you here."

"I know you didn't. And I think Lucy was right, that you didn't write that letter either."

"What letter?"

"It's not important."

"Armand," Ambri said after a moment. "The 'master' forger. Whatever you read came from him. But I did try to break your heart, and for that I'm so very sorry."

"It's breaking now," I whispered.

"Stay on topic, please. We're talking about *me*."

I smiled weakly. "My bad. Please continue."

His tone grew warm and serious. "Thank you for my portrait, Cole. I never told you. It's perfect. It's everything I could've hoped for. And thank you for finding a record of my birth. For un-erasing me."

"You're a Gemini, but I think I could've guessed that one."

"Ah yes, humans and their astrology. I'll tell you a little secret. It's one hundred percent real."

I sniffed a laugh. "Of course, it is."

Ambri frowned. "We never celebrated your birthday."

"September ninth. It hasn't happened yet. You want it to happen without you? Impossible. I can't let you go."

"Yes, you can. Sleep. And when you wake up in the morning, it'll be like a dream. Only you'll have a legacy. Legions of admirers—"

"I won't have you. I won't survive it."

"Yes, you will. You're so much stronger than you know. Even now, you're willing to dive into the abyss for me. But I can't let you do that. I need you to promise me something," he said and grimaced as pain shuddered through him. "You can't let yourself fall into despair, and if you do, find help. Talk to Lucy. Talk to anyone, but don't suffer in silence. Demons work in the dark, in solitude. Talking about their insidious whispers is like turning on the light and watching the roaches scatter. Don't let them make you doubt yourself. Promise me." With supreme effort, he lifted his hand off the sheet, his little finger extended. "The most sacred of promises. Pinky swear to me that you'll seek help if you need it."

"Ambri…I can't stay here without—"

"Swear it, Cole," he cried, anguished now, the tears falling. "Please. If you love me at all…"

I could hardly see through my own tears, but I hooked his finger with mine.

"I swear," I whispered.

Instantly, the tension left his body, and he sighed in relief, sinking deeper into the pillows.

"You're a miracle, Cole Matheson, and I am so bloody grateful for you. And I'm not afraid. Because I love you. I didn't know I could feel something this good. Or that I deserved to. I will gladly suffer whatever they have in store for me if I know you're safe. I'll suffer it a million times over. Because I feel your love too. I feel it and it will carry me through whatever is to come. I promise, you don't have to worry about me, okay?" He squeezed his finger, still linked in mine. "Pinky swear."

I leaned over and kissed his forehead, his cheek, his lips. "I love you, Ambri. Always and forever."

"Love you, Cole. Always and forever." He closed his eyes. "I'm so tired."

"I know you are, baby," I whispered. "Rest now, okay?"

He didn't answer, but I presumed the pain had made him too weak, since he couldn't sleep. But I could. My eyes were getting heavier, and I nearly let myself fall under.

No! I can't let him go.

I started to sit up when it felt like a hand was pressing me back down, gently but with all the strength of a mountain.

You promised him you'd live, mein Schatz, and he has to finish what he started. Where he goes now, you cannot follow.

I struggled against the sensation, but it was useless. The harder I tried to stay awake, the faster I slipped under.

No! Ambri, I love you. I love you and I'm so sorry!

I cried out to him or maybe I only thought I did because I couldn't move anymore. Couldn't speak. I was stumbling down into darkness that was limned in blue light. Like falling backward into a warm sea.

The last thing I saw were the shadows in the room. They crawled up the walls, over the bed. They grew long fingers and I tried to scream because they reached for Ambri…

thirty-two

Ambri

I woke up, which was impossible, because demons don't sleep. I sensed I was in my human form, but I felt different. My body felt different. Lighter, somehow.
There's no pain.
I sighed into the pillow. I'd almost forgotten what it felt like to take a breath without stabbing agony.
But I was tired. So tired.
With effort, I opened my eyes. The light in my bedchamber told me it was the darkest hour, just before dawn. My hand was near my face, my little finger still curled…but Cole was gone, and that's when I smelled the smoke.
I sat up and noticed I was dressed in the clothes I'd died in nearly three hundred years ago.
"An interesting development."
Shadowy figures swarmed the room—the Vices and Eisheth, and yet I wasn't afraid. Eisheth screamed in rage—a good sign that things were not going her way.
"You'll burn, Ambri," she screeched. "If we can't have you, you'll burn all over again…"

The darkness seemed to broil and swirl like dark water. The demons dissolved away while the room filled with billowing gray vapor. I could hear flames chew through the other rooms of my flat.

I'd have imagined the thought would cause me some concern, but I was strangely calm.

Because Cole was safe.

I didn't know how I knew that, but it was true. He was safe and so nothing else mattered.

I smiled and thought about trying to escape, but the smoke was quite thick now and I was so tired. I lay back down and watched the gray curls move across the ceiling. I could hear the fire coming closer. The flat was burning. My books were burning. Cole's portrait of me was burning. A shame to lose it but he was so bloody talented; he'd paint another. Paint whatever he wanted because he was safe.

My eyes fell shut again. Love for Cole Matheson infused every part of me, making me warm.

Or maybe that was the fire.

I coughed and grew sleepier. I curled around the pillow and thought of Cole. How happy he'd made me and how grateful I was for our short time together. How much I loved him. It was incalculable. Like a deep blue sea of warm water that had no end.

And I was drifting down into it. Safe. Happy.

Arms went around me. A woman's arms, like a mother's embrace. One I'd never had. They held me close as I sank into the blue infusion.

My brave boy. My brave, brave boy...

thirty-three

Cole

"Ambri!"

I came awake with a gasp and fear lancing through me. I'd fallen asleep. I'd failed to protect him and now they had him. They had him and now he would hurt forever...

Slowly, the room began to resolve around me, and I shivered. A cold draft was blowing in from somewhere and everything was dim and murky. And eerily familiar.

My glasses were on the nightstand next to the bed, on top of my heavy art book. As I reached for them, my old basement flat in Whitechapel came into sharp clarity.

"What the fuck..."

My phone lay on the book too, and I grabbed it. It told me the time was 4:33 on the morning of November ninth. I stared around in disbelief. Against the wall were my portraits from my time at the Academy. Those that I'd lost in the flood. Across the way was my tiny bathroom, the door ajar. Upstairs, I heard Ms. Thomas shuffling around, making her early morning tea.

I threw off the covers and reached for my sketchbook and flipped through it frantically. A few sketches, a few studies of hands or faces. No demons.

No Ambri.

"No…"

Dawn was breaking. I threw on the nearest pair of jeans—old, paint-spattered ones—and a sweater, my coat that wasn't warm enough, and tore out of my flat.

I started to hail a cab but checked my wallet. Empty.

Because it never happened. The gallery shows, the tour…none of it happened.

But I remembered everything. Every second with Ambri was imprinted in my heart. He had been here. *We* happened.

Then I began to run.

I ran until my lungs were on fire in the cold air, and a stitch stabbed me in the side. It was insanity—Chelsea was hours away on foot. No sooner had the thought crossed my mind, than I saw the twenty-two bus rumble to a stop. I jumped on, and it took me to Sloane Square where I jumped off and ran again. I sped through the early morning that was hazy with clouds.

And smoke.

Clouds of gray smoke were billowing up a few blocks away and the sirens broke the early morning quiet.

Ambri…

I rounded the corner to see the entire Chelsea Gardens building engulfed in flames.

"No," I cried and raced toward the inferno that several firetrucks and a host of emergency vehicles had surrounded. Terror practically blinded me, and I crashed headlong into someone.

"Oh dear!" a woman cried.

Instinctively, I'd tried to cushion her fall, grabbing her and rolling to take the brunt of it on my shoulder as we went down in a heap.

When I could breathe again, I helped her to sit. "Are you okay?"

"I'm fine, darling." She sat up like Alice in Wonderland after landing in the rabbit's hole—legs splayed and smoothing down her blue dress. She was mid-thirties but with a delicate, almost childlike face and pretty eyes. Her blond hair was messy and tied with a blue bow.

I sat beside her, watching the building burn, huge chunks collapsing. Nothing—and no one—inside could have survived.

"I'm too late," I whispered, the pain wrapping around my heart in an iron grip. "I'm too late…"

"Now, now, that's no way to think. Help me up, dear."

I got to my feet and pulled the woman to hers.

"You mustn't think like that," she said. "It's never too late, mein Schatz."

I jerked my head to look at her. "What did you say?"

She smiled coyly and leaned in to kiss my cheek. I smelled perfume—old and expensive—as she patted my coat. "Go to him, darling. He's waiting for you."

She tilted her chin over my shoulder, and I looked behind me. The firefighters had pulled someone from the building and were carrying him by his feet and under his arms. I saw a flash of red coat and blond hair, and then I was running again.

"Whoa, whoa." A police officer barred my way from getting close to the scene that was a chaos of flames, smoke, and water-slicked streets from the fire hoses' steady streams. "You can't be here, son."

But I could see Ambri, soot-covered and unmoving. Eyes closed. A crowd of paramedics circled him, working with an urgency that made my blood run cold.

"Please. I have to get to him. Ambri…"

He followed my gaze. "You know that guy? Don't know what he was doing in this building; it's been condemned for years."

"Condemned…?"

The officer walked me closer—close enough to see that Ambri wasn't responding. The men were doing chest compressions, and another had an oxygen pump over his face.

Then one paramedic shook his head at another who said grimly, "I think we lost him."

"No!" I tore past the cop and pushed into the circle. "Don't give up on him. Please."

"He's been in there for too long," said a paramedic.

"Keep at it, Wilson," said another, and the CPR began again. For long, agonized moments, I hung in limbo between fear and hope, until a third paramedic shouted, "I have a pulse!"

In that instant, Ambri arched off the ground and sucked in a deep breath, then coughed as if he were being turned inside out.

Relief—so profound it made me dizzy—washed through me. I tried to reach him, but the paramedics went into a different set of actions. They moved him to a stretcher, constantly relaying information to each other about his status. Ambri didn't open his eyes, but he was breathing. They put an oxygen mask on his face and hurried him to the ambulance.

"I need to go with him, please…" I said, nearly begging. But that felt like an older version of me. One that didn't fit anymore. I squared my jaw. "I'm not leaving here unless it's with him."

"You family?"

"I'm his boyfriend."

The word sounded too weak to describe what Ambri meant to me, but it got me in the ambulance. Or maybe it was the look in my eyes, that I wasn't going to take no for an answer.

The officer jerked a thumb. "Go ahead."

Inside, the medics were moving efficiently but seemed calmer. Less frantic.

"Sit here," one said kindly—the one that hadn't given up. He indicated a seat on the bench on Ambri's left side. "Talk to him. Let him know you're here."

I nodded and took Ambri's hand in mine. "Ambri? Hey, can you open your eyes? Please, baby. Open your eyes."

And he did. Those blue-green eyes fluttered and found me over the oxygen mask.

"Hey, there he is," said the medic, beaming. "Thought we'd lost him."

"He's not out of the woods yet," said the other. Wilson. "Prolonged smoke inhalation. I'm shocked we brought him back, honestly."

I heard the subtext. Ambri might have complications or struggles we didn't know yet.

I don't care. I'll take care of him no matter what.

"One thing at a time," the kindly medic said. "It's a miracle he's alive. A bloody miracle."

I bent over Ambri. "You're safe now, okay? You're safe. I'm right here."

His hand in mine tightened, he smiled, and then went back to sleep.

———⋗

At Chelsea and Westminster Hospital, Ambri was whisked away, and I was led by a social worker to a Critical Care Unit waiting room.

"I understand you're with the man who was brought in from the Chelsea fire?"

"Yes, he's Ambri. I'm Cole Matheson."

"Hi, Cole. I'm Annette. I'm hoping you can help us. We can't find any identification for him. Can you give me a last name, date of birth, national ID number?"

"Umm…" I floundered. They'd probably want to examine *my* head if I told them he was born in 1762. My hands were bunched in my coat pockets because I was a ball of stress and fear. I felt something in the right one and pulled out a…*passport?*

"What…?"

I flipped it open and there was Ambri's photo—looking as sly and beautiful as ever. All of the numbers were up-to-date. He was going to turn twenty-five—again—next June.

"Perfect," the woman said. "May I?"

Bewildered, I handed it over to her.

"Ambrosius Edward Meade-Finch. Quite a name. Ah, there's his birthday." She handed the passport back to me. "And do you have his address?"

"He lives with me," I said without thinking, then gave her my Whitechapel address, only because it seemed like the right answer. Just as I knew the woman I'd crashed into had put the passport in my pocket.

And that she'd been talking to me for months now.

The social worker left, and I eased a sigh, a small one, and waited for the doctors to come out and tell me I could see him. Until that happened, the rest of this craziness could wait.

What felt like an eternity later, a doctor—middle aged and balding—approached. He was frowning as he read the chart in his hand. I stood up on shaking legs.

"You're here for Mr. Meade-Finch?"

"How is he?"

"Frankly, I've never seen anything like it." The man's frown deepened. "He's fine."

I blinked. "He's…fine?"

"Perfectly healthy. Vitals strong, oxygen levels normal, toxicology is clean, CT scan is clear, and he passed a mental examination with flying colors. All of which has left the team a tad baffled, to be honest. The field report states he was clinically dead for four minutes."

I winced as if I'd been punched in the gut, but the doctor was busy studying his chart.

"Given how long he was unconscious in a burning structure, we'd expect to see severe burns, lung damage due to smoke inhalation, and possible anoxic brain injury. He's clean as a whistle." He shook his head. "I'm not a religious man, but…it's rather a sort of miracle."

I barely heard, as if my tears blurred my eyes and ears, both. "Can I see him?"

I was led to CCU room number nine where Ambri lay in a hospital gown, the bed partially inclined. A nasal cannula was in his nose, and monitors on the wall beeped and displayed his vitals. I approached slowly. The last image I'd had of Ambri, his back had been torn open and shadows were reaching for him. I wanted to burst into tears of joy, but it was all too surreal.

A nurse smiled at me. "He's resting now, but I'm sure he'd love to hear from you."

I nodded faintly and sat beside him. I took his hand in mine and just held it for a few moments. I traced the lines of his fingers, his palm, then pressed the back of his hand to my lips, forcing my senses to believe this was real.

I glanced at the nurse who gave me a final parting smile, then left us alone. When my gaze returned to Ambri, he was awake and staring at me.

"Hi, baby."

"Am I dreaming?" he whispered.

"I don't think so, but honestly, it's hard to tell. What do you remember?"

"All of it," he said. "But the worst parts…like the Other Side…are hard to grasp. It's like a nightmare that's fading away." Tears filled his eyes and spilled down his cheeks. "I'm not…what I was anymore. I'm…free."

He broke down and I climbed onto the bed beside him and pulled him close. He clung to me, trembling, and I held him as he cried. My chest ached; I wanted to let go too, but I couldn't.

What if this isn't real?

Ambri sat up and wiped his eyes. "Look at me. Handful of moments as a human, and I'm already a sobbing mess."

"I love you as a sobbing mess."

"You'd better, because it's your fault," he said and settled against my chest. "I've never felt this happy before. It's so powerful, I'm scared it isn't real. That this is a trick or ruse, and I'm going to be hauled away from you at any moment."

"I know what you mean," I said, holding him tighter.

He pulled back to look at me. "Are you happy too?"

His hopeful uncertainty nearly broke my heart, so I kept my fears to myself. I bent and kissed him softly. "I'm so fucking happy right now, if you hooked me up to that heart monitor, doctors would come running."

"Because there's no place for me to run anymore," Ambri said. "No Other Side I can hide in when things are tough. It's just going to be me, all the time."

"That's all I've wanted since the moment we met. You, all the time."

Please let this be real.

Ambri smiled, soft and full of love, and laid his head back down. "I think I'm falling asleep. It's nerve-wracking to just…drift away. Will you stay?"

"I'm not going anywhere."

He settled against me. "I love you, Cole. I love you more than I can ever say. But I'll try. I'll try every day, to make sure you know…"

"I know, Ambri. I feel it. And I love you. So much." My voice grew thick. "Forever and always."

thirty-four

Cole

The night's shadows had stretched and grown long, then faded away with the coming light. I'd remained in his hospital bed, awake and watching. Standing guard.

It took longer than expected, but by late that afternoon, he was discharged. I'd reluctantly run home to fetch him a pair of plaid flannel pants and my bulky NYU sweatshirt. Ambri put on the clothing and scowled at my laughter.

"What's so bloody funny?"

"I've seen you in nothing but three-piece suits for months. You are so damn cute right now, I can't handle it."

"I'm so glad this is amusing to you. I look like a pile of laundry." He heaved a dramatic sigh. "I suppose I lost everything in the fire. We'll go shopping at once and then see about new accommodations."

"Yeah, about that. Your flat wasn't the only thing that was wiped out yesterday."

I explained to him that we were in November of the previous year, and that my fame and fortune had never happened.

"A police officer told me your Chelsea building had been condemned and vacant for years."

Ambri put his hands on his slender hips. "That's a pisser. Why didn't you tell me before?"

"You'd just woken up in the CCU. I didn't want to stress you out. But I think, maybe, the slate's been wiped clean. For both of us."

Ambri nodded. "Perhaps. Perhaps, there's a price to pay for a second chance. I turned to the darkness, and I had to pay my dues to get out."

I nodded, hoping that was true. That he had nothing left to pay.

He's suffered enough.

The light was growing dim by the time we arrived back at my little flat in Whitechapel. It seemed even shabbier and danker than before.

Ambri glanced around. "Not quite the Four Seasons, but it will do."

"Will it?" I asked and rubbed the back of my neck. "It's not much. And I get what you were saying yesterday. I don't have anything anymore. It's just…me."

"You, who would have followed me into hell." Ambri moved to me, and his eyes were dark and dilated. "Cole…"

I could only nod because words failed me too. He was here. We were together, and now it seemed that the only thing left to do was prove it to each other.

Ambri's hands slipped around my shoulders. I pulled his hips to mine, and his lips parted in a gasp. His tongue flicked out to taste me, and I lost any semblance of control. I crushed my mouth to his, devouring him, invading and tasting him, knowing I'd never be satiated.

He kissed me back with equal fervor, drawing me in with the delicious sucking pull of his mouth. Our clothes melted away, and we stood chest to chest, naked, our hands roaming, both of our erections straining for the other.

"You just got out of the hospital," I said. "Don't you need to rest?"

"Do you *want* me to rest?"

"Good point."

We climbed into bed, bundled into the blankets, then reached for each other again.

"What do you want?" I asked between breathless kisses.

"I want you, Cole. I want to feel you around me and inside me, so I know that this is real."

I needed that too. That part of me still refused to concede that he was here to stay. I wanted his body, to infuse my every nerve and cell with the sensations of him, to leave no doubt of his permanence.

I rolled over so I was on top of him, kissing him, exploring every inch of his mouth with my tongue. I let the moment simmer and worked our need to a frenzy, our cocks rubbing and dripping, my hips thrusting as if I were inside him already.

"Bloody hell, Cole, I'm going to come."

"I want you to," I growled. "All over both of us. Then I'm going to fuck you and you're going to come again."

His face became a grimace of pained ecstasy, my words forcing his body to obey, his release spurting hotly. I felt it against my stomach and slid my body along his, rolling my hips, smearing his cum between us, wanting as much of it on me as possible.

"Dirty," Ambri said approvingly and kissed me hard. "Now fuck me before I get mad."

I grinned and reached in the nightstand drawer for a bottle of lube and a condom.

"The hospital gave me a clean bill of health," he said with a nod at the condom.

"It sure did. You're a fucking miracle," I said. "I'm good too. You're the only person I've been with in years." I pulled back, holding his face in my hands. "I've been waiting for you."

"I'm here," he whispered.

He's here. God, let him be here...

He kissed me hard, reigniting the fire between us. We rolled back on our sides, and he took the bottle of lube and poured a few drops over my fingers, then slung his leg over my hip. He stroked my cock with his slick hand as I moved my hand between his legs, using a finger to loosen him.

Ambri groaned as I breached his tight ring of muscle, his face pressed to my neck, planting soft kisses, then little bites, then soothing the sting with his tongue. I added a second finger.

"Yes," he murmured, his hand sliding over my length in long, leisurely strokes. "God, you're big. And perfect. And all mine."

I took my time kissing and touching and when I could move my fingers in him easily, he rolled over, his back to my chest.

"I want you like this," he said. "I want to be wrapped in you completely while you fuck me, Cole."

I understood what he meant. The safety but the heat and need too. The love and lust. All of it. I wanted to hold him and cherish him while unleashing myself against him and inside him, fucking him and loving him in equal measure.

I kissed his neck, his back, and the places over his shoulder blades where those awful wounds had been. Now there was only smooth, perfect skin, and I started to let myself believe his hurting had ended.

"Please, Cole," he gritted out. "I need you…"

I aligned myself while he inhaled deeply, then let it out, relaxing slowly as I pushed in. I groaned as the incredible pressure of him gripped me. I tried to move slowly but Ambri, impatient as ever, pushed back until we were skin to skin.

"Cole," he breathed. "It's so good with you. How is it so good?"

Because you're the other half of my soul…

But I could hardly speak, overwhelmed with him. I wrapped him in one arm. With the other, I gripped his muscled thigh, holding his leg as I moved in and out of him. He reached one hand back and sunk his fingers into my hair, then craned his mouth to mine.

"I'm going to come again," he whispered between broken kisses.

"That's right," I managed. Being inside him with nothing between us was its own fucking miracle. "You're going to come for me."

I reached one hand around him, fingers still slick from the lube, and stroked his cock that was hard again. Every part of him was magnificent.

And all mine…

Ambri grabbed a tissue from the nightstand, then put his hand on mine, and together we worked his cock until he shuddered against me, his head thrown back, exposing his beautiful neck, corded and tense with the strain of taking me. His Adam's apple protruded, masculine and beautiful. He was everything I could ever want. Everything I would ever want for the rest of my life.

He caught his release in the tissue and tossed it aside, then reached to kiss me again.

"Now you. Fuck me, Cole. Just like that. Come inside me and let me feel it."

His words spurred me, and I clutched at his hip as my orgasm rocketed through me. I came hard and fast, spilling into him. He moaned, and my thrusts slowed, and then I held myself still, savoring the sensation. The tightness of him around me and the slick heat of my release inside him.

Slowly—reluctantly—I withdrew from him, and he rolled over to face me, and then he was back in my arms, and I felt the dam finally begin to crack.

"What is it?" Ambri asked. "What's wrong?"

"I thought I lost you. Twice." I struggled to hold the tears back. "I'm sorry…"

"Don't be sorry," he said thickly. "No one's ever cried over me."

I held him tight to me, my lips against his warm skin. "I swear, I'm going to take care of you. No one is ever going to fucking hurt you like that again."

And I didn't know if I meant his uncle or the demons. All of them. Anyone.

"We'll take care of each other," he said, pulling back to brush the hair from my forehead. "Through richer or poorer, in sickness and in health, and all that."

"Are you proposing?"

"Absolutely not. There will be no proposals without jewelry."

I sniffed a laugh and dried my eyes. "I hate to break it to you, but I don't think there's much jewelry in our future. According to my calculations, this place is going to be flooded in about a week. We're going to be homeless."

"That is concerning," he said. "Tomorrow we should see if I have any fortune left. I suspect I won't, but…c'est la vie. So long as I have you."

We kissed, and I left the bed long enough to clean us up, then climbed back in to wrap him in my arms.

"I'm going to sleep listening to your heart," Ambri said, resting his head on my chest. "Every night. And every beat will remind me of this second chance I've been given. I'm so bloody grateful for you Cole."

"Me too. Grateful you're here with me."

"But…all of your beautiful paintings," he said sleepily. "You lost everything too."

I kissed his forehead. "I didn't lose what matters most."

The next morning, Ambri and I found a Barclays bank, and he marched up to the teller in my flannel pants and sweatshirt that were both a tad too big for him. His hair was mussed from our nocturnal activities that had resumed after a short nap and lasted all night.

"Yes, good day, I was wondering if this institution still has all of my money."

I smiled showing all my teeth. "He just got out of the hospital."

The woman behind the counter gave us both a look. "Name?"

"Ambrosius Edward Meade-Finch."

Her keyboard clacked and she shook her head. "I'm sorry. I don't have a record of anyone with that name ever having an account with us. Are you sure you have the right bank?"

Are you sure you're allowed to be out in public?

"Thank you, ma'am." I tugged Ambri's sleeve. "Come on."

Outside, he frowned. "Well, that's that. We're starting from scratch, apparently."

"We could go back to your place and see if there's anything left."

He looked at me sharply. "Last night, I dreamt we did exactly that."

I stared back. "So did I."

In the few minutes of sleep between bouts of celebration, I'd dreamed that we were carefully picking our way through charred rubble.

"But nothing happened in the dream," I said. "I didn't find anything."

"Me neither. Maybe that was the point. To make us curious."

We took the bus to Chelsea. It was Ambri's first excursion on public transit, an experience he declared "dodgy at best." We approached what was left of his building. Police tape was strung up to keep people away, and a bobby was on duty, marching back and forth.

I clutched Ambri's arm. "Is that…Jerome?"

The bobby turned and gave us a stern look. "What are you doing here? Can't you see the tape? No one's allowed in."

Ambri and I exchanged glances, and then he put on his most winning smile. "Might you make an exception for us, old chap? For old time's sake?"

Jerome frowned but then nodded, once. "Make it quick."

"Thanks, Jerome."

He tapped his nightstick to his helmet. It might've been my imagination, but I could've sworn he winked.

"This is getting weirder and weirder," I said as we picked our way through the rubble. Four stories had collapsed, but the only items we found came from Ambri's flat. His furniture, books, the couch...all charred or destroyed completely.

"I'm sorry, Ambri," I said. "I came to feel like this place was my home, too. This must be so hard for you."

"On the contrary. Last night I was laid spectacularly by the man I love. *Thrice.* I'm cracking."

I grinned. "When you put it that way..."

He bent down suddenly and picked up a small iron box. "I don't recognize this. Yours?"

"Not mine," I said and touched a finger to the fleur-de-lis engraved on the lid.

"Still warm." Ambri opened the box. Inside was a small black velvet bag with a note tied in the drawstring like a little scroll.

> Bonjour boys!
> I think you know what this means....
> Ha! I've always wanted to write that, turnabout being fair play and all. Here you'll find a little gift from me to you. I'm not supposed to. The fresh start was supposed to be enough, but I couldn't help it! I just had to do something a little extra and help you begin your new lives. Spend it wisely, and perhaps think of me as you do, for I will always be watching over you, my sweet boys. My treasures.
> All my love,
> M.A.

Ambri and I exchanged a glance. He undid the drawstring and dumped an enormous square-cut diamond into my palm. Seven or eight carats, at least.

"Holy shit. That's a big effin diamond."

"M-A…" Ambri murmured, thinking. Then his eyes widened. "Oh, bloody hell, that's impossible. It can't be…Marie Antoinette?"

I stared. "Get the fuck out."

"It is. I can feel it in my bones." He picked up the diamond from my palm. "This is from the Affair of the Necklace. But why? I helped ruin her."

"I'm no expert on angels, but it seems like forgiveness might be one of their superpowers. The biggest."

"The blue fairy," Ambri whispered to himself, then shook his head, disbelieving. "All this time, she's been the voice in my head."

"Mine too," I said. "I've been hearing her for months."

"She was always telling me to not give up hope and to just love you," Ambri said softly. "And to let you love me."

"She told me not to give up on you. Not that I ever could." I smiled. "But she said *mein Schatz* a lot. Antoinette was the Queen of France, right? That sounds German."

"Bloody hell, Marie Antoinette was born in Austria. German would have been her native language." Ambri shook his head with a smile. "Well played, darling."

"What does that even mean, mein Schatz?" I pulled out my phone and Googled it. Then my heart dropped. "Oh my God."

"What?" Ambri asked. "It means *little shit*, doesn't it? I knew it…"

"It means *my treasure*. Holy crap." I read the letter again. "M-A…*Margaret-Anne*." I looked to Ambri. "My grandmother."

Ambri stared back, his mouth agape. "No…"

"You said yourself we all live more than one lifetime. She's been watching over both of us." I smiled, wiped my cheek. "Our guardian angel."

Ambri put an arm around me. "We're a blessed pair, Cole Matheson."

"You can say that again."

I dropped the diamond back in the bag, and he tucked it into his pocket.

We were making our way back to the street when we came across the burnt remains of Ambri's portrait. The frame survived, though tarnished and warped, but the canvas was burned to ash.

"Oh, Cole," Ambri said. "I'm sorry. I understand why it had to be brutal for me, but you? Your success? All your beautiful work. Why did that have to be erased? You didn't do anything wrong."

"I don't think it's about right or wrong; it's about showing me what's important. I cared too much about what people thought. I was paralyzed by it. I let it get in the way of the work." I turned to him, my heart full. "My art was lost. *I* was lost. Until you, Ambri. You gave it all back to me. You gave me everything."

Ambri smiled, and the sharp edges he showed everyone else melted away with me. "You remember what I was. You can start again."

"No, no more demons. There'll be some other subject that grabs me, I have no doubt." I reached out and brushed my fingers over his cheek. "After all, I have the most beautiful muse."

epilogue

Ambri
Two years later

I strolled down the hallways of the Winthrop School and paused outside Cole's classroom. The school for the arts was built in 1889 and smelled of old wood and paint, the wide, pine-floored halls ringing with the talk and laughter of children.

Cole stood at the front of his classroom in jeans, a tweed sports jacket, and a plaid button down, looking every inch the art professor. His hair was still moppish, but he no longer wore glasses. He'd gotten contacts only because I told him his eyes were too beautiful to hide. Moreover, they'd become a liability when I attacked him as he walked in the door after a long day of teaching.

I waited in the doorway, a lunch sack in my hand, and listened. Twenty ten-year-olds stood behind twenty little easels; twenty pairs of eyes peered at the bowl of fruit and a white water pitcher arranged on a table at the head of the class.

"Notice how the light changes the color and even the texture of the fruit," Cole was saying, wandering among them. "A grape in the shadow has a different quality than the grape in the sun. Play with the color tones. Play with your shading."

I smiled, my heart so full of love for that man, it was rather astonishing. Like a fathomless sea that stretched out into forever. I'd never reach the end of my love for him. Not in a million lifetimes.

I leaned against the door jam, content to watch Cole share his gifts with the artists of the future. But the old wood creaked, and the twenty little faces swiveled to me.

"*AMBREEE!*"

Pandemonium, as they surrounded me and pulled me into the classroom.

"Hello little ones." I looked to Cole. "I didn't mean to interrupt."

He smiled, and bloody hell, if my heart didn't swell. It'd been two years, but Cole's smile for me was as happy and rich as if it'd been ages instead of hours since we'd last seen each other.

"It's fine," he said. "Lunch is in about five."

The little nuggets tugged at my hands.

"Ambri, are you staying?"

"Are you going to have lunch with us?"

"Come look what I did!"

I spent the next few minutes wandering from easel to easel, admiring their work. They were all talented for having gotten into this school, but Cole was an extraordinary professor. You can't teach talent, but he was able to shape the skills they had, and he encouraged them to tune out the noise. *"Believe in yourselves and love what you do,"* I once heard him say. *"Make those thoughts louder than any other."*

The bell rang and they screeched for the door, waving their little starfish hands at me. "Bye, Professor Matheson! Bye, Ambri!"

Alone in the classroom, I went to Cole and kissed him. "I don't know how you do it for hours a day."

"They give me life," Cole said, beaming. "What's the occasion?"

"I brought us lunch," I said, holding aloft a white paper bag. "I have two bits of news and I didn't want to wait until you came home."

Home was our modest little flat in Marylebone. Two bedrooms—one for us and one for Cole's studio—with white walls and plenty of windows. We'd been extremely careful with the gift our guardian angel afforded us, saving and working as much as possible.

Cole had found the job at Winthrop, teaching during the day and working on a new collection at night and on and weekends. It was my job to do all the tedious networking he hated. I made the calls and sent out photos and emails because I believed in him utterly. Because his talent had not been wiped away in our little time loop but had flourished. He'd made several big sales and had an upcoming show at a small gallery. There was even a rumor that Jane Oxley was interested and would attend.

His friend, Vaughn Ritter, was coming too.

Two years ago, after the shock of what we'd found in the rubble had worn off, Cole called Vaughn and kept close with him, checking in and being there for him. He and his new wife were frequent dinner guests at our home.

Because Cole is in the business of saving lives.

Mine, especially, but his too. He kept his promise to me and found a therapist he trusted to prevent my former associates from getting too close again. And because the abuse suffered at the hands of my "uncle" wasn't magically wiped away, I did the same. Hard moments still came and facing them sometimes felt like standing naked before a firing squad. But talking through them felt like learning how to put on a suit of armor, and it grew stronger and stronger every day.

We took our lunch outside and sat at a bench under a brilliant May sun. From the bags, I pulled out two tuna fish sandwiches with cranberries, two ice teas, and two bags of crisps.

"So what's your big news?" Cole said.

"I've been discovered."

"By what?"

"A modeling agency. I was standing in line at Pret-a-Manger, fetching this feast, when a man in a Brioni three-piece hands me his card. He wants to take photos of me day after next."

"I'll bet he does," Cole muttered warily. He took the card. "Holy shit. This looks legit. This is one of the biggest agencies in Europe. This could be huge."

"I hope so. It'd be nice to be clad in designer couture again. Do you think I'll suffice?"

"Suffice? Ambri, you have to be one of the most gorgeous men on the planet. They'd be fucking idiots not to sign you."

"I adore you, Cole Matheson. I think it's rather perfect for me, actually."

"I agree," he said dryly. "Sitting around, doing nothing but being admired all day is exactly your skill set."

"Then why do you look less than thrilled?"

"It's…nothing."

"Tell me."

"Well, modeling is an exciting life. And my career might be about to go somewhere." Cole shrugged one shoulder. "It sort of feels like everything is starting up again. Not that I'm complaining but…" He smiled weakly. "We've been there before."

"That 'exciting life' hasn't happened yet. And in any case, Cole, *you* are my life. I've been given a second chance. The last thing I'd ever do is succumb to whispered temptations from our old friends. It's not even possible. I love you too much."

"I wouldn't either. Sorry, I'm just being weird about the upcoming show. And maybe part of me is a little jealous. You were my muse, and now you're going to be the muse of a hundred different photographers."

"I won't cease my tireless work as your manager," I said. "I'll take a job here or there but nothing international. No prancing up and down runways with an oil barrel on my head or some such nonsense. Just for the extra income. And the clothing, of course."

"Of course." Cole smiled. "And what's the second piece of news?"

"Casziel called me today. He said we need to go to Hever Castle immediately."

Our friends across the pond had had to be told about me for a second time and everything that had transpired after. Given that we'd all been sucked backward through some sort of celestial wormhole, Cas and Lucy took it rather well. The four of us had become very close, taking turns popping over to visit each other as often as possible.

Cole was frowning. "Is going to Hever a good idea?"

"My first thought was *absolutely bloody fucking not*, but then I considered it. Perhaps I need to look directly into my old pain instead of letting it haunt me from afar. Don't you agree?"

"Well, yes and no, Ambri. There's no need to torment yourself with horrible memories just to prove some point." He reached across the table and took my hand. "But if it's important to you, then yes, of course we should go."

Lord have mercy, this man.

Cole's consideration and protectiveness of me was a constant. Unwavering. He deserved every happiness. No doubts or fears or uncertainty. Not ever.

"Did Cas say what's at Hever?" he asked.

"No. He said we must see it for ourselves. Tomorrow, I think. He sounded rather urgent." I stood up. "But I must go."

Cole frowned. "You just got here."
"Yes, but I realize I have an errand to run."
"Can't it wait?"
"Not one more minute."

I threw my uneaten lunch back in the bag, then leaned over the table and kissed Cole. A quick kiss on the mouth and then another, a longer one, while I held his face.

"I love you."

He smiled. "I love you too."

But now there was uncertainty in his eyes. Not that Cole didn't trust me—his concern was of the same tenor as that which plagued me at times. That things were too good, that we were too happy. Surely something must be waiting around the corner to muck it all up.

I walked away, across the school's green grass.

"I'll die first," I muttered. "Again."

The following afternoon, Saturday, we took the Southern train to Hever Castle and Gardens. It was a beautiful, sunny day, and we followed a line of tourists into my former abode. As we approached the entrance, Cole slipped his hand in mine.

Crossing the threshold was like stepping back in time, but instead of the dark and drafty castle I'd known, there was electric lighting in the rooms, polished wood walls and floors, and elegant furniture. A tour guide informed a group of listeners that William Astor was responsible for the restoration of Hever in the twentieth century. He took it back to the Tudor era to invoke something of what the castle was in Anne Boleyn's time. She was the main attraction, of course, but I found I had none of the old jealousy of having been forgotten by time.

"How are you doing?" Cole asked, checking in as we passed through the lushly furnished Drawing Room. "If it's too hard, we can go."

"It's somehow both more and less modern than when I lived in it," I said. "It's a strange feeling to see that your home has become a museum. Though it wasn't actually my home for very long, and it never felt much like one anyway."

We made our way to the Long Gallery that was lined with paintings—most of them Tudor-era. But at the end was a section of previous owners.

Cole's hand in mine tightened as we came to my family's portraits, and then he gasped and fell back a step. "Holy shit…"

My father's portrait hung beside my mother's, then my older sister, Jane's…and then there was me.

Cole's portrait of me, done over those precious months we were together before the tour and the demons that pried us apart, hung with the rest. I was un-erased after all.

I looked to the placard below it.

Ambrosius Edward Meade-Finch, 1762–1786

"Artist unknown," Cole said with a chuckle. "They got that right at least. But I don't understand it. The canvas, the paint…none of it was contemporaneous." His gaze darted to me. "Oh, baby, are you okay?"

Tears blurred my vision. "I thought I'd never see it again. I thought your work…it was lost in the fire." I smiled. "One last gift from our guardian angel."

"Come on," Cole said, after a moment. "Let's get some air."

I nodded vaguely and we went out to the courtyard. We sat on a concrete bench in front of an elaborate fountain.

"You did that," I told Cole. "You gave my life back to me. Both of them. The first one, all those years ago, and now this one."

"I didn't do anything you haven't done for me a thousand times over, Ambri."

His smile was charming and beautiful, but I had to make him understand.

I got down on one knee and reached into my coat pocket for the box I'd been carrying around all day.

Cole's eyes widened. "What are you doing?"

"I was going to do something adorable and charming with your students, like in that comedic American movie? *Meet the Fuckers?*"

"Fockers," he said faintly. "It's *Meet the Fockers,* the sequel…"

"But that would've taken all sorts of planning and I couldn't wait anymore. I couldn't wait one more second."

I opened the box to show a small but wide band of platinum tucked in blue velvet. I inhaled deep, conscious that a small crowd had formed to watch at a respectful distance.

"Cole Matheson, I love you. I love every bloody last thing about you. I love the little vein under your left eye that pops out when you're angry, which is almost never. Even when I'm being a prat, which is frequently. I love my reflection in your beautiful dark eyes. I love how you see me. As if I'm enough, just the way I am. I've never been with anyone who made me feel that way, and that is true happiness. I want to spend the rest of my life giving that back to you, if I can. Will you marry me?"

Cole's eyes were full. The crowd waited with bated breath. My heart felt like it had stopped too and wouldn't start again unless he said yes.

"Yes," Cole said, first a whisper and then louder. "Yes, Ambri. I'll marry you. But you already give me all the happiness I could want. You don't have to try."

He pulled me to my feet, and we kissed, smiling through tears. The small crowd burst into applause and offered congratulations.

I took the ring out of the box, more nervous than I could ever remember feeling.

"It's engraved." I showed him the underside where *Always and forever* was written in small script. "And it goes here." I slipped the ring over his right pinky finger.

Cole was staring at the ring and then at me, disbelieving.

My face grew hot. "I know it's rather plain, but our actual wedding bands can have a little more pizzazz, and—"

"It's perfect," Cole said as I sat with him on the bench. "How did you know?"

"How did I know what?"

He glanced around, then slid his hand into his pocket and drew out a box of his own.

My heart crashed, and it was my turn to have tears flood my eyes. "No…"

"I don't want to overshadow your proposal," Cole said. "It was the most beautiful thing I've ever heard. But you should have this too."

He opened it to reveal a gold band, also wide and small. Too small for any finger but one.

"It's engraved too," he said with a teary laugh. "Bet you can't guess what it says."

A half sob, half laugh burst out of me. "Our angel is still whispering in our ears. She's a cheeky one, isn't she?"

Cole slipped the ring on my right pinky finger, then took my face in his hands. "I'm going to love you forever, Ambri."

He kissed me, and I kissed him back with all the love I had in my human soul, which was infinitely more powerful than any darkness. And in that moment, I knew that my long exile was over and that my heart was home at last.

the end

author's note ii

I try to put a piece of my story in every single one of my books, but this book was one that almost didn't get written. The grief from losing my daughter had sunk deep teeth in me, and the prospect of living that way for the rest of my life was an exhausting one. I can't write about the dark until I can also write about how to find a way out of it, so this book was put on hold until I could do just that.

Every mental hardship Cole Matheson endures in this book is taken directly from my own experiences—the self-doubt, the hopelessness, the desire to run and not stop. I wasn't active in escape, but I had thoughts that asked if it wouldn't be such a bad thing if I sat the rest of this one out. Depression felt like my own brain had turned against me, whispering insidious thoughts, day in and day out. It took me some time to decide I didn't have to (or deserve to) continue suffering. I sought help and with a lot of hard work, found my way out of the dark.

The demons in this book stand in for those destructive thoughts but fictionalizing them does not minimize or trivialize their power. They're not literal demons, but they are separate from our true selves. It's my hope that this story helps illustrate that and show that speaking shadows into the light can help dispel them. We so often suffer in silence but if you are, please know there is help and that you deserve to feel better.

With love.

Suicide and Crisis Hotline, call 988

Additional resources at their website: www.988lifeline.org

acknowledgments

Thank you to my Gal Friday, Melissa Panio-Petersen, for keeping the ship afloat even when it seemed like it wasn't going anywhere. Love you forever.

To my sensitivity reader, Robert Hodgdon. Thank you for your insight and guidance, and for your love of these boys that encourages me so much to tell their story. Love you so much!

To my beta readers, MJ Fryer, Joanne Goodspeed Ragona, Shannon Mummey, Marissa D'onofrio, and Terri Potts for reading my boys early. Your encouragement and kind words during the most nerve-wracking of times always sees me through. Thank you and with all my love.

To Lori Jackson for hitting the cover out of the park in one try—AGAIN! You're batting a thousand, lovely. Thank you for always being there to bring my visions to life.

To Nina and her team at Valentine PR. Thank you for going along with me on this crazy journey and supporting me no matter what kind of story my own muse insists I tell. Love you!

Every demon in this book is "real" thanks to Theresa Bane and her *Encyclopedia of Demons*, from which I was able to cast this motley crew of infernal bad boys and girls. I'm grateful, not only for her extensive research into the underworld, but for every new or crazy idea for the book that came with it.

To the Entourage and to the readers, bloggers, and members of the romance community at large. Since June of 2018, you all have become so much more to me, supporting and comforting me through all the ups and downs. And there have been many. Thank you for making me feel seen and heard as I navigate this life and try to describe a little of what it's like through my books. With love.

And to Robin Hill. My gratitude for you, your friendship, love, and the immaculate work you put into my book babies to make them what they are, is boundless. Thank you and I love you, always and forever.

also by emma scott

Duets
Full Tilt ✦ All In

Bring Down the Stars (Beautiful Hearts #1)
Long Live the Beautiful Hearts (Beautiful Hearts #2)

Series
How to Save a Life (Dreamcatcher #1)
Sugar & Gold (Dreamcatcher #2)

The Girl in the Love Song (Lost Boys #1)
When You Come Back to Me (Lost Boys #2)
The Last Piece of His Heart (Lost Boys #3)

RUSH (RUSH #1)
Endless Possibility (RUSH #1.5)

The Sinner (Angels and Demons #1)
The Muse (Angels and Demons #2)

Standalones
Love Beyond Words ✦ Unbreakable ✦ The Butterfly Project
Forever Right Now ✦ In Harmony ✦ A Five-Minute Life
Someday, Someday ✦ Between Hello and Goodbye

MM Romance
Someday, Someday
When You Come Back to Me (Lost Boys #2)
The Muse (Angels and Demons #2)

Novellas
One Good Man ✦ Love Game

about the author

Emma Scott is a *USA Today* and *Wall St. Journal* best-selling author whose books have been translated in six languages and featured in *Buzzfeed, Huffington Post, New York Daily News,* and *USA Today's Happy Ever After.* She writes emotional, character-driven romances in which art and love intertwine to heal and love always wins. If you enjoy emotionally charged stories that rip your heart out and put it back together again with diverse characters and kind-hearted heroes, you will enjoy her novels.

Printed in Great Britain
by Amazon